Before he could stop himself, Raleigh started to glance around. The muzzle of the pistol swung just enough away from Bowie, who yanked the Greener up out of the snow with his right hand, praying that the barrels weren't plugged with snow and that the gun wasn't going to blow up and kill him if he had to shoot. His left hand streaked to the fore end and his right thumb snapped the hammers back. By the time Raleigh realized he'd been had he was staring into the twin maws of the short-barreled shotgun from a distance of roughly fifteen feet.

"Drop it, Raleigh!" Bowie snapped at the stunned bounty hunter. "You might miss but I damn well won't." The two men stared at each other, and for the briefest moment Bowie was sure that Raleigh was going to do what he'd been told. Then desperation flickered in Raleigh's eyes and his finger tightened on the trigger.

The silence around Bowie was deafening. When Bowie had disappeared into the brush, Bronco had quit trying to make mincemeat of the black horse with his rifle and stopped shooting so he could reload. The only sound was the chuckling of the creek over the rocks and the slightest of breezes whispering through the willows.

Bowie watched the knuckles of Raleigh's trigger finger whiten and said, "It doesn't have to be this way," but in the tension of the moment he felt like he could see the trigger moving.

"Ah hell," Bowie muttered to himself, and squeezed the triggers of the Greener.

Tyler's Law:
The Deputies Book 2

A novel of the West

Chuck
"Charlie MacNeil"
Buchanan

Sisley Creek Press
Durkee, Oregon

Sisley CreekPress
33369 Sisley Creek Road
Durkee, Oregon 97905

This is a work of fiction. Any resemblance between the characters and any person, living or dead, is purely coincidence.

ISBN 978-0-9824580-1-3

Acknowledgements

Every writer needs a support staff and I'm no different. Without the understanding and encouragement of my lovely and longsuffering wife Cheryl, none of my writings would ever have seen the light of day. Because she told me to go for it, to take a shot at living my dream of becoming a published author, the first book in the Deputies series, Complications, became a reality. And it's because of Cheryl that the book you hold in your hand is in print. Thanks, Babe. I couldn't have done it without you there to cover my back.

Thanks also to Beverly Coomer for her copy-editing and for taking the time to help me see my work from the point of view of someone who doesn't read westerns. Her comments and criticisms have helped me grow as a writer.

And of course I need to thank all of the loyal readers out there who are always asking, "When's the next book coming out?" whenever I see them. They spurred me on to what I hope are greater heights in this book. To all of you, here it is.

Chuck "Charlie MacNeil" Buchanan
January, 2010

~ 1 ~

Four snow-crusted shadows appeared out of the darkness. The frosty white plumes of their breaths swirled away on the banshee wind. Their heads were bowed and scarves tied under their chins held their hats on as the riders pushed ahead into the teeth of the storm. Their shoulders were hunched inside their coats. The cold had gnawed deep into their very cores, and the leader of the small band had begun to despair of ever being warm again. His feet were like blocks of ice, and the gloved hand that held the reins of his exhausted horse was the same. As he rounded the shoulder of rock that stood against the wind into the relative calm of the cove beyond, Bob Morton slipped the glove from his right hand. He reached inside the sheepskin-lined coat he wore to tuck his numb fingers into his armpit in an attempt to restore some warmth and dexterity to them.

Ahead of the four men, the welcoming glow of lantern light in the cabin window flickered through the early fall blizzard. The four exhausted men drew to a halt; their bloodshot eyes were dull and watery. Morton stepped down and shucked his Winchester from the scabbard under the offside stirrup. He held the reins out toward Abel Barnes, who happened to be nearest. "Take my horse to the corral," he told Abel over the shriek of the wind through the rocks at the top of the cove. "I'll have a look inside, make sure we don't have unwanted company."

"Take yer own damned horse," Barnes replied with a sneer. "I've got my own to look after." He jerked his tired sorrel savagely toward the shelter of the lean-to shed that stood with its back to the swirling fingers of wind that reached into the cove. Snow had piled into drifts at the base of the wall.

Morton took two long strides and grabbed the headstall and pulled the sorrel to a stop as Barnes cursed. "You're the reason we're late, Barnes. Because of you, we had to nearly kill our horses getting away from that posse. Right at the moment I'm on the verge of shootin' you myself, so don't give me any lip. And if I ever see you treat a horse that way again I'll kick your ass into next week. Just shut up and do what you're told." Morton released the bridle and turned away. As he went back toward his own horse, Abel's hand moved stealthily toward the Colt in the crossdraw holster in front of his left hip. "Don't even think about it, Barnes," the words drifted on the wind. "You draw that pistol and I'll take it away from you and make you eat it."

Startled, Abel could do nothing but drop his hand and lean forward to pick up the reins Morton had let fall into the snow. Over the shriek of the wind overhead Abel thought he heard a chuckle. He snapped his head around but the other two shadows were turning away. He didn't know for sure who had found the whole situation humorous, but he had his suspicions. He would bide his time and wait for his chance to get even. Abel Barnes was a good hater.

The snow was soft and heavy underfoot as Bob walked tiredly toward the cabin. "Hallo the house!" he called. He stood just out of reach of the light from the oilskin-covered window cut into the wall next to the door and waited with the Winchester held down beside his leg. The door swung inward and Max Horner lifted a lantern and its rays illuminated the hulking, snow-covered figure.

"Is that you, Bob?" Max called. The leveled Colt in his other hand gleamed dully in the lantern light.

"Yeah, it's me," Bob said. He moved forward into the light. "Are you alone?"

"Just me and Colonel Colt's finest," Max chuckled. "Come on in." He moved back into the room, favoring his right leg. He holstered the pistol and hung the lantern from a hook on an overhead beam. Bob stopped on the stone stoop to stamp the snow from his boots, and the smell of coffee, biscuits and beans drifting through the open door made his knees sag. It had been the better part of two days since any of them had a decent meal. He, Abel Barnes, Jake Carver and Ben Terrell had spent most of that two days dodging a very persistent posse with a very good tracker. They'd finally managed to get away from the men trailing them only because of the snowstorm that had suddenly blown in and covered their trail. Or he was pretty sure they had lost them.

The interior of the cabin was almost too warm after the cold of the storm. A fire crackled merrily in the stone fireplace and the warm glow of lantern light was in sharp contrast to the spartan furnishings. A simple plank table, flanked on both sides by rough benches, stood to one side of the room. Four bunks stood in pairs along the back wall and a single bunk formed an L against the sidewall under the only other window. Max had obviously been using that one; it was neatly made up. The others were merely frames laced with rope. A set of rough-hewn shelves near the fireplace held some beans, a sack of Arbuckle's coffee, and a sack of flour. Some pots and a large frying pan took up most of the bottom shelf, accompanied by a stack of mismatched plates, cups, and eating utensils. A crane held a pot of beans close enough to the fire to keep warm and a scuffed enamelware coffee pot sat on the edge of the hearth with wisps of steam drifting from the spout. A pan of biscuits was on the table alongside a book laying open face down.

Bob reached in and set the Winchester against the wall just inside the door and unbuttoned his coat. He shrugged the snow off of his coat, then took off his hat and slapped it against a porch post to knock the crusted snow and ice from it. He stepped into the cabin and hung his coat and hat on a peg near the fireplace. He stretched his hands out toward the flames and rubbed them together, working the tingles out as the feeling crept back into his stiff fingers. Max was setting plates, spoons, and coffee cups on the table. "You boys are a bit late, aren't you?" Max asked quietly in a concerned tone.

Bob looked over at him. "We need to talk about that. That trigger-happy wannabe gunslick you saddled me with..." Just then the door swung open and he fell silent. The others came in, shedding their coats and hats and stomping snow from their boots.

"Come on in, boys," Max called. "Coffee's on and the biscuits are ready." He smiled and reached out to shake hands with Jake and Ben. Abel turned away from the proffered hand, grumbling to himself, and moved up to the fireplace. Max' green eyes narrowed and he gave Abel a thoughtful look then turned toward the fireplace himself. He picked up the big coffeepot and poured for all of them. His eyes met Bob's in silent communication; a slight nod signified that he felt that they did indeed need to talk.

~ 2 ~

Whistling loudly and somewhat on key Deputy Bowie Tyler strolled along the boardwalk that lay beside the wide dusty main street of Barlow. His spurs were jingling in time with the music and as he walked he was contemplating the fine, sunny afternoon. A light breeze stirred the dust of the street and somewhere out of sight someone was hammering. It looked like he should have good weather for the long ride back to Laramie. He turned in through the open door of the local law office, banged the door shut, and came to a tuneful halt in front of the paper-littered desk of Sheriff Orville Hartley.

Sheriff Hartley had long since come to the conclusion that the Mexicans were onto something with the whole idea of the siesta. Consequently, he was slumped comfortably in his seat-sprung swivel chair with his booted feet propped up on a spur-scarred desk drawer and his hat down over his eyes. Sheriff Hartley tipped his hat back with a finger and opened one eye, glared at Bowie, and rasped, "Tyler, you'd best have a good reason for all the noise. You are interruptin' my rest."

Unfazed, Bowie just grinned at him. "That I do, Sheriff. I've come to take that gent quartered in that cell yonder off your hands." He pointed toward the back of the building. "Got a telegram from headquarters and they want this little lost sheep to come home."

"Huh!" Hartley grunted. He got to his feet and lifted a ring of keys from a drawer of the desk. "Kinda late to be headin' for Laramie, ain't it Tyler?" When Bowie just grinned at him he snorted and said, "Well, come on then. The sooner you an' that critter back there go on down the trail, the sooner I can get back to my nap. Things were a lot quieter around here before you got here an' I expect they'll quiet right back down again after you're gone." He walked to the barred door in the back wall of the room. He unlocked the door, swung it open, and motioned for Bowie to precede him.

Though he didn't look the part, Bowie Tyler was a special deputy for Judge Randolph Martin. He stood only about five feet four inches in his sock feet, and his ample waistline made him appear to be almost as big around as he was tall. His ash blonde hair was worn short and parted in the middle when it was combed, which wasn't often. His boots were run down and there was a crude patch, put on with rawhide string, on the shoulder of his grubby buckskin shirt. A pair of ragged suspenders held up his britches, which he wore tucked into his boot tops. Altogether, he presented a less than convincing picture of a lawman, and that was just the way he liked it. But appearances can be deceiving, as a number of gents whose faces had graced wanted posters hither and yon had found out to their chagrin. Bowie Tyler was tougher than rawhide and cat-quick on his feet, and his draw was a sight to behold. When you're built somewhat along the lines of a pumpkin you have to learn to fight or you have to learn to run, and Bowie never could get the hang of running. His legs were too short.

Bowie generally carried a Starr double-action Army revolver that had been converted to fire metallic cartridges. It was practically an antique, but it fit his hand and shot where he looked. He carried the Starr butt forward, high on his right hip, and he could draw it equally as fast with either hand. Tucked into a sheath inside his shirt collar was a razor-sharp throwing knife with a leather-wrapped hilt that had brought more than a few jackrabbits to the cook fire when he needed to maintain the peace and quiet of his surroundings and still be able to eat. The Arkansas toothpick he carried in his boot top was for chores that required a heavier blade.

Bowie stepped up to the door of Bert Harper's cell, grabbed the bars, and gave the door a shake. Harper, who obviously had had nothing better to do, had been working on a nap of his own, and the rattling of the cell door jarred him from a sound sleep. Startled, he reared up and hit his head on the bunk above. Harper sat holding his head in his hands and proceeded to curse Bowie, his ancestry, and any possible future he might have, then went on to ask, "What the hell do you want, Tyler? Go away and leave me alone." Harper started to lay back down, with one hand on his now aching head, and Bowie rattled the door again, louder.

"Rise and shine, Bertie," the deputy said cheerfully. "Your

presence is requested in Laramie. Judge Martin's ready for your day in court. You're not just in this cell for your health, you know."

Harper reluctantly swung his feet to the floor and reached for his boots. "And just how do you plan on me gettin' to court, Tyler?" he groused. "Seein' as how you shot my horse and all."

"I shot your horse after you ran him into that rock slide and broke his leg, Bertie," Bowie replied coldly. "I should've shot you instead and brought the horse in. Now get your sorry butt up off that bunk and let's go meet your new mount."

Harper stood, picked up his hat and put it on, then moved to the cell door as Sheriff Hartley unlocked it and swung it open. Hartley kept a hand on his gun and a watchful eye on Harper. In spite of Bowie's apparent good humor Bert Harper was nowhere near being a model citizen. Harper had killed a homesteader and his family, burned their cabin, and run off and sold what little stock they had. Along the way he'd also robbed a small trading post and pistol-whipped the proprietor when that elderly gentleman didn't move fast enough to suit him. The old man had been more than happy to identify Harper and the horses he had with him.

A pair of manacles lay near the cell door and Bowie squatted and picked them up, never looking away from Harper. He fastened the manacles to Harper's wrists and motioned for Harper to precede him back to the office. Sheriff Hartley closed the cell door and followed the two men back to the other room. He reached into a desk drawer and took out a sheet of paper and a pen. He dipped the pen into a bottle of ink and held the pen out to Bowie. "Sign on the bottom line, Tyler. And, nothin' personal, but I'd just as soon not see your smilin' face around here for a while. You're too much trouble."

"I don't have the foggiest idea what you're talking about, Sheriff," Bowie replied with a smile. "But I plan on leaving your fair city just as soon as I can get my traveling companion here mounted up. Take care, now."

Hartley watched Bowie and his prisoner go out the door then settled back down in his chair. Tyler and Harper had only been in Barlow for two days, but in that time Bowie had been in two fights. Admittedly, the fights had been short ones and the deputy had only been defending himself, but he had broken two chairs with other people's heads. His short stature and rotund appearance just seemed to bring out the worst in the patrons of the Buckhead Saloon. Though he would deny no man the right to defend himself, Sheriff Hartley would just as soon not have to deal with such goings on. He settled back into his chair and propped up his feet on the desk drawer again to resume the nap that Bowie had so rudely interrupted.

Bowie and his prisoner walked down the main street of Barlow toward the livery stable. Bowie was whistling as he strolled along, seemingly without a care in the world. Beside him Harper looked madder than a stepped-on baby. His hands were shackled in front of him, but his legs were unfettered and he stomped along the boardwalk. His black expression dared anyone to get in his way. "Slow down, Bertie," Bowie laughed. "You'll hurt yourself."

"Never you mind about my health, Tyler," Harper snarled. "Just get me on a horse and get me out of here. The sooner we get goin', the sooner I get shut of you an' that infernal whistlin'".

"Oh, we'll get you mounted, alright," Bowie said. "But it may not be to your liking once you're there."

At the livery stable Bowie pulled Harper to a halt. "You wait here. I'll go find the proprietor of this establishment. He should have your mount saddled and ready to go." Bowie moved up to the wide-open double doors of the big barn and peered into the cavernous interior. He left Harper standing there staring dumbfounded at Bowie's back. He couldn't believe that Bowie would just walk off like that.

Thinking he was seeing his chance to escape, Harper ever so slowly slid his left foot ahead, then his right. As he moved he listened with bated breath to see if his manacles were going to make a noise and give him away. He had managed to cover about three feet of the straw-littered sand in that manner when he heard a clicking sound that stopped him stock-still in his tracks. He had just lifted his foot to move forward again and he stood there uncertainly with his foot just clear of the ground. He slowly turned his head toward the source of the noise and looked directly into the unblinking black eye of the muzzle of Bowie's revolver that stared into Harper's own suddenly wide-open eyes. The hammer of the Starr was eared back and Bowie's finger was near the trigger, but Bowie was still looking intently into the dark interior of the livery barn. Harper dropped his foot back to the ground.

"Hallo in there!" Bowie called. He didn't look around to see if his prisoner was still moving or not. He just took it for granted that Harper had stopped trying to get away. "Anybody home?"

From inside the barn a voice said, "Is that you, Deputy Tyler? Got your mounts right here." A husky fellow of about thirty, whose left leg ended in a wooden peg below the knee, came stumping from the barn. He was leading Bowie's black horse, which carried the rather unimaginative handle of Black. One of Tyler's Unwritten Laws was "never give a pet name to something you might have to eat". Tethered to the horn of Bowie's Texas-rigged saddle was the ugliest excuse for a brown mule to ever see daylight. A McClellan saddle was cinched on the mule's back and a rope halter and lead connected the mule and the stocky-built Black. The mule was bony and old, and its muzzle was gray from nostrils to eyeballs. Its ears were flopping in time to its steps.

"That ain't a horse, an' that ain't my saddle," Harper sputtered. "An' I ain't gettin' on that beast for nobody."

Bowie turned to face Harper with the revolver still in his hand. "Well, Bertie, the way I see it you can do one of two things. You can either get up on that 'beast' or you can walk to Laramie. It's your choice. But think about this: if you decide to walk you're gonna be tethered to my horse. He ain't very tall but he's a fast walker, and we're a long ways from Judge Martin's courtroom. So what's it gonna be?" Bowie waited calmly for Harper to decide; it didn't take long for him to climb up on the mule.

~ 3 ~

The lantern had been blown out in the mountain cabin and the fire was burning low. A pocket of pitch in a stick of wood flared in the fireplace and sent shadows dancing around inside the cabin walls. A chorus of snores came from the direction of the three blanket-shrouded forms in the bunks built against the back wall of the room.

The wind outside had died down, and only the occasional gust moaned around the eaves of the cabin or swirled down the chimney to stir the embers of the dying fire. The snow still fell outside but not with the stinging intensity of earlier in the day. Instead, it came down in a feathery silence, frosting the trees and filling the mountain passes. In the corral against the rock wall of the cove the tired horses dozed under the lean-to shelter, content to share the warmth the close surroundings brought.

Inside the cabin, Bob and Max sat at the table sipping coffee in silence. Bob stared, brooding, into the flickering fire. The two men had been friends and saddle partners for a lot of years; Max knew that eventually whatever was bothering the big man across the table would come out. Over beans and biscuits earlier he had intentionally steered the conversation away from the last few days, knowing something had gone very wrong. So now Max waited with his back against the wall and his right leg stretched out on the bench where he sat.

Bob stirred. With a grimace he swallowed the last sip of the cold coffee in his cup and lifted his eyes to Max's. "Where'd you find that trigger-happy bastard?" he rumbled quietly.

"Bronco Jarvis," the higher-pitched answer came back, just as quietly. "He came through here, said he knew a good man he could get word to easy. You'd already left for Sycamore Springs so I told him to have Barnes meet you there and gave him a note Barnes should have showed you. I know you don't like to go into a job short-handed. So what'd he do?"

"He shot the banker's wife..."

Three riders came into Sycamore Springs from three different directions. It was late in the day and businesses were beginning to close up. One by one, the three men stepped from their saddles at three different places along the street. The biggest of the three stepped down from a long-legged bay and tied it loosely in front of a solidly built brick building with "Cattleman's Bank and Trust, Ronald J. Searles, Founder" lettered in gilt on the windows. He stepped up onto the boardwalk and stretched the kinks out of his back while he nonchalantly perused the street. The only other people he saw anywhere were two small boys chasing a slat-ribbed mongrel dog at the far end of the street and a man in a flat-brimmed hat, cloth coat, and crossdraw holster sitting on a bench in front of the saddle shop next door. The man looked intently at the big rider for a moment then stood and moved toward him.

Bob Morton casually hooked a thumb over his belt near his holstered Colt and waited for the man to speak. The stranger looked around quickly, almost furtively, and asked in a nasal twang straight out of the Missouri hills, "You Bob Morton?"

Bob looked him up and down, then asked, "Who are you?"

"Name's Abel Barnes. Max Horner sent me. Said you needed another man."

"How do I know Max sent you?"

Barnes reached into his jacket and Bob's hand went to the butt of his gun.. Barnes ever so carefully brought his hand back out with a piece of paper between his fingers. He handed the note to Bob, who recognized Max's scrawl. "Alright. Where's your horse?"

"Behind the bank."

"Good. Go on in, and act casual. I'll be right there." Barnes nodded once, stiffly, and went into the building. For a moment longer, Bob stood and let his gaze drift up the quiet, late afternoon street. The horses the other two riders had come into town on had vanished, which was just right. He mentally checked that step off of the list he kept in his head and followed Barnes into the bank. He left the bay tied at the rail.

According to Bob's information, the bank should be holding several thousand dollars in gold, silver, and paper. The fall roundup was on, hands would have to be paid, and cattle buyers would be cashing checks. With any luck this one last big strike would see Bob retired to his own ranch far from here.

Inside the bank, the only sounds were the ticking of the Regulator clock on the wall and the scratch of a pen on coarse paper from the tall desk where a balding man in sleeve garters and a green eyeshade tallied accounts behind the teller's cage. A discrete wooden sign painted with "Ronald Searles, President" in gold script hung loosely on a door that stood ajar near the desk.

At the sound of the two men's boots on the puncheon floor, the clerk looked up from his work and a smile began to form on his face. "Can I help you, gentlemen?" he asked as he stepped down from his stool and moved to stand behind the window.

Bob drew his pistol and stepped up to the window. "You sure can, friend. You can open up the safe for us. We need to make a withdrawal."

The clerk's face paled and he swallowed loudly. "I can't do that," he stammered. "The safe is in Mister Searles' office and he's the only one with the combination."

"Then I reckon we'd best go see him, hadn't we?" Bob asked mildly.

The back door to the building swung open, startling the clerk. Ben Terrell and Jake Carver stepped inside the bank with several sets of saddlebags draped over their shoulders. Jake had some canvas bags tucked in his belt as well. "All clear," he said.

"Alright, Mister..." Bob said, looking at the clerk.

"J-j-jacobs," the man stammered. The poor fellow was deathly pale and he was sweating profusely.

"Alright, Mister Jacobs. Let's go see Mister Searles. Time's wastin'." Bob indicated the door to the office and stepped through the gate in the low wall that separated the lobby of the bank from the teller's area. "Wait here and keep an eye out for trouble, Barnes." Jacobs pushed open the office door and stepped inside with Bob right behind him.

The slender fellow in shirtsleeves and vest who was seated at the rolltop desk just inside the office door looked up sharply. "Here now, what do you want?"

"Uh, sir, this gentleman would like to make a withdrawal," Jacobs said with some difficulty due to the dryness of his mouth.

"Then take care of it," the seated man snapped.

"A withdrawal out of the safe, Mister Searles, if you don't mind," Bob said. He moved from behind the teller so that Searles could see the gun in his hand. "This gent tells me you're the only one who can open it."

Searles swallowed loudly. The act of swallowing seemed to help him regain a small measure of his composure. "And I suppose you'll shoot us if we don't give you what you want?"

"No, but I am prepared to blow the safe, and this building, to Kingdom Come if need be. It's your choice."

Reluctantly the banker rose from his seat. "I suppose I'd better take the less violent alternative. Just a moment." He knelt in front of the large iron safe and began to turn the dial on the front. He turned the dial back and forth. There was a single loud click of the tumblers as the lock released then Searles pulled the door open. The shelves of the safe were piled with bags of coins and stacks of bills. Ben and Jake moved in and began rapidly and expertly filling saddlebags and canvas sacks. As each sack was filled one or the other of the two young men carried them out to the waiting horses.

While Ben and Jake were taking care of the money, Bob was trussing up the banker and the teller. He gagged them and laid them side-by-side on the floor. When he had them securely bound he straightened up and started toward the office door. He heard the tapping of footsteps crossing the lobby floor and a female voice called out, "Ronald dear, are you here?" Immediately a shot shattered the late afternoon silence followed by a piercing scream and the thud of a falling body...

"Everything went to hell in a hand basket from there," Bob told Max. He stared down at his hands on the tabletop. "That shot started people yelling in the street, wantin' to know what was goin' on. Fortunately for me, Ben had gone around and got my horse and brought him to the back, so we lit out of there with what we had, which was less than half of what I'd planned on taking out of that safe." He sighed. "By the time we got to the box canyon where we'd left the extra horses that posse wasn't all that far behind us. About all we had time to do was change horses and head out. The wrong direction. We didn't even have time to unsaddle the ones we'd ridden into the town. We had to just turn 'em loose." He stopped talking and his eyebrows knitted in anger and frustration.

"Dammit Max, that's the first time in all the years I've been in this business that anybody's gotten hurt, and it was a woman to boot. I came damn close to shooting Barnes myself on the way back here. The snow's the only thing that let us get away and we came real close to killing our horses to do it."

In the shadows of one of the bottom bunks Abel's eyes were glittering slits in the dim firelight. He had been feigning sleep for the last several minutes while he listened to Morton's account of the robbery. Abel loved it when a plan came together and this one was coming along nicely. He'd just been supposed to stir things up, shooting a woman hadn't actually been part of it; that had been an added bonus. On top of that neither Morton nor Horner had noticed that he was awake and that was just the way he liked it.

"I don't know what I can do about all that now, Bob," Max said softly, "except to have a heart to heart talk with Bronco Jarvis first chance I get. And I intend to do just that as soon as my leg heals some more. He's the one who got Barnes there in the first place."

"Speaking of which, how is your leg, Max?" Morton asked. "I should've asked sooner."

"It's still sore as a boil and I've gotta be careful about bending it, but it's coming along." Max had gotten crossways of a pissed-off puma about three weeks before and had gotten his right leg torn up. He'd gotten off one shot when the cat jumped him and he'd ended up finishing the cat with his belt knife after he lost his pistol. The hide was stretched on the cabin wall outside. Unfortunately for Bob, Max had been stuck in the cabin when Morton and the others had gone to Sycamore Springs, which was the reason he'd had to do some recruiting. He'd promised Jarvis that he'd pay whoever Jarvis had been able to find a hundred dollars to go along and be the lookout. Max truly disliked Bronco Jarvis, but he'd been desperate to help Bob so he'd made a deal with the man. Obviously it was a bad deal and one that Max would set right when he got the chance. Abel Barnes wasn't supposed to shoot anyone, least of all the banker's wife.

Bob regarded Max with concern. "How soon can you ride? We may have to clear out of here before too long, especially if any of that posse knows this country at all. If they do, they'll be showing up here as soon as the snow starts to go off if not before. That ignorant hillbilly shootin' that woman'll have them after us for real this time. All the other times it was just about money and we never took it all, so most of the posses didn't chase us all that hard. But I've got the feeling this bunch is gonna be chasin' us for all their worth, along with every other Tom, Dick, and Harry that can get astride a horse and pull a trigger."

~ 4 ~

Bowie and his reluctant traveling companion moved slowly down the main street of Laramie. It had gotten dark on them two hours before, but being that close to town Bowie had decided to keep riding. He was hungry, tired and dirty, and he wanted to get rid of Bert Harper in the worst way. He was afraid that if he spent any more time in Harper's presence he might just shoot the man and save the Judge the trouble of a trial. Or shoot himself just so he didn't have to listen to the complaints any more. At the courthouse Bowie turned his horse and Harper's mule down a side street and pulled up in front of a barred door in the side of the building. "Harry, open the door," Bowie called. He stepped down onto the packed dirt in front of the door. "I've got a present for you." There was no sound to indicate that the jailer was anywhere around, so Bowie kicked the door hard three times. The thumps echoed into the depths of the building, and shortly a shuffling sound and the jingling of metal on metal could be heard from inside.

"Hold yer horses, I'm comin'," a querulous voice said. A key rattled in the lock, and the door swung open to reveal a heavy-set man in his late fifties whose once strong frame was bent and twisted. Harry Koller had been one of Judge Martin's deputies until a horse had slid off the side of a ridge with him. The horse had rolled over him, breaking his back and leaving him permanently crippled. Rather than turn a good man out into the street, Judge Martin had made Harry the jailer.

Harry opened the door with his key ring held in one hand. One or the other of those keys would open any lock in the lower part of the building, and to make sure he was the only one with access to them Harry carried a cut-down twelve-gauge shotgun that had been shortened into what was essentially a double-barreled pistol. In his strong hands it looked like a toy; however, to date, no one had ever gotten his keys away from him. A bandoleer of shells was across his chest, and despite his physical condition he could still reload that gun in a hurry if necessary.

"I shoulda known it was you, Tyler," Harry said with a smile. "You're the only one who doesn't ring the bell." He pointed at a sign on the outside wall near a small rope. The sign said, "Ring bell for admittance". "Just once, I wish you'd surprise me."

"I might do that someday, Harry," Bowie said. "But for now why don't you take Mister Harper here off my hands so I can go get a bath and something to eat. I'm tired of listening to him complain." He went on in a fair imitation of Harper's voice. "This saddle's hurtin' my butt. Ain't you got nothin' but jerky ta eat? How much farther is it?" Lapsing back into his own voice he said tiredly, "Get down, Bertie, it's time for you to see your new lodgings. And don't get any ideas about Harry here. He can't run very fast, but he don't have very far to shoot and that cannon he's got there ain't just for show."

Harper reluctantly dropped to the ground and walked up to the doorway where Harry waited. "After you, Mister Harper," Harry said, gesturing with the hand that held the shotgun. "I'd offer to shake hands but mine are full and yours appear to be busy." He pointed the way down the hall with the shotgun. His voice and demeanor suddenly went deadly cold, and Harry went on, "Third door on the right, Harper. Go in, move to the bunk, and set. Do not move from the bunk until I tell you to. This is my jail, and I make the rules, and you will obey those rules. Period. Once the cell door is locked you will move to the door and put your hands through the bars, at which point Deputy Tyler will remove the manacles. You will then move away from the door and go back to the bunk. Do you understand all of these instructions? I certainly hope so because your very life depends on your understanding."

Harry looked at Harper who was glaring at the floor. Suddenly he thrust the muzzles of the gun up under Harper's chin, forcing his head up. Harry's big thumb cocked both hammers of the sawed-off shotgun at the same time. Harper's eyes widened and he swallowed as best he could under the circumstances. "I asked you a question, Harper, and I expect an answer! Do you understand my instructions?" Harper nodded and the gun moved up and down in unison with his head. "Good. Now move down the hall, do what you're told, and we won't have any trouble."

A thoroughly cowed Bert Harper moved away rapidly and

practically threw himself into the cell and onto the bunk. Harry winked at Bowie and said quietly, "Works every time, don't it?" He shuffled to the cell door and swung it shut. When it was locked he nodded to Harper, who brought his hands through the bars. Bowie took off the manacles and with them dangling in his hand turned back toward the door and his waiting horse.

"You gotta sign the papers, Bowie," Harry told his retreating back. "You can't leave yet." With a sigh Bowie turned back toward Harry and the two men moved out of earshot of the occupied cells.

"Forge my signature like usual, okay, Harry?" Bowie said tiredly. "I'm about dead on my feet."

"Someday Judge Martin's gonna start comparing signatures and we're both gonna be in trouble," Harry told him. "Go on, get out of here and get some sleep. I'll take care of it." Bowie thanked him and went out to his horse and stowed the manacles in a saddlebag. He mounted and reined Black toward the stable next to the Greek's bathhouse. The lights were still on at the Greek's, so the place was probably still open.

The next morning Bowie opened his eyes and reached for his watch, which lay on the chair near the head of the bed. From the brightness of the room, even with the shades drawn, he was pretty sure he'd overslept. One look at his watch confirmed that he was indeed late, as the rabbit in that book he'd read last spring had said, "...for a very important date." He threw off the blankets, yawned and stretched, and swung his feet to the floor and got up. The pitcher on the dresser was full and he poured water into the bowl and washed his face, trying to wash some of the cobwebs out of his brain at the same time.

His trail clothes were in a heap at the foot of the bed, piled atop the rundown pair of boots he'd worn into town. He wrinkled his nose at the condition of his buckskin shirt. Gingerly he picked it up with two fingers and moved it to a hook on the outside of the closet door. His pants he'd leave here for Missus Bleeker to wash, along with the drawers and socks he'd been wearing when he had ridden into town. He'd changed into his last clean ones after his bath at the Greek's place down the street last night.

Missus Bleeker's boarding house offered baths as part of the amenities he got with his rent, but it had been late enough when he finished eating last night that he knew the fire would be out under the boiler and Missus Bleeker would be asleep, so he'd bathed at the Greek's, then tiptoed into the house and gone to bed. As near as he could tell he hadn't moved all night; he was pretty sure he had fallen asleep as soon as his head had touched one of Missus Bleeker's fine goosedown pillows.

Bowie trotted down the stairs dressed now in a blue linen pullover shirt and black canvas britches with the legs tucked into the tops of his mule ear boots. When he came to the dining room it was empty and the dishes had been cleared, which was pretty much what he'd expected. As he was passing through the house headed for the front door he heard Missus Bleeker's voice from the kitchen. "Slept through breakfast again, eh, Mister Tyler?"

"Yes ma'am, I reckon so," he replied sheepishly. He turned and went into the dining room.

Missus Bleeker appeared in the doorway leading to the kitchen with a cloth-wrapped bundle in her hand. "Well, it's beyond me why I do it, but once again I've saved you some food," she said sternly as she held out the bundle. The rich aroma of sugar-cured ham wafted through the room. "You take it and get. You've kept Judge Martin waiting long enough. And mind you bring back my napkin." Her smile belied the stern words.

"Thank you, ma'am," Bowie said. He smiled, ticked the brim of his hat with a finger, and was on his way. From past experience he was pretty sure of what he'd find inside the fragrant bundle. There would more than likely be two of Missus Bleeker's flapjacks there with a slab of ham between them. He'd had the same room for a few years now and he and Missus Bleeker had been through this routine before.

Dorothy Bleeker was a railroad widow who ran a neat and orderly establishment. She didn't seem to mind Bowie's coming and going at all hours of the night and day, though. In fact, she treated him more like she was the mother he'd never really known than his landlord. For his part, Bowie could generally count on just such things as the food in his hand although he really didn't purposefully take advantage of it. One of Tyler's Unwritten Laws was that "sometimes things just happen"

~ 5 ~

The fire crackled merrily, and the smell of coffee was beginning to drift on the wisps of steam escaping from the spout of the big enamelware coffeepot as the water inside began to boil. "I suppose there's a reason for you waking me up at this ungodly hour?" Max' voice drifted from the pile of blankets heaped on the single bunk. "I was planning on sleeping in and having the butler bring me my breakfast in bed about ten-ish." Outside the cabin, the eastern sky was growing rapidly lighter while in the hollow the shadows slowly retreated, fighting a losing battle with the coming day. The storm had blown itself out some time during the night and stars glittered in the frigid air.

"Time you got up anyway," Bob chuckled. "Folks die in bed, ya know."

"Yeah, but that generally takes place after they get old," Max snorted. His tousled hair and intense green eyes emerged from under the blankets. The cabin was slowly warming and Max sat up and swung his injured leg out over the edge of the bunk with a wince.

"When's the last time you changed the bandages on that leg, Max?" Bob asked with a look of concern on his face. "It ain't getting infected, is it?"

"I changed 'em yesterday morning. It seems to be healing pretty well, actually."

"That's good. I'm thinkin' we need to be getting out of here about tomorrow. It's too early for this snow to stay on now, so if we head west and get out of it our tracks should melt out. Once we're out of the snow we'll head north. You remember that place we hid out in up yonder about ten years ago?" Max nodded and Bob said, "I was by there last summer. The cabin's still there, an' it looks to still be weather tight. I didn't see any sign that anybody'd been there in a long time. I cached some supplies there, some tinned meat, beans, flour an' such, but we'll have to take what's here when we go. Especially with an extra mouth to feed." He paused, thinking about the trip ahead of them. If their luck held they could make it to that cabin in about a week, by the roundabout way Bob planned to go.

"Speakin' of feed, I'll go feed the horses if you wanna start some grub. And you can roust out those chuckleheads and start 'em makin' up some packs." Bob stood and lifted his buffalo coat down from its resting place on a peg on the wall and shouldered into it. He put on his hat, lifted the latch bar, and started to swing the door open.

The creaking of the leather strap hinges was drowned by the blast of a shot and a screaming whine as the bullet ricocheted off the edge of the doorframe and thudded into the thick slab door. Morton stumbled back into the cabin and slammed the door, then dropped the bar back into place while pawing at the wood chips the impact of the bullet had sprayed into his face. Outside there was a shouted curse followed by a volley of rifle shots and the thump of lead into the door and walls of the cabin. Somehow the posse had found them in spite of the snow that covered their back trail.

This particular cabin had been built extra stout for just such an eventuality by Bob and a good friend who had spent a whole summer putting it up. The log walls, the shutters, and the front door had all been built to withstand anything short of a Sharps Big Fifty, and the back of the cabin was pressed tight against the sheer cliff behind it so it was unapproachable from the rear. While the other three scrambled out of their bunks and into their clothes, Bob and Max calmly began putting packs together for the trip out of the canyon while the bullets hammered on the wood outside.

Abel was crawling around on the floor gathering his gear, his pursed lips white and bloodless. He wasn't too keen on the idea of shooting it out with someone he could see let alone a whole posse. He'd rather do his shooting from cover, and the constant boom of rifles and shotguns outside was unnerving. "How the hell do you plan on getting out of here, Morton?" he demanded from a position on his back on the floor as he tugged at his still damp boots.

"You just hang tight a bit, and I'll show you," Bob replied. "We're safe enough in here for the moment. It don't sound like they've got anything out there big enough to bother us in here."

Just then there was a deep-throated BOOM and a huge slug smashed through the door and blasted chips of granite from the stones of the fireplace. The big hunk of lead screamed off the hearth and ripped splinters from one of the top bunks before coming to rest in a log near the ceiling. They all stared in amazement at the finger of daylight that crossed the room and made a bright dot on the floor, then all four men redoubled their efforts to gather up food, clothing, and guns. They hastily slung the supplies into makeshift packs and it was a matter of only a minute or two before they were ready to go.

When they were as ready as they were going to get in the time they felt like they had, Bob said, "Jake, reach in behind the back leg of the bunk that jasper just blew up and you'll find a piece of chain. Give it a yank." Jake bent to reach into the shadowed area near the back wall and pulled on the section of chain that hung there. With a jingle and creak the bunk pivoted, taking a section of wall with it. A three by three foot hole let in a rush of cool air. "Let's go boys," Bob said. "Unless of course you wanna wait for that Sharps to start in on us again." He didn't have to say that twice. With a rush the men were out of the cabin and rising to their feet in a crack in the rock behind the cabin. Bob stayed behind to pull the door back into place and drop a pin into a hasp. Once the posse was in the cabin it probably wouldn't take them long to figure out where the men had gone, but he didn't plan on making it any easier for them than he absolutely had to.

Following the way the others had gone Bob soon came to where the men were hastily saddling horses. The corral with yesterday's horses was out in plain sight, but these horses were fresh and were hidden undercover where the shooters couldn't see them. Abel scrambled into his saddle and started to turn the horse he was riding. "Hold up a minute, Barnes," Max said. "You don't know which way we're going out of here." Max gingerly stepped into his own saddle, favoring his injured leg, and held Bob's reins out to him. "Ready, Bob?"

Bob mounted up and led the way out the back of the hidden corral, keeping to the deep sand of the crack in the rock. The crack gradually widened as it wound down into lower ground until at last it petered out on a wide expanse of shale at the bottom of a slide a half mile away and a thousand feet below the cabin. Here the snow cover was much thinner than it was in the area around the cabin. Stopping to make sure everyone was present and accounted for, Bob listened. The firing at the cabin had pretty much faded out and he knew it wouldn't be long before the posse would be in the cabin. "We'd best get movin', boys. That posse's about figured out there's somethin' kind of off kilter up yonder. Jake," he indicated the young man in buckskins, "get us to some bare ground and get us under cover. You know this area better than the rest of us." Jake led out and the party spread apart, weaving their trails through the brush, trying as much as possible to cover their tracks while still making time away from the posse.

An hour later Bob and his men were on dry ground below the snow line. They went on for a few more miles until they came to a stretch of granite sand that pointed toward the top of the mountain above them. A pass off to the left beckoned. Bob stepped down and began to rummage in the packsack on one of their two packhorses. He came out with a handful of pieces of leather. "Lace these on your horses' hooves, it'll make their tracks harder to see." he told the men. "And let's get shut of this posse."

~ 6 ~

Bowie trotted up the stone steps of the courthouse and pulled open the heavy oak door. His footsteps echoed on the parquet flooring of the hallway inside. He winced as the sound reverberated throughout the building. Judge Martin's office was at the end of the hall on the right, and Bowie hurried through the door and skidded to a halt under the disapproving gaze of Missus Eunice Carstairs. Missus Carstairs was Judge Martin's secretary and the guardian of the Judge's day.

"You are late for your appointment, Mister Tyler," Missus Carstairs intoned. Her considerable bulk was ensconced behind a large Victorian table that served her as a desk. An array of wooden cabinets along the wall behind her held court records and other important papers and the only keys to the cabinets hung by a heavy golden chain on Missus Carstairs' substantial bosom. She had been Judge Martin's secretary since he took office fifteen years before and was always fashionably dressed in the styles of the day. Bowie normally referred to her as "The Dragon Lady", though generally not to her face.

"Good morning to you too, ma'am," Bowie said cheerfully. "Destroyed any peasant villages lately?"

"Your saucy tongue will be your downfall one day, Mister Tyler!" Missus Carstairs huffed.

Before Bowie could reply Judge Martin barked from his inner office, "Get in here Tyler, and leave the lady alone!" Bowie gave her an innocent smile and went through into the Judge's office. "Close the door." Bowie hastily did as he was told; the Judge did not sound happy.

Bowie came nearly to a position of attention in front of Judge Martin's desk. The Judge looked him up and down slowly. His lips were pursed and his fingers tapped on the desktop in front of him. At last he shook his head and said, "Tyler, you don't really realize how thin the ice you're skating on is, do you? Antagonizing

Missus Carstairs is not exactly in your best interests, you know. In addition to her other duties, she's the one who takes care of pay records. Think about that."

Before Bowie could reply Judge Martin went on. "Don't let this go to your head, but you are one of my best deputies. However, it might be a good idea for you to remember where you were just a few short years ago."

He's got you there, Tyler, Bowie thought to himself, remembering. Remembering growing up with whatever family would take him in after cholera took his parents when he was hardly more than a baby. Remembering running wild, rebelling against the work he had to do wherever he lived, because frontier families often didn't have anything extra to give to someone who wouldn't work. And remembering rustling his first steer.

After his parents died Bowie had moved from family to family. He had lived with, and worked for, anyone who would take him in. When he was fourteen, he got tired of working from daylight to dark and left Wilson Carter's farm. In addition to the clothes on his back and a navy Colt with a bent firing pin, Carter's favorite saddle horse had left with him. Three days later, Bowie had sold ten head of steers that didn't belong to him to a butcher in a small town twenty miles away. At the general store he'd traded the defective Colt for the Starr he carried now.

By the age of eighteen he was extremely proficient with both guns and knives and he'd robbed a trading post on the edge of the badlands. And shortly after his twenty-second birthday he'd found himself standing in Judge Martin's courtroom wondering what his sentence was going to be, and knowing it couldn't possibly be good. Surprisingly, the Judge had offered him a job, telling him, "I've heard that it takes a thief to catch a thief. You must be a good one, because you've never been in my courtroom before. The way I see it, you can either come to work for me or you can break rocks in the territorial prison for the next fifteen years." The Judge had taken out his large gold watch, popped open the cover, and sat calmly looking down at the hands. "You have thirty seconds to decide." It took Bowie about three of those thirty seconds to decide that he'd rather be a deputy and have his freedom than to be just another convict with a sledgehammer in his hand. He was twenty-six years old and he had been chasing outlaws for four years. Four pretty successful years, if the truth be known.

Judge Martin removed his spectacles and placed them carefully on his desk then folded his hands and stared hard at the deputy in front of him. "I realize you just came in last night, but I have another job for you. Bob Morton and his gang robbed the bank in Sycamore Springs several days ago. The banker's wife was shot. I have had no further word on her condition. The banker," the Judge consulted the notes in front of him, "is a Mister Ronald Searles. He has said that he saw four men. He claims to have identified Bob Morton and Ben Terrell. The others he couldn't identify. He claims it was Morton who shot his wife. The shooting is unusual in that Morton is known to take pains to make sure no one is hurt during one of his robberies. Apparently this time he slipped up. I want you to bring in Mister Morton and as many of his men as possible. They are to be brought in alive if possible, dead if necessary. But I especially want the man who shot Missus Searles. I leave it to your discretion how you accomplish this."

Judge Martin picked up his spectacles and settled them on his nose, then picked up a document from his desk and began reading. Bowie didn't move. The Judge looked up. "Are you still here, Mister Tyler? I believe I gave you a job to do."

"Do I get any help on this, or am I on my own against four men?"

"All of your colleagues are on assignment, Mister Tyler," the Judge said somewhat severely. After a moment he relented, and went on in a softer tone, "I realize this is a big job, Bowie. But I wouldn't give it to you if I didn't think you could find a way to get it done. Obviously, I don't expect you to bring them all in at once. If you could do so that would be excellent. If not, as I said, I leave it to your discretion. If I had anyone to send with you I wouldn't hesitate to do so. Unfortunately that isn't possible at this time. Do what you can. See Missus Carstairs for traveling funds. And try not to antagonize her too much, if you don't mind. I really am getting a bit fed up with having to listen to her complain about you."

The Judge went back to his paperwork and Bowie went back into the dragon's lair. "I have your funds here, Mister Tyler," the Dragon Lady said, handing him an envelope. "Please sign here, acknowledging receipt of those funds." She turned a sheet of paper toward him and indicated with the pen in her hand where he was to sign. Bowie was unusually silent when took the proffered pen and quickly scratched his name on the dotted line. Bowie pocketed the envelope containing his travel money, saluted Missus Carstairs with a tick of his finger to his hat brim, and left Judge Martin's office and went out of the courthouse, deep in thought. The Judge had given him quite a lot to handle, but his natural enthusiasm and confidence soon came to the fore and he strolled down the street to his boarding house, whistling as he went.

When Bowie stepped inside his room, he found his buckskin shirt cleaned and neatly patched once again. His canvas britches were clean and folded, as were his drawers. As usual, Missus Bleeker had taken care of him. Smiling, he quickly changed into what he thought of as his "traveling cowboy" clothes and hung the others neatly in the closet. He took the gunbelt with the holstered Starr down from a peg in the closet and slung it around his waist, settling the belt comfortably so that his hand came naturally to rest on the grip. He drew the pistol and checked to make sure it was loaded then snugged it back into the holster, which was custom built for the gun and held it securely without a hammer thong. The thong was there if needed, but in three years it hadn't been needed. The throwing knife went into the sheath sewn in the back of the shirt below the collar and his big dagger-bladed camp knife went into the boot sheath. A razor-sharp skinning knife was tucked into a beaded and quill-decorated sheath on his belt.

The next thing out of the closet was a full-length saddle scabbard. Protruding from the scabbard just far enough to allow him to get a good handhold on it was the stock of a model of 1873 Winchester rifle. The stock had been cut down to fit his physique, as had the barrel, and the same gunsmith who had converted the Starr to cartridges had worked on the action of the '73. Bowie's weapons were his one vanity. He knew his life depended on them and he made sure that he had the most reliable guns and knives money could buy. Many looked down on the Starr as being obsolete, but it fit Bowie's hand and, with the work that had been done on it, was deadly accurate and tough enough to use for a hammer. It had yet to fail him, and had in fact pulled him out of several tight spots. Bowie started to swing the closet door shut and stopped. He looked down at the rifle in his hand, then stood it back in the corner of the closet. He had the strangest feeling that he might need a weapon a bit more intimidating than the rifle so he reached in and brought out a different scabbard.

This second scabbard held a Greener coach gun. Its two

short barrels didn't give it a lot of reach but it was deadly at close range. He slipped the shotgun from the scabbard and started to hang the scabbard back in the closet, then changed his mind and took it back out. He lifted a bandoleer of shotgun shells from a hook, slung it over his shoulder, and loaded the shotgun. The Winchester he left in the closet.

A sheepskin lined coat, wool gloves, and a beat up black hat completed Bowie's ensemble. It was still relatively warm here in the city but he didn't have any idea how long he would be gone. With fall progressing fast and the first snows already in the high country he thought he'd best be ready for anything. An hour later he was in the saddle of his black horse headed for Sycamore Springs to talk to Ronald Searles. He wanted to hear the story for himself.

~ 7 ~

"Alright, hold 'em up, let's give 'em a breather." Bob Morton raised his hand to stop the string of horses and men following him up into the mountains. They'd finally traveled far enough that they could cross the mountains away from the snow. The vegetation here just below timberline was sparse and composed mainly of lichens and wind-twisted pines, and the occasional stunted mountain huckleberry bush struggling to exist in the lee of a rock. They were halted in the shade of a rock outcropping where they would be hard to see.

Bob reached down to his saddlebag and brought out his spyglass. He pulled it out to its full length and scanned the country behind and below them, looking for dust or any other sign of the men who had attacked them at the cabin. Knowing how far light could flash in the clear air of the high country, he was careful to keep any reflection from the lens or the brass of the tube. With a grunt, he collapsed the glass and returned it to the saddlebag. "I think we lost 'em."

"Good," Max said through gritted teeth. "I'm ready to take it a little easier." Bob looked quickly at his friend. Max' face was pale; it was easy to see he was in a considerable amount of pain.

"Once we get through that pass yonder we'll hole up for the night." Bob pointed up the slope above them. "I'd hate to stop on this side and have another storm blow in and trap us. Can you make it another three or four miles? Jake should have camp set when we get there."

"I reckon I can if I have to," Max replied. He didn't see the calculating look Abel cast his way.

"Alright then, we'd best be moving on. It's gonna be dark before too long, and I don't wanna go through this pass without at least some daylight to help."

Abel looked up the mountain and snarled, "I don't see no pass, Morton. I think you're leadin' us into somethin' we can't get out of."

"Barnes, don't make me regret not shooting you back yonder. Just shut your mouth and follow me." Bob turned his horse up the mountain and heeled him into motion. Abel sat still, seething, until Ben Terrell's horse bumped into the rump of his mount.

"You going, or staying?" Ben asked. "If you're going then get that cayuse on up the trail. If you aren't then get down and hand me your reins. That's my extra horse you're sitting on, and either way he's going up yonder."

"I'm goin', I'm goin'," Abel snapped. He yanked the horse's head around, unmindful of the glare Ben fixed on his retreating back; he hated seeing a horse mistreated. That was a damn good horse, and if Bob didn't shoot this hillbilly maybe Ben would himself. But for now they had bigger fish to fry, like getting completely away from that posse. Ben heeled his own horse into motion, tugging on the lead rope of the packhorse behind him. The two packhorses were roped nose to tail, and both were good, mountain bred mustangs. Bob led off, followed by Jake and Abel. Ben brought up the rear with the packhorses. Soon the only sign of the men was a few slowly settling wisps of dust and a few dimples in the bed of granite sand they rode on.

Four days later they reached the cabin. When Bob called a halt at the edge of the forest, the cabin and the surrounding forest were dark and silent. The cabin was a dark shadow among other shadows at the edge of the clearing where it backed up against the trees. The only sound was the far-off hooting of an owl and the swish of a nighthawk's wings as it swooped through the little clearing in search of flying insects. A horse stamped impatiently, smelling grass and water ahead. It swung its head and the bit chains tinkled softly. The first crescent of the new moon tinted the trees with the faintest hint of silver.

Jake Carver drifted up to Bob, materializing like a wraith out of the darkness. His soft voice carried just far enough for Bob to hear him say, "Corral's empty and the chimney's cold. If there's anybody here, I ain't findin' no sign of 'em. Far's I can tell, you were the last one here."

"Good," Bob said. Exhaustion was evident in his voice. They had left the posse on the other side of the mountains four days ago and had ridden straight through, stopping only to rest the horses. They'd lived on jerky and dry biscuits, napping in the saddle as they rode, and both men and horses were all in.

"Alright boys, let's go on in, but look alive. We've come too far to get stupid now." Bob heeled his horse into motion with the reins in his left hand and his right hand on his leg near his holstered Colt. He stopped his horse alongside the cabin then stepped down and groundtied the bay. He stepped up to the cabin door and listened for a minute. He heard no sound so he stepped to the side of the door and tugged on the latchstring. He gave the door a push and it swung open on creaking leather hinges. He stood a moment longer, giving anyone inside time to get antsy, but nothing happened.

Bob drew his pistol and slipped into the cabin with his back to the wall. He heard the scrabble of tiny clawed feet on wood as a mouse scampered away from the intruder, but there was no indication that the cabin was occupied by anything bigger. Bob relaxed and holstered the Colt then reached into his pocket and brought out a match and a stub of candle. The candle soon sat flickering on one corner of the rough pole table.

He turned back to the door. "We gettin' down or not, Morton?" Abel's nasal voice grated out of the dark. "My butt feels like it's done grown to this damn saddle."

Bob ignored the complaining voice and walked up to where Max sat slumped in his saddle. A twinge of alarm went through Bob at the sight of his old friend, and he wondered if he'd pushed too hard. Then Max' head came up and his white teeth flashed in the dim light as he said, "Are we there yet, Dad?"

"Yeah we are, son," Bob answered in the same vein. "Get down and go on in. I'll take care of your horse." Max half stepped, half fell from the saddle as Bob reached out to grab his arm. Max stood with his head down and both hands clamped on the saddle horn for a moment, then he straightened up with an obvious effort.

"I'll be alright, Bob. You go on and get the horses settled." Max took a step and fell flat on his face, out cold. Bob and Jake scrambled to his side and rolled him over gently. Max's face was ghostly pale and his breathing was shallow.

"Let's get him inside, Jake. Ben, you and Barnes get the horses unsaddled and bring the packs in. Corral's back yonder and there's good water and grass. We'll take care of Max." For once Abel was silent, but an unseen look of calculation passed over his bony, unshaven face as he turned away toward the corral.

~ 8 ~

Bowie's tired black horse came into the west end of the main street of Sycamore Springs with his head low and the reins swinging loosely on his neck. They'd been pushing hard since leaving Laramie several days ago. It was now nearing midnight and the town was, for all practical purposes, closed for the day. The houses standing back from the street were dark, all the townsfolk in their beds. Even the saloon had only a single dim light showing inside, and a flickering lantern outside. Inside, the swamper was cleaning up the place, sweeping the floor, emptying the brass spittoons, and generally sprucing up for the next day's business. It wasn't the fanciest place in the territory so he didn't have to work all that hard at it. The man came out onto the boardwalk and dumped a bucket of dirty water over the rail.

As he turned to go back inside, the swamper caught a glimpse of the tired horse and its drooping rider. The horse stopped of its own accord in front of the saloon. Bowie jerked up into some semblance of wakefulness and saw the old-timer standing there looking at him, holding an empty bucket in his hand. "Any chance for a meal and a drink, amigo?" Bowie asked. He was figuring that it was probably a waste of time, but at the same time he knew that the worst the answer could be was "no".

"I reckon there might be some beans left on the stove in yonder," the fellow answered. "Fire's been out for a while so they probly ain't too hot but you're welcome to what's there. I've done had mine. Can't do nothin' about the drink though. Boss'd have my hide if I... Aw, hell, come on in. He'd probly do more if I turned away a payin' customer. Y'are gonna pay, right?"

"Oh yes, I'll pay," Bowie replied. "And right now I'm not too particular whether the grub's hot or not as long as it's at least remotely edible." He stepped down from Black and led him to a nearby trough. "Don't founder yourself, you idjit," he told the tired horse as the white-streaked muzzle plunged into the welcome coolness. The horse slurped in several large swallows of water, then Bowie drug its head back up. "Come up for air, why don't ya?" He let the horse have a bit more water then led him to the hitchrail and tied him securely.

He turned back to the swamper, a grizzled old-timer with one eye that seemed to be looking at everything but what his snout was pointed at. The old man was stoop-shouldered, and his nose showed the broken veins of the longtime alcoholic in the light of the guttering lantern flickering from a nail driven into the front of the building. His clothes were tattered, the sole of one boot flapped when he took a step, and his ragged britches were held up by a piece of rope in lieu of the suspenders he'd probably sold to buy whiskey. "Lead on, MacDuff," Bowie said with an airy wave.

"Who the hell's MacDuff, mister? Name's Cooner." The old man glared at him then shrugged and reached inside his ragged shirt to scratch his bony chest. He'd long since given up on figuring out what most people were talking about anyway. He turned and went into the saloon, holding the batwing door for Bowie. Bowie stifled a laugh and followed Cooner inside. Soon he was digging a spoon into a heaping bowl of beans and venison and washing it down with beer.

Between bites Bowie asked, "Where can I put up my horse for the night? You don't happen to be offering livery services along with this fine cuisine, do you?"

"Not hardly," the old man snorted. "Yer on yer own for that. Livery stable's down the street. I reckon you can turn your horse in most any stall down there, an' Ol' Man Perkins'll be more than happy to take yer money. Or yer horse if ya don't show up in the mornin' to pay him. He's sold more than one man's mount out from under him fer not payin'. An' he ain't too patient about it, neither. You'd best not wait too long ta git him some dinero."

"I'll try to remember that," Bowie laughed. "Say, old timer, you wouldn't happen to know anything about a robbery hereabouts a week or two back, would you?"

"How'd you hear about that? What are you, the law or somethin'? "

"Or something. Word gets around the trails, you know. I heard it was Bob Morton and Max Horner."

"Well, you heerd wrong, mister. It was ol' Bob all right, but that Horner weren't with him. Them boys had some other feller with 'em instead. It was that other feller that shot the banker's wife."

"Is she dead?"

"No she ain't, but the sawbones don't figure she's gonna last much longer. That feller done gutshot her."

"How'd you know it was Bob Morton? And how do you know Max Horner wasn't with him?"

"I was out yonder in the bresh when they rode out. I've known Max for nigh on ten year, an' ol' Bob longer'n that. The townsfolk's been sayin' that Bob shot that woman. I know better, but folks hereabouts don't pay me much mind. I will say, Bob ain't never shot no woman, ner 'lowed one ta be shot, in all the time he's been makin' off with other folks' money. Never hurt nobody else, neither. That other feller took it on hisself ta shoot Missus Searles, an' if I ever see him again I'll gutshoot him m'self. There ain't no kinder er gentler soul in this town than Missus Searles."

"Would you recognize him again if you saw him?"

"I should smile. He set right over yonder on that bench for half the day." Cooner pointed across the street to where a bench could just barely be made out against the wall of the saddle shop.

"What did this other gent look like? And how do you know he shot the woman?" Bowie asked.

"He looked like the Missouri hill trash he more'n likely is," Cooner snorted. "Ya know what I'm talkin' about?" He looked at Bowie, who nodded. "He was kinda medium-sized and kinda scrawny lookin', with a big Adam's apple that bobbed around a lot when he swallered an' when he talked. He was wearin' a homespun shirt and them kinda dark wool pants like ya git off the store shelves, only these was patched like he'd had 'em a while. He had on a old frock coat an' mule ear boots with little blue stars up by the top that he wore with his pants tucked in. He carried his pistol in a crossdraw holster an' kept his hand on it the whole time he was settin' there. Reason I noticed him was 'cause he was actin' real nervous-like. Kept lookin' at his watch like he was waitin' on somebody. Then Bob Morton rode in an' the two of 'em went into the bank. It weren't but a few minutes later Missus Searles was shot an' them boys come a hellin' out from behind the bank an' rode off up the country. Bob was acussin' that feller up one side an' down the other. That's how I know who shot Missus Searles. I heard ol' Bob givin' him what for about it."

Bowie drained his glass, then stood and dropped a dollar on the table. He'd gotten a lot of information in a hurry, all of it information that he hadn't had before. At least now he had some idea of what the unidentified man looked like. "That pay for the grub and the beer, old timer?" he asked, knowing full well the money would go in the old man's pocket as soon as he was out of sight.

"I reckon. But a mite more might make the boss a little happier in the morning," Cooner said with a sly smile on his whiskered face.

Bowie laughed and dropped another dollar on the table. "I reckon I'll get my horse on down to Mister Perkins' establishment and take my chances on keeping him," he said. "Adios, and thanks." Bowie went out the door and untied Black from the rail. As the deputy went out of sight in the darkness, Cooner's hand snatched up the two dollars and dropped them in his pocket with a cackle, then the old man went back to his work.

Bowie was standing on the boardwalk the next morning picking the remains of his breakfast ham out of his teeth when the posse straggled in. Their horses were shuffling through the powdery dust of the street and the horses' coats were streaked with salt and dried mud. One man lay belly-down over his saddle and several others had bandages on various parts of their anatomy.

What hair could be seen under the lead rider's hat was streaked with gray, and his walrus mustache was powdered with dust. The once shiny star that peeped out from under his heavy sheepskin lined coat was scuffed and dirty. Sheriff Cosby drew rein in front of the Branding Iron Café and stepped stiffly down into the street. The dapple he was riding stood hipshot with its nose to the ground, too tired to wander away. Cosby's hands went to the small of his back and he grumbled, "I'm gettin' too old for this crap."

Bowie stuck his toothpick in the corner of his mouth and stepped forward. Cosby ignored him and turned to the men who sat their horses in a ragged line behind the gray. "You men might's well go on home. Ain't gonna do no good ta just sit there. You," he pointed to the man leading the dead man's horse, "get him to the undertaker. Town'll pay for his buryin'."

A crowd had gathered by this time. "Did them outlaws kill Bart?" a voice asked.

"No, the damn fool's horse rolled on him crossin' a shale

slide a day or two back. Those outlaws led us clear to hell and gone back up into the mountains yonder, then dropped us like a dirty shirt," Cosby growled.

"Did ya ketch them no-good murderers, Sheriff?" another voice wanted to know.

"What the hell did I just say? Do you see any of 'em layin' across any saddles anywhere here? I sure as hell don't." He turned back to his horse in disgust as the riders began to disperse. "You people go on about your business," he ordered the small crowd of townsfolk. "Show's over." He pulled the gray's nose up out of the dirt and started toward the livery stable. "Come on, horse."

Bowie stepped down into the street and fell into step with the sheriff. "Mind if I join you, Sheriff?" he asked.

"It's a free country, ain't it? Who're you, and what do you want? I'm not much in the mood for small talk."

"My name's Tyler, Sheriff. Bowie Tyler." He waited for Cosby to introduce himself, but the sheriff just walked on. "I'd like to talk to you about Bob Morton."

"Why?" As tired as he was, Sheriff Cosby wasn't planning on wasting any more words than he had to. He and the posse had been out for seven long hard days. Like a damn fool, he'd figured on one day, maybe two at the most, even though he should have known better. As a result, they'd long since run out of grain for the horses and food for themselves. Yesterday they'd run out of coffee. The only thing that had saved them was a young mule deer buck too naïve to know he should be afraid of the men on horseback. Sheriff Cosby's plans for the immediate future included nothing more than a bath, a bottle, and a bed, and not necessarily in that order. He'd get with that program just as soon as his horse was put away. He'd worry about eating after he woke up, which event would preferably take place in about a week.

"I'm planning on bringing in Morton and the rest."

The matter of fact way Bowie made his statement finally got Cosby's attention, and he stopped walking to stare at Bowie. "What in Sam Hill makes you think you can do that?" he rasped.

"It's what I do," Bowie said quietly.

"You some kinda bounty hunter?" Cosby asked suspiciously. Distaste was evident in his voice.

"I'm a special deputy for Judge Martin's court."

Cosby looked him up and down then snorted. "Right. And

my Aunt Martha's the Queen of England." He turned away and went on toward the livery.

Bowie stood thoughtfully watching him go then came to a decision. He reached inside his vest and brought out his badge. A few steps later he was again beside the sheriff. He cupped the badge in his hand and held it where Cosby could see it. "Here's my bona fides, sheriff." Startled, Cosby looked at the silver star then looked at Bowie.

"Is that thing real?"

"Yes it is. Now will you talk to me about Morton or not? Winter's coming, and I'd kind of like to get back to Laramie before Christmas if I can."

"Let me get my horse put away and we'll go back to my office and I'll tell you what I can, which ain't much. Them boys are damn good at hidin' a trail."

~ 9 ~

Inside the cabin, Bob hurriedly threw together a pallet of blankets near the stone fireplace. He and Jake had brought Max into the cabin and they laid him on the pallet. Jake went to work getting a fire started and Bob covered Max with another blanket. Tinder, kindling, and firewood were already laid, ready for a match, and soon the orange light was casting weird shadows on the walls. "There's water right outside," Bob told Jake. "I walled up a spring, and dug it over to the corner of the cabin. Made a little pool there big enough to dip a coffeepot into."

Jake went out the door with the coffeepot and a kettle in hand. He brought them back full and put them in the edge of the fire to heat. Bob laid a hand on Max's forehead. "Damn, he's burnin' up with fever," he said, looking up from where he knelt on the floor. "We gotta do somethin'." Jake stood there awkwardly, not knowing what to say.

Bob looked down at Max's right leg. It had swollen until the bandages visible through the split seam of the pants had cut deep into the flesh. Angry streaks of red connected the bandages like an evil spider's web. "You damn fool," Bob said softly. "You just had to keep goin', didn't you? Wouldn't take a chance on slowin' us down." He shook his head sadly and looked up at Jake again. "Is that water hot yet?"

"It ain't boilin', but it's purty hot."

"Good. I gottta change these bandages and get something on this leg or Max is gonna lose it." Bob went to work uncovering the wounds. The knots that held the bandages were stretched tight, so he eased the blade of his knife under each one and carefully cut them away, lifting the pads they held as gently as he could. Most were stuck tightly to the skin and had to be worked loose a little at a time. The smell of suppurating flesh turned his stomach but he went doggedly on. Abel Barnes and Ben Terrell came in with the packs and stacked them in a corner away from the fire.

"Ben, break out some more bandages," Bob ordered. "There's a sack of corn meal with 'em. Stir up some mush for some poultices for this leg. And somebody get me a bottle of whiskey." Ben dug into one of the packs and came out with a handful of linen strips and a cloth bag. He quickly stirred the corn meal into the kettle of water until it was almost too thick to stir.

Bob took the bottle of whiskey from Jake and liberally doused the wounds in Max's leg. He used a piece of linen to wipe away the crusted blood and other matter, trying his best to be as gentle as possible and still get the job done. He expected the pain to rouse Max but the only sign that the unconscious man felt anything was an occasional twitch of his lips. Ben looked over at Bob. "Corn meal's ready if you are, Bob."

"Alright, wrap it up in the cloth and let's get it put on these claw holes." They quickly bound the poultices to Max's leg then covered him with some more blankets. Ben built up the fire, and Bob sat back on the floor. He picked up the bottle and took a long swallow of the whiskey. The burn of the liquor made him cough. He'd done what he could for Max; the rest was in the hands of Divine Providence.

"You men get some sleep," Bob told the others. "I'll sit up with Max." The three men were too tired to argue; they merely unrolled their blankets and dropped on them without taking time to pull off their boots.

Bob leaned back against the wall and stared unseeing at the firelight on Max's face. He was looking back down the years at the trails he'd covered with Max. They had been riding together for fifteen years. They had met down in Texas, at a small border cantina, and each had recognized a kindred spirit in the other. They'd been robbing banks together pretty much ever since. Sometimes it seemed like they'd spent their entire lives running from posses and hiding out.

There had been hungry times and cold times. They'd patched each other's wounds and covered each other's backs. And through it all, they'd acted as honorably as they knew how, never injuring anyone in any of their robberies and never taking all there was to take. They'd always left half of what was there, knowing that a lot of the money belonged to those who couldn't really afford to lose all they had.

Now Max was in bad shape and there wasn't much that

Bob, for all his great strength, could do about it. A feeling of helplessness washed over him and he gritted his teeth, fists clenching. At last he laid his head back against the rough logs of the wall. His eyes slowly closed and he fell asleep, lulled by the warmth of the nearby fire.

Abel Barnes' eyes glittered in the firelight. He watched carefully as Morton's head fell back and his eyes closed. Soon Morton was snoring softly. Abel slowly and carefully threw back the blanket he'd pulled up around his face to keep Morton from knowing he was awake and sat up, doing his best not to bump either Ben or Jake. The last thing he needed was a witness to what he was about to do.

Abel got to his feet and eased across the floor in his socks. He stood for a moment looking down at Max and listening to his labored breathing. He knelt by Max' head and listened again to his harshly drawn breaths then he reached down to the rolled blanket that served the injured man as a pillow. Max had shifted his head and now barely lay on the end of the roll.

The outlaw from Missouri looked around at the others and saw that Ben and Jake were still sleeping soundly. Morton stirred and Abel caught his breath and silently willed the big man to go back to sleep. Morton's arms came up and crossed on his drawn up knees and his head fell forward. His forehead rested on his crossed forearms and he began to snore again.

Abel quietly released the breath he had been holding and grasped the blanket roll in both hands. He brought the rolled blanket up and over Max' face and leaned all his weight on it. The wounded man bucked and fought. His hands came up to try to grab Abel's wrists and take the blanket from his face, but the long ride had taken its toll. Max' struggles grew rapidly weaker and soon his hands relaxed their grip.

The killer kept the blanket pressed to Max' face. He knelt there watching Max' chest heave as he tried to draw in the air that he couldn't get. Max' chest quieted and all movement ceased as Max died. Abel looked around the cabin to see if the commotion had awakened the others but no one stirred. Abel replaced the rolled blanket under Max' head and crept back to his own bed, well satisfied with his night's work.

~ 10 ~

The Sheriff's office was cold inside when Sheriff Cosby and Bowie walked in. "Ain't been anybody here since the posse rode out," Cosby said by way of explanation. "There's generally not enough law work around here to warrant hirin' a deputy unless I got somebody locked up back yonder." He hooked a thumb back over his shoulder. "Then I got a fella that comes in nights."

"Back yonder" consisted of a strap iron grid fronting a small room with two wood-framed bunks bolted together out of four by four lumber, and a honey bucket. A door stood open in the middle of the wall of iron. A large, rusty padlock hung open from a loop next to the opening.

"Sit down, deputy." Cosby pointed toward an ancient swivel chair that sat by the scarred desk. He went behind the desk and dropped into his own chair with a heartfelt sigh. "Damn, it's nice to sit on somethin' that ain't movin'." He leaned forward, slid open a desk drawer, and brought out a bottle of rye and two glasses. He poured two fingers of the whiskey into each glass and nudged one toward Bowie. The other he emptied down his throat in one long swallow, coughing as the liquor burned its way to his stomach.

"Hoo boy, I needed that!" Cosby exclaimed, then poured another two fingers into his glass. He tipped the bottle toward Bowie who shook his head, no. Cosby drove the cork back into the bottle with the heel of his hand, leaned back in his chair, and asked, "What do you want to know, deputy?"

"Call me Bowie, Sheriff." He held out his hand.

"I'm Jim," Sheriff Cosby said, reaching across the desk and shaking Bowie's hand.

"First off," Bowie went on, "I'd like your version of the robbery, or at least your version of the pursuit. I already heard about the robbery from somebody else. And I may talk to the banker. What I'd mostly like to hear about is what went on while you were chasing Morton and the rest."

Cosby drew in a deep breath and let it out slowly. He took a sip from his glass then said, "What went on was a helluva wreck, mostly. After Missus Searles was shot, them boys lit out like their tails was on fire. They ran their horses plumb into the ground gettin' outta here. But they had fresh mounts hid in a canyon about five miles out, already saddled. Couldna taken 'em more than a minute or two to get gone from there.

"It took me a while to get a posse organized, and by the time we found where they changed horses it was startin' to get late. We did find where they went into the river, and we thought we found where they came out. It was pretty much dark by then, so we camped for the night.

"The next mornin' at first light, we took in after 'em again..."

The posse was out of their blankets well before it was light. Benson got a fire started and coffee on. It had been a restless night for all concerned. Some time after midnight a cold wind had come up and clouds had blotted out the stars, and the men had huddled in their blankets wishing for sunup. But sunup was long in coming and they had finally given up trying to sleep.

They gathered around the fire with their hands outstretched toward the flames. A few chewed jerky as they waited for the coffee to be ready. Adams, the dentist, had a blanket wrapped around his skinny body. He'd found that his cloth coat was woefully inadequate to block the keening wind. Most had their hats tied on with scarves in an attempt to keep their ears warm.

Sheriff Cosby returned from saddling his horse. "You men better saddle up while you're waitin' for that pot to boil," he said. "As soon as we can see tracks we're leavin'." There was a great deal of grumbling but the men did as he said. By the time the coffee was ready the camp had been struck and they were ready to go look for the outlaws' trail.

Tracks were plain where the outlaws had come out of the river. Just plain wrong. Allston was the first one to figure it out. "These ain't the same tracks we were followin' yesterday," he said, reining his horse in. He was the best tracker of the lot. "There's too many of 'em, and none of these horses have got riders. The tracks ain't deep enough. And none of 'em's shod, neither. This here's somebody's brood mare band or somethin'. It sure ain't Morton and his gang. They musta come outta the water somewheres else."

Sheriff Cosby disgustedly led the posse back to the river. "Benson, you take Adams, Fox, and Carter, and ride back to where we hit the river. Two of you take each side. When you get back there, keep goin' for a mile or two, and look sharp. If you find somethin', send somebody back here. We'll go the other way."

Fox and Carter trotted their horses through the shallows to the other bank and the four started back the way they'd come. Adams was shivering under his blanket. Sheriff Cosby took his own horse across the river, followed by Arlen Jackson, and the rest of the posse started upstream, checking carefully for any sign of the outlaws' passage.

The four riders moved downstream; three of them were looking carefully at the banks and the surrounding foliage, while the fourth just tried to stay warm. Yesterday they'd been hurrying and had just plain overlooked whatever clues there might have been. Today that wasn't gonna happen, at least as far as Benson, Fox, and Carter were concerned. Adams was so cold and uncomfortable that he didn't really care one way or the other whether they found anything or not. He was ready to turn around and go home. For what seemed like forever they moved along. All but Adams were peering intently at scuffs in the sand, broken twigs, and anything else that might give them some indication of the outlaws' trail. But their searching eyes found nothing.

They came up to the sandy beach where they'd struck the riverbank the day before. The sand was churned up, as was the gravel of the river bottom, where the posse's horses had milled around while their riders tried to decide which way to go. Yesterday, upstream had seemed like the logical way to go. Some of the rocks visible through the crystal clear water had seemed to be disturbed in that direction, so they'd turned that way. Then, this morning, they'd found out that the tracks they'd thought were going to lead them to the outlaws weren't the right ones.

"Alright," Art Benson said. "We're back where we started. Anybody see anything?" The other three shook their heads. "Sheriff Cosby said to go downstream for a ways before we turn around, so let's get to it. The longer we set here the farther those murderin' scum are gonna get."

Far downstream the very tops of a group of cottonwoods

could be seen over the rolling terrain. The four riders approached the copse carefully with rifles in hand. The underbrush was thick and grew right down to the water's edge so that visibility was poor. Benson reined up at the edge of the brush and told the others, "You boys wait here and cover me. We don't wanna tromp on the tracks if there is any." He stepped down, keeping his rifle aimed in the general direction of the wooded area in front of him and his horse between himself and the trees.

The wind in the cottonwoods made a sighing sound, and one of the horses stamped a foot. Somewhere a bird chirped once and was still. "I don't think there's anybody in there," Adams said to no one in particular. Benson ignored him as he moved cautiously past his groundtied horse and up to the edge of the brush.

Benson parted the bushes with the barrel of his rifle. He gripped the Winchester tightly, his knuckles white. He took one hesitant step then another. The bushes were wiry and snagged at his clothes and gun. He was sweating in the cool air and the moisture was beading on his forehead. Benson reached up and tipped his hat off his head to hang down his back by the rawhide string.

"See anything, Art?" Don Fox asked. They were all nervous, expecting the thunder of gunfire at any moment, and knowing that they were right out in the open if anything did happen.

"Shut up, dammit," Benson snarled back over his shoulder. He faced front again and wiped his hands, one at a time, on his shirtfront. He gripped his rifle again with his right thumb on the hammer and took a step forward.

With a thunder of wings a covey of quail burst out from under Benson's feet. He fell back cursing, unconsciously yanking back the hammer of the Winchester. His finger closed convulsively on the trigger and the rifle boomed. Instantly, the other three posse members opened up on the thicket, rifles blasting. Bullets were clipping twigs and whining off of tree trunks.

Benson scrambled for cover, yelling less than complimentary words at the shooters. A bullet sprayed bark into his face and stung his cheeks. Another slug burned across the top of his right shoulder, tearing through his vest and shirt and splitting the skin. "Stop yer shootin', you ignorant jackasses!" he roared. "You're about to kill the wrong man!" Gradually his words, combined with the epithets he was shouting, sank in, and the firing tapered off. White clouds of powder smoke drifted on the breeze.

"Are you alright, Art?" Buck Carter jumped from his fidgeting horse and ran forward with his eyes wide and alarm on his face. He stopped dead in his tracks at the sight of the blood on Benson's vest.

"Do I look alright to you, Buck?" Benson snarled. "What the hell did you think you were doin'? You idiots damn near took my head off."

"We thought somebody was shootin' at us, Art," Fox said.

"That was me, you dern fool. My foot slipped and my gun went off." He reached up to his shoulder with his left hand, wincing. "Adams, you're the doctor. Get your butt off that horse and see if you can stop the bleedin'. Carter, you go look for tracks."

Adams started to protest that he was a dentist, not a doctor, but Benson stopped him with a glare. Besides the fact that he'd nearly been killed, he was embarrassed that it had actually been his own damn fault. He'd fired the shot that had set the rest off, so he tried to cover his fear and chagrin with bluster. Carter asked, "What if there's somebody in there, Art?"

"After all that shootin', anybody in there is either dead or hightailin' it outta the country. Just go do it. Adams, get over here." Benson slipped off his vest and unbuttoned his shirt. By this time, the bleeding had essentially stopped of its own accord. He felt around the cut on the top of his shoulder and drew out his hand. A few small smears of blood were on his fingers, but he had an idea that the bleeding wouldn't amount to much. He'd gotten extremely lucky. "Never mind. It's done bleedin'."

From the thicket Carter called, "I think I found the trail."

~ 11 ~

Cosby yawned mightily, his jaw creaking. It was still and quiet in the room. Outside, a freight wagon rumbled past. The crack of the teamster's whip echoed off the buildings, and Cosby went on with the story. "Fox rode back upriver and got the rest of us. We headed on back down to where Benson and the rest were waitin'. You ain't gonna believe what we found when we all got back together at that thicket." He paused and took a small sip of whiskey. "You probly been in some of those alder thickets that grow along the rivers around this country." When Bowie nodded he went on. "Well, Morton and the rest left the water in the middle of one of the thickest alder tangles I've ever seen. Left it mighty slick and quiet, too, from what we could tell. They didn't hardly turn a leaf. Looked like they came up out of the water one at a time, on different deer trails.

"So anyway, when I got there, Carter was all ajangle, wantin' to show me what he'd found. And it was the damnedest thing, but somebody was actually markin' the trail for us."

"Seriously? Marking the trail?" Bowie was having considerable trouble believing what Cosby was telling him.

"That's right. I told you it was hard to believe. But there it was, plain as day. Off to one side of one of the deer trails, somebody had bent a couple of branches into a arrow, and tied 'em with string, pointin' the way. Otherwise, I don't think we ever would've figured it. That alder tangle was about five acres, and there was deer and cattle trails all through it, and those boys took advantage of ever one of 'em..."

Cosby, Jackson, Ralph Allston, and Wally Barrett, the proprietor of the livery stable, rode up to the alder tangle where Benson and company had found what they thought was the outlaws' real trail. Carter was on one foot and then the other in anticipation. As soon as Cosby brought his horse to a stop Carter was at his stirrup. "You gotta see this, Sheriff. Dangedest thing I ever seen!"

"Alright, Carter, alright. Let me tie up my horse, and I'll go with you." Cosby looked for a convenient branch, and finally ended up just handing the reins to Bart Adams, who seemed to have become the designated horse holder. The dentist looked thoroughly miserable and he gave Cosby a wan smile as he took the gray's reins. "Thanks, Bart," the Sheriff said. He turned back to Carter. "Alright, let's go." Carter turned toward the thicket.

The Sheriff followed Carter into the brush for about thirty yards before Carter stopped and pointed. At first, Cosby just looked around in confusion, trying to figure out what it was that he was supposed to be looking at. He was just about to ask when he saw, just above head height, two relatively freshly broken alder branches tied together at the tips with string. The arrow they formed pointed a little west of north. "See, Sheriff? It's just like Fox told you. Somebody left us a trail marker."

Cosby studied the marker. It was unobtrusive enough that it was apparent that whoever had left it didn't want anyone but the posse to see it. What bothered Cosby was why it was there. He couldn't for the life of him figure out why someone who was running from a posse would be letting that very same posse know where he was headed. It was a sure bet that it wasn't Morton who left it. What wasn't so sure was who else it might be. Cosby shrugged and turned back toward where the others were waiting. Regardless of who had left the marker, Cosby sure wasn't going to look a gift horse in the mouth; at this point they needed all the help they could get. "Allston. Find us a trail to follow."

Ralph Allston was a trapper and part time wolfer. He was slightly built, with stooped shoulders and one leg that didn't quite work right. He had been around for the big beaver boom, but lately the market had been poor. He'd done some hide hunting and some scouting for the Army. For the last couple of years he'd taken to hanging around Sycamore Springs, trapping and hunting wolves for the ranchers in return for food and drinking money. His greasy buckskins stank, and he was seriously in need of dipping and clipping; but when he was sober, which wasn't often, he was a good tracker. Yesterday he hadn't been especially sober; today he was sober and hungover and more than a little pissed about both conditions. Sheriff Cosby had found his bottle at last night's camp and confiscated it.

Allston stood under the arrow and looked around. His rheumy blue eyes were still sharp, and it didn't take him long to find a smudged track in the deep leaf litter. He bent nearly double, almost like he was sniffing out the tracks, then stood and pointed. "They went yonder, Sheriff." Cosby saw a gap in the trees and brush and nodded.

"Alright. We'll head that way. But just remember that bunch of unshod horses you followed last night." Cosby raised his voice. "Bart, bring me my horse. The rest of you men come on. We'll have to walk until we get out of this crap." He didn't see the look of pure venom the wolfer aimed at his back as he took the gray's reins and started through the alders on foot, and wouldn't have cared if he had seen it. It took a lot more than Ralph Allston's attitude to bother Sheriff Cosby.

The posse made its way through the alder tangle, leading their horses and following an occasional smudge of a track until the trail ended on a wide outcropping of hard rock. As near as any of them could tell, it just stopped dead with no trace of where it went from there. The men cast about in circles, looking for anything that would tell them which way the outlaws had gone, but it was like their horses had sprouted wings and flown out of there.

It was the dentist who found the marker. At the edge of the rock slab, someone had piled three rocks on top of each other and made an arrow pointing away. The small stack was only a few inches high, and Adams had only found it because he'd needed to answer the call of nature. He'd been kicking through the grass to discourage any reptiles or other wildlife from sampling his behind when he squatted, and he'd kicked the small pile over. The clattering of the rocks as they fell had caused him to jump back thinking he'd found a snake. "Over here," he called. "I think I found another marker."

Cosby walked over, leading his horse. He looked at the marker and called out, "Alright. It looks like they headed west, at least for now." He looked up at the sky, which was growing grayer by the minute as clouds gathered overhead. "We'd better get moving. There's a storm comin'." He toed the stirrup around and swung up on the gray. He sat waiting while the oth-

ers mounted then told Allston, "Lead out Ralph. Keep lookin' for another marker." The wolfer booted his paint out onto the short grass and rode slowly, looking for any other sign of the outlaws.

A slow couple of hours later he stopped. Just ahead of them a small creek cut through the land; on the near side, willows and other brush grew down to the water's edge. Allston cursed Bob Morton and the men riding with him. They were making this job damn hard, when all he wanted to do was get it over with and get back to his ramshackle cabin and a bottle. And now he had another creek to unravel. To make things even harder, the first snowflakes were skating down a raw north wind. The flakes were more ice than snow, and stung where they struck exposed flesh. If it snowed much they might never find the trail again. These early fall storms could drop a foot of snow in just a few hours, and if that happened they might as well go back to town. He said as much to Sheriff Cosby. "I don't think we're gonna find 'em, Sheriff. An' if this snow gets to goin' like you an' me both know it can, we fer sure ain't gonna even get close. All they gotta do is lay up somewhere an' their trail'll be gone."

"I know that," Cosby snorted. "Just keep goin'. I'm starting to think somebody in that bunch wants us to find 'em." Cosby turned up the collar of his coat and raised his voice to be heard over the keening of the wind. "You men look for markers. It's getting on toward sundown and I'd like to know which way to look for their trail in case this storm gets serious." The men grumbled, but they spread out and started searching.

In a skirmish line they moved toward the bed of the small creek. Their rifles lay across their saddles as they rode. A thin line of willows, live oaks, and chokecherry brush blocked their view of the banks and the wind made it hard to hear. Allston was the first to push his paint through the screen of vegetation into the relative calm of the creek bed. His head was swiveling as he tried to look in all directions at once. A few snowflakes swirled around him. "Ain't nobody here," he called to the rest of the posse. The men broke through the wall of brush into the creek bed and the small grove of cottonwoods that lay across the thin trickle of water. In the last few minutes the snowfall had gotten heavier.

"Alright, fan out and see what you can find," Cosby told them. "Keep an eye out for someplace to camp too. We need firewood, and grass for the horses." The men scattered, some up-

stream and some down. A sudden call from Buck Carter brought them all quickly back together. At a bend several hundred yards upstream, he could be seen standing in his stirrups and waving his hat. When he saw the rest moving toward him he sat back down in his saddle and rode out of sight. A thin trail of smoke, whipped away instantly by the wind, told the tired posse members that Carter had found a place to camp. He'd also found another marker.

~ 12 ~

The gray light of dawn was barely lightening the cracks in the shutters of the cabin when Bob Morton awoke with a start. The fire had gone out hours before and only a few wisps of smoke drifted up from the stone hearth. Bob rubbed the back of his stiff neck and tried to straighten his back. He'd been exhausted and had slept through the night sitting up with his back against the logs. His creaking muscles were telling him in no uncertain terms that he was too old to do that kind of stuff any more.

He yawned and rubbed his eyes, then ran a hand across the stubble on his jaw. Bob was a man who liked to be clean-shaven as much as possible, but for the last few days hygiene had gone out the window. Maybe today he could at least wash up good, and scrape the bristles off.

Bob rolled himself toward the fireplace and got up on his knees. With a partially burned stick he scraped together a few embers and laid a handful of pitch slivers over them. He leaned down and blew gently on the glowing red spots. A sliver started to blacken and curl then a tiny tongue of flame sprang up. He blew again, and the flame grew and spread to another sliver. In short order Bob had a small blaze going and he fed it larger sticks until he was sure it wouldn't go out.

Bob turned to where Max lay on his back with the blankets up under his chin. At first he was sure that Max was asleep, and he was thankful that his old friend could get some kind of rest. Then it struck Bob that something wasn't right. It didn't look like Max was breathing. He watched closely, but the blankets covering Max's chest weren't moving and there was no sound. Bob reached over and touched Max's shoulder. Even through the blankets he could tell that Max was cold. He quickly felt for a pulse in Max's neck but there was none. "NO!" he suddenly roared in anguish.

Ben and Jake came out of their blankets with their guns drawn, looking wildly around for the source of that sudden shout.

Bob was down on his knees alongside of the body of the man who had been his best friend. His head was in his hands and his eyes were closed as he rocked in silent pain. Behind Ben and Jake, Abel was smiling to himself as he watched the big man's grief.

Bob rose heavily to his feet. His pale face was a blank though his eyes glittered with unshed tears. "Ben, you and Jake wrap him up. I'll go start diggin'." He took his coat and hat from the pegs they hung on near the door then shrugged into the coat and set the hat on his head. He swung the door open and went out, leaving the door open to the cold morning air.

"Bob," Jake called.

"What?" Bob asked without turning around.

"I'm awful sorry about Max. He was my friend too. We'll get him ready." Bob nodded curtly.

"Thanks." Bob picked up a shovel that stood against the corner of the cabin and moved off into the woods. He stopped at the top of a small rise that looked down on the meadow in front of the cabin and kicked and scraped the litter of pine duff away and started digging. His mind was empty as he dug and the mechanical rhythm helped him to put Max's death aside for a little while. Here the soil was deep and it wasn't long before the hole was nearly at Bob's waist.

"I'll dig for a while, Bob. You better go get somethin' to eat. Jake's got bacon and tortillas in yonder." Ben Terrell's voice broke into Bob's reverie and his head jerked up. He'd been concentrating so hard on the simple task of digging that he hadn't heard the young man come up. When Bob stopped shoveling, he realized that he was soaked with sweat, despite the coolness of the air, and that he was shaking with hunger.

"Alright," he said, tiredly. "I'll go get somethin' to eat and be right back."

"Don't hurry on my account." Ben watched Bob heave himself up out of the hole, then jumped lightly down and began to dig. The dirt flew as he dug the spade in. Bob picked up his coat; he didn't even remember taking it off. He turned toward the cabin, walking slowly with his head down. At the cabin door he automatically stamped the dirt from his boots before opening the door.

Max's blanket-wrapped body lay against the far wall when Bob walked into the cabin. He looked at it for a moment then looked away, fighting back the grief and the pain that the shoveling had temporarily dulled. There would be time enough for that after he'd eaten. The smell of bacon made his stomach rumble. He sat down on the log bench beside the table and Jake set a cup of coffee and a plate with a couple of tortillas and some bacon in front of him. Bob ate mechanically, not really tasting what he was chewing. When he was finished he sat for several minutes staring into his empty cup before he shook himself and got slowly to his feet. "Jake, I'd appreciate it if you'd help me get him outside."

"Sure Bob. Whatever you want." The two men each took an end of the shroud and carefully carried the last mortal remains of Max Horner to his grave. Ben stood silently beside the mound of dirt with his hat in his hand. Two lariats were stretched out on the ground near the hole and Max's body went on top of the two ropes. Gently the men used the ropes to pick up the body and lower it into the ground.

Bob took up the spade and scooped a shovelful of dirt into the hole. Silently he handed the spade to Jake, who did the same thing then handed the shovel to Ben. Bob took back the spade and began to fill the hole. For some reason his vision was blurred and he was having trouble breathing. He stopped and stood there with wet streaks down his face, unable to keep going. Jake took the shovel from him, eased him aside, and took over the job of filling the grave.

When the grave was full and the soil was well tamped down, Jake Carver stuck the spade in the ground nearby and went to where Bob stood with his hands in his pockets. "You gonna say somethin' over him, Bob?"

"I reckon. I ain't sure what, but I guess I'd best say somethin'." He stood silently for a moment then took off his hat. Ben and Jake did the same. No one made mention of the fact that Abel wasn't with them; no one particularly cared. He wasn't really a part of the group. "Lord, we're sendin' you a mighty good man," Bob said quietly. "He mighta been an outlaw in the eyes of the law, but he never hurt nobody who didn't have it comin'. He was a man of his word, and the best friend I ever had. He'll be missed down here, Lord, and all we ask is that you show him a little of your mercy, like he showed mercy down here. Thank ya. Amen." Bob put his hat back on his head. "Let's see if we can round up somethin' to use for a marker. He was too good a man to lay in an unmarked grave."

~ 13 ~

Sheriff Jim Cosby ran his fingers through his hair and exhaled tiredly through pursed lips. “After that, it seemed like every time we lost the trail we found another marker. But with the snow it still took us two days to catch up with ‘em. We found ‘em in a cabin up yonder under the Caveney Rim, and got ourselves set up. I told the posse not to shoot until I did, but when Bob Morton started to come out of the cabin that damn wolfer fired anyway. The stupid bastard was shakin’ so much from not havin’ had any whiskey for a couple of days that he missed. Morton dove back inside and slammed the door, and the whole damned posse emptied their guns into the walls of that cabin before I could get ‘em shut down. Near as I could tell, the only bullet that went through the door or the walls either one was the one from Wally Barrett’s Sharps. He punched a hole in the door but that was it.

“Turns out Morton had a whole other bunch of horses hid out that we didn’t know about, and a back door out of that cabin we couldn’t see. Nobody shot back at us, so after while we went on down there and found out that Morton and the others was gone. It didn’t take long to figure out how they got out. We trailed ‘em after a fashion for about a day and a half and finally lost ‘em completely way the hell and gone back out in the mountains. There’s about half a dozen passes they could’ve used, and in the process of us traipsin’ around tryin’ to figure out which one they did use, Bart Adams let his horse roll on him. After that the rest of ‘em just wanted to come on home. So now you know as much as I do.”

Cosby poured more whiskey into his glass and took a sip. Bowie sat quietly thinking. “I was gonna have a talk with the bank president,” Bowie said. “But I kind of doubt that I’ll get any more from him than I got from you.” He looked over at the sheriff. “Can you point me to where you lost their trail? I guess that’s where I need to start. I’ve got a map back at the hotel if that’ll help.”

“Bring me your map and I’ll give it my best shot,” Cosby

said. "I ain't tried to read a map since the Army, but I'll see what I can do."

"I'll be right back." Bowie got up out of the chair and went at a fast walk back to his room at the hotel. The map was right where he'd left it, spread out on the bureau. He rolled it into a tight tube and left the room. He went down the stairs and across the lobby and out the door, and trotted down the street back to the sheriff's office.

When he stepped back into the sheriff's office, the thump of his bootheels on the puncheon floor brought Cosby's head up from where it had been resting on his chest. Cosby snorted and rubbed his face with a calloused hand as he tried to bring himself back to life. "Sorry about that, Deputy."

"No problem, Sheriff." Bowie unrolled the map on Cosby's desk and pinned the corners down with whatever objects he could find. Cosby stood and looked over the well-creased sheet of paper for a minute while he got himself oriented.

"Alright. Here's Sycamore Springs." His blunt finger touched the dot that marked the town. His finger moved across the paper. "Here's where they went into the river, and here's where we found the first marker." He traced as best he could the route the posse had followed to the cabin. From there he showed Bowie which way the posse had gone until they lost the trail for the last time. "Up in there is the best I can do, Deputy," Cosby said, indicating an area on the map that was blank except for the word "uncharted" in black ink. "Like I said, there's a wagon load of passes they could have used, and I never did figure out which one was the right one. I guess you'll just have to try 'em all until you find some sign that they've been there. If it don't snow you might get lucky."

Bowie rolled the map back up and stuck out his hand. "Thanks for your help, Sheriff. I appreciate it. I reckon I'd best be on my way." The two men shook hands and Bowie left the office. As he swung the door shut he looked back over his shoulder. Cosby was sitting slumped in his chair staring at nothing. The man looked, in his own words, "too old for this kind of crap." Bowie shut the door quietly and turned toward the livery stable.

Bowie strode briskly into the barn where he'd left his horse. The hostler was in the back cleaning out stalls. "What's it gonna take to get my horse outta debt?" Bowie called to him.

"Four bits, stranger," a tenor voice said, practically at his elbow. Bowie jumped aside and turned and his hand went to his pistol. An unshaven, lath-thin fellow in a tattered black frock coat with patches on the elbows stood in front of the open door to a small office. His hands were stretched as high in the air as he could get them and still have his feet on the ground. His dented derby was on the ground behind him where it had landed when it fell victim to a blow from his rapidly rising arms. "Don't shoot, mister. I didn't mean to startle you. I'm the proprietor of this establishment." As Bowie relaxed and moved his hand away from his gun the man slowly brought his hands down. Shaking, he held one hand out toward Bowie. "My name's Perkins. Joshua Perkins." Bowie ignored the outstretched hand and reached into his pocket and brought out some coins.

"That's a good way to find yourself taking up residence in Boot Hill, Mister Perkins," Bowie said. "I'd like my horse saddled and taken to the hotel if you don't mind," he went on. He dropped the four bits in the man's hand. "And I'd like him to be there in the next few minutes. I've got a long ride ahead of me."

Perkins nodded sharply. He was starting to regain his composure. "If you want that kind of service, it will cost you another two bits!" he snorted.

"I don't think so," Bowie snapped in return. "After you took two years off my life, I think you owe me. What I gave you is all you're getting."

"Oh alright," Perkins said reluctantly after a moment's thought. "But don't think I do this for every two-bit drifter that comes in here! I'm only doing this out of the goodness of my heart."

"From what I hear, you don't have any goodness in your heart," Bowie said with ice in his voice. "Or much of a heart, neither. By the way, my horse is that black over yonder." He turned sharply to leave the barn. He could feel the heat of Perkins' glare on his back as he went out of sight.

Bowie stomped out of the livery barn and down the street. He was thoroughly disgusted with himself, first for not paying attention to what might be behind him, and second for reacting the way he had to the liveryman's voice. He'd nearly shot the poor sucker for nothing. Of course Perkins had no business sneaking up on Bowie like that, and should have known better, but still Bowie had overreacted. Maybe when he got back to Laramie he'd better talk to Judge Martin about getting some time off.

Bowie gathered his gear from his hotel room and went back down to the lobby. The hostler from the livery was waiting for him with his hat in his hand. "I got your horse right outside, mister," he said. "Mister Perkins said to tell ya he's sorry for what happened. He even sent some grain fer yer horse." The man grinned. "You musta really spooked him. I ain't never seen him do nothin' like that before."

"Thanks." Bowie smiled and tossed the man a dime. He went out to where Black was tied to the rail. Sure enough, a small cloth bag hung from the saddlehorn. Bowie slung his saddlebags and bedroll behind the cantle, tied them down, and slid the shotgun into the scabbard behind the offside stirrup. He snugged up the cinch, pulled the rein loose from the hitchrail, and mounted. He touched a finger to his hat brim in thanks to the hostler and tickled Black with his spurs.

Noon found him fifteen miles from town. Bowie stopped at a small spring-fed pool and watered his horse then went on. He was chewing on a piece of jerky as he rode. He hoped to be somewhere close to the trading post at Riverbend by dark; Bowie didn't mind sleeping out, but he much preferred having a hot meal of some sort in his belly when he went to bed. Jerky would only take a man so far. He'd heard that the gent who ran Riverbend had a wife who could really cook and he meant to find out for himself.

It wasn't quite full dark when Bowie came over a rise and saw the lights of the trading post in the near distance. Two saddled horses stood hipshot at the rail by the door so Bowie turned Black off the trail and circled to come up to the long rambling building from the rear. He kept to soft ground where he could, and there was no indication that anyone saw or heard him come up. He stepped down and led Black to a nearby water trough for a drink then tied him to a corral pole across the fence from where two brown mules and a rawboned sorrel stood switching a few brave flies.

Bowie moved cautiously around to the front of the building. In the splash of light from the windows he could just make out the brands on the horses. One horse had a Lazy B Bar on its hip and the other had a Rafter S on its shoulder. Bowie had no idea if the horses and riders were from a local ranch or not, but the animals appeared to be of better quality and in better condition than most ranch horses. These two were built for speed and bottom.

Bowie paused just outside the open door and let his eyes adjust to the brightness, then stepped into the trading post. Across the room a long counter was backed by shelves filled with canned goods and sacks of coffee, dried fruit, and other staples. A blanket-covered doorway at the left end of the counter led to another room. To the left of the doorway shelves held a selection of trade blankets and a few bolts of brightly-colored cloth. At the other end of the counter a stack of dried furs of various sorts and a similar collection of deer hides lay under a wall rack that contained a few well-used rifles and one short-barreled coach gun in what looked like ten gauge. A pot-bellied stove with a pot of coffee on its top stood in the middle of the room.

Bowie turned to his right and sauntered toward a bar made of two planks laid across whiskey barrels. Outwardly he was relaxed, but inside he was anything but. Sitting at a table with his back to the room was a man with a scar on his neck. Bowie had hauled him into Laramie on an assault charge two years ago. Assault and robbery both, actually. Charlie York was his name, and he'd severely beaten a miner and robbed the man and his partner. York had gotten eighteen months in prison for his efforts, and he'd sworn that he'd get Bowie when he got out.

Bowie didn't know the scrawny fellow sitting across the table from York and he hoped he could have a drink and a meal without having to fight York first. He was tired and hungry and just not in the mood.

The man behind the bar was tall and lanky, with red hair and freckles. A walrus mustache, well stained with tobacco, covered his upper lip. The sleeves of his gingham shirt were rolled up and he had a moderately clean bar towel tucked behind his belt. He put down the glass he was polishing and greeted Bowie with a smile and a fusillade of words. "Howdy stranger. What can I getcha? Drink? Meal? Supplies? We got it all here, by golly. Have ya come far? Guess so. Ain't too many folks live around here close. Been here five year, myself. Name's Red Hanlon..."

Red stopped to take a breath and Bowie cut in. "I'll take a drink and a meal and some supplies, all three, Red. And send those gents yonder one of whatever they're drinking." He pointed over his shoulder at York and his tablemate, hoping York would take the drink as a peace offering instead of a challenge.

"Yessir, here ya go." Red brought a bottle with no label on

it from behind the bar and poured a glassful and set it in front of Bowie. Bowie picked up the glass and held it up to the light. He couldn't see through it, but at this point he really didn't care what was in it as long as it was alcohol and he could be fairly sure it wouldn't kill him. He shrugged and took a drink. How bad could it be, really?

When he got his breath back, he looked at Red's grin and said, "Damn, that's moose turd pie!" He sucked in another breath. "Sure is good though. Did you make that yourself?" Red nodded, and with a somewhat puzzled look on his face took the bottle to York's table. He reckoned he'd have to have the stranger explain to him just what his good homemade whiskey had to do with a moose turd pie.

Red went back behind the bar and commenced polishing glasses that didn't really need polishing. He glanced at Bowie then looked back to where Charlie York and his companion were sitting. The clink of a bottle on glass was loud in the quiet room. The gurgle of poured whiskey and a deep gulp were equally as loud as the muttered curse that followed the drink. A chair scraped on the floor and Red's eyes widened. A hand fell on Bowie's shoulder and yanked.

Bowie turned with the force of the yank and the Starr appeared in his left hand. York's fist was drawn back to punch when the muzzle of the pistol came to rest a little north of his belt buckle. "Now Charlie," Bowie began quietly as York tried to swallow the sudden lump in his throat. "I don't really wanna kill you because there's just too much paperwork involved. And I'm relatively certain that you don't particularly want to be dead. So why don't you just put your arm down and go have another drink, then you and your playmate can ride on out of here. I'll forget that you laid hands on me if you just stay off my backtrail, okay?"

York nodded mutely and lowered his hand. His face was pale. He backed a couple of steps with his eyes on the pistol then turned and stomped to the table. He poured his glass full and gulped the dark liquor down. "Come on, we're leavin'." His traveling partner started to protest that they'd just barely got there and besides it was dark out and where did Charlie plan on camping tonight? York just looked at him for a half dozen heartbeats then walked out the door in mid-protest.

Bowie holstered the Starr. The man at the table glared at

Bowie. "He wasn't gonna do nothin' but thump on ya some. He wanted ta git even with ya for arrestin' him. Why'd ya run him off?"

"Maybe I just don't feel like being thumped on tonight," Bowie replied. He leaned back on his elbows on the bar. This wasn't always possible because of his height, or lack of it, but this bar was not especially tall. "Let me suggest that you might be a mite more comfortable elsewhere too."

The man looked at him, dumbfounded. "I didn't do nothin' to ya!" he exclaimed.

"You didn't do nothin' for me, either." Bowie strode to the table. "Now scat!"

"Nobody tells me where to go or what to do! I don't give a rip if you are a lawman!" The man pushed himself to his feet and reached for his gun. Bowie came around the table and slapped the reaching hand aside with his left hand. His right hand balled into a fist that slammed into the man's jaw. The man went backwards over his chair and landed in a tangled heap of splintered wood with his gun hand trapped behind him.

Bowie plucked the Colt from the man's holster and calmly shucked the cartridges out of the cylinder while his fallen opponent struggled to quiet the bells ringing in his head. Bowie dropped the Colt on the table and reached down. He got a solid handful of the man's neckerchief and drug him to his feet. "Just for the record, what's your name?"

"You go to hell!" the man snarled.

"That's entirely possible, friend," Bowie replied, then delivered a hard, open-handed slap to the man's jaw. "Just answer the question." His voice hardened. "Now!" He drew his hand back again.

"Awright, awright! You don't fight fair! My name's Shaw. Sam Shaw."

"Well Mister Shaw, if you can't fight any better than that I think it would behoove you to straddle your horse and light a shuck out of here before I really get mad. I'm tired and I'm hungry and I want you gone." He pushed Shaw toward the door. "Now git!"

Shaw stopped at the door. "What about my gun?"

"Chalk your loss up to bad judgment on your part," Bowie replied curtly. The door slammed behind Shaw and Bowie turned back toward the bar. Red was staring at him. He handed Shaw's pistol to Red. "And now..."

"I-I-I'd like to stay, if that's okay with you," Red stammered uncertainly.

"You live here, remember?" Bowie said wryly. "How about another drink and something to eat? My belly's thinking my throat's been cut."

~ 14 ~

Red Hanlon set an inch-thick venison steak and a plateful of spuds and gravy in front of Bowie, along with some cornbread and a pot of honey. "You realize, a course, that them feller's are probably gonna be waitin' to drygulch you someplace out there, right?" Red asked. He poured a cup of coffee and set it on the bar next to the plate.

"Uhm hm," Bowie mumbled around a mouthful of food. He chewed and swallowed then said, "But I'm figuring that I can make 'em miss."

"Now just how in the world are you gonna do that?" the storekeeper asked in surprise.

"I'm not sure yet, but I'll think of something." Bowie went on eating. He paused to swallow then asked, "You got a back door out of this place? And someplace I can sleep tonight?"

Red hooked a thumb over his shoulder. "Back door's out yonder through my house," he said. "I'll show ya when ya get done eatin'. Ain't got no extra rooms, but you're welcome ta bunk down in here by the stove, or out yonder in the haybarn. It ain't much of a barn, but the hay out there'll be softer sleepin' than the floor in here." Bowie nodded his thanks and went on eating.

Mary Hanlon came out of the kitchen, wiping her hands on her apron. The burr of her Scots accent was pleasant to the ear. "Would ye like some pie, mister? We have nae fresh fruit this time of year so it's dried apple, but the mister here seems to like it." Bowie's mouth was full so he settled for nodding as politely as he could. The lady smiled at him and went back into the kitchen. She came back with a quarter of a pie on a plate and set it in front of him. "I do like to see a man eat," she said.

"This food is well worth the eating too, ma'am," Bowie said. "I imagine the pie will be the same. Thank you."

"Oh, go on with you!" she said, then turned back to her kitchen, smiling to cover the blush on her cheeks.

Bowie stuffed the last of the pie into his mouth and washed it down with coffee. He pushed his plate back with a quiet belch and a sigh. "That, my friend, was good eats. That lady should be running a fancy restaurant in a big city somewhere, not pushing grub in a trading post in the middle of nowhere."

"I think so too, but Mary, she won't hear of it. She likes it out here. Says she likes to listen to the coyotes howlin' and the wind blowin' through the sagebrush, an' she wouldn't have none of that if she lived in town. So I reckon as long as she's happy here we'll probly be stayin'." He gestured toward the coffeepot. "More?"

Bowie declined with a shake of his head. "I'm so stuffed I can hardly move," he groaned. "I think I'll put my horse up and hit the hay, so to speak. It's been a long damn day."

"Back door's back this way." Red led the way into his living quarters and pointed. "The back porch's in the shadows. We'll blow out the lamp so's ya can get out without nobody seein' ya."

Bowie nodded his thanks to Mary, who blew out the lamp. He waited a moment for his eyes to adjust then slipped soundlessly out the back door. He stood with his back to the wall and listened to the night. When he had come out, the crickets had gone silent, but it wasn't long before their song started again. He could hear the stirring of the horses and mules at the corral and the swoosh of a bullbat out beyond the barn, but no other sounds marred the stillness.

He walked over to Black and untied him from the rail. By this time the horse should have gotten well enough acquainted with the storekeeper's animals that he could be turned into the corral. Bowie quickly stripped off the saddle and blankets and threw them up on the top rail. Judging by the abundance of stars twinkling overhead it probably wasn't going to rain. He watered Black once more and turned him through the gate. The horse immediately dropped to his knees and rolled onto his back, working back and forth to scratch his itchy hide. He rolled back to his feet and shook the dust off then trotted to the manger and began munching hay.

Bowie untied his bedroll from behind the cantle of the saddle and slid his shotgun out of the boot. He carried both to what Red had optimistically called the haybarn but which was in fact more of a big shed stuffed with prairie hay. He moved some of the hay around until he had a nice soft bed built and spread his blankets. He took off his boots and gunbelt; the Starr went near his head and the Greener was laid across his boots alongside his blankets. It wasn't long until he was asleep.

Back in the trading post kitchen, Mary Hanlon had relit the lamp. If Bowie could have heard the conversation between Mary and her husband he would have smiled. "Yon fellow is not the normal range tramp we get in here," she said.

"He's some sort of lawman," Red answered. "Them boys he sent packin' said somethin' about him arrestin' one of 'em back down the trail somewheres."

"Really? He's very polite. I never would have taken him for an officer."

"Me neither, but you shoulda seen the way he handled them fellers. He don't look like much, as chunky as he is, but I got an idee he's a lot tougher than a fella might think. He seems kinda lazy, but he moves purty dang fast when need be, too. He drew that pistol before that gent even knew he done it, an' he got over there an' took the other'n's gun without even breakin' a sweat. I don't know who he is, but I'm glad he ain't an outlaw. There's enougha that sort around here as it is."

Miles away from where Bowie slept in Red's barn, Bob Morton was wide-awake. He lay in his blankets in the cabin hideout with his hands behind his head, thinking about the events of the past weeks. As far as he could tell they'd gotten away clean from the posse from Sycamore Springs, but it had cost them. He still couldn't believe Max was really dead. He guessed maybe that death was a sign that it was time for Bob to disappear, to retire from the outlaw trail.

Bob owned a ranch up in the Idaho mountains under another name. The hands who rode for him knew him as Donald Gordon, and they all thought he was a railroad surveyor. He'd actually done some surveying in a past life and he used that as the explanation for both his absences from the ranch and the extra cash he could afford to spend on the place.

Bob had thought very seriously about turning Abel Barnes in to the authorities for shooting the banker's wife. It would probably have been for the best, but for some strange reason he just couldn't bring himself to do it, and it probably wouldn't have changed anything. He figured he must be getting soft in the head. If that was the case it made retirement look that much better. So that was it; he'd break the news to the boys in the morning. With his mind made up Bob drifted off to sleep.

~ 15 ~

Bowie woke up when the first rays of the sun poked their way into the barn. He sat up and stretched and rubbed his hands over his face. Several hens and a bedraggled rooster scratched and clucked in the dust around the bottom of the haystack. Bowie threw the blankets off and reached for his boots. The sudden movement startled the chickens, who clucked in alarm and scuttled off. Bowie grinned as he upended his boots to dump out any unwanted company that might have taken up residence there during the night. Chickens just might mean eggs for breakfast.

A plume of smoke rose from the chimney of the trading post kitchen, pointing straight up in the still morning air. By the time Bowie had rolled his bed and tied it behind his saddle, the smell of boiling coffee and frying bacon drifted to his nose and his stomach growled in response. He knocked on the kitchen door. The door swung inward and Bowie was greeted by Mary Hanlon and a steaming cup of Arbuckle's. "Thank you, ma'am," he said politely.

"Come in, Mister, uh..."

"Tyler, ma'am. Bowie Tyler."

Mary looked him in the face and said, "I understand that ye are a law officer, Mister Tyler. Is that correct?"

Bowie nodded uncomfortably. He really didn't want to answer her question but Charlie York had kind of let the cat out of the bag last night. "Yes, ma'am, I am. I'm a special deputy for Judge Martin down yonder in Laramie."

"If ye don't mind me saying so Mister Tyler, ye don't really look like a deputy."

"Please ma'am, call me Bowie. And I try not to look much like a deputy. I find it makes my job easier." He was saved from any further explanations by the sudden appearance of Red in the doorway to the trading post proper.

"Yer horse'll be out front when ya finish breakfast, mister. I took the liberty of puttin' some supplies, some dried apples an' jerky an' such, in your bags. There's some venison and some of Mary's good fresh bread there too. If there's anythin' else ya think ya might want or need, just let me know."

"Thanks, Red," Bowie said. "It sounds like you've pretty much got it covered." Mary called them to breakfast and Bowie reached into his pocket and brought out a five dollar gold piece. "Will that handle things?"

"That's more than plenty," Red answered. "I'll go git your change."

"Keep it," Bowie told him with a smile. "I might be broke the next time I come through and I'm generally in need of a good meal." He held Mary's chair for her then sat down himself. "We'd better sit down and eat before this good food gets cold."

When the meal was done and the dishes scraped and put in the sink, Bowie thanked his hostess and sauntered outside. He figured that by this time York and Shaw, if they were waiting for him to surface, would have gotten really tired of waiting for him to show up and would have ridden on. He was half right.

Bowie led Black to water and stood with his hands in his pockets while the horse drank, then Bowie pulled the cinch up tight and stepped into the saddle. Red came outside to see him off and Bowie waved as he turned the horse and booted him out past the corral. The short-coupled mustang wanted to run so Bowie let him have his head for a half mile or so then pulled him down into the ground-eating jog that was the main reason Bowie had the horse. Sunrise was an hour old when the trading post disappeared from sight behind him.

By mid-morning Bowie was starting up into the foothills. He had a good idea where to go from Sheriff Cosby's description and from what he'd seen on the map though the map wasn't as good as it maybe could have been. As he moved higher the bunchgrass and buckbrush of the lower elevations gave way first to junipers and mahoganies, then to pines and firs. A few scattered tamaracks glowed yellow in the afternoon sun as he climbed higher. Just before dark Bowie stopped Black at a spring at the edge of an aspen grove.

Bowie led the horse to water then unsaddled him and picketed him on a patch of lush grass that grew near the spring. A fitful breeze rustled what leaves remained on the white-trunked trees for a moment, then was still. Off in the distance a coyote wailed and was answered by another equally as far away. In a small clearing below where Bowie stood stretching the kinks out of his back a doe, followed by this year's fawns who were nearly as big as their mother, stepped cautiously out into the open and sniffed the air for intruders. She stood totally still for a moment as the breeze swirled a few dry leaves into the air, then with a snort she bounded back into the brush followed by her children.

A magpie that flew down and landed at the edge of Bowie's clearing saw the black horse standing there alone. The bird scolded for a moment then flew to the top of a nearby currant bush and began to pick the dried berries from the branches. Bowie was nowhere to be seen. Only his horse and saddle remained in the clearing.

To the west of the clearing a twig snapped, then clothing rustled on smooth white bark as whoever was out there brushed against an aspen trunk. The magpie jumped into the air with a squawk and Bowie quietly drew the Starr and held it pointed in the opposite direction from where the sound had come. He was laying behind a newly-downed aspen trunk and he had burrowed under those few branches that still held some leaves. He strained to hear the telltale sound of movement through the trees and brush behind the clearing; the tiniest scrape of boot leather on stone told him where the second man was.

Bowie shifted the Starr to his left hand and wiped his right hand on his sleeve. The movement jarred a branch on the downed tree and dried leaves rattled. There was the blast of a shot and a bullet threw a spattering of bark in his face then whined out over the mountain slope. Bowie fired twice in the direction of the shot then rolled to his left. He dropped down into a shallow depression under the tree trunk and lay still.

The magpie was long gone, and the clearing was still except for the anxious stamping of the black as he milled around his picket rope. Bowie lay listening in the hollow under the tree. Quietly he slipped the empty shells out of the Starr and reloaded. He heard a moan and a scraping sound then silence. With no warning at all a boot crushed the dead leaves six inches from his hand and a voice said in a harsh whisper, "Sam! You alright? Sam?"

A stout branch lay under Bowie's hand. He carefully laid the Starr down on a clump of grass and took a tight hold on the branch with both hands. He rolled up onto his left side and slammed the branch into Charlie York's shins. York came crashing down with a yell, dropping his pistol when he hit the ground. He thudded down on his face and Bowie clubbed him unconscious. Bowie picked up his own pistol and rolled to his feet with the gun pointed in the direction of the moan he'd heard.

Just beyond Bowie's saddle Sam Shaw, the man who had been with York at the trading post, lay on his side with his knees drawn up and his hands clasped to his belly. His pistol lay out of reach behind his head. A dark stain on his shirt continued down into a crimson pool on the ground beneath him. As Bowie watched, Shaw drew a last shuddering breath and went still. Strangely, he seemed to shrink in on himself as he died.

Bowie calmed his upset horse, cussing under his breath the whole time. He cussed Charlie York for not leaving well enough alone, and he cussed himself for letting the two men get so close. Now he had two choices: he could bury Shaw and do his best to put the fear of God into Charlie York and get the man off his back-trail, or he could take them both back to Laramie, where he would have to bury one and jail the other. Of the two choices the first was the most palatable. It was a long way back and he had better things to do with his time than play nursemaid to a corpse and an idiot for however long it took to get them to Laramie; he had a bank robber to catch.

York was starting to stir, so Bowie walked over to him and kicked him in the head. "Get up, you ignorant ass," he grated. "I've got half a notion to shoot you and leave you for the magpies and the coyotes."

York rolled over and tried to sit up. He had a knot the size of a hen's egg on the back of his head. He groaned and held his head in his hands for a few seconds then reached down and pushed himself to his knees. "Where's Sam?" he asked haltingly.

"The stupid bastard's dead," Bowie told him. "You two just had to follow me, didn't you? What in the name of all that's holy were you planning to do? Just kill me and ride off? You'd have had the whole territory hunting you!"

"There weren't supposed ta be no bloodshed," York said plaintively. "We was just gonna beat on ya some like I was gonna do back yonder."

"Well, your plan fizzled," Bowie said disgustedly. "Your pard got anxious and it cost him a .44 slug in the belly. He bled out and now you get to bury him. So get your grubby butt up off the ground and get him outta my camp."

"But I ain't got nothin' ta dig with," York protested.

"You've got a belt knife, don't you? Use that."

York rose grumbling to his feet. He looked around for his pistol and saw it tucked behind Bowie's belt. He stumbled over to where Shaw lay and looked down at the dead man with his hands in his pockets as if trying to decide how to go about getting hold of him. It was obvious that York's head was hurting and he really didn't want to bend over far enough to grab onto the corpse. He finally bent and grasped Shaw's ankles, and began walking backward dragging his dead partner across the dirt. When he got to the edge of the clearing Bowie said. "That's far enough. Now get at it." It looked like York had a long night ahead of him as he dropped to his knees and began to stab his knife into the loamy soil.

Some time in the wee hours of the morning York finally got his deceased partner covered up. Bowie was back in the shadows beyond the now dark fire ring with his back to the lone pine tree that stood among ghostly white aspens. He'd napped off and on throughout York's ordeal, and was lightly snoozing when a small twig snapped to his left.

Bowie's eyes snapped open but he kept his head still and his breathing slow. His hat brim shadowed his face; York was out in the open and fully visible. Moonlight glinted along the edge of the wide-bladed knife in York's hand. York slipped closer and his hand drew back to stab. He stopped dead in his tracks when something cold prodded him in the crotch. He was afraid to look down. He heard the multiple clicks of the Starr's hammer being drawn back and sucked in his breath. "Bad idea, Charlie," Bowie said. He tipped his hat back off his forehead and pushed York back with the barrel of the pistol.

Bowie got carefully to his feet. He made sure that the muzzle of the pistol stayed where it was, mostly because it tickled his funnybone to see the look on York's face. "Drop the knife, Charlie." York's hand opened, and the blade clattered to the ground. "Now lay down on your belly and tuck your hands in the back of your pants."

"Why the hell..." York began to protest.

"Because I'm gonna turn you into a soprano if you don't, is why! You do know what a soprano is, don't you Charlie?" Before York could speak, Bowie answered his own question. "Probably not. Just hit the dirt." York did as he was told and was soon trussed up like a hog for the slaughter. "I'm gonna be right over here, Charlie. You just get some shuteye and come daylight we'll discuss your future. 'Night." Bowie went back to his tree, leaving his camp companion hog-tied in the middle of the clearing.

The morning sun found York snoring loudly on his side a few feet away from Bowie. Bowie stood and stretched, then rudely kicked York in the ribs. "Come on, Sleeping Ugly. Time to rise and shine." York woke with a snort and rolled up onto the seat of his pants.

"Whadda you gonna do with me, Tyler?" he growled. Charlie never was very easy to talk to before he'd had his morning coffee. Sleeping on the ground without blankets and with his hands tied behind him and his feet bound didn't especially improve his disposition any either.

"I haven't really decided yet, Charlie. I did think seriously about just hanging you, but then I'd have to either bury you or haul you into a town somewhere. I don't have time for either one." Bowie paused and appeared to come to a decision. "So here's the deal. I'm gonna cut you loose and give you back your pistol. Empty. I know you've got more ammo somewhere in your goods. Then I'm gonna give you a head start. If you're not out of my sight and heading anywhere but where I'm heading within about a minute I'm gonna shoot you off your horse and bury you, and nobody will ever know what happened to you. Deal?"

York could see that he really didn't have a great deal of choice in the matter. He didn't care for the idea of swinging from a tree limb, or for the idea of being buried in an unmarked grave like his ex-partner. And while he'd been digging he'd been developing a hankering for some warmer weather. "Alright, deal. Now cut me loose." He pushed his hands out behind him. Bowie bent and cut the rawhide strings holding York's wrists together then stepped back to wait for him to untie his own feet. He made a show of shucking the shells from York's pistol then handed it to him.

York took the gun without a word and headed for his horse at a trot. A minute later the clatter of his horse's hooves was fading in the distance, heading south.

~ 16 ~

Quiet reigned in the midnight dark streets of Hobart. The barest hint of a breeze drifted between the buildings and teased puffs of dust from the street. A striped tomcat slipped through the shadows in search of an unwary mouse or some other tidbit. And behind a building whose sign identified it rather unimaginatively as the First Bank of Hobart a small group of horses stood dozing on their feet.

A nervous young man in a dark duster stood near the horses. Only his darting eyes showed between the bandanna tied over his face and the pulled-down brim of his hat. He nervously shifted his weight from one foot to the other. The screech of a night-hunting predator in the trees by the creek nearly stopped the young man's heart.

The bank's back door creaked open and three men strode out. The biggest of the three, an outlaw named Riker, walked up to the sentry. "Move the horses on back an' hold onto 'em real tight," he said. "It's about ta git real noisy around here." The boy, for that was all he really was, gathered the reins and led the animals back a hundred yards or so. The other two men followed at a distance. One of the men watched the buildings on the street behind them as he moved.

The big man had gone back inside the building and he suddenly reappeared on the run. A rumbling blast split the night and knocked him rolling. He scrambled to his feet and ran up to where the others fought to keep the panicked horses under control. Behind him, shattered boards and splintered shingles rained fire down on the nearby buildings. Orange and red flames licked at the dry wood and, liking the taste, began to burn in earnest.

In the course of just a few moments, the First Bank of Hobart had ceased to exist as a coherent structure. The iron safe that had once been an impregnable bastion of security was now a twisted wreck of charred metal in the middle of an inferno. The nearby hills rang with the echoes of the explosion and the flickering orange light from the fire reflected from the nearby buildings.

All over Hobart, lights appeared in windows and people jarred from their beds by the blast ran half-dressed out into the firelit streets. Some of the townsfolk shouted questions while others shouted for water to douse the flames. In the shadows along the creek there was a chuckle and Riker asked, "Did you put the flyer where I told ya to?"

"Yep," Bronco Jarvis answered. "Come mornin' those folks yonder are gonna be real mad at Bob Morton." The four men mounted and eased their horses across the creek and disappeared into the darkness.

By ten or so the next morning, the fires were finally out. The exhausted citizens of Hobart had managed to save the buildings surrounding the bank, but just barely. Buildings and people alike were singed and soot-blackened and smoke still drifted from the smoldering ruins of the bank building.

A group of men had gathered behind the ruins. Their voices were angry as they tried to figure out who would do such a terrible thing. Robbing the bank was one thing; totally destroying it was something else entirely. A fluttering movement on the early morning breeze caught Davy Brewster's eye. He left the group to pick up a piece of paper that was caught under a burned timber.

The page was charred and tattered, but the print on its face was still legible. When Davy picked it up somebody who the flyer identified as Bob Morton was looking back at him. Whether or not the likeness was really Bob Morton remained to be seen; The name was enough. "I know who done this," he called to the group. "It was Bob Morton." He walked up and showed the men the Wanted flyer he'd found. "He left a callin' card."

"You're fulla crap, Davy," one of the men said. "Morton ain't never done nothin' like this before. An' besides, why would he leave that layin' around?"

"He ain't done nothin' like this that we know about!" Davy retorted hotly. "That don't mean he ain't done it somewheres else. I say we get up a posse and go after 'em!"

"Where are ya plannin' on lookin' for 'em?" someone else asked.

"There's tracks yonder headin' for the crick. I'll get Yancy and we'll follow 'em. You boys get your horses saddled." Davy turned to go for his horse and the tracker named Yancy. He stopped dead at the sound of another voice.

"I'd like ta know who died an' left you in charge," one of the men said stiffly.

Davy turned slowly and leveled a stony gaze at the group. His fists were clenched and he gritted, "We ain't got a sheriff here and somebody's gotta go after Morton. If one of you *ladies* wants to take the lead then you can have right at it. If not, then all of you git your horses and be back here in ten minutes armed and ready to travel."

Davy waited with his hands at his sides but no one stepped forward and no one spoke. He turned with a snort of disgust and stomped off toward his house. He'd get his horse saddled then go find Yancy. The tracker was more than likely at the General Store this time of day, waiting for it to open so he could try mooching a meal from the storekeeper. The man had money, but he seemed to get some sort of strange fun out of finagling food and drinks out of people.

It was closer to thirty minutes than ten by the time the group had gathered again. They were milling around and stamping out what tracks might have been left near the buildings when Davy rode up to them with Yancy beside him. "You men wait here," Davy ordered. He and Yancy rode down to the creek and Yancy stepped down and handed Davy his reins.

Yancy was rather flamboyantly dressed in tailored whipcord pants tucked into high-topped star boots and a white linen shirt with billowing sleeves under a beaded buckskin coat with long fringes. A long red sash was wrapped around his waist. Tucked behind the sash was a pair of Colt Navy revolvers. "If it's good enough for Hickock, it's good enough for me," he would tell anyone who would listen. The man might be more than a little bit windy, but there was no getting around the fact that he could track. Davy figured that he could put up with Yancy's eccentricities if he could help them catch the men who had demolished the bank.

Yancy knelt and ran his finger around the edges of several of the tracks in the trail crossing the creek. "There were four of them," he intoned. "One big man, the others not so big. They headed west on the same trail they came in on." He stood and dusted off the knee of his breeches and reclaimed his horse. He mounted and sat looking at Davy.

"What're you waitin' for?" Davy asked irritably.

"I'm waiting for you to tell me you're ready to go, and for you to summon the rest your posse. I plan on riding hard and I wouldn't want to leave anyone behind," Yancy answered mildly.

Davy turned and shouted, "Let's go!" The others reluctantly spurred their mounts forward. Davy turned back to see Yancy guiding his horse into the creek and up the far bank. The tracker looked back over his shoulder and saw the others coming. He nodded curtly to himself and spurred his horse first into a trot and then into a lope.

The trail was plain and easy to follow. *It's almost like these men we're following want to be caught*, Davy thought to himself. He shrugged the thought away and spurred his horse after Yancy, closely followed by the other eight members of the posse.

Early morning turned to early afternoon. The only stops the posse made were for short rests for the horses and to give them a little water. Horses and men were dusty and tired but the trail still led arrow-straight across the plains. Ahead the first hint of greenery could be seen above the banks of a small creek and the scent of water was on the wind. The horses quickened their pace, and the riders relaxed in their saddles as they looked forward to a break and something to drink that was colder than the water in their canteens. It's been said many times that the opera ain't over 'til the fat lady sings; unfortunately for the men of the posse, the music was about to start.

~ 17 ~

Bob Morton waited until breakfast was done and everyone had a cup of coffee in front of him to make his announcement. "Boys, I got somethin' to tell you, but first let me say that a man couldn't ask for better men to ride with than the two of you." He looked at Ben Terrell and Jake Carver and pointedly ignored Abel Barnes. "We've rode some rough trails together but those days are over. I'm retirin'." He stopped and waited for his words to sink in.

Bob turned a level gaze on Abel. "Barnes, Max told me promised you a hundred dollars. I'm gonna honor that promise instead of just shootin' you, even though it goes against my better judgment." He stacked five double eagles on the table. "There's your money. I'd appreciate it if you'd saddle your horse and hit the trail. I don't care where you go as long as it's away from here. And don't let me catch you on my backtrail or you're dead. You got that?"

Abel stood and reached across the table for the money without saying a word. Bob's big hand clamped down on his wrist. Abel tried to yank his hand away and Bob's grip tightened until Abel's face went white. "I asked you a question," Bob said with no hint of strain in his voice.

Abel jerked a nod and tried again to pull his wrist from the big man's grasp. "I can't hear your head rattling. Say it!" Bob growled.

"Yeah, I got it," Abel rasped. Bob let go of his wrist and Abel yanked it back and began trying to work some feeling back into his numb fingers. "Don't think this is the end of things, Morton!" he blustered.

Bob rose casually to his feet with his thumb hooked over his gunbelt near his holstered Colt. "It ends here, one way or the other," he said mildly. "You can leave here sittin' on your saddle or layin' over it. It makes me no never mind one way or the other. It's your choice." Abel glared at him for a long count of thirty then turned away and started rolling his blankets.

"I ain't got no grub," he mumbled.

"Never let it be said that Bob Morton sent a man away from his camp hungry, even if the man is a coyote," Bob said. He reached down and picked up a cloth sack and tossed it toward Abel who let it fall to the floor with a thump.

Jake Carver came in from outside. He had slipped out during Bob' conversation with Abel. "His horse's ready to go, Bob," he said. Abel picked up the sack of supplies, threw his blanket roll up on his shoulder, and stomped out of the cabin without another word. A short time later they heard the clatter and thump as Abel reined his horse around and galloped away from the cabin.

Ben Terrell had been sitting silently, watching the whole show from his seat near the wall by the fireplace. "You ain't seen the last of him, I'm thinking," the young man said quietly. "It mighta been better for all concerned if you'da just shot him."

Bob shrugged and a rueful grin crossed his face. "I reckon you might be right," he said. "Maybe I'm gettin' soft in my old age." He sat back down and reached for his coffee cup and took a sip of the cold brew. "Damn, that stuff tastes even worse cold than it does hot." Bob threw the cold coffee out the door and refilled his cup. He sat back down at the table. At the moment he could feel every one of his fifty-two years. He took a sip from his cup and set the cup back on the table. "You boys been with me what, four, five years?" He went on without waiting for them to answer. "We've had a pretty good run of luck in that time, at least 'til now. What with that trigger-happy gunsel shooting that woman in the bank, and that posse catching up to us the way they did, I feel like our string's run out so I'm cutting you boys loose. If you'll take an old outlaw's advice, you'll get on outta here and go back East where nobody knows you, or at least what you've been up to. Buy a place, get married, settle down, tell some lies about your adventures out West." He drank some more coffee as the two young men shared a look.

Ben Terrell and Jake Carver were cousins although they couldn't have been more different in appearance. Jake was fair with an unruly mop of reddish hair that seemed to constantly need cutting, and that caused any woman who got close to him to want to run her fingers through it. His boyish face had a sprinkling of freckles across the cheeks that made him look younger than his twenty-three years. He was slender and moved with a feline grace. Jake preferred to dress in buckskins and a Winchester rifle was his favorite weapon.

Ben was just the opposite. His dark complexion, black hair and dark eyes had caused him to be mistaken more than once for a Mexican. He was nearly as tall as Bob, though he was not as wide in the shoulders. He wore his hair short and neatly combed. His bushy mustache hid an easy smile. He often dressed in black broadcloth, and his double holster rig carried two short-barreled Colt Army revolvers. He was fast with either hand and a dead shot to boot.

"Bob, you've been right good to us," Ben began. "We've been sending money back home right along..." Bob looked up sharply and his mouth opened to protest. Ben stopped him with an upraised hand. "Our folks think we been minin', an' they've been puttin' it away for us. In fact," he grinned, "we're already landowners back home. We each got a hundred sixty acres of good farm ground with a crop in and a cabin built. We just been waiting for you to decide you were done so we could go home."

Bob didn't trust himself to speak for a moment as he looked back and forth between the two young men. After a minute he nodded and said, "Will wonders never cease? Here I thought you boys spent all your money on whiskey and women!"

"Nope. You taught us to look ahead so that's what we been doin'. We got enough put by to get along fine," Jake said.

"You'll still get your cut of this last job," Bob said. They began to protest and he said, "It's no use arguing. You'll need some travelin' money if nothing else." He sat back feeling like a load had been lifted from his shoulders. It was a relief to know that he'd been worried about his two young friends for no reason.

~ 18 ~

The posse slouched in their saddles as they rode toward the small creek. From the creek bed four pairs of eyes watched them come. Bronco Jarvis was on the far right and Riker, the big man who had set the dynamite charge in the bank, was to the far left. Between them was the young man who had held the horses, Lonnie Grable, and a husky fellow who was currently answering to the name John Smith.

The young man wiped his sweaty palms on his shirtfront and picked up his rifle. He licked his lips nervously and looked over at Riker. “Are you sure about this, Riker?” he whispered hoarsely.

“Yeah, I’m sure, kid. Just shut your yap an’ get ready. Don’t shoot ‘til I do, but when I shoot you pour it to ‘em, you hear me?” Riker waited until Lonnie Grable nodded his understanding then went back to watching the posse.

“Whatsa matter kid, conscience botherin’ ya?” Smith sneered.

Before the boy could answer Bronco said, “Leave him alone, Smith. He’s just young. He’ll do alright.” Smith’s glare was met by a smile that didn’t quite reach Jarvis’ eyes. Smith turned back to watch their intended targets come toward the ambush site.

Yancy stopped his horse a hundred yards from the creek bed. For all his flamboyant manner and his taste in clothing, he was actually a rather astute outdoorsman and something about that creekbed bothered him. He scanned what he could see of the banks in front of him for the tenth time while the others gathered around him. His horse tugged at the bit, wanting to go to the water it could smell.

“What’re we waitin’ for?” Davy asked.

“Something’s not right,” Yancy answered. His eyes never stopped their scanning of the creek bank.

“Ah, you don’t know what yer talkin’ about,” another man

said. "Come on, fellers. Let's go get us a drink of water." He spurred his horse forward and the others followed suit. Davy looked at Yancy.

"Whatta you mean, somethin's not right?"

"It's too quiet."

Riker watched the approaching riders over the sights of his rifle. The rifle's forearm rested easily on a willow branch and the blade of the front sight was centered on the lead rider's chest. The tip of his finger curled around the trigger as he thumbed the hammer back and took a deep breath. He breathed out and the rifle roared. White powder smoke billowed along the bank of the little creek as the others took their cues from him and began to pour lead into the riders as fast as they could lever and fire.

Out on the grass the lead rider's horse suddenly tossed its head and the bullet meant for the man thumped into the horse's head. The horse went down headfirst in a boneless heap, sending its rider rolling through the grass. Bewildered, the man jumped to his feet and a bullet slammed him back to the ground. All around him horses and men were being shot to pieces as the outlaws fired again and again into the confused mass of riders. Blood spattered the grass and dead and dying horses lay in tangled heaps. Those few men not killed in the opening volleys tried to return fire and were shot down where they stood.

Davy spun toward the creek when the first shot sounded. He watched in horror as Bud Winslow's horse went down. He could only stare in shock when Bud jumped up only to be shot down a moment later. Coming back to himself, Davy pulled his rifle from the scabbard under his leg and jacked a shell into the chamber.

Beside him Yancy reached up and stuck the reins in his teeth and drew his Navy revolvers from his sash. "I told you something was wrong!" Yancy mumbled around the leather in his mouth.

"What the hell are you doin'?" Davy yelled.

With a muffled "Yeehaw!" Yancy spurred his horse into a run toward the puffs of white smoke. The chestnut gelding was well-trained, and Yancy used his knees to move the big horse on a zigzag route toward the creek. He was firing with both hands as the horse charged.

"Well, will you look at that!" Bronco exclaimed to no one in particular. He stood watching, fascinated, as the Hickock wannabe in front of him charged forward through the carnage. The rider swayed in the saddle when the chestnut jumped one of the dead horses but came on unperturbed while lead bees buzzed around his ears. The horse slowed just a bit at the edge of the bank then leaped down into the creek bed. The gelding spun toward Bronco and the man's guns swung in his direction.

The chilling sound of a pair of pistols' hammers falling on empty chambers was loud even in the midst of the gunfire. Bronco nonchalantly drew his pistol and watched Yancy's eyes widen. "Don't ya just hate it when that happens?" Bronco asked. Without waiting for an answer he shot Yancy between the eyes, bowling him backward over the bay's rump.

Davy saw Yancy's horse jump off into the creek bed and saw Yancy go down. He raised his rifle to his shoulder to fire. A bullet slammed into the side of the action and his face was spattered with stinging fragments of lead. He dropped the rifle and pawed at his eyes and cheeks while at the same time he pulled his horse around to run. He kicked the horse into a gallop back toward Hobart and a bullet slammed him forward onto his horse's neck where he clung with all his remaining strength. With a determined effort he stayed mounted, and he managed to stay conscious long enough to tie himself to the saddle before the world went black.

A few hours later, Davy's horse trotted into town and stopped in the middle of the street in front of the saloon. The rangy gelding stood patiently waiting for its rider to dismount. When Davy stayed slumped in the saddle the horse pawed the dirt and nickered. The nicker roused Davy slightly and he tried to straighten himself and step down from the saddle but his swollen hands were tied to the saddlehorn. He fought the strings that held him there for a moment then once again lapsed into unconsciousness. The horse pawed the dirt and nickered again. He was tired from their headlong flight from the scene of the battle on Gratton Creek and ready to be unsaddled and fed.

Inside the quiet saloon, Joe Harris and Barney Wilson were sharing a bottle of rye and a platter of beans and tortillas at a table by the window. The two men had just finished a three day trip at the lines of two freight wagons loaded down with merchandise for the general store. Another drink or two and the teamsters would be heading for their bunks. Joe heard the horse nicker and looked out the window. He wondered for a minute why the rider was just sitting there, then decided that whoever he was, the man must be too drunk to get down from his horse.

When the horse nickered again and pawed the dirt Joe looked a little closer. His eyes widened when he recognized Davy slumped over his horse's neck. "Holy Mother o' God!" he gasped. He jumped to his feet and went charging out the door and ran up to the tired horse. "Davy! What happened?"

The sound of his name brought Davy back to some semblance of life and he started fighting his bindings again. Joe yanked his belt knife from the sheath and cut the strings holding Davy in the saddle. Davy's feet were out of the stirrups, and when his hands were freed he lost his balance and fell from the saddle. Joe caught him and gently eased him to the ground as the horse ambled away.

"Barney!" Joe called. Barney's startled face appeared over the batwings doors of the saloon, and Joe yelled, "Bring me that bottle!" Barney disappeared, then reappeared with the bottle of whiskey. He trotted up to where Joe knelt in the dirt cradling Davy's shoulders on his arm and one knee.

"What happened to Davy?" Barney asked. A crowd was gathering around the injured man and everyone wanted to know the same thing.

"He's done been shot, you dern fool!" Joe retorted. He took the bottle from Barney's hand and held it to Davy's lips. The wounded man sipped a small amount of the liquor and coughed. A red stain appeared on his lips and his eyes opened.

"Am I home?" he whispered.

"Yeah, Davy, you are," Joe said gently. The young man's eyes fluttered closed again. "You just take it easy while we git the doc here ta look at ya." A young boy had pushed his way to the front of the crowd of onlookers and was staring wide-eyed at the scene in front of him. Joe pointed at him. "You, boy. Go git the doc. And hurry! This man needs help, an' soon!" The boy nodded and ran off down the street.

A short time later a baritone voice shouted, "Make a hole, people. Move over! Dammit, let me through!" A portly, balding man with a pair of spectacles perched on his red-veined beak of a snout pushed through the crowd, stepping on some toes and elbowing the more reluctant bystanders out of the way. He used the black leather bag in his hand as a battering ram to clear a trail through the mob.

Doc Stevens knelt down beside Davy. "Who did this?" he demanded. "Why wasn't I called earlier?"

"We ain't got no idea who done it, and we couldn't call you any earlier 'cause he just rode in," Joe snapped. "Are you gonna sit there and ask questions like some kinda idjit, or are ya gonna help him?"

Doc gaped at the teamster for a moment then shook himself and got down to business. "You're right, of course," he said. "You men," he pointed at two of the bystanders. "Get something here we can carry him on. And snap it up. This man is seriously hurt." The two Doc had pointed to hurried into the saloon. The sound of breaking wood and a shout from the bartender was heard then the two men reappeared carrying a legless table. The splintered remains of its supports could be seen underneath it.

The two men put their makeshift stretcher down next to Davy; Doc and Joe carefully moved Davy from the dirt of the street onto the wood then the four men picked up the table and its passenger and started down the street to Doc's house. The table wouldn't fit through the door of Doc's house, so they laid it down and Joe picked the young man up and carried him into the house behind Doc.

"Put him on that table there," Doc ordered. He pointed to a narrow, cloth-covered table in the middle of the room. "You other men, get out. I don't need an audience. Martha!" he called. His wife appeared with a bundle of bandages and a teapot that steamed in the cool air. She set the hot pot on a nearby counter, picked up a pair of scissors, and began to cut Davy's shirt away. Doc poured water into a washbasin and washed his hands. He soaked a cloth in the hot water, wrung it out, and began to gently wash the caked blood away from the hole in Davy's chest.

"Doc, is he gonna make it?" Joe asked. He stood in the doorway with an anxious look on his face. He and Davy had been friends for a long time.

Doc had been about to snap at the teamster, but the look of anguish on the big Irishman's face stopped him, and he said quietly, "I don't know, Joe. Young Davy's lost a great deal of blood. I believe he may have a hole in his lung as well. I'll do what I can but whether he lives or dies is in the hands of Almighty Providence. At least the bullet went clean through." He turned back to his patient for a moment, then looked back at Joe. "If you want to help you might consider prayer."

After Davy disappeared Riker stepped up out of the creek bed with his rifle raised. He smiled in satisfaction at the carnage in front of him. "That oughta get ol' Bob some attention," he said to no one in particular. Here and there a horse struggled to get up, and Lonnie went from horse to horse and put the wounded animals out of their misery. Their riders were mute bundles of dead flesh around them.

Smith had been riding the kid the whole time they'd been with Riker and took every opportunity to pick at him. This time was no exception. "Hey kid," Smith sneered. "You got a soft spot in yer head fer them worthless brutes? Let the coyotes finish 'em and save a bullet." He stood poised with his feet apart and his rifle butt on his hip, daring the younger man to take exception to his words.

Lonnie finished replacing the spent cartridges in his pistol then holstered the gun and looked at Smith. He never said a word; he just started walking forward. Smith watched him come with a confident smirk twisting his lips, but when the boy had cut the distance in half Smith shifted his feet and looked quickly over to where Riker and Jarvis stood. His gaze shifted back to Lonnie. This was not going exactly as he wanted it to. He'd been planning on goading the kid into drawing so he could kill him, but the kid just kept coming.

Lonnie came on with his gaze locked on Smith's. His hands were hanging at his sides. He stopped a yard short of where Smith stood and said quietly, "Put down the rifle."

"What?" Smith asked. The stocky outlaw couldn't believe his ears.

"You heard me. Put down the rifle."

"Yeah, John, put down the rifle," Bronco taunted. Smith's eyes flicked across the smile on Bronco's face then back to Lonnie. "You aren't afraid of a kid, are you?"

"I'll put it down, alright," Smith snarled. He swung the barrel of the rifle down and his thumb found the hammer and cocked it on the way down. Lonnie slapped the muzzle aside with his left hand and Smith's finger tightened on the trigger. The rifle blasted smoke and flame and sent a bullet out across the grass. Lonnie's right fist smashed into Smith's jaw and knocked him sprawling. The rifle was jolted from his hand.

Smith's hand went to his holstered Colt, but before he could draw he found himself staring down the barrel of Lonnie's pistol. Lonnie's face was pale and his eyes were wide. His voice shook, but the hand holding the pistol was rock-steady. "Leave. Me. Alone." he said, making three sentences out of the three words.

Smith carefully lifted his hands. "Okay, okay. I hear ya." He waited for the pistol to move away from his face. Beads of sweat were popping out on his forehead and he was sure he was about to die. Lonnie nodded sharply then stepped back, but he kept the Colt in his hand while Smith got to his feet and made a show of slipping the tiedown over the hammer of his pistol. Lonnie holstered his gun and walked toward the creek bed.

"My, my, my," Bronco said after Lonnie had gone out of sight. "Looks like you pushed that boy a bit too far." Smith whirled to glare at him. "You don't want a piece of me, John," Bronco said lightly. "I won't stop with just knockin' you on your butt. I'll kill you."

Smith stared at him for a moment. "Ah, you can go ta hell." Smith picked up his rifle, wiped some dirt from the action, and stomped off toward where his horse was tied.

Lonnie rode out of the creek bed and up to Riker. "Mister Riker, I'm ridin' out." Riker just looked at him, so he went on. "I never hired on for somethin' like that." He pointed across the grass. "I think we'd all be better off if you find somebody else to ride with you." He stopped and waited for Riker to say something.

The big man looked up at him and nodded. "Alright, boy, if that's the way ya feel." Bronco started to protest and Riker silenced him with a look. "You got money comin' from the bank in Hobart."

"Keep it, Mister Riker. I don't want it. I've got a little cash, and enough grub to tide me over 'til I can get somewhere and find a job. And in case you're wondering, no, I ain't goin' back to Hobart."

Riker nodded and held out his hand. "I can see you ain't cut out for this kind of life," he said kindly. Lonnie leaned out of the saddle to take the proffered hand and Riker clamped his hand down hard on the boy's and snarled, "But if I even hear so much as a whisper that you said anything about this to anybody, anywhere, any time, I'll find you an' gut you like a fish. You hear me?" Lonnie's face was pasty white as he nodded. "Alright. Go on now."

Riker stepped back and Lonnie pulled his horse around and trotted away, looking back over his shoulder until he was out of sight.

~ 19 ~

After Charlie York rode out Bowie started a small fire and made coffee. He still had some of the food Mary Hanlon had sent with him so he made his breakfast out of that. He saddled Black and rode deeper into the mountains following the route he'd marked on his map back in Cosby's office.

Just short of noon he rode up to the cabin where the posse had found Morton and his gang. From the description and from the bullet holes it was easy to see that this was the right place. He stepped down and trailed his reins and stepped up onto the stone stoop. The cabin door had been left unlatched and was swinging in the wind, and when he stepped inside he heard the scurry of small clawed feet. *Don't take long for squatters to move in,* he thought with a grin.

Bowie looked around but there wasn't much to see. He found the outlaws' escape route and had to take a minute to admire the ingenuity of the door and the passageway out.

Bowie stepped back outside and shut the cabin door. He made sure that it was latched this time. There was no reason that he could see for letting a well-built cabin like this one go to wrack and ruin if it could be helped. He might even decide to come up here and settle some day, if he ever got tired of chasing down lawbreakers.

Bowie stepped into the saddle and went on. A cold breeze was stirring and he took the time to untie his sheepskin coat from behind his saddle and slip his arms into the sleeves. Overhead, clouds were gathering and off in the distance to the west he could see the first wispy tendrils of rain falling. At least he hoped it was rain. This time of year it could rain or snow or both depending on Mother Nature's whim of the moment. He thought for a moment about turning around and going back to the cabin, but by now he was an hour or more away from it; if it did rain he'd be soaked by the time he got there. He'd be better off finding a place to hole up somewhere ahead.

Down the ridge he was riding on, a thick stand of lodgepole pines had grown up in the aftermath of a fire. The mares tails of falling rain ahead of him had drifted closer and the wind tasted wet. Bowie kicked Black into a trot toward the pine thicket. An opening showed as a darker shade against the green of the needles and Bowie turned in that direction. He stopped the horse and stepped down from his saddle where a game trail went into the thicket then he went on, leading the horse and pushing his way in among the trees.

When he was far enough into the stand of trees that he could no longer feel the wind, he stopped in a small clearing where a huge charred log had kept the smaller trees from growing. Bowie looked around in satisfaction and started pulling the tops of some of the smaller trees together and tying them with some rawhide strings from his saddlebag. In short order he had a serviceable shelter made of living pines, situated with its back to the oncoming storm.

Bowie stripped most of the boughs from the inside of the cave and used them to thatch a roof for the shelter. The charred log formed a half wall at the front of the hut and would make a dandy reflector for his fire. Bowie stripped the saddle and blankets from his horse and carried them to the back of what would be his home away from home for the foreseeable future then picketed Black where the gelding could reach some of the ankle-high grass that grew in the clearing. He'd watered the horse not long ago at a small seep he'd come across so he figured that he'd be fine until morning.

In the near distance, thunder rumbled quietly like an old man muttering in his sleep and the first tentative drops of rain began to fall. Bowie pulled some dry pine needles together along with some small twigs and slivers from the underside of the log and started a fire. By the time the rain began in earnest the fire was crackling merrily and the smell of frying bacon was filling the snug little lean-to.

Sometime after midnight, the cold woke Bowie from a sound sleep. A hushed stillness had come over the night and he could no longer here the patter of the rain that had lulled him to sleep. At first he thought that the sun must be rising, but he soon realized that the light he saw was a sliver of moon reflecting off of the snow that covered everything. He sat up in his blankets and leaned over to drop some pine needles on the last of the embers he could see winking from his fireplace. He was shivering with the cold, but he doggedly blew on the embers until a tiny flame flared up. He laid some small pieces of pitch wood he had found on the flame and it gradually grew and slowly pushed the cold back.

By the time the eastern sky began to lighten, the temperature had dropped to close to zero. Bowie had spent the rest of the night huddled in his blankets next to the fire, keeping it going and trying to stay warm. The horse had moved up as close as he could get as well, as if taking comfort from the flames.

Bowie shook the snow that had drifted in through the cracks in the roof of the lean-to from his blankets and got to his feet. The sky overhead was black, but he could just see the faintest hint of lighter color over the tops of the trees around his clearing. He had just leaned over to put what little wood he had left on the fire when his horse suddenly spun to face the trail into the thicket, blowing in alarm. The Starr appeared in Bowie's hand and he dropped below the top of the log and crept forward to peer around the end of it.

He heard a low growl from the mouth of the trail and saw a pair of yellow eyes reflecting the light from the fire. In a moment another pair of eyes joined the first, and the two wolves moved side by side into the edge of the clearing. They were clearly intent on the horse, which by now was nervously stamping a front foot and shaking its head. Bowie quietly eared back the Starr's hammer, but not quietly enough; the smaller of the two wolves looked his way. Before Bowie could do anything else, the bigger wolf snarled and launched himself at the horse.

Bowie couldn't get a shot at the big male but he did get the female. As the Starr was coming level and the male made his attack, Black spun and kicked out with both hind feet. One steel-shod hoof slammed into the big predator's shoulder, knocking him away and rolling him across the small clearing. His mate had followed him in on the attack, and Bowie's bullet hit her in the neck and turned her aside. She rolled over and over trying to bite at the pain in her neck. Bowie shot her again and she went still.

The male had regained his feet. A growl rumbled deep in his chest, and his teeth were bared as he faced off with Bowie and the horse. A flap of skin dangled loose on his shoulder where the sharp edge of the steel horseshoe had torn it. Bowie scrambled to his feet. "Go on, git!" he yelled. "I don't wanna shoot you too. GO ON!"

When Bowie yelled the hair on the wolf's neck stood up, making him look even bigger. Bowie leveled the pistol, taking careful aim just above the bridge of the wolf's snout and between his eyes. The horse was stamping and neighing, and Bowie was afraid that this standoff was going to fall apart when the horse broke loose and stampeded. He yelled again, adding a few words the wolf more than likely didn't understand in a tone of voice that left no doubt of Bowie's intentions. Still the wolf stood his ground.

After what seemed like an hour, but couldn't have been more than a minute or two, the wolf finally turned away. He whined once, looking toward where his mate lay, then limped off back the way the pair had come. "Damn!" Bowie cursed. He felt bad about killing the female but he needed his horse. He wished he'd had more time to try and deflect the attack but the pair had given him no choice. They'd come on too fast.

Bowie stepped over the log and went to calm the black horse. Black was unhurt, but the smell of wolf and blood in the clearing kept him stirred up. Finally Bowie gave up, threw snow on what remained of his fire, then saddled Black and led him out of the clearing, taking the widest possible detour around the dead wolf.

Outside the thicket, the first gray light of dawn was spreading across the white landscape. Bowie brushed off the snow that had fallen on his saddle coming through the trees and mounted up. At the first creek they came to he'd stop and make some coffee. He was kind of like Charlie York in that he was never at his best without his morning coffee.

~ 20 ~

Davy Brewster was dying. Doc Stevens had done all he could for the young man but the bullet had caused too much damage and the loss of blood on the ride back to Hobart had taken its toll. It was a miracle that Davy had lasted as long as he had. He lay on the bed in the back room of Doc Stevens' house with a sheet over him and bandages wrapping his chest. His breathing was shallow and would sometimes catch for a moment; the doctor would be sure it was the end of Davy. But after a moment his chest would rise again and he would take another breath.

Somewhere outside a rooster crowed, greeting the sunrise. Joe Harris jerked awake and rubbed his neck, trying to rub out the kinks from spending the night in a chair by Davy's bedside. He listened to Davy's labored breathing and watched his friend's face, wishing there was something he could do and knowing that all he could do was pray and be there for the young man if he did wake up.

In a lucid moment, Davy had told them what had happened near the creek bed. He'd told of Yancy's last heroic charge and his death, and of how the other members of the posse had been gunned down by the men whose tracks they'd followed across the plains.

Doc came in with a pot of coffee and two cups. He set the cups on the sideboard and poured them full and handed one to Joe. The teamster took it and warmed his hands for a moment then took a sip of the hot brew. "That's good, Doc. I never have been able to make a decent cup of coffee." He took another sip. "He ain't gonna make it, is he?" he asked anxiously, nodding toward Davy.

"I'm afraid not," the gruff old man in front of him replied. "I've done all I can, but he's lost so much blood I'm afraid my best isn't good enough. I'm really surprised he's survived as long as he has."

“If he dies, I’ll follow Bob Morton to the ends of the earth and I’ll shoot him dead!” Joe declared vehemently.

Doc turned sharply. “What makes you think Bob Morton had anything to do with this?”

“Who do ya think that posse was followin’?” Joe demanded. “Who else could it’ve been?”

“You were bringing in that last load of freight. How do you know it was Morton?”

“I got ears, Doc. I know Davy found a flyer with Morton’s picture and such on it. I know there was four men, and that’s how many they say is in Morton’s gang. And I know that the men in this yellow-livered town let Davy and the others go out and get killed. I don’t need ta know nothin’ else.”

Davy died an hour later. Doc Stevens put the time of death at 8:05 AM by the Ingersoll watch he wore on a silver chain strung across the front of his vest. He reached and pulled the sheet up over the pale face that would no longer show the lines etched by the pain of the bullet wound that had killed the young man. He turned away from the bed and saw Joe standing there with his fists clenched at his sides and a frown on his face. He started to speak and the big teamster turned away. “I’ll go get the undertaker,” Joe said in a monotone. “I already got the marker and the coffin made up.”

Joe stomped down the street in a stormy silence. The townsfolk hurriedly cleared out of his path when they saw the dour look on his normally cheerful face. At the undertaking parlor he went inside and addressed the grim-faced individual across the room. “He’s gone, George. I’d appreciate it if you take yer wagon and Davy’s box on over to Doc Stevens’. I’ll go on to the graveyard and finish diggin’ the grave.” He’d already dug part of it, although at the time he’d hoped he wouldn’t have to finish. George Borland just nodded and reached for his hat, then went out the back door to the stable and hitched his team to the hearse that stood gleaming quietly in the shadows. The coffin was already loaded.

When Joe judged that the grave was deep enough, he tossed the spade up onto the pile of dirt and climbed out of the hole. He brushed the dirt from his clothes and went back into town. He lived in a small house near the freight yard and he went inside and over to a small trunk that stood near his bed. When he opened the trunk he stood looking down into it for a few moments then took out a paper-wrapped parcel that smelled of mothballs. Inside the parcel was the black broadcloth suit he'd last worn at his father's funeral five years before. In his line of work there wasn't much call for broadcloth, so the suit had lain in the trunk ever since.

He unfolded the suit and hung it up in a vain attempt to get some of the creases out while he undressed down to his drawers. He put on the suit then used his bandana to wipe the worst of the crud from his boots. He wet his unruly hair and combed it somewhat into obedience in front of a cracked mirror on the back of the door of the one-room shack. Satisfied that he'd done all he could, he went out and down the street.

At the saloon he pushed his way through the batwings and announced, "Davy Brewster's dead. When he's buried I'm goin' after them that killed him. If there's any man in this God-forsaken town that ain't afraid ta go with me he's welcome ta come. The rest of you can stay here and rot." He turned and went back outside, leaving a stunned silence in the room behind him.

At Borland's he went inside. Davy was laid out in his best shirt and britches with his hands crossed on his chest. His hair was combed and his face was composed. Joe nodded and the undertaker placed the lid on the coffin and fastened it in place. He and Joe carried Davy outside and slid him into the hearse. George climbed up onto the seat, lifted the reins, and clucked to the team. The hearse moved slowly toward the cemetery with Joe walking behind.

At the cemetery a small crowd had gathered. The town preacher was there, and he read some Scriptures as Davy was lowered to his final rest. When the preacher was done speaking Joe laid his jacket aside and wordlessly began to fill in the grave.

~ 21 ~

Ben Terrell and Jake Carver were saddling their horses. They would be leaving for Ohio as soon as they were ready. To the best of their knowledge, no one knew the two young men's names in this part of the world, so they probably didn't have to worry about posses between here and there, but they'd be careful nonetheless.

Bob stood with his back against the corner of the cabin watching the two young men's preparations. They'd stalled as long as they could, not wanting to leave, but if they didn't get gone they might as well wait another day. As it was they were going to be coming down off the mountains in the dark. Finally he'd told them, "You two git. Hanging around here isn't doing any of us any good. As soon as you're gone, I'm headed for Idaho."

At last the horses were ready for travel and the two men walked up to where Bob stood. Jake stuck out his hand and said, "Bob, I really ain't got the words..."

"Me neither," the big man answered. "You boys just be careful. And if you need anything, send a letter to Borden City. You know the name to use." He shook the outstretched hand then drew the young man to him in a hug. "You boys have been the sons I don't figure on ever having," he said with a catch in his voice. "And I expect some grandkids." He smiled as Ben stepped up and stuck out his hand.

"So long, Bob. We'll do right by you," Ben said.

"No more bank robbing, you hear me?"

"We won't need to. You've done set us up already." The two turned away and mounted their horses. Jake took a turn of the packhorse's lead rope around his saddlehorn then clucked to his horse. At the top of the first ridge he and Ben turned back to wave at the man who still stood watching them go. Bob raised a hand in farewell then stood watching until the two had faded out of sight.

Bob turned and went into the cabin. He'd spend the night

then head north in the morning. His gear was packed and the cabin spruced up, ready for the next occupant; Bob hoped it wouldn't be him. As far as he was concerned, he was done with the outlaw trail and was ready to settle down and live a normal life. He wanted to give something back for all that he'd taken over the years. Looking back he regretted some of the things he'd done, but he could point with pride to the fact that he'd never hurt anyone, at least not physically, in all the bank jobs he'd pulled. But he deeply regretted the financial injury that he knew now that he'd caused.

At first, the bank robberies had just been a way to make a living. After while, it had seemed to kind of take on a life of its own until he couldn't seem to get out of the life if he tried; so he just quit trying. But as time went on he'd found himself thinking more and more of making enough to buy a ranch. He'd managed to put by enough over the years to do exactly that. A number of years ago he'd bought a place up in Idaho, stocked it with cattle and hired a crew. Now he was done with the outlaw life. He was going north and wouldn't be back.

The next morning Bob saddled the long-legged bay that waited patiently in the pole corral behind the cabin. He carried enough food in his saddlebags for a couple of days if he ate sparingly. The rest, except for some things he'd left in the cabin for emergencies, he'd sent with Ben and Jake. Barring any unforeseen happenings, he would be to a town early the day after tomorrow and he could resupply then. He stepped into the leather and turned the bay toward a new life.

A week later Bob rode into Borden City. He'd stopped a few miles out of town and changed into the clothes he'd bought at a small town back down the trail. The Colt he'd been wearing on his hip was now in his saddlebag along with the gunbelt and holster, and a cut down Remington rode in a holster under his arm. His white shirt was buttoned to the top and a ribbon tie was knotted around the button-on collar of the shirt. His gray vest and coat showed some dust and some wrinkles but he didn't mind. It made his story of being gone on a surveying trip more believable. Here he was Don Gordon, and Don Gordon often wore white shirts and ties, and he didn't carry a gun on his hip.

He pulled the trail-worn bay up at the hitchrail in front of the Crystal Palace Saloon, the grandiosely named two-story combination dancehall and drinking establishment on Main Street. He stepped down into the dust of the street and put his hands in the small of his back, trying to stretch some of the kinks out, while he cautiously examined the street from under the brim of his hat. The street looked like it always had, other than what appeared to be a church that was going up yonder past Boker's Dry Goods. "Will wonders never cease," he said to himself. "Next thing somebody'll be wantin' to close down the Palace."

Don Gordon stepped up onto the boardwalk and through the crooked doors of the saloon. He paused for a moment with his back to the wall to let his eyesight adjust then stepped up to the bar. The room was empty except for Sheriff Johnny Parker, who was leaning on the end of the bar with a cup of coffee in front of him talking to the bartender. Both men looked around when they heard the doors creak. "Long trip, Don?" Parker asked. The man now known as Don Gordon nodded and came forward to shake the outstretched hand Parker offered.

"Sure was," he replied. "I hope I don't have to leave home for a while now. Winter's coming on and I'm ready to light in one place for a while." He looked over at the bartender. "How 'bout some of that sourmash I know you've got hiding under the bar?"

The bartender, whose name was Del Scott, reached down and brought up a bottle then snagged a glass with two fingers and set bottle and glass on the bar in front of Gordon. Don pulled the cork from the bottle and poured the glass half-full and drank it down in one swallow. "Damn, I needed that," he said with a sigh. "That jughead out yonder pert near beat me to death. He travels good in the back country but he's rough on the butt." He poured another drink and took a sip. "Anything I need to know about before I head out to the ranch, Johnny?"

"Got a telegram a few days ago," Parker replied. "Seems Bob Morton blew up the bank in Hobart then ambushed the posse that took in after him, and shot 'em up bad. Killed seven men on the spot, and the eighth one died a few days later. Folks down there are mighty upset."

Don Gordon struggled to keep his face from showing his shock. First Barnes shoots the banker's wife, and now this. "I reckon they would be," he said after a moment. "Getting their bank blown up and that many men killed has to be rough." As he talked his thoughts were whirling. Somebody was setting him up for something, but he didn't have the first foggiest idea who it might be or why. He'd best get out to the ranch and sit down and contemplate. If what Parker said was true, and he had no reason to doubt it, then Don's retirement plan was definitely in jeopardy. He stretched again. "Well, I reckon I'll ride on out to the ranch. I'm ready to sit on something that isn't moving and eat something that I didn't have to cook myself. Thanks for the news. See ya."

Don turned and walked out to his horse, tightened the cinch, and stepped into the leather. It was still several miles out to the ranch; if he hurried he could get there in time for supper.

~ 22 ~

Riker was feeling very satisfied with himself. By now, the word would be spreading that Bob Morton had turned bad. Riker figured that the telegraph lines had to be humming with the news. Now he could sit back and see what kind of hornet's nest he had stirred up.

Riker, Smith, and Jarvis were camped in a canyon on the backside of nowhere, waiting for Abel Barnes to show up. Their lean-to shelter was comfortably dry, so when the snow came they just holed up and waited it out, figuring that it would all melt off once the sun came out. Their canyon was sheltered enough that their horses could graze with minimal effort due to the thinness of the snow cover. There was also a jug of whiskey in Riker's saddlebag for company. Riker's theory was that a sitting man leaves no tracks; so they sat.

Abel Barnes reined up at the mouth of the canyon and looked around carefully. He saw no sign of anyone around, so he heeled his horse into a walk and moved into the canyon slowly with his hands in plain sight. He'd ridden with Riker before; he wasn't taking any chances on getting shot by accident.

Abel's horse passed a nest of boulders a good distance into Lost Creek Canyon and a chuckle from behind him nearly stopped his heart. He spun to look toward the source of the sound and saw a rifle barrel pointed at him from between two rocks. "Damn you, Jarvis," he blustered. "Some day yer sick sense o' humor's gonna get you killed."

"Not by the likes of you, hillbilly," Bronco answered, rising to his feet behind the rocks but keeping his rifle trained on Abel. "All you're good for is shootin' women." He chuckled again when he saw the color rising in Abel's face. He didn't know how close to home that comment had come.

"Where's Riker?" Abel asked, ready to change the subject.

"He's up yonder," Bronco pointed with his chin. "He's been

wonderin' where you were."

"I've been on my way. That posse from Sycamore Springs chased us a damn long ways, an' Morton took us even farther gettin' away from 'em. I had to go the long way around to get here."

"Well, you might oughta get a move on. Riker ain't exactly a patient man even when he's in a *good* mood, which generally ain't too often."

Abel heeled his horse into motion and went on. Behind him, Bronco dropped back down into his hiding place and leaned his rifle against a rock. He leaned back against another rock whose slanted surface made a natural backrest. Smith should be down shortly to take over guard duty.

Abel reined up at the edge of the camp and got down from his horse. "Where the hell have you been, Abel?" Riker demanded roughly. "You shoulda been here three days ago!"

"You said to lead the posse on," Abel replied. "It wasn't easy to do with that blizzard screamin' down our necks." He shivered again in memory of the storm. "Then one o' them damn fool posse riders got antsy an' shot too soon, an' missed Morton. So we ended up ridin' a hunnert miles the wrong way before I could get shut of Morton an' the rest." He stopped, and a smile creased his thin lips. "But Morton's got one less friend in the world now." He waited for Riker to ask him what he meant, and he wasn't disappointed.

"What's that supposed ta mean?" the big man asked.

"You know the reason Morton was lookin' for somebody in the first place was 'cause Horner was hurt, right?" Riker nodded and Abel went on. "Well, by the time we got away from the posse the last time, Horner was in a bad way. Morton an' that kid that does the scoutin' for him did what they could for Horner, an' then they fell asleep." He smiled again. "Whilst they was asleep, I put a rolled up blanket over Horner's face an' smothered the life outta him." Riker cursed and started to get to his feet. Abel raised a hand and Riker settled back down. "Them boys never knew a thing. They just thought he died in his sleep. They buried him the next day an' split up. Morton paid me what Horner promised an' sent me on my way, an' here I am." He turned to his horse and started to loosen the cinch with a self-satisfied smirk.

Behind him Riker sat staring thoughtfully into the fire. "You were supposed ta stay with Morton an' find out where he was headin', Abel," Riker said.

"I didn't have no choice in the matter," Abel replied without turning around. "It was get out or get shot. Morton was really pissed about the banker's wife."

Riker got to his feet behind Barnes. "What banker's wife?" he asked quietly.

"The one I shot in the bank job. You told me to do somethin' to get the townsfolk after us."

"I also told you to stay with Morton. You shoulda known that shootin' a woman would make Morton mad." By now Riker was behind the oblivious Barnes. Riker dropped his big hand onto Abel's shoulder, spun him around, and sank his fist into the thin gunhand's belly. Abel doubled over, retching, and sank to his knees gasping for breath. The horse danced sideways as the reins dropped from Abel's hand. "So now we're no closer to findin' Morton's hideout than we ever were." Riker hooked a boot toe under Abel's chin and tipped his face up. "Give me one good reason why I don't kill you right now, Abel."

Abel stuttered and stammered while his mind raced frantically around in circles trying to come up with a reason why he should stay alive, and not having a great deal of success in the endeavor. He was so sure that Riker was going to kill him that he finally just shut down the whole process and waited for the bullet. Riker lowered his foot in disgust. "Damn, you're just about totally worthless, ain't you?" he growled. "I can't for the life of me figure out why I trusted you in the first place."

"Because he's what we could find on short notice, remember?" Bronco said as he strolled into camp. "Sometimes beggars can't be choosers."

Abel suddenly staggered to his feet and stumbled off into the rocks behind the camp; they could hear him retching. He came back into the camp wiping his hand across his mouth. He'd never come that close to dying in his whole miscreant life, and he'd been so scared he'd lost his breakfast and nearly emptied his bladder. But while he'd been out yonder he'd made himself a promise. If there was any way possible to make it happen, Bob Morton was going to die. As far as he was concerned it was all Morton's fault that Riker had nearly shot him, and he would get back at Morton for the sheer terror he'd just gone through. It never dawned on Abel that what he'd just gone through had been his own damned fault. It was easier to just blame Morton.

"So what's next on the agenda now that this critter's back?" Bronco asked. Riker turned back toward where Bronco stood with a half-smile on his lips.

"It's time to turn up the heat," Riker said. "This jackass didn't do what he was told, so we can't go to Morton. I guess we'll just have to bring Morton to us."

"What'd Morton do to put the burr under your saddle anyway?"

"He's my step-brother," Riker replied.

"And?" Bronco prodded.

"And I've always hated him ever since the day my ma married his pa. He was always the fair-haired boy, even with my ma. An' I've been waitin' for years ta git even. His pa beat me an' my ma let him." What he didn't say was that his stepfather had usually had a good reason for the whippings he'd doled out.

"After my ma died I din't have no place else to go. Morton left when he was sixteen, but I had ta stay for a while longer. What Morton don't know is that I got some of my own back. He thinks his pa rode out after cattle an' never come back." Riker's twisted smile was pure evil. "He rode out all right, but I rode out right behind him. You shoulda seen the look on that old man's face when that rope come tight. The folks that found him think his horse dumped him an' he got drug. But the horse that drug him was mine. Then I rode off an' never looked back. I been plottin' ever since. I'm either gonna kill Morton myself, or do my damnedest to make sure the law does; I don't care which. It's just that up 'til now I haven't been able to find him."

Bronco whistled quietly to himself. "Hoo whee man, you're serious about this, ain't ya?"

"That I am. I'll see Morton dead one way or the other." Riker turned toward the lean-to and picked up his saddle and blankets. "Go git Smith an' git your horses saddled. We're leavin'."

The four rode out of the canyon and turned toward the northwest. Somehow Riker had the feeling that was the way they needed to go.

~ 23 ~

Bowie and Black meandered down the main street, such as it was, of Stanson late in the morning. There wasn't much to the town, but he was fairly sure that it had a telegraph office. He'd seen the wires as he made his way down out of the hills to the west. Right at the moment he was pretty much at a loss as to how to proceed. He hadn't found hide nor hair of Bob Morton, so he'd decided to wire Judge Martin and see if Morton had surfaced anywhere else recently. As far as Bowie could tell the man had dug a hole, crawled into it, and pulled it in after him. He was no closer to finding Morton than he was when he left Laramie. With any luck, he could get a good meal and some supplies here and maybe get some indication of where he needed to head next.

He tied Black at the hitchrail in front of the ramshackle telegraph office and stepped inside. Behind the counter an old codger wearing sleeve garters and a green eyeshade was dozing in an old rocker. The man had his feet propped up on another chair and was snoring gently. There was a bell on the counter and Bowie tiptoed quietly up to it then began to hammer mightily on the clapper. The telegrapher gave a snort and his eyes popped open and he jerked upright in his chair. In his hurry to get to his feet he nearly fell on the floor but managed to achieve an upright position with a minimum of bodily injury.

"What in tarnation'd ya do that for?" he asked in a reedy voice. "Ya dern near scairt me outta ten years of my life! An' I ain't got any extry years ta spare!" He glared at Bowie.

Bowie gave him an innocuous smile. "Sorry about that old timer. I just wanted to make sure you weren't dead."

"Hmph," the man snorted. "I'll give you dead, young feller. You just drop that pistol an' we'll see what's what." The man put up his fists and waved them at Bowie.

"Easy there, pard," Bowie said as he raised his hands up, palms out. "I just want to send a wire, I don't need to get my butt kicked."

"Next time you'd best think before ya hammer on the bell then," the old-timer said, somewhat mollified. He turned a pad of paper around toward Bowie and tossed a pencil on the counter. "Get her writ, an' I'll send it."

"Thanks, mister," Bowie said and began to write.

The telegrapher was reading as Bowie wrote. When he came to the part where Bowie was asking about Bob Morton, the old man said, "Where you been for the last week boy, under a rock? The whole damn country knows that Bob Morton done blowed up the bank in Hobart an' bushwacked the posse that was chasin' him from there. Shot 'em up bad an' killed most of 'em on the spot. One of 'em made it back but he died later on. The wire's has been buzzin' ever since it happened."

"Are you sure it was Morton?" Bowie asked.

"Why sure I'm sure," the man replied. "He done left part of a wanted flyer outside the bank."

"Why in the world would he do that?"

"How should I know? Maybe he wanted folks to know who done it."

"That sure doesn't sound like the Bob Morton I've heard about," Bowie said. "I understand that he generally makes sure nobody gets hurt."

"I guess maybe any man can turn bad, stranger." The telegrapher read a bit more of what Bowie had written. He saw Judge Martin's name and lifted his head. "You one a them special deputies I've heerd tell about? You sure don't look like no lawman."

"I try not to," Bowie replied. "And I'd appreciate it if you didn't spread it around." He turned away from the counter. "I'll wait for the answer, if you don't mind." He wanted confirmation of the telegrapher's information before he decided what to do next.

"Help yourself, deputy. That chair yonder's purty comfy. We even got magazines that's less than a year old."

An hour later the telegraph key began to chatter. The message was from Judge Martin and confirmed everything the old man had said. Five minutes after that Bowie was out the door and riding east.

Lonnie Grable had sat by his small fire most of the night staring into the flames. The young man had a lot on his mind.

The happenings of the past few days were weighing heavy on his conscience. He'd originally started riding with Riker and Jarvis because he was bored in the small town he was living in and the oultaws offered excitement. They'd swaggered into town, acting like they owned the place, and to a young man with dreams of adventure they'd seemed to have what he was looking for. For the first month it had been pretty exciting. He'd held the horses while the two men had robbed a small bank back down the line, and his cut had been more money than he'd ever seen before in his life. He'd bought a new pistol, and some better clothes, and even sent some home to his folks, who thought he was on his way north with a trail herd.

But blowing up the bank in Hobart, even though no one had gotten hurt there, was something else entirely. That had been just wanton destruction for no visible gain. They hadn't even taken much of the money. And ambushing the posse was more than he could handle. He'd stood there with his rifle in his hand until Riker had snarled, "You better start shootin', boy," then Lonnie had fired a few rounds over the posse's heads as they were falling. He'd gone out and killed the wounded horses then saddled his own horse and left, with Riker's parting words echoing in his head.

On the one hand, he knew that if he said anything to anyone, Riker would kill him. Riker was a man of his word. On the other, he just couldn't let something like this slide. He was going to have to tell someone, somewhere, and take his chances on Riker, and take his chances on going to jail. As soon as he came to a town he was going to turn himself in. With his mind made up, he rolled up in his blankets and went to sleep. In the morning he'd start looking for a lawman to surrender to.

Bowie had been gone from the telegraph office for about four hours when he saw another rider coming towards him from the south. He pulled Black up between two spruce trees and waited with the Greener across his thighs and his thumb on the hammers. He'd already made sure it was loaded. He took a drink from his canteen then hung it back on the saddlehorn.

The rider went out of sight beyond an aspen thicket. Bowie could hear the man's horse picking its way through the trees. Finally the sweating sorrel horse appeared, weaving through the white trunks of the trees. Its rider was concentrating on not banging his knees against them and not on what was around him. Bowie could tell by the way the horse was moving that it had come a long way in a hurry. When the rider was twenty yards or so away, Bowie touched Black with his spurs and moved out into the open. He lifted the Greener so it was level and pointed mostly in the rider's direction. "Afternoon," he said cheerfully. Lonnie Grable yanked his horse to a stop; his hand went to his holstered gun but froze in mid-air when the yawning muzzles of the Greener appeared in front of him.

The young man's hands slowly rose to shoulder height and he said, "Easy with that thing, mister! I saw a man shot with one of 'em once and it wasn't pretty."

Bowie chuckled. "Nope, it ain't pretty. But it is pretty damned effective. Settles crowds down real nice, too." He let the muzzles of the shotgun sag just a bit and rested the forestock on his saddlehorn. "You wouldn't happen to have seen four men with bloody hands back there behind you now, would you?" The boy, for that was what he was in reality, suddenly went ghostly pale and swallowed nervously. His knuckles were white where he gripped his reins. "What's the matter?" Bowie asked. "You look like somebody just walked over your grave!"

Lonnie started to speak, then stopped and tried to swallow the lump in his throat. He finally got his voice going and answered, "Nothin's the matter, mister. That was just kind of a strange question. About the blood I mean." Despite the coolness of the day, the young man was sweating. "No, I ain't seen nobody. Why, you some kinda bounty hunter or something?"

"Or something," Bowie said. He looked at the boy, who was getting more antsy by the second. "You got a name, pard?"

"Grable. Lonnie Grable."

"Well, Mister Grable, just what exactly did you see back yonder that's got you so fuzzed up?" Bowie gestured behind Lonnie with the shotgun. While he was talking he was keeping a close eye on the kid in front of him. If he so much as looked like he was thinking about drawing, Bowie was going to empty that boy's saddle with the Greener.

The boy stared tensely down at his hands where they were now folded on his saddlehorn for a minute then he suddenly relaxed as if he had come to a decision. "Mister, you don't happen to know if there's a town with a lawdog of some sort in it anywhere's close to here, do you?" Bowie looked at him sharply. "I got something I need ta tell somebody and the law's probly the best one ta tell it to." He looked up at Bowie and Bowie suddenly grinned.

"There's a town about four hours in front of you, depending on how fast that horse of yours can travel, but as far as I know there ain't any lawman there. Or at least I didn't see a sheriff's office or anything like that. But you're in luck. I just happen to be a bonafide, honest to Goshen lawdog myself, and if you've got something to say you just go right ahead and spill it."

Lonnie stared at him in astonishment, then his mouth closed with a click. "Yeah, right," he said. "And so's my momma. You don't look like no lawman. If you're a lawdog, where's your badge?"

Bowie reached into his vest and brought out his badge. Its silver face flashed in the afternoon sun. "There you go. Now what say we make an early camp and you can tell me what's so all-fired important for you to get off your chest that you've about run that horse into the ground to get somewhere to tell it."

~ 24 ~

The boy was silent while the two rode on toward a small creek nearby. On the grassy banks of the creek they unsaddled their horses then led them to water. Lonnie's sorrel had cooled down enough while the two had been talking that he could drink without getting sick. When the animals had drunk their fill, the men picketed them on a nearby meadow and began to gather sticks for a fire. Bowie scuffed out a bare spot back from the water and soon had a small fire crackling merrily and the coffeepot starting to heat.

Bowie leaned back on his saddle and waited for the coffee to cook and for Lonnie to speak. Neither took place very fast. Finally Bowie asked, "So are you planning on talking, or are you just going to sit there like a wart on a frog and brood?"

Lonnie looked up at him. "I'm tryin' to decide where to start."

"The beginning might be nice."

"I guess you're right," Lonnie said slowly. "I've been riding with these three fellas for about a month or so. They rode into town, at least two of 'em did, and had money to spend. Things were way too dull around home, and I hooked up with 'em 'cause I thought it might be exciting. I found out in a hurry that there's such a thing as too much excitement." He stopped and watched the flames for a minute, then went on. "I was holdin' the horses when them boys knocked over a crackerbox bank back yonder." He waved vaguely back the way he'd come.

"They give me more money from that than I'd ever seen in one chunk in my whole life. I thought I was really onto somethin' there. Never gave no thought to the fact that I'd have the law after me from there on. All I could think of was the money. So when we rode on toward Hobart, I didn't think nothin' of it. But then I started hearin' some stuff that I wasn't too sure about."

"These boys have names?" Bowie asked quietly.

Lonnie sighed. "Yeah, they got names. Leader's name is Riker. Big fella, real fast with a pistol, and meaner'n hell. He told me he'd kill me if I told anybody about 'em. That's why I was pushin' my horse so hard. I wanna get as far away from Riker as I can git. That man scares me! From some stuff I overheard, he's got it in for another outlaw named Bob Morton for some reason, and he's doin' his level best to get the whole territory stirred up. That's why he blew up the bank in Hobart. Do you know about that?"

"I just found out this morning. But the way I heard it, Morton and his gang did it. Then they bushwhacked the posse that was chasing them and killed everybody." Bowie looked intently at Lonnie. "And now you're telling me it wasn't Morton?"

"Mister, I can dead solid guarantee you it wasn't Bob Morton that wrecked that bank. It was Riker!" the boy exclaimed.

"Who else is with him?"

"There's a gent name of Bronco Jarvis"- he paused when Bowie said an ugly word- "and another one that goes by Smith, but I'm pretty sure that ain't his name. Jarvis mean something to ya?"

"Yeah, he's been on the list for quite a while. Sucker's too slick to get caught though. He's never where you think he's gonna be. What's this Smith fella look like?"

"He's kinda short, and blocky-built. No fat on him, just solid meat and bone. Carries a Colt in a cut-down holster, and has a Winchester in his hand most times."

"You're right, his name's not Smith. It's Daltrey. I'm betting that he's got a long-legged paint horse and he's riding a Texas-rigged saddle, right?"

"How'd you know?"

"He's on the list too, only I heard he got killed down in the Nation. I guess I heard wrong."

Bowie hated to do it, because the young man in front of him didn't seem the type, but he had to ask about the posse. "Were you there when they ambushed that posse?"

"Yeah, I was there." Lonnie stopped and stared into the fire. "But I didn't shoot nobody, and that's the God's honest truth! I wasn't gonna even pull the trigger, but Riker saw me just standin' there, and the way he looked at me I figured it was either shoot or die, so I shot over their heads. Riker and them shot the horses first, then shot the riders when they tried to run." He swallowed hard then went on. "All the men got killed except one that hung back and got away while the shootin' was going on. I think he was wounded too. He was ridin' all humped over."

"He died a couple of days ago," Bowie said.

Lonnie went on like he hadn't heard. "I went out and put down a couple of horses that weren't already dead. Smith called me on it, and I slugged him and stuck my pistol in his face." He was staring down at his folded hands and didn't see Bowie's startled look at his words. "Then I got in the middle of that sorrel horse yonder and rode out. I told Riker I hadn't banked on anything like that and didn't want no part of it. He let me go but he told me if I told anybody he'd find me and kill me." He looked at Bowie. "I just couldn't let somethin' like that go by. My conscience has been eatin' me alive ever since I took off. So now you know what happened, and I'm ready to go to jail if you're ready to take me there."

"So far, all I can see that you're guilty of is being young and foolish," Bowie said. "How old are you, anyway?"

"Seventeen. But I've been doin' a man's work since I was fourteen."

"I reckon so. Did this Riker say anything else I maybe should know about?"

"I think he had somebody ridin' with Morton. I know he talked about a man named Abel somethin' or other that was gonna have some information about where Morton holes up when he ain't settin' up a bank job. But that's it."

"I think I know a little something about the mysterious Abel," Bowie said. "I think he was in on Morton's last job, the one Morton actually did pull, and I think he's the one that shot the banker's wife. It'll surprise me if that gent ain't dead. From what I hear Bob Morton prides himself on never having hurt anybody in any of his robberies."

"Now how would you know that, mister?" Lonnie asked with surprise in his voice.

Bowie winked at him and said, "I didn't always ride on this side of the law. Now I've got job for you," Bowie said thoughtfully. "I need you to ride for that settlement yonder and send a wire for me."

"A wire to who?" Lonnie asked. "And where you goin'?"

"The who is Judge Martin in Laramie. And the where is that I'm gonna backtrail you and see if I can't pay Mister Riker and company a visit."

"He'll kill you, mister."

"I might just take a sight of killing, my young friend," Bowie replied.

~ 25 ~

Throughout the course of the evening Bowie quizzed Lonnie about the country he'd just come through. He was trying to get a feel for where Riker might be headed. When he'd gotten all the boy had to give, they sat over coffee, each lost in his own thoughts. After a long silence, Lonnie suddenly spoke up. "You ever heard of a place called Lost Creek?"

Bowie shook his head no. "I don't think so, why?"

"Riker mentioned somethin' a time or two about a Lost Creek Canyon or some such. It kind of sounded like maybe that's where he was headin'."

Bowie spread his map where the firelight would fall on it. He searched the whole map but there wasn't a Lost Creek anywhere to be seen. Finally he gave up the search and folded the map. "I guess I'll just have to take my chances," he sighed. He reached into his pocket and brought out a piece of paper. "Here's what I want you to send to the Judge in the morning," he said as he handed the slip to Lonnie. "You got some cash to pay for it?"

"Yeah. It's the least I can do to try to make up for all I done."

"I told you, you haven't *done* anything yet. You got out before you got down to their level. I think Judge Martin will think so too."

Lonnie looked up at him. "Whadda you mean, Judge Martin'll think so? How's he even gonna know?"

"'Cause you're gonna go tell him, that's how. As soon as you send that telegram, you're gonna point that red horse toward Laramie, and you're gonna keep him going that way until you're standing in the Judge's office confessing. Tell him I sent you, he'll understand. He might even put you to work." Bowie sat back with a grin.

"Are you nuts, mister? Why would I want to do somethin' like that?"

"Because otherwise I'll have to hang you myself," Bowie replied seriously. “You’ve done told me what a bad boy you’ve been. I can’t see any other way to stop your criminal career, and I don’t have time to take you back to Laramie myself. Either you’ll have to go to Laramie on your own hook or I’ll have to string you up right here.”

Lonnie gaped at him while he tried to decide if Bowie was serious or not. Bowie sat with a stern look on his face and watched the play of emotions cross the boy’s features. Finally he couldn’t stand it any longer and broke out laughing.

“What’s so dern funny?” Lonnie wanted to know.

“You should’ve seen yourself. You’d be laughing too,” Bowie answered. “You didn’t know whether to crap, scream, or cry, and it’s pretty obvious you still don’t. I just couldn’t take it any longer.” He chuckled again. He was starting to like this kid.

“Hmmph,” Lonnie snorted, and turned away. This character got more annoying every minute.

Lonnie and Bowie parted company at daylight the next morning. Last night Bowie had kept Lonnie awake until he knew everything the boy knew about where he’d been and what Riker’s plans might be. Finally Lonnie had told him, “I don’t know nothin’ else, mister. You’ve got it all. Now I gotta get some sleep.” He’d gone to his saddle, unrolled his blankets, and laid down with his back to Bowie and the fire.

The next morning, the crackling of the fire and the smell of coffee and bacon brought Lonnie out of a sound sleep. When he sat up, Bowie said, “Ah, the dead have arisen. I was about to come over and kick you and see if you were still alive.”

“Are you always this blasted cheerful first thing in the mornin’?” Lonnie groused, rubbing his hands over his face. “And it ain’t morning yet anyway.” He looked around. “It’s still dark.”

“A journey of a thousand miles begins with a single step, my son. And you have a long journey ahead of you,” Bowie intoned solemnly.

“Oh, shut up,” Lonnie answered politely as he rolled out of his blankets and started putting on his boots. Bowie just grinned and turned the bacon. A half hour later they split up; Bowie rode toward where he thought Riker might be, and Lonnie went toward Laramie by way of the telegraph office in Stanson. Or so Bowie thought.

Lonnie rode into Stanson and went straight to the telegraph

office to do what that obnoxious deputy had told him to do. He stepped down in front of the ramshackle building, tied his horse to the splintered hitchrail, and shoved the weather-warped door open. From the looks of the walls, and the door itself, the whole thing had been slapped together out of green lumber that had dried unevenly in the wind and sun.

The bottom of the door scraped loudly on the floorboards and startled the grizzled gent behind the counter awake. He snorted and sat up. The momentum of his feet falling off of the small table where they'd been resting bounced him to a standing position. He rubbed his eyes and yawned, belched loudly, and asked, "What can I do fer ya, young feller?"

"I need to send a wire to Laramie," the young man replied. "It's important."

The telegrapher scratched his whiskers and said, "Can't do 'er."

"Whatta you mean, you can't? Ain't you the telegrapher?"

"Oh, I'm the wire mechanic, alright. Ain't none better, if I do say so myself." The man showed a gap-toothed grin. "But the wire's down somewheres. Got a feller out lookin' for the break but he ain't found it yet that I know of. Leastways I ain't heard nothin' from him yet."

"But I need this telegram sent!" Lonnie growled in frustration.

"Yer welcome to wait here until the wire's back up if you want," the telegrapher told him, "But I can't tell ya when that'll be." The old man thought a minute then said, "Say, I'll tell ya what I'll do. You leave yer message with me, an' when the wire's fixed I'll send it for ya. An' it'll only cost ya an extra two bits." He grinned slyly.

"Two bits? For what?"

"Why, special handlin', of course. What'd ya think it was for?"

"Ah, hell, I don't know," Lonnie said in resignation. He reached into his pocket and brought out Bowie's message. "Here. What do I owe you, including the 'special handling'?"

The telegrapher counted words and looked up. "That'll be a buck an' a quarter. An' I'm givin' you a deal, seein' as how it's a law matter."

"Some deal," Lonnie grumbled. He reached into his pocket

and brought out some coins and counted out the money for the telegram. "Just don't forget to send it, alright?" Without waiting for an answer he turned and stomped out. He nearly sprained his wrist trying to slam the door and finally settled for dragging it most of the way shut then stomped to his horse. He mounted the sorrel and turned him toward Laramie.

Lonnie's back trail was easy enough for Bowie to follow. All the kid had been worried about was putting distance between himself and Riker, so the sorrel horse's tracks were plain enough that Bowie kept his own horse at a trot. He finally called a halt just before full dark on the banks of a small creek. He'd pick up the trail in the morning. He figured he'd gained several hours and should be at the ambush site some time late the next day.

Bowie turned out to be a pretty fair fortuneteller. It was just about straight up four o'clock by the Ingersoll watch in his vest pocket when he came to the creek bed. He watered Black then tethered him to a small tree and began to cast around for tracks and other signs. He knew that a lot of the tracks would have been tromped out by the men who had come to take the dead posse members back to town, but he figured he should look around anyway. He should at least be able to find out which direction the outlaws had gone when they left here.

He found the empty shell casings where the bushwhackers had been standing. The shooters definitely had the oncoming posse in their sights. The carcasses of the dead horses were scattered on the grass beyond the creek. His arrival hadn't disturbed the prairie cleanup crew in the least. Magpies and crows squawked and squabbled over the bounty while a golden eagle stood aloof sentry on one of the carcasses.

Bowie started to scramble up the bank to where the dead horses lay. A cold voice stopped him halfway up and left him balanced on one foot with both hands wrapped around clumps of grass. "Hold it right there, mister. I got this here rifle pointed right at yer back and there ain't no way in hell I can miss from here."

~ 26 ~

"You have me at a disadvantage, my friend," Bowie said casually, while plans and thoughts flashed through his head. It sounded like the voice had come from a small thicket of sand plums to his right. His boot slipped a little in the loose soil and he said, "I'm not sure I can stay here for long, friend. I'm starting to slide back down."

"Come down slow," the voice said. "And don't try nothin'." Bowie had the man's location pegged now and he quickly glanced that way. He saw a flash of sunlight on steel and let go of his handholds. He lunged sideways and rolled down the slope, drawing the Starr as he went. He heard the blast of the shot and saw dirt fly up from the bank where he'd been standing. He rolled behind a downed cottonwood and waited.

His wait was short. Another shot thumped a bullet into the log and he almost fired back then shouted instead, "What in the world did I do to you, friend?" As soon as he spoke he rolled to his right toward where the log gave more cover.

"Yer one o' them that killed Davy and the others!" Joe Harris snarled. "And now I'm gonna kill you!" He fired again and the bullet caromed off the log with a whine.

"I've never been here before!" Bowie protested as he looked along the log for a way out of his current predicament. "And even if I was one of 'em, why would I come back?" Joe answered with another shot. Those were big slugs, and Bowie was afraid this character would eventually find a soft spot in the log and get one through. Bowie finally decided that if he was careful and kept his arse down he might be able to weasel his way around behind the shooter, whoever he was, and get the drop on him. He really didn't want to shoot this jasper; after all, the man just wanted to avenge his friends. On the other hand, ending up dead himself would definitely put an end to his mission so if push came to shove he wasn't averse to putting a bullet in the man in the bushes.

Bowie low-crawled down alongside the log. When he came to where the it crossed the small creek, he took off his hat and cautiously peeked up over the log. A bushy plum tree that still had most of its leaves blocked the shooter's view so Bowie slipped over the log and moved into the thicket. It wasn't long until he was standing behind the shooter. Bowie eased up behind him, tucked the muzzle of the Starr behind the teamster's ear, and drew back the hammer. "Mister, I don't wanna kill you, and I'm pretty sure you don't wanna be dead, so you just pitch that cannon out yonder and get your hands where I can see 'em."

Joe stiffened when he felt the cold steel touch his head. When he heard Bowie's words his shoulders slumped. He was thoroughly disgusted with himself as he tossed his battered .56 Spenser out onto the sand. He should've known something was wrong when there were no return shots. His hands came up to shoulder level and he felt his pistol being lifted from his holster. The pistol barrel left his head and prodded him in the back. "Step on out in the open there, friend, and let's have a look at you."

Joe stepped down out of the thicket and turned around. "Who are you and why are you bushwhacking innocent travelers?" Bowie asked, keeping the Starr pointed in the general vicinity of his prisoner's belt buckle.

"My name's Joe Harris. Davy Brewster was my friend and you bastards killed him!" Joe turned his head and spat.

"I already told you," Bowie reminded the man, "that I've never been here before. And besides which, I'm one of Judge Martin's deputies. I'm most definitely not a bank robber." Joe paled, and Bowie gave him a smile. He could almost see the thoughts racing madly around the teamster's brain. "It's not nice to try to shoot a member of the law enforcement community."

"How do I know you're a lawdog?" Joe blustered. "You don't look like no depitty."

"I haven't shot you yet, have I?" Bowie asked. He holstered the Starr and pulled Joe's ancient open-top Navy revolver out of his belt. He shucked the cylinder out of the pistol, dumped the shells out in his hand, and returned the two parts of the gun to their rightful owner. The cartridges he put in his own pocket. "Now would you mind explaining to me just what the hell you think you're doing here?"

Joe started to put his pistol back together, but when he saw the look on Bowie's face he elected to holster the pistol and shove the cylinder into his vest pocket instead. "I'm gonna find them that done this," he waved a hand toward the dead horses, "and kill 'em!" He stood there defiantly and waited for Bowie's answer.

"You do realize, I hope," Bowie told the teamster in a reasonable tone, "that if I'd've been one of the bushwhackers you'd be dead right now. From what I hear about those boys, they don't waste around any when it comes time for shooting."

"I don't care," Joe said stubbornly. "They gotta pay for what they done ta Davy."

"Oh, they'll pay alright, but I'm not sure you're the gent that's gonna be able to do the collecting. And what're you doing out here alone? Doesn't anybody back where you came from like you well enough to come with you?"

Joe spat again and the look on his face was that of a man who had just bit into something nasty. "Ah, them yella-bellies back yonder are too scairt to do anything. I came out here by myself 'cause they was all too lily-livered ta come."

"Maybe it's not cowardice," Bowie said quietly. "Maybe they're smart. The men you're planning on chasing aren't greenhorns. Those men are stone cold killers. You throw down on them the way you did me and you'll get shot full of holes. And they won't care which side of you the holes are on." He stopped and looked at Joe. "Go home, Mister Harris. Leave these men to me."

"There's only one of you," Joe protested. "How's that different from me goin' after 'em?"

"It's different because I do this sort of thing for a living, and you don't. And," he gave Joe a big smile, "I cheat. Now get up on whatever critter brought you here and you head for home while you're still able."

Joe grumbled to himself then picked up his rifle and disappeared into the brush. He emerged a few moments later astride a big sorrel mule. "I ain't scared of you er your badge, lawdog," he said, trying to salvage something of his shredded ego. "And I ain't afraid of dyin', neither."

"If that's the case then you're dumber than you look," Bowie told him.

With a snort Joe started to boot the mule up the bank and Bowie said casually, "I don't suppose you've ever heard of Lost Creek Canyon, have you?"

Joe drug the mule to a halt and looked slyly at Bowie. "Well, maybe I have, and maybe I haven't. Why, is that where them no-accounts is headed?" He stopped and waited for Bowie to speak.

"Nah, it's just some place I heard about," Bowie said casually, but he could tell the lie wasn't working. "I thought it sounded interesting, and I thought maybe if it was someplace around these parts I'd look around a bit." He gave Joe another smile.

"Mister, I ain't as dumb as you think I am, and on top of that, you're a damn poor liar," Joe told him. "Somebody's done told you that them fellers are headed for Lost Creek Canyon but you ain't got no idea how to get there. It looks to me like you're holdin' a busted flush and you need some cards." He gave Bowie a smile of his own and sat back in his saddle with his arms smugly crossed on his chest. "There ain't no way you're gonna find it without my help, so what's it gonna be?"

Bowie cursed under his breath. "Alright, you got me on that one. But why can't I find it if you give me directions?"

"'Cause I ain't gonna give you no directions, that's why. The only way you're gittin' to that canyon is if I take ya there."

"Dammit, you're gonna get yourself killed, but I guess that's your business. It's a free country," Bowie said in resignation. "Let me get my horse and let's get started."

~ 27 ~

Riker, Bronco Jarvis, Smith, and Abel Barnes topped out on a sage-covered ridge. Below them, in the lowering light of evening, they could see a small fire that twinkled and sent up delicate wisps of smoke. On the grassy meadow beyond the fire a small horse herd grazed, watched over by a man on a stout buckskin. Near the fire three beds were rolled out and the man's companions lounged near the fire drinking coffee and talking quietly.

Riker pulled his horse back into the shadows near a wide-spreading juniper tree. "Alright, time to turn up the heat. We'll ride down yonder an' kill them cowboys and scatter that horse herd. I want the one on the buckskin left alive to tell the tale, so make sure you watch where yer shootin'. An' make damn sure that gent hears that Bob Morton done the deed before anybody shoots him. Got it?" He looked around at the others.

Bronco was quietly checking his guns. Smith had his rifle out of the scabbard and balanced butt-down on his thigh with his hand around the stock. Abel just swallowed nervously and licked his tongue across his suddenly dry lips. He nodded and waited for Riker to make his move.

"Bronco, you ride on down yonder a ways," Riker pointed to the west, "an' come in from that way. That'll bring you in behind 'em. Me an' Barnes'll come in from the east. Smith, you stay up here. Yer purty proud of that rifle of yours, so when you hear me shoot you put a bullet in that fella out yonder with the herd. Just make damn sure you don't kill 'im."

The Thornton brothers and their neighbor, Shorty Grimes, had spent two weeks gathering the horses in the meadow beyond their fire. Then they'd spent a few more weeks getting them tamed down enough to handle. They could even ride a couple of them. Now the three men were on the way home. They had a good stud horse waiting back at the home ranch for the mares they'd gathered, and they were just about to be in the horse business.

Dillon, the oldest Thornton and the oldest of the three in general, looked up from where he'd been contemplating the fire and the future when he heard the clank of a steel-shod hoof on rock. Out on the meadow Shorty and the mares were still visible in the last of the daylight but the sound hadn't come from the meadow. It had come from the slope to the east, and a moment later two men rode into the open at the edge of the meadow. "Hallo, the camp," Riker called. "Mind if we come in?"

"Light and set, stranger," Dillon said, straightening from where he'd been laying back on his saddle. "Coffee's on, and ye're welcome to it."

His younger brother Jaren sat up and tipped his hat back on his head. "We done et all the bacon we had cooked, but there's a bit of biscuit left if you gents're interested."

"Much obliged, friend," Riker said as he stepped down from his horse. "You men've got a nice bunch of horses out yonder. You from around these parts? I might be interested in buyin' if you're sellin'."

"Them mares ain't for sale, Mister, uh..." Dillon began.

"Morton. Bob Morton," Riker cut him off.

"Bob Morton the outlaw?" Shorty asked from behind Riker.

"That's right," he said, and drew his pistol. He fired a shot into Dillon and heard the blast of Smith's rifle and the thud of the bullet into the man on the buckskin horse. Beside him, Abel had pulled his Colt and was firing at Jaren Thornton. Behind the camp Bronco suddenly appeared and shot Dillon twice in the back as he struggled to pull his pistol. The impact of the bullets knocked him onto his face in the fire, scattering the coals and tipping the coffeepot on its side. Then Jarvis turned his gun on the younger Thornton but Riker had already finished him.

The three men turned toward the sound of galloping hooves and saw Shorty disappear into the high sage that surrounded the grassy opening. There was blood high on the back of his shirt and Riker nodded in satisfaction. "That oughta do it," he said to no one in particular. He turned back toward the camp and pointed at the body of Dillon Thornton. "Abel, drag that one outta the fire an' rustle up some grub. I'm hungry. Surely they've got somethin' left to eat in those packs." He pointed at the canvas-covered panniers that lay to one side then turned away to lead his horse to water.

"Why do I gotta be the one to get all that done?" Abel began.

"'Cause I'll kill ya if ya don't," Riker answered matter-of-factly over his shoulder. Bronco chuckled and Abel jerked as if he'd been beestung. He added Bronco Jarvis' name to the list of men he planned to kill someday.

Smith came clattering through the rocks on the side of the ridge and into the camp. "Good shot," Riker said. Smith just looked at him with no change of expression and began to unsaddle his horse. Grumbling to himself, Abel drug the two dead men out away from the camp then began to paw through the supplies in the packs.

"There ain't much here, Riker," he said. "Bacon an' a little hardtack's about it. These here rawhiders were about down to nothin'." He dug a little further and came up with a stone jug with a corncob stopper firmly pounded into the mouth. Abel held up the jug. "Well, lookee here, boys. They weren't *completely* outta good stuff." He worked the stopper out of the jug and tilted it to his mouth, holding it on the crook of his elbow. The first taste of home-brewed corn liquor had barely hit his tongue when the jug was snatched away.

Abel whipped his head around with an enraged squall only to see Riker tilt the jug to his own lips and take a mighty swallow. The fumes of the powerful brew made the big outlaw's eyes tear as the liquor burned its way into his belly. "Damn, now that's good," he said, with an uncharacteristic smile on his face. "You done good for once, Abel." Riker passed the jug to Bronco, who took a swallow then passed the corn squeezings on to Smith.

"Ain't much left," Smith said as he took a drink. The jug at last came back to its discoverer and Abel tilted it up. The last mouthful flowed down his throat and he swallowed in satisfaction and some disgust.

"You gents coulda been a little more generous," he groused. "I am the one that found this here jug, ya know."

"Just be happy you got any at all," Riker growled. "Now git some grub started."

Later, Bronco belched and wiped his greasy fingers on his pants. "You cook bacon right well," he told Abel. He looked over at Riker where the big man was lounging against his saddle. "We gonna gather them horses, Riker?" he asked.

"Nope," Riker replied. "Whatta you think we'd do with a

bunch of green-broke broomtails? I got better things to do than nursemaid a bunch of horses across the country. I got a man to find and kill."

~ 28 ~

Bob Morton, the man Borden City knew as Don Gordon, woke at first light the next morning, no closer to a solution as to what was going on than he had been when he went to bed. When he'd ridden in last night, the hands were just coming in for dinner and the cookhouse was abuzz with speculation. The cow country grapevine had brought the news of the destruction of the bank in Hobart at least as fast as the telegraph wires could. It was downright amazing how quick, and even how accurate, the news could get from one cowboy to another.

As for him, he couldn't think of a person, other than a few lawdogs here and there around the country and maybe a banker or two, who might have it in for him. At least not enough to get a bunch of killings and the destruction of a bank blamed on him. He lay in his old brass bed in the big log ranch house for a while, pondering, while the sky outside his window got brighter. He imagined he could hear the rattle of stove lids and the squeak of the pump as the old cook got the stove burning and coffee started. The thump of bootheels on pine and the creaking of the leather hinges of the bunkhouse door would be signaling the first trip of the day to the outhouse out back by one of the hands. Don smiled to himself. That would be Jeff, his foreman. Jeff was just about always the first one up and he seemed to take it personal if one of the other men made it to the outhouse first.

With a sigh, Don flipped the blankets aside and swung his feet to the floor. He sat for a moment rubbing his hands over his face then reached for his socks. With a grimace he stuck his finger in a hole in one of them then pulled them on his feet. He'd get new socks the next time he was in town. He stepped into his britches and pulled his suspenders up over his shoulders then stamped his feet into his boots. He pulled on a coat then went across the yard to the bunkhouse and stepped inside. "Alright you cow nurses," he yelled, "Time to rise and shine." He grinned at the chorus of groans and catcalls that erupted from the lumpy blankets in the bunks. "Folks die in bed," he called.

"Yeah, an' folks have been known ta die of lead poisonin' when they interrupt a man's sleep, too," groused Joey Nelson. "I just can't reach my shooter right at the moment."

"If you shot me, who'd pay you boys your wages?" Don asked cheerfully. "Billy's got coffee on and daylight's a-wastin'." He went on into the cookhouse and poured himself a cup of coffee.

By the time the men had eaten, roped out the day's mounts, and saddled up, the sun was chinning itself on the hills to the east of the ranch buildings. Don stepped into the leather on a long-legged dun and rode the kinks out of the young horse in front of an appreciative audience of his ranch hands. He'd been watching this gelding develop over the course of the summer, and it seemed to be developing into the kind of mount he liked. His bay was tired from the long days and long miles he'd just covered, so Don had roped out this one.

When the dun had finished crow-hopping around the ranch yard Don reined him toward where the hands waited. He'd gotten a report on the cattle and the range last night from Jeff and the two of them had come up with a plan for the coming days. He'd been reading in some of the cattlemen's journals about weaning calves in the fall and feeding them up separately, letting the cows put on flesh for the winter without having to worry about feeding a big calf. He'd decided to give it a try. It never hurt to put some extra pounds on a calf before it was sold.

The ranch had a pasture well fenced with some of Mister Joseph Glidden's new-fangled barbed wire, some of the first in the area. Don and the hands would gather the cows and calves, separate the calves from their mothers, and put the calves in the pasture. The cows would be left near the calves until the calves were weaned. The pasture was well watered, with abundant grass that had cured on the stem, and should keep the young bovines in good shape. Don figured on putting a hundred head in there and seeing how they did. If it worked this year, he'd do it with some more next year.

"You boys mount up and let's go see about separatin' some cows from their babies," Don said. "Jeff, you, Marco, Sam, and Dix take the north side. The rest of us'll go east and we'll meet you on the flats at the bottom of Rooster Comb." The men nodded and turned their mounts to leave. "And keep an eye out for wolves. I saw where they killed an elk about two miles from here when I was ridin' out from town last night."

By noon Don and the men with him had fifty or so pairs gathered and started toward Rooster Comb. The snow that had nearly gotten him killed down south apparently hadn't come this far north yet and the fall weather had been mild, so the cattle were scattered to hell and gone. They'd had to ride a lot of miles for what they had. In addition, Don had noticed that there seemed to be a number of cows without calves. Don didn't even want to think about what that might mean.

Gordon's fifty head were the first to get to the meeting place so the men let the cattle scatter on the lush meadow grass while Don stepped down and built a fire for coffee. Toby and Scott stayed mounted to keep the cattle from drifting too far while the others stepped down and eased their cinches. The lowing of the cows and the bawling of the calves gradually diminished as the pairs found each other and settled in to graze. When everything was relatively quiet Don waved the other two men in toward the fire.

Before the two could dismount, the bawling of cattle announced the arrival of the rest of the bunch. Toby and Scott cut out to help settle the newcomers while the other men with Don finished their coffee. Jeff rode up to where the horses were hobbled on a patch of grass and stepped down. He had a worried look on his face when he walked up to where Don stood. "Is it just me, or is there a bunch of cows without calves out yonder?" he asked without preamble.

"I noticed that too," Don said quietly. "Did you see any sign of wolves in your travels?"

"I seen a few tracks," the foreman replied, "But nowhere near enough to account for that many missing critters. I think we're being rustled."

Oh damn, Don thought to himself. *That's the last thing I need, with the rest of what's going on.* He turned to Jeff and asked, "How many'd you get gathered?"

"We got about sixty head." Jeff looked out over the meadow with the lifelong cattleman's practiced eye. "Looks like you got about the same, maybe a little less. I'd say we got enough for what you wanna try." He brought a coffee cup out of his saddlebag and bent to pour it full of the dark brew. He took a sip and looked up at the sky. "I reckon we got just about enough daylight left to get these critters home."

A couple of days ride to the southeast of where Don and Jeff stood discussing the lack of calves on the ranch, Jackie Gowan and Stan Hall were pushing a small herd of said calves in front of them. They'd been patiently working the calves away from their mothers over the course of the last week or so. A week seemed like a long time and a lot of work for no more animals than they were pushing but these were prime critters. With any luck they'd have the twenty head of almost yearlings pushed into Buckhorn Canyon and the brands changed before the next morning. Don Gordon's Rafter B would be relatively simple to change to a Diamond 8, at least for Jackie's brother Billy, who was an absolute artist when it came to using a running iron.

"How many head you reckon we can get before them boys start getting wise?" Stan asked. "These are damn good calves."

"We've already got forty or so. I'm thinkin' we're probly good for another forty or fifty," Jackie answered. "Most folks don't do much roundin' up this time of year." Little did he know that Don Gordon wasn't "most folks".

The two men lounged in their saddles. By now the calves were pretty much trail-broke and followed the old longhorn steer the rustlers had brought with them as if he was the youngsters' mother. The old steer had led many a rustled herd down many a trail, and had a memory like a homing pigeon. Put him on a new pasture for a few days, drive him to where you wanted to go, and he'd lead whatever herd you found back to that same pasture. If the truth be known, that old brindle could probably have been hung for rustling along with his owners.

Riker stopped his horse and raised a hand. The others reined in their mounts and waited. From somewhere ahead came the bawl of a calf and the clink of a steel horseshoe on rock. He motioned for the others to drop back into the cover of a copse of alders that stood to one side of the trail while he sat his own horse where he had stopped.

The small herd of young cattle came into view around a shoulder of rock. The rustlers saw Riker and yanked their horses to a stop. Their hands drifted casually toward their guns and they eyed the newcomer suspiciously. Riker gave them a wolfish grin. "Now hold up there, gents. Let's not do anything we all might regret. I'm just lookin' for a little information." His gaze strayed to the brands that stood out on the reddish hides of the calves. "You boys ride for the Rafter B, huh?"

The two looked at each other uneasily for a moment then Jackie said, "That's right mister. We're drivin' these younguns to market for the boss."

"Horse puckey!" Riker barked. "You boys're stealin' those calves!" His pistol appeared in his hand as Jackie's mouth came open to protest.

"We ain't doin' no such thing. We're sellin' these for the boss."

Bronco walked his horse into the trail behind the two men. "I think Riker's right, boys. You're rustlers! And if you ain't stealin' these critters, tell us who the boss is and we might just let you go on about your business." He sat with an insolent grin on his face as he watched the two men trying to keep an eye on both him and Riker at the same time.

"Uh, his, uh, name's Barlow," Stan stammered.

"Yeah, that's right, Barlow," Jackie agreed.

"I don't think so," Riker snorted. "But I'll tell you what I'll do. You boys tell me what I want to know, no beatin' around the bush, an' I might let you live; I might even let you take these baby beeves to wherever you're headed. How's that sound?"

It took the two all of about thirty seconds to make up their minds that they had enough of Don Gordon's calves, and that if they wanted to live to profit from their acquisition they'd best give these two whatever they wanted. It wasn't that the two were lacking in guts; it was just that they were bucking a stacked deck, and they both knew that neither one had decent cards in his hand. "Whatta you wanna know, mister?" Jackie asked.

"First off, whose brand is that?"

"It's a fella name of Gordon, back up yonder," Jackie answered. "He's been bringin' in some high grade bulls, and we figured he had a few more calves than he needed so we helped ourselves to some."

"Gordon, huh?" Riker mused. "So what's he doin' brandin' Rafter B? Most folks use their own initials."

"I ain't got a clue," Jackie said. Stan kept his mouth shut, perfectly content to let Jackie do all the talking. "I just stole these critters, I didn't register the brand on 'em."

"And just how far, and which direction, is this Gordon's ranch?"

"It's about two days ride up that way." Jackie pointed to the northwest. "If you follow our tracks to Beaver Crick, then turn upstream, you'll eventually come to Borden City. Gordon's spread is a few miles on beyond the town. Now can we go on? I've done told you everything I can."

Riker looked him over for a minute then nodded abruptly. "Go on, git. I reckon I can find it." He reined his horse off the trail and watched as the two suddenly relieved rustlers gathered their charges and began pushing them on. The cattle had scattered out on the grass in the little basin and it took several minutes to get them together and moving again. While this went on, Riker sat his horse silently. A short time later the cattle were out of sight.

Bronco rode up to Riker as Smith and Abel appeared from where they'd been sitting their horses out of sight beyond the alders. "What was that all about, Riker?" Bronco asked quietly.

"Those were Morton's cattle," Riker answered.

"Now just how in the hell would you know that?" Bronco asked.

"That's his iron," the big man said. "I oughta know, I put it on enough cattle before I left Morton's old man's place."

"That brand could be anybody's," Bronco protested.

"It could be, but it ain't. Old man Morton made that iron special, so it wouldn't look like anybody else's in the world. That's it." He reined his horse around and kicked it into a jog. "Let's go. We know where to look now," he said back over his shoulder. The others turned their horses to follow.

~ 29 ~

"Damn! A day late and a dollar short!" A string of ripe curses echoed through the abandoned camp in Lost Creek Canyon as Joe Harris stamped through the small clearing. He and Bowie had ridden carefully up to the mouth of the canyon an hour earlier and found that the only remaining horse tracks were exiting the slot in front of them. Still, they'd tied Bowie's horse and Harris' mule out of sight and slowly and carefully entered the winding defile on foot only to find that, like Old Mother Hubbard's, their cupboard was bare; the outlaws were gone. So Bowie sat patiently on a tilted slab of sandstone near the cold ashes of the outlaws' long-dead cooking fire and watched Harris' tantrum with a look of wry amusement on his face.

"Joe, if you don't settle down you're gonna do yourself an injury," Bowie chuckled. "At least we know somebody's been here recently." He looked around the camp area. "And I'm sure it was them. I recognize some of the tracks from back yonder, horse and man both. We just have to find out which way they went when they left."

Joe finally got his temper reined in enough to allow him to stop discussing the ancestry of Riker and the rest and listen to what Bowie had to say. He scrubbed his hand across his face and looked over at Bowie. "I ain't no tracker," he said roughly. "I got ya this far, it's up ta you ta find their trail from here." He glared at Bowie impatiently. "So you gonna just sit there, or are you gonna start trackin'? The day ain't gettin' no younger, ya know!"

Bowie looked at the slant of the sunlight into the canyon. Shadows were rapidly moving across the canyon floor as the day came to a close. The two men had already made one dry camp on the way to this canyon, and he didn't relish the prospect of two in a row. "I've got a better idea," Bowie said after a moment. "What say we go get our mounts and use what little daylight we've got left to get them in here? Then we can get after Riker first thing in the morning we're all better rested."

Joe's temper had cooled, but not that much. He snapped at Bowie, "Yeah, and while we're settin' here havin' a pink tea party, them murderin' skunks're puttin' country between us and them!"

"It would surprise me if they're not camped already," Bowie answered patiently. "It's been my experience that if nobody's chasing them, most outlaws are basically lazy. And those boys think they killed the only posse that's come after them. We'll figure out which way they went tonight, and start tracking at first light tomorrow."

"How in hell'd you know how lazy outlaws are?" Joe demanded.

"I didn't always have this badge, ya know."

Joe considered Bowie's words for several long minutes, then said grudgingly, "I reckon you might be right. I guess there ain't no sense takin' a chance on losin' the tracks in the dark." He turned and started down the canyon.

Bowie got up from his perch near the fire ring and followed Joe down the narrow trail that snaked through the brushy canyon bottom. Before long he could see the tops of the rocky shoulders that marked the canyon's mouth. Joe was nearly to the opening when the clink of steel on rock brought Bowie up short. "Wait!" Bowie hissed. He reached out and grabbed the teamster's shoulder. Joe turned his head and his mouth came open to ask a question, but he froze when he saw Bowie standing with his finger to his lips.

Joe's eyebrows rose questioningly. "Somebody's right outside there," Bowie said softly. He pointed toward the mouth of the canyon then stepped to one side and motioned for Joe to move behind him. At first he thought the stubborn muleskinner was going to refuse, but finally Joe moved back up the trail.

Bowie was carrying his short-barreled Greener, muzzles down, hanging from his shoulder by a leather strap. Now he hooked his thumb in the strap and smoothly brought the scattergun up and into his hands. He draped his thumb over the hammers and eased forward, walking on his toes and being careful not to step on any of the twigs that littered the ground. He reached up with his left hand and tipped his hat off his head so that it hung down his back by the rawhide chin strap.

Again Bowie heard the sound of steel on stone, accompanied by the jingle of bit chains and the creak of a saddle. Then a familiar voice said, "Stand still, horse. I'm tryin' to see where they went," and Bowie moved a little further forward until he could see the rider without being seen himself. He listened intently for sounds of more than one horse but the rider seemed to be alone.

Bowie braced the butt of the Greener on his hip, barrels pointed up, but kept his thumb on the hammers. He stepped out behind the rider and said loudly, "This must be my week for picking up strays, and dumb ones at that. I could've sworn I sent you to Laramie."

With a start Lonnie Grable pulled his sorrel around to face Bowie, who smiled amiably when he saw the look on the young man's face turn from fear to relief. "Dammit, Tyler, you tryin' to scare me to death?" Lonnie asked. His eyes were wide and his hand was on the butt of his holstered pistol.

"No more attention than you were paying, I probably could've snuck up and clubbed you to death," Bowie said tartly. "Damn, kid, you better start looking behind you." He paused. "What're you doing here, anyway? You're supposed to be on your way south."

"I thought maybe I could help," Lonnie answered defensively.

"You'll get yourself killed, more than likely!" Bowie retorted. "From what you told me about Riker, if he sees you again he'll blow you outta your boots and never look back. Is that what you want?"

"I can take care of myself," the boy said stubbornly. "And besides, I know what he looks like and you don't."

He had Bowie on that one. The man Lonnie knew as John Smith's face graced a Wanted flyer or two here and there, and so did Bronco Jarvis'; but Riker was an unknown quantity. It might help to have somebody along who would recognize the man if they did happen to see him. Of course the other side of the coin was that Riker knew Lonnie too, and if he saw him he'd know something was up. Bowie frowned and slung the shotgun back on his shoulder. "Alright, you can stay, but you do what I tell you to do, when I tell you to do it. You got that?" Lonnie nodded eagerly; Bowie just shook his head resignedly and started for where he'd left his horse.

Joe appeared, leading his mule and Bowie's horse. "I figgered since you didn't shoot that young feller right off that you probly weren't goin' to, so I went and got these critters. You figure out which way them others went yet?"

"I haven't had time..." Bowie began.

"They went northwest from here," Lonnie offered smugly. "Or at least the only tracks other than yours that I saw went that way." He grinned, unable to keep from showing off just a little when he saw the look on Bowie's face. "I've seen all those horses' tracks before but one. You ain't the only one that can track, mister. How do you think I found you?"

"For all I know a little birdie coulda told you," Bowie grumbled. "Come on, let's go make camp." He took his reins from Joe and led his rapidly growing entourage back into the canyon. For a gent whose unwritten laws included one that said "Always work alone" he seemed to be gathering quite a collection of helpers.

~ 30 ~

The buckskin horse was confused. When he'd been spurred out of the meadow and away from the popping of pistol shots his rider had been in firm control. But now the man on his back was slumped forward and the reins were slack. Not knowing what else to do, the gelding kept moving. The smell of water on the night breeze led him on.

A sudden nicker out of the darkness near the tiny flickering remnants of a fire made the buckskin quicken his pace, eager to be with others of his kind. He was young and the herd instinct was strong. When he whinnied in reply, the blanket-wrapped figure near the fire rolled over and made a beeline for the shadows with his boots and pistol in hand.

Raleigh Smithers had never been a trusting soul. He'd always figured that the Lord helps those who help themselves even if you had to lie, cheat, and steal so when his horse's greeting was answered immediately, he didn't waste any time getting out of his blankets. Only when he lay prone in the dark next to the big pine near his bed did he stop to assess the situation. As he watched, the buckskin horse stepped out into the open and walked up to where Raleigh's chestnut was picketed.

Raleigh was startled to see the rider; he'd expected to see somebody's stray horse. He watched the man for several minutes but the only movement was the slow rise and fall of the rider's chest. A dark stain that appeared black in the last flickers from the nearly dead fire had oozed down across the horse's pale hide. Raleigh was sure that the stain was blood.

Raleigh reached out for a handful of dry needles from the tree he lay next to and tossed them onto the fire. A small plume of smoke went up as the needles heated. Then the needles caught fire and light flared, sending shadows dancing. In the sudden burst of light he could see what looked like a bullet hole high on the rider's right shoulder. When the flames died back down Raleigh rolled behind the tree and got to his feet. He quickly pulled on his boots and peered carefully around the side of the big pine's trunk.

"Mister, you alright?" Raleigh asked softly, though he already knew the answer. His pistol was up and pointed at the dark shape in front of him but his eyes darted all around. He was listening so hard he was surprised his ears weren't bleeding. The rider didn't answer; the only sound was the gentle creak of saddle leather as the horse shifted its weight from hoof to hoof. Satisfied that the rider was alone Raleigh stepped around the tree with his gun still in his hand. He spoke softly to the buckskin as he walked up. The young horse shied away from this stranger that had suddenly appeared from the dark and his rider swayed in the saddle.

"Easy, boy," Raleigh said softly. "You just stand fast now and let's see about your boss there." He holstered his pistol and stepped up alongside the horse. He reached up to take the man down and saw that he had somehow managed to tie himself into the saddle. The knots had pulled tight, so Raleigh reached into his back pocket for his jackknife, opened the sharpest blade, and carefully cut the man loose. When the last of the rawhide strings parted Raleigh suddenly found himself flat on his back with the injured rider's slack-muscled bulk pinning him to the ground. The buckskin horse danced away, spooked by the sudden commotion.

Raleigh gently rolled the man to the side then got to his feet. He reached over to his small woodpile and picked up a small piece of the pitchwood he had found earlier and laid it on the fire. When the fire began to burn in earnest, he added more wood then went to the nearby spring for water. He set the pot on the fire and turned to the wounded man.

Even though Raleigh had broken his fall, the jolt of falling from his horse had brought Shorty Grimes partially back from the dark well his consciousness had fallen into. He could tell by the damp feeling on his chest and back that the holes where Smith's bullet had passed through him were bleeding again. He looked up just as the stranger turned away from putting a pot of something on the fire. Through the foggy shroud that enveloped his brain Shorty thought he heard the man speak, but the words made no sense. Shorty's eyes closed.

Raleigh turned from the fire in time to see the momentary dull gleam of orange light in the man's eyes before the lids closed. He walked over and untied the bedroll from behind the man's saddle then rolled out the blankets near where he lay. As gently as he could, Raleigh moved the man onto the blankets then unbuttoned and opened the man's vest and shirt. A blood-soaked handkerchief was stuffed into what looked like the bullet's exit hole and a trickle of blood slid silently down the pale skin.

Working as carefully as he could Raleigh eased the cloth out of the wound. The puckered edges of the hole were crusted and the fabric gave way reluctantly. Raleigh whistled to himself, silently. As big as that hole was, the man was lucky to be alive. "What in hell'd they shoot you with, pard?" he asked the unconscious man, knowing full well he'd get no answer. When the water was hot Raleigh went to work cleaning the wounds. It was awkward working on the entry hole on the man's back with one hand while he held him up with the other, but it couldn't be helped. At last Raleigh had the wounds cleaned as best he could. He dumped the bloody water out of the pot and reached into his saddlebag for the small bottle of whiskey he kept there for emergencies. He pulled the cork and took a small sip. He wrapped a strip of muslin from his meager supply of bandages around a small straight stick he'd found then poured some of the whiskey over the cloth. "This is gonna hurt you a whole hell of a lot more than it does me," he told his unconscious patient then proceeded to shove the whiskey-soaked cloth through the tunnel the bullet had made in the man's flesh.

The searing burn of the alcohol woke Shorty instantly. He sucked in a deep breath; his eyes snapped open and he groaned. The muscles in his neck stood out like cables as he strained against the pain. He heard a voice say soothingly, "Easy there, friend. It's gonna burn for a bit but it's the best thing. Had to get that hole cleaned out."

Shorty turned his head stiffly as the pain began to recede. His tormentor was kneeling beside him, holding him up off the ground. Shorty slowly relaxed as the waves of agony finally faded to the dull gnawing ache that he'd grown accustomed to since he'd been shot. "Who're you?" he croaked. His throat was parched and he had to force the words out.

"Name's Smithers," Raleigh answered as he gently laid Shorty back on the blankets. "Your horse brought you here and I've been trying to fix you up. As soon as you're up to it, I'd be interested to know who you are and how you ended up in this predicament. Somebody obviously disliked you enough to shoot you in the back." Raleigh brought out some more bandages. "I gotta get that shoulder wrapped and see if I can stop the bleeding again, and I can guarantee you it ain't gonna be fun. You want a drink of this whiskey before I start?"

Shorty nodded and Raleigh lifted him up so he could drink. The liquor burned all the way down and caused him to cough; the sudden jolt brought a grimace to Shorty's face. "I reckon I'm as ready as I'm gonna git, mister," he rasped. "The sooner you git at it the sooner you'll git done." He reached back with his left hand and pushed himself the rest of the way up to a sitting position while his face went white. "But you'd best hurry ever' chance you git, 'cause I can't guarantee how long I'm gonna be with ya on this trail."

Wordlessly Raleigh placed a pad of cloth over each of the bullet holes and wrapped them in place with a long strip of cloth. Shorty was pale and sweating when he finished. Raleigh buttoned the shirt across Shorty's chest and helped him lay back down. "Damn if that wasn't entertaining," Shorty said through clenched teeth. "D'you think I could have some water?"

After a long drink that eased the dryness in his throat Shorty laid down and closed his eyes. Raleigh had unsaddled the buckskin and moved Shorty's saddle over near the fire. The wounded man was partially propped up on it. The first hints of dawn were stealing over the horizon when he opened his eyes. Raleigh was sitting across the fire from Shorty, with a cup of coffee in his hand, staring into the flames. The planes and angles of his face stood out in sharp relief in the flickering yellow firelight. Shorty's shoulder was stiff and he tried to move to ease the stiffness. The movement caught Raleigh's attention and he looked at Shorty. "I'm almighty grateful for your help, mister," Shorty said haltingly. "What'd you say your name was?"

"Smithers," Raleigh replied. "Raleigh Smithers."

Shorty looked at him. "You're that bounty hunter, ain't ya?" he asked.

Raleigh nodded. "I've been known to bring in a wanted man or two." He sipped his coffee. "I'm hunting Bob Morton at the moment. The banker in Sycamore Springs put up a big reward for the man who shot his wife." He paused. "I've got some soup here, if you think you're up to it."

"I could use somethin' to eat," Shorty said. "But you're gonna have ta help me. I don't think I can handle it on my own."

After Shorty had managed to down a small amount of jerky broth, Raleigh eased him back down on the saddle and covered him with a blanket. "What day is it?" Shorty asked.

"I think it's Wednesday."

"Then I know where Morton was two days ago." Raleigh's camp was high on a pine-mantled ridge, and he had turned to study the land below, looking for any sign that Shorty had been followed. The sunrise lent a sharp contrast to the terrain. Raleigh turned back and looked at Shorty.

"Oh really? How would you know that?" he asked in surprise.

"'Cause it was one of his boys that shot me," came the succinct reply.

When nothing else was forthcoming Raleigh asked, "And you know this because...?"

Shorty related the tale of the shooting of the Thornton brothers and of how he himself had barely escaped with his life. He used few words, but few were needed. When he finished, Raleigh sat looking at him thoughtfully. "That doesn't sound like Morton," he mused, almost to himself. "Of course, shooting a woman doesn't either. Something's not quite right about this whole thing." He shrugged and threw out the cold dregs of his coffee. "But then I reckon that's not my problem. There's a hefty reward for Morton's hide and I intend to collect it. If you can get me on a fresh trail I'll give you a percentage when I run him down."

By the time Raleigh was sure he could find the horse camp, Shorty was exhausted. His eyes closed and slid into an uneasy sleep. His eyelids fluttered and he groaned often; whether from the pain or from something else Raleigh didn't know. All Raleigh knew for sure was that having to nurse the wounded man was letting Bob Morton get further and further away, if it was indeed some one from Morton's gang who had shot Shorty. In spite of the lure of the reward money, Raleigh couldn't help but wonder about Shorty's story. The killing of the Thorntons didn't match up with the stories Raleigh had heard about Morton.

The next morning Shorty's condition had improved considerably. The wound was still red and inflamed but there no longer seemed to be any danger of serious infection. When Shorty's eyes opened, the bounty hunter was saddling his horse. His bedroll lay on the ground near his saddlebags, along with a fringed and beaded elkhide rifle scabbard. A small cloth sack that looked to contain food of some sort was near Shorty's head and Shorty's canteen lay, glistening with water droplets, next to the sack.

"I take it you're goin' after Morton, eh?" Shorty asked.

Raleigh nodded and reached down for his gear. He slung the saddlebags and bedroll behind the cantle of the saddle, tied them down with the saddle strings, and picked up the rifle. When all was stowed to his satisfaction he said, "I've done all I can for you. There's what food I can spare in the sack there," he pointed with his chin, "and I've filled your canteen." He pointed back in the brush. "The spring's back yonder. There's a kind of a town about two days ride south of here. There ain't much there beyond a beanery and a store of sorts, but there'll be food and other folks there. I gotta get on. The trail's getting colder by the minute."

"I'm much obliged to ya, Smithers," Shorty said. "I wouldna made it without you patchin' me up. An' I hope you catch that murderin' cur an shoot him down like the animal he is!" he finished viciously.

"I've been thinking about what you told me," Raleigh said as he reined his horse toward where the Thornton brothers were killed. "And I'm not so sure that Morton's the one who did this." He raised a hand to silence Shorty's protest. "But I intend to find out. Vaya con Dios, friend." He tapped the chestnut with his spurs and left the camp at a trot.

~ 31 ~

Gray shadows stirred in Lost Creek Canyon as the three mounted men moved out into the open. “Dang it, this is the second time you’ve got me up before the sun,” Lonnie groused. “I think you’re just doin’ it to aggravate me.”

“Yep, you’re right,” Bowie said seriously. “Getting you outta bed in the dark just tickles my funny bone.” He let Black pace forward. He was watching Lonnie out of the corner of his eye as he rode. Just when the younger man was going to say something he no doubt thought was scathing, Bowie interrupted him with a chuckle. “Actually, I’d get up this early even if you weren’t with me. Haven’t you heard that the early bird catches the worm?”

“Well I ain’t no bird, and I sure as heck don’t need no worms,” Lonnie said. Behind him he heard Joe’s stifled chuckle. He gave Joe a hard look over his shoulder that made the teamster laugh louder. “You can both go straight to hell!” Lonnie said then booted his horse into the lead. The tracks they needed to follow were in soft dirt for a ways and were easy to follow even in the dim light.

Even after the sun rose and the day grew warmer, the tracks of the four outlaws remained easy to follow. Riker and his men had no reason to think anyone was following them, because of the effort they’d put out to lay the blame on Bob Morton; so they’d been no more than marginally careful to cover their tracks. After all, wild horses ran this country, and a few small ranchers were beginning to try their hand at making a living out here now that the worst of the Indians had been either killed off or moved onto reservations. The way Riker had figured it, a few more horse tracks one way or the other shouldn’t be a cause for comment. By noon Bowie and his makeshift posse had gained a couple of hours on Riker and the others.

Just enough daylight remained when Bowie and the others topped the sagebrush-covered ridge that the three men could tell something tragic had happened below. Magpies, crows, and one lone golden eagle were perched in the trees near the stream, and the snarls of coyotes fighting over scraps echoed up the slope. Without a word the three men spread out. Bowie pulled the shotgun from the scabbard and braced the butt on his hip with his thumb on the hammers. Joe and Lonnie each drew his rifle from the scabbard and lay it across his saddlebows; at a nod from Bowie they started down the slope.

The scene that greeted them made Lonnie turn aside. He hung off his horse's side as his stomach rebelled against the stench, and even Bowie was put off by the sight that greeted them. As they rode up to the camp, a pair of coyotes slunk off into the brush leaving what little remained of the Thornton brothers to the newcomers. Around them birds scattered with a rush of wings and loud vocal protests.

Bowie swallowed loudly. "Joe, see if you can find a shovel around here, why don't you?" he said. "Otherwise we'll have to find some other way to cover these gents up. I'll see if there's anybody else around." He swung Black aside and began to circle the camp. He could see three scattered beds around the long-dead fire ring, so there had to have been one more man along. On the far side of the circle he found tracks where a rider had come up to the camp then jerked his horse around hard and fled with the horse running all out. "There was one more, but he got away," Bowie called. "Kid, are you gonna be up to this?"

"I'm alright," came the shaky reply. "It just caught me off guard for a minute."

"Good. If Joe finds a shovel, you can help him dig while I see if that other man's still here somewhere." Without looking back he moved Black out to follow Shorty's trail. The tracks led straight away and there was no one in sight, and Bowie wanted to find out as much as he could around the camp before dark, so he turned back. When he rode up to the camp the remains of the Thornton brothers had been covered with blankets and Joe was standing up to his waist in a hole in the ground.

"That's deep enough," Bowie said. "Let's get these boys in the ground and get some words said, and get settled. We've still got a long ways to go tomorrow."

"You're about a callous bastard, ain't you?" Joe asked. He spit in the bottom of the hole in disgust.

"What do you want me to do, tear my clothes and throw ashes on my head?" Bowie demanded. "Surely this isn't the first man you've had to bury trailside is it?" Without waiting for an answer he went on. "If I stopped to cry for every pile of bones I came across in my travels I'd never get anywhere! I might as well stay in Laramie. Don't worry, I feel it, but my job isn't to mourn every damn fool that gets himself killed out here. My job is to get the men who did the killing! In this case I know who the killers are because we tracked them here, and that gives me a leg up on this job. And besides which, they don't know I'm following them, and that gives me even more of an advantage."

He stopped to let his temper cool a little. Most times he was pretty jolly, but sometimes when someone like Joe, who knew absolutely nothing about him or his character, started in on him, he just had to let off a little steam. "So," he concluded, "If you don't like my methods, there's the door. Just don't let it hit you in the ass on the way out because that can get a mite painful." He looked Joe full in the face and the teamster couldn't hold his gaze.

"Sorry," Joe mumbled, "I guess I was outta line."

"I guess you were," Bowie snapped, then turned to the blanket-covered bodies. He began to matter-of-factly go through their pockets to see if they had anything on them that would let him know who they had been.

Raleigh had been pushing his horse hard all day. He'd let the chestnut catch his breath a few times when they came to water; other than that they'd kept moving. He was feeling the pressure of time; considering the fact that the reward was big enough to bring every lowlife who thought he could pull a trigger out of the woodwork, he was sure that there had to be more than just him chasing Morton. He wanted to make sure he was the lowlife who got there first.

By sundown, Raleigh was pretty sure that he was only a mile or two from where the Thorntons had been killed; that is if Shorty had told him right. As open as the country was he was pretty sure that he could find the camp even in the dark, so he pressed on.

Raleigh heard the voices before he saw the men. He reined in his horse and sat listening. Whoever the men were, they were in the Thornton's camp. They were talking quietly, so he could only catch a word or two now and then. There was an occasional scraping sound and once he heard the clank of metal on stone ahead of him as he eased the chestnut closer. He reached down and lifted the thong from the hammer of his Colt and nudged the horse out around the meadow. He drew to a stop in the shadows of a clump of willows and stood up in his stirrups to look into the camp.

The click of a pair of gun hammers drawing back to full cock dropped him back into his saddle with a hand on his pistol. "Mister, you'd best not try to pull that pistol unless you wanna get shot out of your saddle," a cold voice said from behind him. "At this range this Greener will cut you in two. Now you move on out where I can see who you are." Raleigh lifted his hands to shoulder height and tapped the chestnut with his spurs.

"You seem to have the advantage of me, sir," he said formally as he came out into the open.

"I'd say so," the same voice said. "That's far enough. Why don't you turn that hayburner around so I can see what I caught. Joe," the owner of the voice called, "hold off on that for a minute and get out here." There was a flurry of movement then footsteps rapidly approached.

By now Raleigh had turned so that he was nearly facing the source of the voice. "Why, Raleigh Smithers, as I live and breathe," Bowie said conversationally. "What brings you to these parts?" Then his voice turned cold again and the muzzles of the Greener never wavered. "And I'd like to know one thing in this blessed world that is gonna keep me from shooting you now that I know who you are?"

"Tyler? What in hell are you doing here?" Raleigh went on and answered his own question. "Morton. Right. It figures that Judge Martin would have to send somebody after him. And I can explain what happened at Tahoe, if you'll just give me a chance."

"What happened at Tahoe is you cost me an arrest, and you damn near got me killed, you greedy snake," Bowie said. He eased down the hammers of the Greener but kept his thumb on them and the muzzles pointed in Raleigh's direction. "I had Bannerman dead to rights until you decided to cut yourself in on the deal."

"Bannerman was worth a lot of money and I needed money right then," Raleigh persisted. "I didn't mean to get in your way. Can I put my hands down now? I feel kind of foolish sitting here debating with you like this."

Just then Joe and Lonnie around the fire. Joe was carrying

his Spenser and Lonnie had his Colt in his hand. "Who's this?" Joe demanded.

"This is a low-life bounty hunter named Raleigh Smithers," Bowie explained. "He'll more than likely cause more trouble than he's worth and I'm trying to decide whether or not to shoot him."

"Now just a minute, Tyler," Raleigh protested. "I did help you get the Carter brothers last year. That oughta count for something."

"It lets you stay alive awhile longer is all, Raleigh. Now you step down from that horse real easy-like, and you step on out ahead of me to the camp. And keep your fingers off that Colt. You know good and well I can cut you in two before you can draw and turn."

Raleigh stepped very carefully to the ground and started to walk toward where Joe and Lonnie stood. He was leading the chestnut and keeping his hands in plain sight. While he walked he was trying to figure out what his best plan of attack, so to speak, was going to be. The last thing he'd expected was to find Bowie and the others here. Finally he decided that open and honest was what would probably let him ride out of here sitting in his saddle rather than draped over it.

"If you've been here any time at all, you probably know there were three men here," he began.

"We just buried two of 'em," Joe interrupted. Neither he nor Lonnie had relaxed their guard in the least.

"The third one rode into my camp in the middle of the night, two nights ago," Raleigh went on. "Or rather, his horse brought him in. He'd somehow managed to tie himself in the saddle before he passed out. He'd been shot in the back by a man he said was riding with Bob Morton."

"It wasn't Morton..." Bowie began.

"I've about figured that out for myself. But whoever shot the two you just buried identified himself as Morton." Raleigh paused while he began to unsaddle his horse. "Somehow this just doesn't seem like Morton's style."

"Like I said, it wasn't Morton," Bowie said. "Young Lonnie here says the gent in question's name is Riker, and Mister Riker seems to have it in for Bob Morton for some reason. He's been pulling some seriously bad stunts around the country and doing his damnedest to make it look like Morton did 'em." He slung the

Greener over his shoulder by the strap. "You're welcome to whichever one of them you can catch, but I'm only gonna tell you this once: you stay out of my way while you're doing it. If you try to pull what you did with Bannerman, I'll stomp you into a mudhole it'll take a team of Missouri mules a week to haul you out of. And you know I can do it. You hear me, Raleigh?"

"I hear you, Tyler." Raleigh was thinking rapidly. For all his jolly appearance and manner Bowie was tough, and he'd no doubt do what he said he'd do. It wasn't exactly in Raleigh's best interests to be laid up for any length of time and he knew that if he took on Bowie he more than likely would be. He'd just have to rein his larcenous impulses in. "I'll make you a deal, Tyler. You let me tag along with you and your playmates here and pick up the pieces and I'll stay back out of the way. All I ask is that you let me collect at least some of the bounty money. I don't know anything about this Riker you say you're following, but there's five thousand dollars on Morton's head and that would set me up for a long time to come." He raised a hand to stop Bowie from snarling at him. "At least think about it, alright?"

"Alright," Bowie huffed. "But you just make damn sure you remember what I said."

~ 32 ~

Riker, Bronco, Smith, and Abel pulled off the trail where a small creek crossed their path and moved back into a willow thicket. If what that rustler had told them was the truth and not just something to get them off his back, they should be no more than ten or fifteen miles from Borden City. Now that they were close Riker seemed to relax. He almost appeared to be in a good mood as he stripped the gear from his horse and led it to water. "Boys," he said, "I'm startin' to feel like this just might be my lucky day."

"Ain't no such thing," Smith growled.

"You think what you want, Smith," Riker said, "but it looks to me like things are goin' our way." Smith snorted and went to unsaddle his horse. He didn't see the feral glance that Riker drilled into his back before the unaccustomed smile returned to the big outlaw's face. It was going to give Riker great pleasure to kill Smith when the time came; and that time would for sure come.

Abel began gathering twigs for a fire. Soon the smell of boiling coffee was wafting through the thicket. While the coffee cooked, he sliced bacon into a skillet; shortly the smoky smell of the fat pork was mixing with the aroma of Arbuckle's best. The breeze, which had been essentially nonexistent for most of the day, began to pick up almost imperceptibly, and the aroma of the cooking food slowly drifted beyond the thicket.

Downwind from the fire, the leader of a band of buckskin-clad riders threw up a hand, halting the group in midstride. Several of the ponies had haunches of venison slung over their withers. The horses milled about as the lead rider, a short, hawk-faced individual whose long black hair hung in a single braid down his back, sniffed the wavering breeze. He'd caught just a whiff of something he was sure wasn't his companions and their horses.

Quartering his horse into what seemed to be the prevailing direction of the freshening breeze, he caught the odor again, a combination of boiling coffee and frying meat. He turned to the other hunters, pointed to two of them, then pointed in the direction the smell had come from. They nodded and dropped silently from their horses, handing their reins to the youngest one of the group, who was on his first hunt with the men. The two slipped off their buckskin traveling shirts and began to move toward the source of the smells.

"When's that food gonna be ready?" Smith asked roughly. His horse had stumbled earlier with him and thrown him into his saddlehorn, and he wasn't in a good mood.

"Just hold yer horses," Abel said in his nasal drawl. "You snarlin' at me ain't gonna make it cook no faster."

"Yeah, why don't you go for a walk or somethin', Smith," Bronco told him. "You can check on the horses, and by the time you get back maybe ol' Abel here'll have you something to eat besides your liver." He grinned coldly back when Smith glared at him.

Smith didn't say a word; he just stomped off into the brush toward where the horses were picketed. In his anger he was crushing twigs and rattling the brush, not caring who heard him and not paying attention to who or what might be around. When the half-naked brave came out of the brush next to the trail with a club raised to strike, the outlaw had no time to do more than take the blow. There was a crushing impact to the back of his head and his world went black as he folded to the ground with a muffled thud.

Running Wolf grabbed the white man by the wrists and dragged him into the brush away from the trail. His partner Little Bear appeared, leading the four horses that had belonged to the whites. Working quickly, the pair stripped the weapons and clothing from the man. They could hear the mutter of voices across the thicket as they hurriedly tied his hands and feet and slung him belly-down over the back of one of the horses. They tied his wrists and ankles together under the horse's belly, then slipped back toward their companions with their prisoner, taking all of the horses with them. Running Wolf had a woman to impress back where the lodges were set; capturing the white man and his weapons and horses would help make him a big man in White Deer's eyes.

The arrival of the two braves and their captive brought a startled grunt of surprise from their leader. He raised an eyebrow in question but decided to wait for an explanation until the group had returned to their camp. He watched quietly while the two men retrieved their shirts and horses then turned his horse and led the way east at a trot.

"Smith! Hey, Smith! What happened, you forget where we left the horses?" Bronco called a few minutes later. When there was no answer he looked over at Riker. "You 'spose somethin's happened to him?"

"Naw, he's just poutin'. He'll be back when he gets hungry enough. Leave him be. An' if he don't come back before the food's gone, it's his own fault. He'll just have to cook his own grub." He reached for another slice of bacon and wrapped it around the biscuit in his hand then swabbed both in the bacon grease in the bottom of the skillet.

When the three remaining outlaws had eaten their fill and Smith still hadn't come back Bronco got to his feet. He wiped his hands on his canvas britches, gave out with a rumbling belch, then said, "I reckon I'll go see what's keepin' that stubborn bastard. Maybe Injuns have run off with him or some such." He loosened his pistol in the holster and strolled nonchalantly out of sight. He came running back into camp a few short minutes later. "The horses are gone an' so's Smith!" he told Riker. "I found where somethin' had been drug off into the brush, and horse tracks headin' off to the east." He paused. "And there was moccasin tracks mixed in with the horse tracks!"

Riker lunged to his feet with a curse and caught up his rifle from where it leaned against his saddle. "Show me!" he snarled. Bronco led the way out of the camp to the scene of the ambush.

The sign left by the band of hunters was easy to read in the bright moonlight. The three outlaws could easily see where Smith had been struck down, apparently without a fight. They could read the rest of the story as well, and they struck out on the trail of the stolen horses at a fast walk. Abel brought up the rear, muttering under his breath as he tried to keep up with Bronco and Riker. It wasn't long until they reached the clearing where the rest of the hunting party had waited; they reached the end of Riker's limited supply of patience at the same time. With a curse, Riker wheeled and the muzzle of his rifle came up under Abel's chin, forcing his head up from where he'd been staring at his boots and grumbling.

"Abel, you'd best shut your yap." The purr in the big man's words was more menacing than anything he could have said. "I've put up with your noise as long as I'm goin' to." He eared back the hammer of the Winchester. Abel's eyes were wide as he stared into Riker's face and his cheeks were pasty white in the moonlight. "You hear me?"

Abel tried to speak but his mouth and throat were suddenly so dry that only a strangled croak that sounded something like a stepped-on frog came out. He settled for nodding as best he could instead."If you shoot him, you'll let whoever took Smith and stole our horses know where we are, Riker," Bronco said quietly.

"Seein' as how they just took off with our horses," Riker answered stiffly, "Don't you think it's just a little bit possible they already *know* where we are?"

"They don't know we're followin' 'em, though. Think about that."

Riker thumbed the hammer down on the rifle and let the muzzle drop. Abel sighed with relief and closed his eyes for a moment then swallowed loudly. Riker turned away. "I spose you're right," Riker said. "Let's git back to camp and make up some packs. I don't care all that much about Smith, but that was a damn good horse that got stole and I really don't feel like going after Morton on foot." He turned back; when he turned, he missed the poisonous glare Abel aimed at his back.

The three men quickly made up packs of jerky and their remaining biscuits, filled their canteens, and checked the loads in their rifles. They piled their saddles in a hollow under a downed tree and covered them with brush. It was a half hour after midnight when they started walking. It never crossed Riker's mind to wait for daylight and to go toward the town they'd been heading for. He'd be damned if he'd walk into town when he could ride, and he was determined to get his horse back.

~ 33 ~

Smith was unceremoniously shoved from the back of the horse he had been laying over for most of the night. He slammed to the ground on his back, and the impact took his breath away. He lay gasping for what seemed like an eternity as his head throbbed in time with the beating of his heart. When he could breathe again, he pushed himself to a sitting position. He was dressed in nothing but his holey drawers, and the night air was chilly on his exposed flesh. Around him the Indian camp was bustling as several of the women relieved the new arrivals' horses of their burdens. For the moment he was largely being ignored, but Smith was fairly certain that wasn't going to last. In fact he was pretty sure that the next few hours were not going to be pretty. He'd buried a few men who'd been entertained by Indians in the past.

While Smith sat contemplating both his headache and his possible fate, a conference was taking place in Hunting Hawk's lodge, with Hunting Hawk doing most of the talking. He was storming back and forth while Running Wolf and Little Bear sat on the hide floor and tried to avoid being trampled by the older man.

"What possessed you to bring him *here*?" Hunting Hawk growled, pointing toward the wall and in Smith's general direction. "Never mind, I know the reason. You wanted to impress White Deer." He stopped and glared at the two young men. "Don't you think the whites' horses and this man's gun would have been enough?"

Running Wolf opened his mouth to protest and Hunting Hawk stopped him with an upraised hand. "We have not had to worry about the pony soldiers for a long time. But now thanks to you two..." Words failed him; then he snorted and went on. "The soldiers will be coming."

Little Bear at last got up the courage to say, "I don't think so, sir." Hunting Hawk whirled on him but Little Bear went on, "I think the whites do not want the soldiers, or the tin stars, to come any more than we do. Their camp and their horses were well hidden, far beyond simple caution. If not for a stray breeze we would not have found them." He waited for another storm but Hunting Hawk stood pondering his son's words.

"Alright," he said after some thought. "Give the man something to cover his tender feet and have the women drive him out of camp. We will see then if the soldiers come. You two had better hope that they don't." The two young men jumped to their feet, glad to have a chance to cover for their mistake. Hunting Hawk's next words stopped them in their tracks. "I will be keeping the white man's pistol and one of the horses. You may divide the rest between you. Next time think of the welfare of the band and not just about impressing one woman." He turned away in dismissal.

Running Wolf's face fell. He had been picturing himself strutting in front of White Deer with the gunbelt around his waist, and eventually, in some misty future, tying a couple of the white men's horses in front of her father's lodge. Now, stepping out of Hunting Hawk's lodge into the first light of day, he could see that future fading away. Unless... An idea came to him suddenly and he smiled. He would talk to Little Bear after the white man was gone from the camp.

Little Bear came from the lodge with a tattered pair of elkhide moccasins in his hand. He pushed through the ring of young boys surrounding Smith and dropped the ragged footwear beside the captive. The boys had been taunting Smith, taking turns darting in and slapping him on the shoulder or head and jumping away. His clumsy attempts to grab his tormentors with his bound hands, and his angry growls at failing to catch them, caused fits of laughter among the boys. "Enough," Little Bear told them. "Go tease your sisters or something."

While Little Bear was dispersing the boys Running Wolf was going from lodge to lodge. Soon a crowd of women and teenaged girls began to gather. Each one had a stick or rawhide quirt in her hand and a smile on her face in anticipation of the festivities to come. Smith watched them, knowing, or so he thought, what was coming.

The women formed two lines, one on each side of the trail leading back to the outlaw camp. The men of the camp stood behind the women to make sure Smith couldn't break through the lines. Hunting Hawk came from his lodge and nodded to Little Bear. The young man knelt beside Smith's legs and brought out his knife. Smith tensed, waiting for the brave to cut him, but instead found his legs freed.

The brave pointed first at Smith, then at the elkhide moccasins. It took Smith a minute to decide that the redskin wanted him to put them on. He raised his bound hands and shrugged. The Indian silently pointed to the moccasins again. Smith clumsily reached down and pulled them on and found himself unceremoniously jerked to his feet. The women began to screech and wave their weapons in the air.

Little Bear shoved Smith in the direction of the trail. "Run, white man," he said in English. Smith looked at him in disbelief and Little Bear drew his knife and moved toward him. "Run!" he repeated loudly. Smith ran.

His feet, which had been tied tightly together for most of the night, were numb and tingling at the same time. With his hands still bound his run was slow and clumsy, more of a shambling trot at first. Then the first rawhide quirt lashed across his buttocks, cutting cloth and hide both and goading him on. He covered his head as best he could and tried to go faster. The taunting of the women and the laughter of the men brought a rush of blood to his face but all he could think of was getting away from these heathen devils.

Smith zigzagged through the gauntlet, trying to dodge some of the multitude of blows falling on him, but most of them struck flesh. When he at last came out into the open grass of the meadow his drawers were in shreds, he was bleeding from numerous cuts, and he was covered with welts. One eye was rapidly swelling shut and he had several knots on his head.

The tumult behind him got louder. He glanced back over his shoulder and saw the women trotting towards him, waving sticks and bloodied rawhide. He hadn't the first foggiest idea where he was, but a tiny voice of logic in the back of his dazed brain told him to follow the freshest horse tracks he could find so that was what he did. It wasn't long before the forest swallowed him up and he left the noise behind.

He could no longer hear the screeching of the women behind him but still he ran, until his breath rasped in his throat and he was drenched in sweat. He had never really felt fear until he'd seen the women gathering and even now that fear would not release its hold. He never wanted to go through anything like that again.

Riker and Bronco, with Abel limping along behind them nursing a blister on his foot, were actually making good time on the trail of their stolen horses. They had come close to ten miles when Riker suddenly stopped and raised a hand. Abel was trudging along with his head down and he nearly collided with the man's broad back. "What the..."

"Shut up, dammit," Riker hissed. "I heard somethin'." He pointed ahead of them towards a small grove of lodgepole pines that had grown up at the edges of a small clearing.

A few gaps in the thick stand gave brief glimpes of the area beyond. A twig snapped and something pasty white with brown accents flashed across one of the small gaps. "It's just a damn deer or somethin'," Abel snorted.

"I don't think so," Bronco said. "I think it's a man, but if it is he's dressed awful funny." He looked again toward the trees. "Or not dressed, in this case," he said. He began to chuckle as Smith appeared in front of them with his still bound hands holding the shreds of his long underwear up in attempt to shelter his more tender parts from the perils around him. Bronco's chuckles turned to full-blown laughter at the sight. Even Riker was smiling.

"It ain't funny!" Smith snorted.

Before Smith could go on, Riker, who had been taking in Smith's physical condition as he approached, asked, "What in hell happened to you? You tangle with a bear, or what? And where's the horses?"

"The horses're back yonder," Smith told him. "A bunch of redskins have 'em. An' no, I didn't tangle with no bear." He paused, wondering how best to tell the story to make himself look better. "I fought my way outta the camp," he finally went on.

"I don't think so," Bronco said as he circled the blustering outlaw. "That looks like a quirt cut on your butt. And so do a bunch of the others." He came back in front of Smith. "In fact, I don't think you fought your way out at all. I think they sicced the women on you, and the ladies of the camp ran you out." He broke out laughing again. "Just tell me I'm wrong..."

"Cut my hands loose an' I'll tell you somethin'," Smith blustered. “I’ll...”

“You’ll what, Smith?” Riker cut in. “Bronco is right, an’ you know it. So pipe down an’ show me the way to that camp. I’m tired of walkin’.” He drew his knife and held it with the edge up waiting for Smith to put his hands out. The keen edge made short work of the rawhide thongs on Smith’s wrists. “Come on,” Riker said, and started walking again, back the direction Smith had come from.

Smith hurriedly used what he could salvage of his bonds to thread together enough of his remaining clothing to cover as much of his tender skin as he could then turned to follow the others.

~ 34 ~

The laughter and the screaming subsided and the women and girls returned to the camp. They were smiling and talking in small groups as they walked. The white man scurrying through the grass trying to cover all his body parts at once had been the funniest thing any of them had seen in quite some time. Just when the laughter would die down one of them would imitate him, and the whole group would start laughing all over again. Back at the camp they dispersed to their own lodges. There were meat and hides to process and winter was fast approaching.

Running Wolf took Little Bear aside. Without preamble he told his friend, "It wasn't right for Hunting Hawk to take away the pistol I took from the white man."

Little Bear shrugged and said, "Why are telling me? Take it up with Hunting Hawk. He's your father." He had a good idea what was coming next but Running Wolf was going to have to say it; Little Bear wasn't going to do it for him.

"We took four horses. None were packhorses. That means four men and four guns, maybe more." He stopped and waited for his friend to comment but Little Bear just looked at him. "I want those guns. We can get them."

Little Bear made a show of looking to both sides and behind Running Wolf. "Who's this we you're talking about?" he asked innocently. "Is there somebody here I can't see?" He laughed at the expression on the other's face and held up his hand. "I've already talked to Two Ponies. He will come with us. But we have to be careful not to let anyone else know we are doing this. If Hunting Hawk finds out what we're planning he will stop us. When do you want to leave?"

"As soon as we eat. We can ride there and back before midday if we hurry." Running Wolf turned away toward the young men's lodge to find some food.

After eating, the three young and impetuous warriors each

took his best horse from the herd. They left at different times and in different directions after manufacturing excuses to tell the boys watching over the herd. They came together in a copse of alders well north of the camp and circled wide to strike the trail to the west. All were veterans of a number of raids on other tribes and of horse-stealing ventures, but they were also relatively young. It never occurred to them that their quarry might be closer than they thought as they heeled their horses into a trot.

By the time the young braves had gotten together and ridden away from the camp, Riker and his men, now accompanied by a half-naked Smith, had gained another mile. Though it galled him to do it, Riker had slowed his pace so that the nearly exhausted Smith could keep up; but he was growling about the delay. Considering how late in the year it was, the early morning sun was hot, and he was definitely tired of walking and wanted to get it over with as soon as possible. Still, he had loaned Smith his rifle, and another shooter was a good thing to have in case of trouble, so Riker decided not to leave Smith behind, no matter how badly he wanted to.

Ahead they could hear a small creek tinkling merrily down through the rocks on the side of a ridge. They had brought water with them, but it never hurt a man to replenish his supply whenever he could. They turned toward the creek, and broke out into the open at the same time as Running Wolf and his companions. All and sundry were stunned into immobility, at least temporarily.

Running Wolf was riding in the lead, so he was the first to see the white men; he was also the first to react. He was outnumbered, outgunned, and out in the wide open; he should have turned his horse and got out of there, but the thought never crossed his mind. Instead, he threw his brass-framed Winchester to his shoulder with a yell and kicked his surprised horse into a gallop. His first mistake was charging instead of retreating; his second was charging straight at Riker. He wouldn't get a third.

Riker drew his pistol and fired three times as fast as he could thumb the hammer back and squeeze the trigger. Two of the bullets bowled Running Wolf over his horse's rump, slamming him to the ground; the third flew harmlessly on. Around him, guns were hammering as the other two warriors foolishly followed Running Wolf's lead.

The sorrel that the charging Indian had been riding thundered past Riker. He dropped his pistol, grabbed the jaw rein and a handful of mane, and vaulted to the horse's back as it swept by. It wasn't the first time the sorrel had heard gunfire so it didn't take Riker long to turn him back to the fight, but the fight was over. The other two horses were running on toward the west and he spun the sorrel on its hind feet and went in pursuit. They needed those horses.

At first the feel and smell of the unfamiliar rider upset the sorrel, but the commanding hand on the rein soon had him running smoothly. He was the fastest of the three horses, and even with a rider the size of Riker it didn't take long to catch the others. Riker turned them into a marshy meadow, and kept them turning until they stopped running of their own accord. For all his gruff ways, Riker was good with horses. He talked to the two in a soft voice, and kept edging the sorrel closer until he could pick up both reins. He started back to the creek leading the horses.

When Riker got back to where he'd started, the three Indians were dead and Smith was dying. Two Ponies had had time to fire his old Springfield once before he was blasted from his horse, and the big chunk of lead had gone through Smith's chest from side to side. He lay now on some soft grass, trying not to cough and trying not to cry from the pain. Bronco and Abel stood over him, looking down. "That boy ain't agonna make it," Abel said softly. Smith watched a leaf spiral down from the trees overhead but he never felt it touch down lightly on his wide staring eye as he died.

Riker slid off of Running Wolf's horse. "Is he dead?" he asked, looking at Smith and already knowing the answer.

"Yeah," Bronco answered. "Him and that last buck killed each other."

Riker picked up his pistol, blew the dirt out of the action, and looked around. They had no tools and no way to bury Smith; it would be simpler just to leave him for the birds and the coyotes, but they had been riding together for quite a while so Riker finally decided to do something about covering Smith up. The Indians he didn't care about. Upstream a short distance, Riker saw a crease in the ground that had been dug by runoff. He handed Abel the reins of the three horses and walked up the creek.

"Bring him up here," he called. The notch in the ground was several feet deep, and the shelving banks were mostly rock and sand. Abel tied the horses to a stout tree and when he turned around, Bronco was stripping the beat-up moccasins from Smith's feet.

"What are you doin'?" Abel demanded.

Bronco looked up at him. "What's it look like I'm doin'? He sure as hell don't need 'em, and we might." He dropped the moccasins on the ground and stood. "Grab on. Let's get this over with." He and Abel each took hold of a limp arm, and together they drug Smith to his final resting place and rolled him in. They caved the banks of the cut in on him and rolled a nearby log on top of the heap of rock and dirt.

"That'll have to do," Riker said, and walked away. He picked up his rifle, untied the sorrel and swung a leg over the horse's back, then sat waiting impatiently for the others to mount up. When Abel finally got himself aboard, Riker glanced up at the sun then turned toward the Indian camp.

"Where're we goin'?" Abel whined. "Ain't we goin' back to our saddles now that we got horses?"

"None of these nags has probably ever seen a saddle before," Riker growled. "I want my own horse back, or at least a horse that's worn a saddle before." He heeled the sorrel into motion towards the east.

"And how, pray tell," Bronco said lightly, "Are you planning on doing that?"

"You're half Injun, ain't ya?" Riker asked. "You oughta be able to sneak in an' get all four of our horses back!"

Bronco stared at him incredulously for a moment then he laughed. "Yeah, my mama was Sioux. But how in hell do you expect me to pick four horses out of a herd in the dark?" He waited for an answer, but Riker just rode on. "You are figurin' on doing this in the dark, right?"

"I am unless you think you can get in there an' get 'em in broad daylight," Riker answered.

"Not hardly."

It was dusk when the three came to the Indian camp. Their first clue was the smell of cooking fires; then they could hear the occasional high-pitched yells of children at play. Riker held up a hand and they slid to the ground in the middle of a lodgepole pine thicket. Abel rubbed his hind parts and vowed that he'd never ride a horse bareback again after today if he could help it. Riker and

Bronco handed him their reins and moved ahead at a crouch.

"Looks like it's dinner time over yonder," Bronco commented quietly. "Might be a good time to look over the horse herd." Riker just grunted and went on with his examination of the camp.

A teen-aged boy appeared, leading a bay horse with two white stockings and a snip of white on his nose, and a flashy paint. Riker nudged Bronco with his elbow. "That's my bay," he whispered. "An' that paint looks like Smith's." The boy brought the two horses to a lodge in the middle of the camp and tied them to a nearby tree. Another boy led up Bronco's chestnut, and a dun they were sure was Abel's, and tied them to the same tree. The two boys disappeared.

"There you go," Riker whispered. "Signed, sealed, and practically delivered. All you gotta do is go get 'em. Just watch out for dogs. There's a few around there." He sat back with a smug look on his face as if challenging Bronco. "You're always claimin' you're a good horse thief. Now's your chance to prove it."

~ 35 ~

As was his habit on the trail, mainly due to the fact that he hated sleeping on the ground, Bowie Tyler came awake before the new day was more than a thin line on the eastern horizon. He lay with his hands behind his head contemplating the twists and turns this case was taking. An old trapper he'd traveled with for a few days once had told him, "If you ain't sure what's what or where yer headin', take time to contemplate." Bowie'd found that taking the old man's advice helped most of the time, so he took time to contemplate now.

One of the things he was contemplating was the fact that this parade he seemed to be leading kept getting longer and longer. He'd started out alone, which was how he liked to work, and now he was dragging a green kid, a muleskinner and a bounty hunter around with him. At this particular point in the proceedings he wouldn't be the least bit surprised to see a brass band step out of the bushes and start playing "Oh, Susanna".

A stealthy movement across the way caught his attention and he carefully turned his head. Raleigh was easing out of his blankets and putting on his boots in the semi-darkness. Raleigh knelt and rolled his blankets then stood and started toward his saddle. "You wouldn't be figuring on getting the jump on the trail outta here now, would you, Raleigh?" Bowie asked conversationally.

Raleigh jumped like he'd been jabbed with something sharp. "Dammit, Tyler, don't do that!" he exclaimed. "You could stop a man's heart for him."

The two men's voices jarred Lonnie and Joe awake and they came scrabbling up out of their blankets reaching for their guns. "What's all the ruckus about?" Joe demanded. He saw Raleigh standing there with his blanket roll in his hand. "Where you think yer goin', Smithers?" Joe's battered Spencer swung in Raleigh's general direction.

Bowie saw Raleigh tense and his fingers ease toward his holstered pistol. "Put the rifle down before somebody gets hurt, Joe," he said. "Raleigh was just rolling his blankets so he'd be ready to go when the rest of us are, right, Raleigh?" Raleigh mumbled something about smartass deputies and Bowie asked innocently, "What was that? I couldn't hear you."

Raleigh ignored him and stomped over to his saddle. Bowie got out of his own blankets, pulled on his boots, and stood up. "Since we're all awake, we might as well get ready to ride, eh, Lonnie?" He said this as cheerfully as he could, knowing full well that the younger man would grumble. Bowie knelt and dropped a handful of dry grass on the few remaining embers of the fire and soon was adding larger fuel to the blaze.

After a breakfast of bacon and coffee the four men saddled their respective mounts and got back on the trail of Riker and his men. Bowie figured that he was at least a day behind the outlaws, not knowing that the four had been unavoidably delayed by the loss of their horses and Smith.

The trail was getting fresher. By midmorning Bowie had found where Riker had talked to the rustlers and he was looking over the tracks with some interest. For some odd reason all of the cow tracks seemed to be about the same size, and smaller than what one usually saw in a herd. He studied them for a minute scratching his head, then it dawned on him that somebody was driving calves rather than cows. And out here in the middle of nowhere the calves were probably rustled. He turned his horse and started following the trail of the calves. "Now where you goin', Tyler?" Joe asked.

"I'm seeing where this bunch of cows went."

"And you're doing this because..." Raleigh put in.

"Because I think those critters were rustled, and I'd like to talk to the rustlers. Riker did." Bowie turned back to face the others. Joe looked like a man who'd just taken a big bite of a green persimmon. "I take it you've got a problem with that?"

"Yer dern right I do," Joe snorted. "Them rustlers didn't kill Davy, this Riker we've been trackin' did. I don't see how followin' a bunch of rustled cows is gonna help us find Riker." He stopped and glared at Bowie but Bowie had been glared at by experts so he wasn't fazed in the least little bit.

"I reckon if you wanna find out how it's going to help, you can come along with me. Otherwise, there's lots of country out that way you can look in." Bowie pointed in the direction they'd been going. "I'm going this way." He turned Black and heeled him into a trot following the trail of the stolen cattle.

Behind him, Joe looked at Lonnie and Raleigh. "I think that there deputy's done gone crazy," he said. "I ain't followin' no cow thieves." Lonnie didn't comment, he just spurred his horse out to follow Bowie. Joe hollered, "Now, where you goin'?"

"Bowie's been right so far," Lonnie shouted back. "I reckon I'll stick with him."

"What about you, bounty hunter?" Joe asked belligerently. "You goin' on this wild goose chase too?"

Raleigh sat for a moment watching Lonnie receding in the distance. "I don't think so," he finally said. "I think I'll stay on Riker's tracks. We could even catch up with him some time today if we hurry." He turned his horse back to Riker's trail. Because of the cow tracks, he never saw that Riker had been alone except for Bronco Jarvis when he talked to the rustlers, and that the others had ridden in after the talking was finished. That oversight would prove to be costly.

After Lonnie left Joe and the bounty hunter, he loped his horse up alongside of Bowie then slowed him to a trot. Bowie looked over at the kid. "You're bound and determined to get yourself killed, aren't you?" he asked.

"Not necessarily," Lonnie shot back. "If you wanna know the truth, I figure the safest place in this part of the territory is right next to you." He grinned. "If nothin' else I can duck behind you when the bullets start flyin'." He sat back in his saddle looking almighty pleased with himself. Bowie looked over at him with raised eyebrow and the youth laughed out loud.

Jackie Gowan and Stan Hall had a calf stretched out on the ground between their horses when Bowie rode up to the makeshift corral by himself. He had sent Lonnie to a nearby clump of trees with orders to "Cover my back". Billie Gowan, Jackie's younger brother, was enveloped in smoke as he worked on changing Morton's Rafter B to a Diamond 8. His branding iron was one he'd made by heating the end of a stove poker up and bending it into an L and he was purely an artist with it. He straightened up and waved the smoke away and his eyes grew as wide as the muzzles of the Greener he suddenly found himself staring into.

Jackie and Stan let their ropes go slack and the calf jumped to its feet and raced to join its mates in the makeshift corral. The calf nearly ran over Billie in the process but the young man didn't move. "Uh, Jackie, you might wanna lay off coilin' that rope for a minute," Billie said.

Jackie looked over at his brother then followed his gaze to where Bowie sat his horse next to the corral fence with the Greener cocked and resting on the top rail. Slowly Jackie dropped his half-coiled rope on his saddlehorn and raised his hands shoulder high. Stan followed suit.

"Howdy, gents," Bowie said politely. "Nice day for a branding, isn't it?" He flashed the three men a smile that did nothing to warm his blue eyes. "Or a brand rewrite, I should say."

"Now don't get hasty, mister," Billie said quickly. "We bought these critters an' we're road brandin' 'em."

"Funny how your so-called 'road brand' covers up the original so well, isn't it? If you bought 'em then I guess you've got a bill of sale you can show me, right?"

"I'll show ya a bill of sale," Stan grated and dropped his hand to his holstered pistol. Before he could draw, the shotgun was pointed at his belly.

"I wouldn't do that if I were you, my friend," Bowie said. "All I want is some information; there's no call for violence. Now get your hands back up where they belong." Stan paled and did as he was told. Bowie went on.

"Back down the trail a ways you boys talked to a big fella on a bay horse. What'd he want to know?"

The Gowan brothers traded looks and Billie shrugged. "I wasn't there," he told Jackie. "You're on your own on this one."

Jackie was getting real tired of having guns pointed at him, but he wasn't dumb enough to buck a shotgun at such short range even if Stan seemed to be. "That was one mean, scary sumbitch," Jackie said. "He recognized the brand on these critters and wanted to know where we got 'em." He paused to see if Bowie believed him. Bowie kept his expression blank. "When we told him they came from a ranch the yonder side of Borden City, he wanted to know how to get there, an' then he rode off."

"I think you boys had best get your branding done and head for wherever you call home," Bowie said. He raised the Greener and rested the butt on his hip but Jackie noticed that the shotgun's hammers stayed cocked. "And keep your sticky fingers off of other folks' cows from now on. If these belong to who I think they belong to he'd hang you if he was here." He let the hammers down on the Greener and turned Black to ride away.

Stan saw his chance to restore some of his tattered pride and went for his pistol. A rifle blasted from a nearby alder copse, and a bullet tore a chunk out of the top rail of the fence then whined off into space. Bowie rode on without looking back. Lonnie called, "Drop it or the next one takes your head off." Stan cursed and dropped the pistol like it was burning his fingers. "Now you gents just stand pat while we ride away. If anybody leaves that corral in less than ten minutes..." They heard the clatter of hooves then silence. Bowie was gone as well.

Stan reached for his rifle and started his horse toward the gate. A rope dropped over his shoulders and pinned his arms to his sides. "Let it go, Stan," Jackie told him.

"Yeah, it ain't worth dyin' over," Billie put in. "You heard that gent." He picked up Stan's pistol and reached up to drop it in the holster. "'Sides, we got cattle to brand." Stan stared at the brothers for a minute then shrugged and reached for his rope with one hand while he flipped Jackie's loop off over his head with the other.

"I reckon you might be right," was all he said.

~ 36 ~

The Indian camp was quiet and dark. The last of the children had been taken into their family's lodges some time before, and the fire in the center of the camp was down to an ember or two and a few wisps of smoke. The four horses stood hipshot and dozing. They'd been watered and fed and were used to standing tied.

The first sliver of moon began to show itself above the ridge to the east. A gentle breeze picked up some dust and swirled it around, then dropped it. A dog at the edge of the camp barked a question to the night. When the night didn't answer, it lay down and went back to sleep. And a shadow moved.

Bronco had begun the slow crawl into the camp while it was still daylight. His dusty clothing had blended well with the frost-cured grass of the meadow. He'd come from the west and the sinking sun had made it that much harder for anyone looking in his direction to discern any movement. It had taken literally hours to cover the three hundred yards into the camp but now he was almost where he needed to be.

Bronco gradually stood up behind the tree the horses were tied to. He didn't want to startle the horses into making a fuss. The four stirred and he gently reached a hand to his chestnut's nose. The familiar smell quickly calmed the horse and its calm settled the others. Moving as slowly as he could, Bronco untied the halter leads from the tree and gathered them in his hands. He clucked almost silently, then eased the horses back until he had room to turn them away from the lodge next to where they had been tied.

After a few minutes that lasted nearly a year, the man and the horses were out of the camp; but the tension kept winding tighter. This was no time to relax so Bronco kept going. Only when he was nearly to the alder thicket where Riker and Abel waited did the strain begin to ease.

A shadow detached itself from the brush and drifted forward. Riker wordlessly held out a canteen and Bronco took it and drank greedily. Despite the chill of the fall night, he'd long since sweated through his shirt and the bandanna he'd tied around his forehead. He lowered the empty canteen and nodded his thanks.

"Alright, let's get mounted an' git back to our gear," Riker rumbled quietly.

"What about these here Injun horses?" Abel asked.

"We take 'em with us," Riker answered.

Abel stared at him. "What in hell for?"

"Because if those horses show up back in the herd without those three bucks ridin' 'em in, we'll have the whole damn village after us," Bronco cut in. "At least if the horses and the riders're both gone, those folks yonder won't be near as antsy. And we can sell 'em when we get to this Borden City place."

Abel subsided, grumbling. He hated riding bareback, and he hated the thought of leading another horse without a saddle to tie it to. And right at the moment he pretty much hated both of his companions, but he knew better than to cross them. He'd have to bide his time, but he'd find a way to get even, just like he'd done with Max Horner. He led his horse over to a fallen log and used it as a step up to swing his leg over the dun's bony back.

It was full daylight when the outlaws swung stiffly to the ground back at their camp. Riker dropped his bay's rope, led the Indian pony to a tree and tied it, then went over to where they had cached their saddles. He moved the brush aside and picked his saddle up and turned back to his horse. Abel stood slack-jawed, watching him. "What're you waitin' for, an engraved invitation? Git your horse saddled if yer comin' with us." Riker smiled an unpleasant smile at the look on Abel's face. "If you ain't comin', hand me that lead rope, 'cause yer walkin' outta here. I ain't takin' no chances on you changin' your mind an' doin' somethin' stupid that'll lead them Injuns to us."

Abel started to protest and a pistol appeared in Riker's hand. "Go or stay, it makes me no nevermind. But you best decide quick 'cause time's awastin'." Abel looked at Riker, then at the pistol, and went scrambling toward his saddle. Riker holstered the pistol and turned to saddle his horse.

The dust of three men's departure had hardly settled when Raleigh Smithers and Joe Harris rode into the little clearing. Since Riker had made no effort to cover his tracks the two had been able to follow the trail easily. What puzzled Raleigh was why the men had stayed in one place for so long; he had no way to know about Smith and the Indians. Instead, he silently turned his horse to follow the new tracks.

"We'd better take it slow from here, Joe," he told the teamster. "It looks to me like they haven't been gone long, and there's more horses. I can't tell for sure if the extras are packing riders or not but there's no sense in taking chances. We'll just trail along behind them and come up on 'em when they camp tonight." He didn't see Smith's saddle under the brush and wouldn't have cared if he did. All he was thinking about was capturing, or, better yet, killing, Riker. Most rewards were for "Dead or Alive", and a dead man was a whole lot easier to transport than a live one.

As dusk was settling over the land, far ahead Raleigh could see just the faintest wisp of smoke as it dissipated through the branches of a willow tree along Beaver Creek. He pulled his horse to a quiet stop and swung down, trailing his reins on the ground. The evening breeze was blowing softly from his left to his right, so he was sure that his horse couldn't smell the outlaws' horses, and vice versa. Still, he kept back. He didn't want his horse smelling the others and whinnying to them. He wasn't ready to let Riker and company know he was there.

"They're right up yonder, Joe," he said quietly. "If it's not..." He paused then said, "Aw hell, it has to be. We trailed them here. You stay back here with the horses, and I'll go make sure."

Joe swung down from his mule. "Not hardly, bounty man. If you go, I go. I get first chance at saltin' that Riker's hide fulla lead. You can pick up the pieces if you've a mind to when I'm done."

"I don't think that's a real good idea," Raleigh opined.

"I don't remember askin' you what you think," Joe retorted. "I'm gonna kill that fella and you can't stop me. So let's go."

Raleigh could see that nothing short of clubbing him unconscious was going to keep Joe there and he figured that would make too much noise so he surrendered to the inevitable. "At least let me go in the lead," he told Joe. "I've got a little more experience at this sort of thing than you do." Joe jerked a curt nod, levered a shell into the chamber of his Spencer, and waited for Raleigh to move.

Abel knelt and added some small sticks to the slowly growing fire. He grumbled to himself while the flames licked the new fuel and a small column of smoke made it's way up and to the side in the breeze, drifting out from under the branches above his head. So concerned was he with his own problems that he never noticed the flag of the smoke waving in the slowly moving air.

"You got coffee on yet, Abel?" Bronco's hectoring voice drifted over the small clearing. He knew that Abel was less than enchanted with his role as camp tender and general errand boy, but he also knew that Barnes would never do anything about it up front. All Bronco had to do was watch his back, which he did as a matter of course. Besides, harassing Abel was, if not fun, at least something to break the monotony of Riker's single-minded quest for his version of revenge.

"I ain't hardly got the fire built yet," Abel snapped. "Just hang onta your britches."

Bronco chuckled, knowing it would bother Abel no end, and went back to unsaddling his horse.

Raleigh eased up to the edge of the clearing. He could see the skinny hillbilly working on getting the fire built but the intervening brush made it impossible to tell if anyone else was around. It was pretty obvious that this man wasn't Riker.

"That ain't him," Joe whispered.

"No kidding," Raleigh replied with as much sarcasm as could be packed into an almost inaudible reply. "I never would've known it if you hadn't've told me." A twig snapped and the two men drew back. Riker stepped out into the open and Raleigh felt Joe stiffen beside him. He put his hand on the teamster's arm to keep him in place as long as he could. He wanted to know where the rest of the riders were. They'd been following a lot of horse tracks.

Riker stepped up to the fire and stood looking down at Abel. "Don't build it up too high, Abel," he said. "Just 'cause we ain't seen nobody but them rustlers don't mean the law ain't out an' about somewhere." He turned away from Abel and found himself looking down the barrel of Joe's Spencer. Joe brought the rifle to his shoulder and stepped out into the clearing.

"Mister, you're gonna die."

Raleigh had been standing beside Joe, so he had no choice but to step out himself. He drew his pistol and pointed it in the general direction of the two outlaws, while inside he was cussing Joe. Damn the man's impatience.

Riker raised his hands. Abel got to his feet and his own

hands shot up to shoulder height. He swallowed loudly as his eyes flicked back and forth between the two men who had just appeared out of the bushes.

"And just who might you be?" Riker asked calmly. "I like to know who I'm killin'."

"I'll do any killin' that gets done around here," Joe snarled. "You and that cur you ride with ambushed a posse and shot the hell out of 'em awhile ago. One of those men was my best friend. Y'all shot him and left him to ride off. He died in my arms, and now I'm gonna kill you." He drew back the Spencer's hammer and his finger tightened on the trigger.

Bronco heard Riker talking to someone he knew didn't sound like Abel. He eased toward the clearing until he could see Riker and Abel standing with their hands in the air and two men pointing guns at them. He heard one of the men tell Riker that it was Riker's time to die, and saw him ear back the hammer on the rifle.

Bronco had no qualms about shooting a man from ambush, especially when that same man was about to cash in Bronco's meal ticket. Since he'd been riding with Riker he'd had it pretty good and he'd just as soon things continued the way they were. He saw the knuckles of the man's trigger finger go white and Bronco palmed his pistol and shot the rifleman square between the shoulder blades.

From somewhere behind him Joe heard the slam of a shot and at the same time felt the burning pain in his back. He jerked the trigger of the Spencer as he started to go down but Riker was already moving, dropping to the ground and drawing his own pistol. Riker's bullet slammed into Joe's chest, lifting him back up on his toes as Joe tried to lever another round into the Spencer's chamber. Blood was dribbling from the corner of the teamster's mouth as he slammed the lever home. The rifle seemed to weigh as much as his mule as he tried to drag it to his shoulder and pull back the hammer at the same time. He succeeded in getting the hammer back but the weight of the rifle was too much. He was shaking, and his vision was dimming, when his finger tightened on the trigger; the big slug slammed into Abel's newly kindled fire, scattering embers in all directions. Riker's second shot killed him dead and he fell on his face on top of the rifle.

Raleigh heard the shot and saw dust puff from the back of

Joe's shirt. Without a second thought he shoved his pistol into the holster and threw himself back and away, and began scrambling through the bushes back toward where his horse and Joe's mule were tethered. Behind him he heard curses and brush breaking, but he had a good start and soon left pursuit behind. He threw himself aboard his horse, jerked the mule's reins loose from where they were tied to a clump of buckbrush, and booted his horse into a trot, dragging the mule behind him. He'd tried to tell that bull-headed teamster to stay behind. It was his own damn fault he was dead now.

Behind Raleigh, Riker got to his feet then shucked the empty shells from his pistol and reloaded the cylinder. Bronco stepped out into the open and did the same. He kicked the dead man in the side. "Who the hell's this?"

"It seems this fella took exception to us shootin' up that posse from Hobart," Riker said. "He's been followin' us with the idea of killin' me an' getting even."

"Who was that with 'im?" Abel wanted to know.

"I ain't sure, but I think it was a no-account bounty hunter name of Raleigh Smithers," Bronco said. "Looked like him from the back, anyway."

"Maybe we'll have to pay that gent a little visit when we get done killin' Morton," Riker mused, almost to himself. He looked at Abel. "Where's the coffee?"

Bronco took hold of the dead man's hands and dragged him out beyond the clearing, into the bushes and out of sight. "Ain't you even gonna bury him?" Abel asked.

"You want him buried, you bury him," Bronco told him. "We'll be outta here before he starts to stink," he said with a smirk. Abel swallowed and looked away. Riker was staring at Abel with a grim half-smile on his lips.

"You ain't turnin' soft on us now, are you Abel?" the big outlaw asked. "'Cause if you are, we can lay you right alongside of that gent."

"No, I ain't," Abel told him, "but it don't seem fittin' to just drag a man out in the brush an' leave him. Why, we buried Smith, didn't we?"

"Only because it was convenient, and because he was one of ours," Riker told him. "Now shut up about it an' get some grub cookin'. I'm hungry." Abel grumbled and turned to the packs and fished out a side of bacon that was only a tiny bit green around the edges and a bag of cornmeal. He sliced bacon into a pan and set it at the edge of the fire to cook.

~ 37 ~

Borden City was peaceful in the late afternoon sunlight. At the hitchrail in front of the Crystal Palace Saloon a pair of saddled horses stood hipshot, dozing in the warmth. Down yonder in front of Grayson's General Store two men were loading boxes and bags in the back of a buckboard. A shaggy brown dog of some indeterminate breed lay in a patch of sunlight, and his tail stirred a puff of dust as Lonnie and Bowie passed by, walking their horses down the main street heading for the better kept of the two livery stables in town. They drew up in front the barn-like structure and stepped down.

"You gents come far?" asked a grizzled gent in neatly patched canvas britches and a flannel shirt, who sat on a tilted back chair in front of the building.

"Far enough," Bowie answered as he tried to stretch the kinks out of his back and legs. He lifted the shotgun sling off over his head and hung the gun, muzzles-up, from his saddlehorn. "Got room for these two nags?"

"I reckon," the man said as he got to his feet. "Two bits a day, all the hay they can eat. Corn'll cost ya extra. The hay we cut out yonder." He pointed past the edge of town. "But the corn we gotta freight in." Bowie pitched him a dollar and the man led the way into the barn.

"See any horses that look familiar?" Bowie asked in a low voice, as he and Lonnie followed the liveryman down the alley between rows of stalls toward the rear of the cavernous building.

"Nope," Lonnie replied. "Either they ain't here yet, or they're stablin' their horses at that other place."

"Or they've got a hideout hereabouts that we don't know about."

"I don't think so," Lonnie countered. "The way Riker was talkin' he'd never been in this part of the world before."

The liveryman turned and indicated a pair of stalls that

faced each other across the alley. "These do ya?"

"These'll work just fine, Mister, uh..."

"Ain't Mister nothin'. Just call me Hank." He stuck out his hand.

"Well, Hank," Bowie began as he shook the proffered hand, "maybe you can tell me something. Have four men come into town together in the last day or so? One of 'em would be riding a center-fire Texas saddle on a flashy paint horse. Could be a big fella on a blood bay leading them."

Hank scratched his chin. "No, can't say as I've seen anybody like that," he said. "Why, they wanted fer somethin'?"

"Oh, no, nothing like that," Bowie said lightly. Lonnie gave him a startled look. "They're friends of ours and we wanted to surprise them. So if they come in, be sure you don't tell 'em we're here, alright? We'll be around and about, so you just come find us and we'll tell them we're here ourselves."

"That kinda service probly should cost extry, don't ya think?" Hank asked. With a sigh, Bowie pitched him another dollar then turned to unsaddle his horse. Hank chuckled when he heard Bowie's sigh and went back to his chair and the last of the afternoon sun.

"What was that all about?" Lonnie asked when Hank was safely out of earshot.

"That was trying to keep Riker and his boys from finding out we're here."

"Why didn't you just tell him you're the law?"

"Because I'd just as soon everybody and their dog not know I'm a deputy. It makes my job a little easier if people think I'm just a drifter passing through."

"Whatever you say." Lonnie stripped the saddle and bridle from his horse, slung the saddle on a stall rail and the bridle on a peg in the side of a stall post and closed the stall gate. "We gonna get something to eat, or is that a secret too?"

"Don't be a wiseass." Bowie slapped the black horse on the hip as he stepped out into the alley and closed the gate. "Unless you're packing a bigger bankroll than you look like you are, you might wanna bring your blanket roll. We're probably gonna be sleeping in the hayloft." He indicated his own blankets. "Unless Hank thinks that's worth a dollar too, in which case we might's well go look for a hotel."

Back at the front of the barn Bowie climbed up the ladder to the loft. He hung his blanket roll on a hook out of the reach of the mice who were more than likely homesteading somewhere in the piled hay, waited while Lonnie did the same, then climbed back down to the ground. He went out the door. Hank silently watched them, still sitting in his tilted back chair. "Where's the best grub for the least amount of dinero in this fine metropolis, pard?" Bowie asked.

Hank pointed to a small building down the block with red-checked curtains in the windows. "Miz Patterson's down yonder is the best eats," he opined. "Purtiest waitress an' cook, too. She does it all herself. But you'd best not get fresh with her or she'll clean yer clock for ya." He laughed. "Why, just last week a young fella went in there all dolled up an' figurin' to get him a kiss. He got kissed alright. By Miz Patterson's fryin' pan. She done knocked him colder'n a wedge!

"Folks around here are mighty partial to Miz Patterson's cookin'. Some of the boys took exception to that sort of behavior, so they hauled that feller outside, stripped him down to his long handles an' tied him on his horse bassackwards. When he come to he was headin' outta town at a high lope, lookin' the wrong direction. He's been mighty humble ever since."

Hank broke into a full-fledged belly laugh and Bowie couldn't help but join in. "Sounds like my kind of place," he said. "I reckon we'll sashay on down there and look in on Miz Patterson. See ya, Hank." He lifted a finger to the brim of his hat and moved on down the street.

The "Huckleberry Cafe', Elvira Patterson, Prop." was neatly painted and clean on the outside, with sparkling windows dressed up with window boxes full of flowers that were not withstanding the fall weather particularly well. Some of them were brown around the edges; the rest were starting to wilt. Bowie reached down and plucked one of the better looking of the petunias and stuck it in a buttonhole on his vest. Lonnie gave him a suspicious look. "You aren't fixing to get us bashed with a fryin' pan and sent outta town in our drawers now, are you?"

"Why Lonnie, whatever do you mean?" Bowie asked innocently. "I'm just trying to spruce up a bit, is all." He turned the cut glass knob and pushed the door open, indicating with a wave of his hand that Lonnie should precede him into the restaurant.

Inside the small room were half a dozen tables covered with tablecloths that matched the curtains and a counter near what appeared to be the kitchen door. A row of stools was neatly spaced along the counter. A few of the tables were occupied by folks in various degrees of finery, from a man who appeared to be a banker to two others who no doubt were cowhands. Unseen by Bowie, a big man in a black frock coat who was sitting at the back of the room, glanced sharply at the two then went back to his food.

When a plump redhead, just slightly taller than Bowie, with rosy cheeks and her hair in a slowly deteriorating bun, came toward them, Bowie knew without being told that this was the famous Miz Patterson. "Welcome, gentlemen," she told them in a lilting brogue as she wiped a strand of hair out of her face. "Would ye be carin' for some dinner?"

Bowie doffed his hat, then nudged Lonnie hard in the ribs with his elbow when the boy didn't remove his own headgear fast enough to suit Bowie. "Indeed we would," he said. "That is, if it's prepared by your own hand. Don't bother to season it, your touch will be enough." As he spoke, he surreptitiously looked for a ring on her left hand, but found neither a ring nor any indication that she had ever worn one. That didn't necessarily mean anything, but it was a good sign.

"Go on with your blarney, m' friend," the lady told him. "I've been sweet-talked by better men than you and have yet to fall for any of their lines." She turned toward a table. "Follow me and watch your step; I've just mopped."

When the two men were seated, with coffee in front of them and menus in hand, and the lady had gone back to her kitchen, Lonnie looked across the table at Bowie. "You tryin' to get us killed?" he asked incredulously. "You heard what Hank said!" Bowie just gave him a smile and went back to looking at the menu.

The big man stood up and reached for his hat, careful not to keep his gaze on Bowie for too long. For some obscure reason, he was sure the short round one in the buckskin shirt was a lawman. He wasn't sure how he knew, but somehow he just did. It probably had something to do with being on the run for as long as he had. The kid he dismissed as being unimportant. The man dropped a dollar on the table and turned toward the door.

"Have a safe trip back to your ranch, Mister Gordon," Miz Patterson called through the pass-through window between dining room and kitchen. Bowie looked across the small space at the man, and something clicked in his own mind. Something about this Gordon fellow made him think that they would be seeing each other again, and soon. And that was the name the rustlers had given Bowie. The man tipped his hat to Miz Patterson then went out and shut the door behind him. He untied a long-legged bay from the hitchrail and stepped into the saddle. He turned the bay's head toward the northwest and heeled him into a jog.

"Did you call that man Gordon?" Bowie asked Miz Patterson when she brought more coffee.

"O' course," she replied. "He owns a ranch outside of town. He also does a bit of surveying for the railroad, and for road building and the like. He goes out on jobs several times a year." She paused and took a notepad from her apron pocket. "Would ye like to order now?"

~ 38 ~

The menu at the Huckleberry Cafe' was much more complete, and the preparer considerably more accomplished, than the bill of fare in the outlaw camp. By now Bowie and Lonnie were the only patrons, it being past the normal dinner hour for most folks in Borden City. Bowie ordered buffalo pot roast with taters and onions and gravy, peas in cream sauce, and biscuits. Lonnie ordered the same. The honey pot was on the table, as was a jar of jam- huckleberry of course- made by their hostess herself. The helpings were generous, and when the two men at last pushed their plates back they were both stuffed. For the first time in recent memory, Bowie had to pass up the fresh-made apple pie that was offered.

"Ma'am," Bowie told Miz Patterson, "that was some of the best food it's been my pleasure to consume in darn near forever, begging your pardon for my language." Lonnie seconded that emotion. He'd been eating camp cooking for quite a while, until even roast possum would've tasted good if somebody else had cooked it.

The lady beamed at them and said, "I do like to see a man eat." She poured them each more coffee then turned back toward the kitchen.

"Ma'am, if it's not too much to ask, what time does this fine establishment close?" Before Miz Patterson could answer, Bowie said, "I'd take great pleasure in walking you home, if you'd allow me to."

"We've yet to be formally introduced, mister," she said. "What in the world makes ye think I'd be allowin' one such as yourself to walk me home?"

"Ma'am, you are most definitely right, I've been remiss in my social obligations," Bowie said gallantly. He rose and said, "Bowie Tyler, at your service," then bowed slightly from the waist, with one arm folded across his middle. "My young companion's name is Lonnie Grable." He ignored the strangled snort that issued from Lonnie's side of the table as the young man struggled mightily to contain the laugh that threatened to burst out of him. Bowie waited expectantly for the lady's answer.

Miz Patterson stood looking at him with a thoughtful expression on her face. She kept him in suspense until the coffeepot in her hand began to get too heavy, then she said, "I canna for the life of me figure out why I'm tellin' ye this, but my name's Elvira, and I generally close about eight." She turned her back on Bowie and went into the kitchen and out of sight.

Bowie dropped back down in his chair, seemingly exhausted from the ordeal he'd just gone through. He looked across the table at Lonnie who was wearing an ear-to-ear grin. "What, pray tell, are you looking so pleased with yourself about?" Bowie wanted to know.

"Oh, nothin'," the youth said. He picked up his cup and took a sip of coffee and said, in a passable imitation of Bowie, "I've been remiss in my social obligations," and started laughing again. Bowie just glared at him over his own coffee cup, which made Lonnie laugh that much harder. He was strangling and nearly in tears with the effort of keeping his voice down. "Looks to me like the big tough deputy has met his match," he finally choked out. "I think Cupid's arrow has done been flung." At last his mirth subsided to a few hiccups and the occasional chuckle.

"Are you done?" Bowie asked. "If you are, then how 'bout this 'big tough deputy' takes you outside and teaches you some manners at the pointy end of his boot, boy?" His face was red and his teeth were gritted in a poor imitation of a grin.

"Oooh," Lonnie said as he held up his hands in mock terror. "Don't hurt me, big tough deputy." He got to his feet, put on his hat, and fished four bits out of his pocket to drop on the table. "I think I'll go find some place to take a bath. I won't wait up." He ducked and made a dash for the door and a biscuit whizzed by his head. "Don't forget, Elvira just mopped." He ducked outside and shut the door as another biscuit bounced off the window.

Bowie got up and retrieved the baking powder missiles from the floor and went back to his seat. "Is there a problem, Mister Tyler?" Elvira asked innocently from the kitchen.

"No ma'am, no problem a good hide-tanning won't solve," Bowie answered. "Just a matter of a certain young man getting a bit too big for his britches is all." He grimaced. "I'll reconcile the matter later."

Thirty minutes later, Lonnie settled into a tub of hot water with a heartfelt sigh. The water lapped up around his chin and he could feel the dirt of too many days on the trail starting to float away. He chuckled to himself, thinking about the star-struck look on the deputy's face back in the Cafe'. It was kind of nice to have the upper hand with Bowie for once. Lord knows the man had made Lonnie feel pretty awkward for pretty much the whole time he'd known him.

"What're you grinning about?" Bowie's voice intruded into the enjoyment of the moment. Lonnie looked around to see Bowie pulling off his boots in preparation for his own bath. The bath-house proprietor's son appeared with a couple of buckets of hot water, and started to fill the other tub that sat in the room while Bowie shucked his trailworn clothes.

"Oh, nothin'," Lonnie said. His grin widened even further when another thought suddenly occurred to him. "Say, don't you have a date with the restaurant lady?" He ducked and Bowie's thrown boot thumped into the wall beyond where Lonnie sat.

"Not 'til eight o'clock," Bowie snorted. "That's still an hour away, if it's any of your business." Bowie stepped into the tub and sat down. "I've got time for a bath."

"More'n likely need one, too," Lonnie said. He held up his hands when he saw Bowie reaching for his other boot. "Hold on, now. You ain't the only one." Bowie subsided and Lonnie said, "'Course I ain't courtin' the restaurant lady later, myself. Why, I'll bet that fella in yonder has even got some sweet-smellin' toilet water you can put on when you get done bathin'."

"Kid, your mouth's gonna get you killed if you don't watch out," Bowie growled as he reached for the bar of soap and the scrub brush that sat on a nearby chair. Lonnie laughed so hard his head slid under the water and he nearly drowned himself. He came up sputtering and pawing water from his eyes. "Told ya," Bowie said dryly. A smile was tugging at the corners of his mouth as his usual good humor was restored by the sight of Lonnie sitting there looking like the proverbial drowned rat.

Eight o'clock found Bowie sitting in the Huckleberry Cafe' with a cup of coffee in front of him. He'd beat as much dust out of his hat as he could and wiped down his scuffed boots. He'd even had a change of clothes in his blanket roll that he'd gotten out and put on. The last patron finally left the table and went out the door; Elvira Patterson locked it behind him and drew the shade. She picked up the man's plate and cutlery and carried them into the kitchen then came back with a broom in her hand and stopped in front of Bowie with the broom extended.

"Don't just sit there like a lump, Mister Tyler," she told him sternly. "There are things to do." Bowie looked back and forth between her face and the broom a time or two then resignedly pushed his chair back, took the broom from her hand, and began halfheartedly sweeping the floor. Elvira turned back toward the kitchen with her lips twitching as she did her best to keep him from seeing her smile. "I don't have all night, you know," she called back over her shoulder. Bowie started sweeping faster.

The moon shone brightly on the strolling couple while a few scudding clouds cast fleeting shadows across the ground. The chilly breeze teased the tails of the shawl Elvira wore over her hair and she gathered the fabric tighter under her chin. Her other hand was tucked in the crook of Bowie's elbow.

They came to a weather-worn picket fence surrounding a small cottage. No lights shone in the windows of the house as Bowie pushed open the squeaky gate and gallantly waved Elvira through ahead of him. A few slates made a walkway to the porch. "I'll be thankin' ye for the escort, Mister Tyler," Elvira said, taking her left hand from his arm and holding out her right. Bowie took her hand in his and raised it to his lips.

"My pleasure, Elvira," he said. "May I call you Elvira?" She laughed lightly as she took back her hand and turned toward the door.

"Goodnight, Mister Tyler."

"Can I see you again?" Bowie asked.

"The next time you're in the Cafe'," she said with a laugh, then went into the house and closed the door. Bowie turned and headed for the street without realizing that the breeze had swung the gate shut. The pickets of the gate hit him at mid-thigh and he promptly did a decidedly ungainly somersault into the street.

Bowie jumped to his feet and looked all around to see if anyone had seen him fall, but no one was in sight. "Bowie, you just better watch out for that woman," he told himself. "And watch out where you're walking, too." He dusted his britches as best he could and headed for the livery and his blankets.

~ 39 ~

In the ranch house on Swale Creek the man the good citizens of Borden City knew as Don Gordon was lying awake staring at the plank ceiling over his head. He couldn't shake the feeling that things were on the verge of going extremely wrong for someone. He just hoped that now, when he was finally retired from his past life and ready to settle down and live the peaceful life of a rancher, that someone wasn't him.

A time or two over the years he'd had the same feeling, and each time that nagging suspicion had turned out to be right. He'd learned to pay attention to it because it had kept him alive and out of jail when a lot of others in his line of work were either pushing up daisies on some two-bit cowtown's Boot Hill or sledgehammering big rocks into little ones on a prison rock pile. So now he was wracking his brain, trying to figure out what kind of storm was coming.

He'd heard the rumors and stories that were floating around; stories about how Bob Morton was supposed to have blown up a bank and ambushed a posse. He'd even heard that a mustanger had come back to civilization with the story that Bob Morton had walked into his camp and murdered his partners, and nearly killed him. News like that seemed to travel on the wind. The mustanger had described the man who'd shot the two men he was traveling with very well, and the description had sounded familiar somehow. But the man the description seemed to fit was supposed to be in prison.

Gordon finally rolled over and closed his eyes. In the morning he'd ride into town and send a telegram. Maybe he could get some questions answered, and maybe he could put at least one ghost to rest.

Don Gordon was saddling his horse by lantern light when Jeff his foreman came into the barn early the next morning. "You're out and about mighty early, ain't ya?" Jeff asked, leaning on a stall post.

"I need to send a telegram," Don answered. "I'll be back either tonight or tomorrow morning." He looked at Jeff. "How're those calves doing?"

"I think that whole 'fence 'em in' idea's gonna work," Jeff told him. "Them calves have settled right down and most of the cows have wandered off back to their pastures."

"Good. Maybe tomorrow we can ease the calves down to the south pasture and get them on some better feed. I'll figure out what I want to do when I get back." He led the horse out of the barn, tightened the cinch, and stepped into the saddle. "See ya, Jeff." Jeff noticed that his boss had tied a blanket roll behind his saddle and the stock of a Winchester stuck out of a scabbard under Don's right leg. That was a bit unusual. Normally the boss didn't go armed except for the cutdown Remington under his arm that most folks didn't know about. Don heeled the horse into a trot as he headed for the trail to Borden City. With any luck, before the day was out he'd have a better idea who the man was that the mustanger had described.

"You gonna root around there all night, or are you gonna get settled and go to sleep?" Lonnie asked Bowie pointedly. "Some of us need our rest. What happened, the restaurant lady stand you up?"

"Just never you mind about me and Elvira," Bowie retorted. "And I'll settle down when I'm good and ready." He pulled his boots off and dropped them with the intention of making some noise but the hay muted the thump to a barely audible tap. He heard Lonnie snicker. "Oh shut up," Bowie told him, which brought another snicker. He rolled over, pulled his blankets up around his shoulders, and went to sleep.

The first glimmers of dawn were painting the eastern sky a myriad of reds and yellows when the rooster in the chicken yard next to the livery began to crow. It was a ragged crow at best; the rooster was old and skinny, and hardly a fit meal for one of the many marauding skunks he'd dodged his whole life- but the noise was sufficient to bring Bowie awake. He looked at the streaks of light starting to slip into the hayloft through the gaps in the log wall, then over to where Lonnie lay snoring in his blankets, seemingly without a care in the world. It pained him to see the young man so blissfully asleep while he himself was wide-awake, and with a backache to boot.

And speaking of boots: Bowie's were right there within easy reach. Maybe that sick-sounding rooster needed a little help rousing the local population. Bowie sat up, rolled over, picked up Lonnie's holstered pistol and moved it out of reach. He picked up his boot by the mule-ear pull straps and started swinging it over his head. The boot soon had a fair amount of momentum built up. At just the right point in the flying footwear's career around his head, Bowie let go. The heavy boot thumped into the wall near Lonnie's head and caromed off the warped timber to knock over a nearby pitchfork that clattered to the floor and threw a wad of hay into the air.

Lonnie bolted to a sitting position in his blankets. His eyes were wide and he was clawing for his pistol, and Bowie was glad he'd taken the precaution of moving the Colt away from the boy's hand. Lonnie looked over at the smiling deputy, then at the boot and pitchfork, and cursed. "I shoulda known you had somethin' to do with all that racket," he groused. "What's the matter now, other'n you not bein' able to stand seein' somebody else enjoy himself?"

"Why, it's time to get up!" Bowie exclaimed. He was enjoying himself immensely. "Can't you hear that sour-voiced chicken yonder saying just exactly that?"

"I'm right on the verge of makin' dumplings out of you and that chicken both," Lonnie groused. "Go away and let me sleep." He lay back down and pulled the blankets over his head. Bowie started to reach for his other boot, and Lonnie's voice came out from under the covers. "You do anything with that other boot than put in on your foot an' I'll throw you down the ladder. I'm goin' back to sleep. You and that stupid chicken are the only ones awake around here."

As if on cue, rusty hinges creaked below them and light flooded into the lower levels of the barn and brought a satisfied smirk to Bowie's face. He listened to the thump and shuffle of someone climbing the ladder to the loft and watched the liveryman's head appear above the hay-strewn floor. "You fellas ready for some coffee?" Hank asked. "It's done boiled an' ready to pour." Lonnie snorted and Bowie laughed.

"We'll be down shortly, old-timer," Bowie told him. "Keep

it hot for us."

Lonnie stuck his head back out of the blankets. "What's this 'we' stuff?" he wanted to know.

"Well, you're awake, so we might as well have some coffee then go get breakfast. It looks to me like we're burning daylight," Bowie told him.

"And just exactly what is there to be in such a rush about, anyway?" Lonnie grumped as he pulled on his boots. His hair was sticking up all over his head and he ran his fingers through it, trying to make it lay down. "Besides you wantin' to visit the restaurant lady, that is. I don't think you need me for that, unless you want me to hold your hand while you talk to her." He paused, and a grin creased his lips. "But I think folks'd frown on that just a bit, don't you?"

Bowie ignored him and stood up. He walked over to his wayward boot and tugged it on his foot. "I'm going down for some coffee. Feel free to join me and Hank at your leisure." He turned and went down the ladder. Lonnie put on his boots and hat and slid down the ladder right behind him.

~ 40 ~

Bowie stepped out of the Huckleberry Cafe' in time to see the big man who'd been in the Cafe' yesterday afternoon ride into the north end of the main street of Borden City. Bowie decided that either the man's ranch wasn't all that far away, or there was something else going on that kept him coming back to town. Bowie didn't particularly believe in coincidence; one of Tyler's Unwritten Laws said that everything happens for a reason.

He watched the man who Elvira had called Mister Gordon pull up and step down in front of the telegraph office then tipped his hat forward and drifted in that direction. It could be interesting to eavesdrop on what message the man might send, if he could figure out a way to do it without anybody noticing. Among Bowie's other talents was the ability to decipher the Morse code used by telegraphers. If he could get there in time to hear what was sent he might just learn a little more about Mister Gordon. For some reason the man intrigued him.

A window beside the telegraph key was open a crack so Bowie drifted past the front of the telegraph office and leaned against the corner of the building.. He could hear voices from inside, but couldn't recognize words. He thought he heard boots on the board floor so he eased back into the alley between the telegraph office and a small dress shop. A door opened and closed and footsteps receded in the distance. Bowie moved back toward the window as the telegraph key began to click.

The rattle of a buckboard passing in the street blotted out part of what was being sent over the wire, but Bowie still managed to catch enough of the message to know that Gordon was checking into the whereabouts of one Albert Riker, who Gordon apparently thought should currently be residing in a prison somewhere. If this was the same Riker that had blown up the bank in Hobart, and Bowie was pretty sure it was, Gordon was going to be a trifle unhappy. He got the impression that Gordon thought prison was the perfect place for Mister Riker. The question now was, how did Gordon know that much about a lowlife like Riker?

Bowie moved down the alley and around the back of the dress shop, strolling casually with his hands in his pockets like he hadn't a care in the world. He reappeared on the street several buildings down from the telegraph office and strolled toward the Cafe'.

Elvira looked at him in surprise when Bowie stepped back inside the eatery; he'd just left a few minutes ago. Before she could say anything, he winked and smiled and sat down at a small table near the door. Gordon was at a table at the back of the room with a cup of coffee in front of him, looking at nothing in particular. His troubled expression made Bowie think he was on the right trail concerning Riker; somehow Gordon knew Riker and was worried about him. And Bowie knew Riker was headed this way. Things were starting to look real interesting, and Bowie planned to be there to pick up the pieces.

Elvira brought coffee to Bowie, and he noticed her puzzled expression. He figured it was due to his sudden reappearance, so he gave her a smile and said, "You make the best coffee around, ma'am. I just had to come back for more."

"Why thank you, Mister Tyler," she replied, apparently satisfied. Inwardly Bowie was sagging with relief at having averted what could have been an awkward moment while outwardly maintaining his cheerful expression.

The room was gradually emptying as the noontime crowd finished their meals and went back to work. Gordon picked at his food for a while, then finally laid his knife and fork in his plate and pushed it away and picked up his coffee cup. Elvira picked up his plate. "I'm hopin' your lack of appetite doesn't mean the food was bad, Mister Gordon," she told him. "Ye usually clean your plate."

"Not at all, ma'am," he told her. "I guess I'm just not hungry today. Got a lot on my mind." He gave her a brief smile as she turned away toward the kitchen.

Lonnie stepped into the Cafe'. "That bounty hunter's here," he said. "And he's by himself." Out of the corner of his eye Bowie saw Gordon jerk like he'd been jabbed with a hatpin then go back to contemplating his rapidly cooling coffee.

"What do you mean, he's by himself?" Bowie asked, though he was pretty sure he already knew the answer. He was watching

Gordon carefully while trying at the same time to look like he was hanging on Lonnie's every word. Gordon appeared to be doing the same thing himself.

"He rode in from the south a little bit ago leading that teamster's mule. Said Joe got the drop on Riker somehow or other, then Bronco Jarvis shot Joe in the back and Riker finished him after he went down." By this time Gordon was leaning forward and there was no doubt that he was listening.

"What else did Raleigh have to say for himself?" Bowie asked mildly. There was an undercurrent of iron behind his words.

"Not much," Lonnie said. "He acted like he really didn't wanna talk about it."

"I reckon not," Bowie snorted angrily. "It's pretty obvious to me that he ran out on Joe."

The door opened and Raleigh stepped into the Cafe' just in time to hear Bowie's last few words. "You repeat that, you little fat bastard, and I'll kick your ass!" the bounty hunter snarled.

Bowie looked him over scornfully. "I'll repeat it whenever and wherever, Smithers!" Bowie snarled. "And as for kicking my ass, you'd best shed that pistol belt because you've got it to do. I've had about all of you I'm gonna take!" He pushed his chair back and stood up. He reached for his belt buckle and said, "What's it gonna be, bounty man? Fight or run?"

Raleigh glared hatred at Bowie. Lonnie could see in his eyes how much Raleigh wanted to go for his pistol. His hands were trembling and his whole demeanor radiated the desire to kill. Slowly Raleigh's hand drifted toward his holstered gun.

"You try to draw that pistol, mister, and you're liable to hurt yourself," Lonnie drawled. "Or Bowie will do it for you. That pistol's tied down."

Raleigh wilted like a lily under the summer sun. He glanced down and the sick realization that he'd been on the verge of what was essentially suicide blew through his mind like a December norther. Then the realization came to him that, even without his pistol tied down, Bowie would have killed him. Even on his best day he was no match for the deputy, and he knew it. He looked back at Bowie.

The smirk on Bowie's face kindled his rage all over again. For too long Bowie had been a thorn in his side, always getting in the way of Raleigh making an honest living. He conveniently passed over the fact that he'd actually been the one in the way more often than not. "Alright, Tyler, you've got your fight. But you'd better make your peace with God, because I'm showing no mercy." He unbuckled his gunbelt and tossed it on a nearby table then stood with his fists clenched and waited for Bowie's next move.

A palpable silence descended on the room and drowned out even the muted sounds from the street. Bowie unbuckled his own belt and laid the Starr gently on the table. "Look after that for me, would you, Lonnie?" he asked, and started forward. The quiet was broken by the whipcrack of Elvira's voice, stopping them all in their tracks.

"If you men be wantin' to tear into one another like wild dogs, I'll not be tryin' to stop you," she said roughly. She came from the kitchen brandishing a large cast iron skillet. "But if you're thinkin' you're goin' to tear up my Cafe' in the process, ye both had best think again! The first man to throw a punch gets this skillet upside his head." She glared at the two men then pointed at the door. "Take it outside. Now." Bowie started for the door. "Oh, and Mister Tyler," she said sweetly, and Bowie looked over at her. "Just be sure ye do a thorough job of it." Bowie smiled and motioned for Raleigh to precede him outside.

"Yes, ma'am," he said on the way out.

~ 41 ~

Outside on the boardwalk the two men stood and looked at each other for a moment. Raleigh was the taller of the two, with more reach. And he was mad. Bowie was short and stout, and appeared to have a lot more padding. But he'd been in a lot of fights over the years that didn't involve weapons, and he was pretty sure the bounty hunter hadn't been in a real knock down, drag out, bare-knuckle brawl in years. If he ever had.

Raleigh charged at Bowie, planning on ending the fight in a hurry. He swung a haymaker for Bowie's chin that Bowie took on his shoulder as he sidestepped; Bowie shot a straight jab to Raleigh's mouth that split his lips and sent stars through his vision. Raleigh backed up and ran his hand across his mouth; it came away red. He rushed again, and connected with a left that knocked Bowie sideways into the street and started bells ringing in the deputy's head. Damn, that hurt.

Bowie rolled to his feet. He quickly brought his guard up and tucked his chin behind his shoulder. Raleigh followed Bowie into the dust of the street and pounded at his arms and shoulders, landing an occasional stinging blow to Bowie's head. Bowie circled and jabbed, slipping punches when he could, then suddenly bulled in and landed a crashing blow to the bounty man's belly that took his wind. Raleigh backpedaled while he tried to suck some air into his heaving lungs, but Bowie closed in relentlessly. It was time to run this pain-in-the-butt bounty hunter out of town.

Raleigh tried to bring his guard up, and Bowie slipped a left into his belly again. Raleigh's arms dropped and Bowie crossed a right to the chin, then the left slammed into Raleigh's belly once again. His knees started to crumble, but from somewhere he found the energy to force himself back up. Although he was having trouble getting air into his heaving chest, Raleigh threw a right that got through Bowie's hands and cut his cheek open; Bowie shook it off and bored in, punching with both hands. The sudden onslaught was more than Raleigh could handle and he panicked.

Raleigh windmilled punches at Bowie but to no avail. Bowie landed another left to Raleigh's gut, then a right and a left to the bounty hunter's face. Raleigh went down hard then rolled to his hands and knees. He gathered his last ounce of strength and threw himself at Bowie's knees, only to meet one head-on as Bowie jerked it up under Raleigh's jaw. He went down on his face in the dirt. Bowie grabbed him by his shirtfront and lifted him to his knees. One of the bounty hunter's eyes was swelled shut and his lips were bleeding. He wobbled in Bowie's grasp, just barely on the edge of consciousness. Bowie dragged him over to a nearby water trough and shoved his head under the water. He held him there until Raleigh's feeble struggles became a full-fledged battle to get his head back out to where he could breathe. Bowie yanked his dripping carcass out of the trough and faced Raleigh nose to nose.

"You listen to me, bounty hunter," Bowie growled through split lips. "You get on your horse, and you ride away. I don't care where you go, but if you ever show up on my backtrail again, I'll make you wish you'd never been born! You got that?" Raleigh nodded weakly. "As far as I'm concerned you're nothing but a two-bit drygulcher who oughta be hung, but I'm gonna let you live, at least for now." He let go and Raleigh slumped to the dirt of the street. "Now git!"

"I need my gun," Raleigh mumbled. Lonnie stepped down into the street and handed him his pistol belt.

"It ain't loaded, bounty hunter," the boy told him. "I'd hate to see you do somethin' stupid." He stepped back and watched Raleigh stumble to his feet and start down the street, weaving drunkenly, with the pistol belt dangling from his swollen right hand. "I reckon that's the last we'll see of him," he said to no one in particular.

"Don't bet on it," Bowie told him, and stepped gingerly up onto the boardwalk. Elvira was standing in the Cafe's doorway with a bemused expression on her face. Bowie looked at her. "Was that thorough enough, ma'am?" he asked. His smile broke off in a wince as his split lips stung him.

"Come inside, Mister Tyler, and we'll see what's to be done about fixin' your face," was all she said, then she turned and went into the Cafe'.

"Yes, ma'am," Bowie said.

Elvira pointed at an empty chair beside a table near the kitchen door. "Sit," she commanded then went into the kitchen. Bowie hear the squeaking of a pump and the gush of water into a pan as he sat flexing his swollen hands, trying to work some of the stiffness out of them while Gordon sat quietly watching.

Elvira came from the kitchen carrying a pan of water and a handful of torn pieces of toweling. She set the pan and the bundle of rags on the table, then picked up one of the rags and sloshed it in the water. After she wrung the excess water from the rag, she reached out to tilt Bowie's head up with her left hand and began washing the blood from his face with her right. "I'm thinkin' that cut will be needin' some stitches. It's very deep," she told him as she dabbed at the split over his cheekbone. "I'll send someone for the doctor. He's a drunken sot but he sews a fine stitch. Or I can do the stitchin' myself." Elvira looked into his face and smiled knowingly at his startled look. "I've sewn up m' father and brothers, more than once."

Bowie composed his features again. A deadpan look was the most comfortable. It didn't pull so much on the cuts and bruises. "Ma'am, I'd be honored," he said solemnly.

"Aye, you'll think honored when I start the stitchin'," she told him tartly. "But if you're thinkin' you're tough enough, I'll do it. It should only take a few." She pressed the wet rag against his cheekbone. "Hold that while I go get m' sewin' basket." Bowie reached up and held the wet cloth pressed against his face.

A quiet chuckle drifted through the room over the sound of Elvira rustling around in the pantry. "You fight pretty good for a man built like a punkin," Gordon called from his table at the back of the room. Bowie tipped his head up to look at the rancher over the swelling below his eye.

"A man built like a punkin has to either learn to fight or take up keeping store," Bowie said. "And I don't like being cooped up indoors. Besides which," he went on, "you can't always judge a horse by the color of his hide. He may just have hidden talents."

"I reckon." Gordon chuckled again and got to his feet just as Elvira came back into the room with her sewing basket in one hand and a bottle of brandy in the other. He dropped some coins on the table, tipped his hat to her, murmured, "Ma'am," and strode out the door.

"Now then, Mister Tyler," Elvira said. "I'll be usin' this

brandy to disinfect the needle and thread, but if you're in need of a wee dram yourself, I'll not take it amiss." Bowie took the hint and picked up a coffee cup from the center of the table. He held it out; she poured it nearly full and he gulped it down, gasping and shuddering as the liquor burned its way to his stomach and ignited a sizeable bonfire there.

"Thank you, I think," he managed to say through the flames. Elvira took the cup from his hand and set it on the table. She poured it full of the brandy again, then reached for a spool of linen thread and a needle. She threaded the needle, nipped the thread with her teeth, and knotted the ends of the thread together. The needle and thread went into the cup and were sloshed around then lifted out.

"If you're ready, Mister Tyler," Elvira said briskly. Bowie lowered the rag from his cheek and concentrated on a spot on the ceiling while he tried to ignore the descending needle he could see with his peripheral vision. The first prick of the needle brought an involuntary twitch to his cheek. But that first pinprick was nothing compared to the burn when the needle penetrated the skin on the sides of the cut and the brandy-soaked thread was pulled through. Tears started from his eyes and he ground his teeth until his jaw creaked as Elvira pulled the edges of the cut together and tied the stitch.

"I'll not tie it so tight that the stitches will pull through," she told him as she snipped the thread with a small scissors and tied another knot in the end. "I know this is going to swell some more, and ye'll not be wantin' the stitches to rip out on their own."

"Uh, ma'am," Bowie said through grit teeth, "no offense, but would you mind sparing me the editorial comment and getting on with the stitching? I'd really like to be done with this."

"Of course," she said apologetically, "I truly am terribly sorry." A few minutes more were all it took for her to put in a few more small, neat stitches. She handed Bowie the bottle and he took several swallows right from the neck.

"Well now, that was entertaining," he said when he could breath again. Elvira took the bottle back from him and poured some on a rag then wiped the blood away from the stitches.

"Would ye like me to try to bandage that?" she asked.

"I don't think so," Bowie told her. "I don't see any way to do that so it won't interfere with my vision more than the swelling already has." He stood and reached for his hat and set it gingerly on his head. "Now if you'll excuse me, ma'am, I need to get some air. What do I owe you for your fine seamwork?"

"Nothing, Mister Tyler," Elvira told him. "It was enough payment seeing you give Raleigh Smithers the beating he so richly deserves."

"You know that lowdown backshooter?" he asked incredulously.

"He and my late husband were cousins, twice removed," she told him. "They were both from the same small town in the northeast, and I've spent more than one evening being regaled by Mister Smithers and his gruesome tales of derring-do, always with him as the hero, o' course. I've also heard the true stories of some of those same adventures. The man is the lowest of the low." With that pronouncement she picked up her medical equipment and went into the kitchen. "I still plan to be closin' at eight, Mister Tyler," she said over her shoulder.

Bowie looked after her for a moment then chuckled and turned toward the door. His next stop was his bedroll. He had a headache and swollen knuckles, and his cheek was throbbing. He'd be in a heckuva fix if Riker and his crew decided to show up in Borden City now.

When Gordon left the Cafe' he went down the street to the telegraph office. He didn't really expect an answer to the telegram he'd sent quite yet, but stranger things had been known to happen. At the very least, it would give him something to do besides sit around.

He stepped into the telegraph office and swung the door shut. The sound brought George Alcott, the telegrapher, from a back room with his coat half on. "Howdy again, Mister Gordon," George said cheerfully. "Got your answer right here. Came in a little bit ago but I had to wait for Marge to get back from the store so's I could come look for you." He held out an envelope.

"I guess my timing was just right then," Gordon said. He lifted the flap on the envelope and took out the message. The message on the page was short and to the point.

Riker released from prison July 31 Stop Last seen in company of Bronco Jarvis and John Smith Stop

Without realizing it, Gordon crumpled the message and the envelope into a wad in his hand. He stared through the man in front of him while his mind raced. He knew for sure now what he'd only had a feeling about before, that he'd been set up and suckered in. Abel Barnes had been a ringer, sent to Sycamore Springs to make sure the posse would keep following them no matter what happened.

Bitterly he realized that Barnes had probably been leaving signs for the posse to follow the whole time; otherwise how else could they have found the hideout in that blizzard? Only the fact that there'd been another exit from the cabin in the canyon, one that Barnes hadn't known about, had saved them. That and the wild ride they'd taken to escape- the ride that had killed Max.

"Are you alright, Mister Gordon?" George's voice cut through Gordon's thoughts and the big man shook himself like a dog after a dunking. Gordon looked at him and smiled but the smile looked pasted on.

"I'm fine, George," Gordon told him. "Thanks." He took a dollar from his pocket and flipped it to George then turned toward the door. As he strode down the street to he horse he realized that the last few miles to the ranch would be in the dark, but it wouldn't be the first time. He needed to think, and he needed to plan. There was no doubt in his mind that Riker was headed straight for him, carrying a grudge that was only in Riker's mind.

Riker and the others rode out at daybreak. They headed up Beaver Creek with their coat collars turned up and their breaths forming misty plumes in the frosty air in front of their faces. The only sounds were the jingle and creak of tack and the occasional sound of a horseshoe on stone. Riker led the way, with Bronco bringing up the rear, riding behind Abel to make sure the hill-billy didn't have a chance to cut and run. Abel had been grumbling under his breath constantly ever since they'd started riding, but Riker had plans that included Abel.

The three outlaws stayed with the creek all day. Late in the afternoon the trail turned into a side canyon and switch-backed out of the canyon and up the side of a steep ridge. On the far side of the next basin they could see a dark smudge and a few faint plumes of smoke. If they rode hard they could make it to the town some time after dark, and Abel turned his horse downhill and tapped it with his spurs, intent on getting to some place with a restaurant. He was getting tired of being the camp cook.

"Where you think you're goin', Abel?" Riker grated. "Nobody told you to move."

"I'm headin' for that town," Abel told him. "Somebody else's gonna cook supper tonight besides me."

"Not hardly," Riker said. "Ain't nobody goin' into that town tonight. We'll camp out down below here along the creek, an' Bronco here is gonna go on in the morning. I don't want anybody seein' three of us come in at once."

Abel glared at him. "What difference is it gonna make if we all ride in at once?" he wanted to know.

"If word that we're headin' this way's been passed as fast as I think it has, the law down there'll be lookin' for a group. They won't look twice at just one man ridin' in alone. Bronco can kind of get the lay of the land and find out where Morton's ranch is then we can all pay him a visit. Until then, we wait." He reined his horse back down the trail and the ready concealment of the willow brush there. "Come on, let's get a fire started and some coffee on. It's been a long day."

Bowie woke up in the loft of the livery just before sundown. His cheek was throbbing and his hands were stiff and sore. He sat up with a groan. "Damn, Tyler," he said out loud. "You must be getting old and slow."

"Uh huh," a voice agreed.

Bowie slowly and painfully turned his head. He could almost hear his neck creaking. Lonnie was sitting with his back against a post and Bowie's shotgun across his lap. From where the kid sat he could cover all the approaches to the loft. "What're you doing here?" Bowie asked him with surprise in his voice.

"Keepin' that bounty hunter off your sorry carcass while you were nappin'," Lonnie told him. "But I was beginnin' to wonder if I was gonna have to call the doc up here to see if you were still alive."

"Oh, I'm alive, alright. But this is one of those times when I almost wish I'd die so I'd feel better." Bowie chuckled then damped it down with a wince. "Damn, that hurts. What time is it?" He reached for his watch.

"It's gonna be dark before long," Lonnie said. "You feel like eatin' somethin'?"

"It's gonna take more than the likes of Raleigh Smithers to keep me from eating!" Bowie reached gingerly for his boots and pulled them on. He stood up carefully, and picked up his pistol belt with stiff and swollen fingers. He swung the belt around his waist and the motion sent pains through his body from his head to his toes. He put on his hat, carefully, and stood flexing his hands, trying to work some of the soreness out. "You gonna leave my shotgun here, or carry it around with you?"

"Oh, I reckon I'll leave it," Lonnie drawled as he stood. "That sucker's heavy." He leaned the Greener against the wall and brushed the hay from the seat of his britches. "Ready when you are."

Bowie gestured toward the ladder. "Lead on, MacGrable," he misquoted.

Lonnie looked at him quizzically then asked, "Did your momma have any normal children, or are they all as strange as you?" He went down the ladder and waited for Bowie to follow.

When Bowie's feet touched the ground, he said, "I'm an only child," and started for the door.

"Well thank the Lord for small favors," Lonnie quipped. Bowie gave him a disgusted look and they headed for the Cafe'.

~ 42 ~

Riker brooded in the shadows with his back against a tree. He had a blanket around his shoulders and a cup of coffee in his hand that he sipped slowly. He was getting close to Morton, he could feel it. All the time he'd been in Yuma prison, all he could think about was killing Bob Morton, preferably as slowly as possible; but quick and painful would suffice as long as Morton was dead at the end of it. And he'd spent the time in prison working out just what he was going to do to Morton if he got the chance.

It had been pure luck that Max Horner had been attacked by a puma, and been too torn up to go with Morton to Sycamore Springs. Max' injury had given Riker the opening he'd needed to get Abel Barnes hooked up with Morton. It was too bad the ignorant hillbilly hadn't been smart enough to figure out a way to stay where he'd been put. Finding the rustlers with a bunch of Morton's calves had been another stroke of luck. If he had only known that Bowie Tyler had found the rustlers as well, Riker might not have felt so lucky. And he might have been able to change what was to come.

The next morning Bronco Jarvis saddled his horse while Abel and Riker sat drinking coffee. "You know what you're gonna do, don't ya?" Riker asked him.

"Yeah, I know," Bronco snapped. He was getting tired of Riker's attitude. "Ride in easy, don't draw attention to myself, and nose around and find out where Morton's ranch is." He looked sullenly at Riker. "That about right?"

"An don't tip him off. Morton's got a nose like a wolf for findin' an' trippin' traps before he gets trapped himself. Just remember that." Riker glared at Bronco and got an insolent grin in return. Bronco stepped into the saddle and heeled his horse out onto the trail.

A couple of hours later he was walking his horse down the main street of Borden City with his hat brim pulled low. Bronco knew his face was on a few wanted posters here and there, but he didn't think they'd made it this far north. Most of his "activities" had taken place closer to the Mexican border. In fact, there were a number of counties in Texas he couldn't go back to even if he should happen to want to. *Ah well*, he thought to himself, *it's too hot and dry down there anyway. This northern country's a lot more comfortable.*

Bronco slouched in the saddle, looking at everything while seemingly looking at nothing in particular. Even so, he didn't notice the short chubby gent in the buckskin shirt who took a step out of the livery barn then slid back into the shadows at the sight of the wanted man. Bowie watched Bronco's nonchalant stroll ahorseback through the town, and his curiosity was aroused when the outlaw stopped in front of the Cafe' instead of the saloon like most men did when they first hit town. This was an interesting turn of events. "Or maybe he's just hungry," Bowie mused.

Bowie had seen some of those flyers with Bronco Jarvis' face printed on them. The last one, which had come in from a town in Arizona, had even been a pretty good likeness. Bowie waited in the shadowy barn until Bronco went inside the Cafe', then strolled casually along the street to a row of chairs lined up on the boardwalk under the windows of the building. He sat down, and tipped the chair back against the wall between two window boxes and settled in to wait.

"I hope that damn kid don't decide to wander down here about now," Bowie said under his breath. "Jarvis knows him." But Lonnie was nowhere in sight.

Across the street in the saloon, Lonnie Grable sat dealing solitaire and talking to one of the girls who worked upstairs. She wasn't much older than he was and she'd taken a shine to him. He'd never approached her about "business", preferring to sit and talk instead, mainly because he was scared to death to even approach the subject. His strict religious upbringing made him hard-pressed to get past the hellfire and brimstone he'd absorbed on the subject of women and other assorted evils as a youngster. He still wasn't sure how he'd ended up riding the owlhoot trail with Riker. It had just sort of seemed like the thing to do at the time.

Lonnie had seen Bronco rein up in front of the Cafe' and go inside, and he had no intentions of going across the street. Not only would Jarvis probably shoot him, just for the hell of it, but

Lonnie knew if he crossed up Bowie on this project he'd probably end up in worse shape than Raleigh Smithers had been in when he finally managed to ride out of town. So Lonnie sat and talked and shuffled the greasy deck of cards he'd picked up off the table, and watched Bowie sit yonder with his chair tilted back and his hatbrim tilted forward.

Bronco came out of the Cafe' almost an hour later, wiping his mustache with a finger and sporting a pleased look on his face. He strolled past the gent napping in the chair by the door, pulled his reins loose from the hitchrail, and stepped into the saddle. He turned his horse and pointed him back toward where Abel and Riker waited for him. The lady in the Cafe' had been more than happy to tell Mister Gordon's cousin how to find the ranch.

When Bronco had disappeared beyond the last buildings at the end of Main Street, Lonnie stacked the cards neatly and strolled to the batwings. He leaned on the top of the doors and looked over at Bowie, who let his chair tip down with a thump. Bowie pushed his hat back and looked over at Lonnie, yawning. Lonnie looked back at him and just shook his head. He couldn't for the life of him figure out how Bowie had managed to fall asleep in that chair, but it appeared to have happened.

Bowie crooked a finger at Lonnie, motioning him across the street. "See ya," Lonnie told the girl at the table. "The master calls." He grinned back over his shoulder at her then pushed through the swinging doors and out into the street. When he was close enough to Bowie for them to talk without raising their voices, he asked, "Are we gonna back trail Jarvis?"

"Nah, I don't think so," Bowie told him. "At least not until I talk to Elvira and find out what he wanted." Bowie stood and stretched and turned toward the door into the Cafe'. He opened it and stepped inside.

Elvira was bustling about the room, picking up dishes and pouring coffee for the half dozen or so patrons who had found time to sit around after their noon meal instead of work. She gave Bowie a brief smile and disappeared into the kitchen, reappearing a couple of minutes later with a piece of apple pie on a plate and a cup of coffee. She brought them both to where Bowie had dropped into a chair and set them on the table. She produced a fork from an apron pocket, sat down with a flip of her skirt and proceeded to start on the pie.

"And here I thought you brought that pie for me," Bowie said with a smile.

"I've not come to likin' ye enough yet to be waitin' on ye hand and foot," Elvira replied with a saucy grin. "And I probably never will. Besides, I'm hungry." She put the last forkful of pie in her mouth and sat back. Bowie looked at her across the table.

"That gent that was just in here, the one with the tied down gun and the mustache?" Elvira nodded that she knew who he meant. "What'd he want?"

"He said he was looking for his cousin, that nice Mister Gordon," she told him. "He wanted t' surprise him with a visit. He asked me not to be tellin' Mister Gordon if I saw him. He wanted his visit to be a surprise."

"Did you give him directions to Gordon's place?" Bowie asked cautiously.

"Why yes I did," Elvira told him. "Is something wrong?"

"No, no," Bowie told her hurriedly. "I was just wondering." He stood and ticked his finger against the brim of his hat. "I'll see you later."

As he was leaving, Elvira called after him, "Will ye be walkin' me home tonight, Mister Tyler?" She was oblivious to the looks of surprise thrown her way by those patrons who knew her reputation.

"Planning to, Miz Patterson," he said as he strolled outside.

Lonnie was waiting for him in the chair that Bowie had vacated. "Well? What'd she say?"

"Jarvis was looking for directions to Gordon's place," Bowie replied. "There must be some connection between Riker and..." His voice trailed off as an idea suddenly dawned in his brain.

"What?" Lonnie asked.

Bowie cursed softly. "Damn, I should have known."

"Known what, for Lord's sake?"

"That Gordon character is Bob Morton! He has to be!" He stood looking down at Lonnie. "I've been trying to figure out why Riker was headed here, and that's gotta be it."

"So what're you gonna do? Go and arrest him?"

"Not hardly," Bowie said thoughtfully. "I think I'll just let things be, and maybe I can get Riker and Morton both. It'd save me a whole lot of gallivanting around the country." He dropped into the chair beside Lonnie.

"So now what?"

"So now we wait and see."

Bronco rode into the outlaw camp a few hours after his visit to the Cafe'. The sun was slanting toward the timber-clad hills to the west. Riker stood up and walked to where Jarvis was unsaddling his horse. "Well, did you find him?" the big outlaw growled.

"Oh, I found him alright," Bronco replied. "He's got a place several miles on beyond the town. I got directions and everything. The problem," he paused as he uncinched the saddle, "is that Morton ain't alone out there. He's got a whole crew of hands that can fight as well as they can ride, an' most of 'em will ride a long ways to find a fight. Not to mention that he's good friends with the local law." He swung the saddle off the horse and led him to the stream. "You take on Morton, and you've got your work cut out for you."

"We'll just have to figure out a way to get him by himself," Riker told him. "Then we can take him down slow and hard."

Abel looked up from where he was sitting by the fire, leaning back against his saddle. "I might just know how ta do that," he drawled.

Riker turned to him. "And how might that be?" he asked skeptically.

"Write him a letter tellin' him one of those boys he had ridin' with him when we pulled that robbery is in trouble," Abel said with a smirk. "That'll bring him out."

Riker stared at him until Abel was beginning to think maybe he'd said something wrong. Then an unusual expression came over Riker's face for just a moment. If asked, Abel would have almost sworn it was a smile, but he couldn't be sure because the usual frown quickly replaced it. "Maybe you aren't such a dumb hillbilly after all," Riker told him. "The question is, how we gonna get a letter to him?"

"Abel can take it in and leave it at the stage station for him. They'd probly be tickled to death to get it to him," Bronco put in with a smirk. "You've been wanting to go to town, haven't you, Abel?"

Riker looked at Bronco, then at Abel. "You got anything to write a letter on, Abel?" Abel nodded nervously, and Riker said, "Then start scribblin'. You can write, can't ya?" Abel nodded again. "Good. You can deliver it tomorrow."

~ 43 ~

The storm began shortly after midnight as a few small snowflakes drifting unobtrusively down through the night. The moon peered fitfully through the slowly gathering clouds and caused the snowflakes to glitter weakly as they fell. The pale light was gradually snuffed out altogether as the falling snowflakes came down faster and heavier, forming a dense curtain of white as they fell. A wandering coyote, feeling the change in the air as the storm drifted down from the north, sniffed the wind for any sign of one last quick meal before he holed up to wait out the storm. When nothing came immediately to his nose, the coyote trotted into the woods toward his den in a nearby rockpile.

All around Borden City, animals stirred nervously in the night as they sensed the same change in the weather that had sent the coyote to his den. Even the human population of the town wasn't immune to the restlessness. In the loft of the livery barn, Bowie Tyler rolled over in his blankets and sat up and scrubbed a hand over his face, careful to avoid the stitches in his cheek. Through a gap between the logs of the barn wall he saw the last of the moonlight disappear, and felt a shiver run up his spine. He lay back down and pulled the blankets up around his shoulders, thankful that he wasn't sleeping on the ground somewhere.

In the ranchhouse on Swale Creek Don Gordon was watching the first flakes drifting down outside his window. He hadn't slept well since he'd gotten the telegram telling him Riker was out of prison, but he was also worried about the coming storm. He had feed put by for his cattle and there were several secluded valleys close by that held good grass that was rarely covered by snow. There was hay stacked in those valleys too, and he hoped it was enough. His instincts told him they were going to need all the help they could get before the storm finally blew itself out.

By the time the first weak daylight was filtering across the town, what had started as a few scattered snowflakes was now a full-out blue norther of the kind that rarely hit Borden City. The snow-laden wind squalled and howled around walls, rattled windows and gnawed at roof shakes. Here and there around the town smoke began to lift from chimneys as early risers stoked up their fires before scurrying back to bed to wait for their rooms to warm.

In the little house behind the picket fence, Elvira Patterson slipped her feet into fur-lined moccasins then pulled her heavy wool coat closed and buttoned it. She'd grown up in snow country and wasn't too worried about a few drifts. She wrapped a woolen scarf over her hair and under her chin. The trailing ends of the scarf went down into the front of her coat and she stepped out into the storm.

Elvira built a fire in the big cast iron range in the kitchen of the Cafe' then went out front to sweep the walk in front of the door free of snow. The way the snow was coming down it wouldn't stay clean for long, but it would let folks know that she was open even though it was Thanksgiving Day. She'd baked several pies the night before, and as soon as the oven was hot there'd be a wild turkey, wrapped in bacon, and a saddle of beef cooking. She'd been putting on a feed on Thanksgiving ever since she'd moved to Borden City several years ago, and a little snow wasn't going to keep her from it this year. If Thanksgiving Day was good enough for Mister Lincoln to make it official in 1863, it was good enough for her!

The bell over the door chimed while she was in the back room changing her shoes and hanging up her coat and scarf. She heard a chair scrape and heard voices; when she came from the kitchen she saw Bowie and Lonnie seated at a table. "The coffee won't be ready for a while," she told them. "I'm afraid I'm runnin' a wee bit late this mornin'." She bustled about the room, getting ready for the day. The married folk of the town would stay home, she was sure, but there were enough of the population of Borden City who were unattached to keep her busy.

By the time breakfast was over, the snowfall hadn't slowed in the least, though it had been over twelve hours since the first flakes had touched down and drifts had piled several feet deep throughout the town. Folks were staying indoors as much as possible, only venturing out and braving the howling wind and the sting of the snow long enough to do whatever chores needed doing, then scurrying back inside.

Bowie finished his breakfast and sat back in his chair with a belch and a sigh, totally stuffed. Elvira had gone all out this morning. It had been awhile since he'd eaten that well, although Red's wife back at the trading post had been a darn good cook. "I think I may have foundered myself," he said wryly to Lonnie, who was in the process of letting his belt out a couple of notches.

"I know the feeling," Lonnie groaned. "I haven't et that good since my momma passed away."

"Speaking of which, I never asked, but I just gotta know: what in the world you were doing riding with Riker?"

Lonnie picked up his coffee cup and stared into it for so long that Bowie started to wonder if he was going to answer. At last the young man sighed and said, still looking down into his cup, "It was kind of by accident, and kind of not. My ma passed away when I was fifteen, and my pa couldn't seem to get himself goin' afterwards." He took a sip of coffee. "I took to runnin' the country 'stead of workin' on the home place, though Lord knows Pa needed my help. I fell in with some ol' boys that were planning all kinds of outlaw stuff, and it was kind of exciting, you know, even though it was mostly all talk. We were all just kids wanting some adventure in our lives, I guess.

"So anyway, Bronco Jarvis came through, and he let it be known he was lookin' for somebody to kind of 'teach the ropes to', you might say. He was mighty impressive to a bunch of small town boys, like one of them outlaws in them penny dreadfuls you find around here and there. He had money he wasn't shy about sharin', and I didn't have any. Somehow or other he heard about me and the rest, and he offered to buy me a drink. Next thing I knew I had new clothes and a new gun and was headin' down the trail with him. We picked up Smith the day before Riker got out of prison; I already told you what happened after that, and here I am." He stopped and looked at Bowie and asked morosely, "What the hell am I doin' here?"

Bowie grinned at him. "Don't look at me," he retorted. "I told you to go to Laramie, remember?"

A hint of a smile crossed Lonnie's lips. "You did, didn't you?" Then with his smile broadening a little he said, "Since we're bein' so all-fired nosy, what about you? What's this 'only child' stuff?"

Now it was Bowie's turn to stare into his cup. He didn't know that he really wanted to go into it, because he wasn't too proud of most of it, but he finally decided that turnabout was fair play. He just wouldn't go into too much detail if he could help it. "I really don't remember much about my folks," he began. "They died of cholera when I was little, and folks have told me I was lucky I didn't die too. I got handed around between neighbors for a while, until I got tired of working from daylight 'til dark for people that only fed me so I could keep working. And pickin's were mighty slim more than once.

"I wanted more than that out of life, so I took up a different line of work, so to speak. Unfortunately, or, as it turned out, fortunately, the line of work I picked ended up with me standing in front of Judge Martin." He stopped when Lonnie burst out laughing. "What?"

When Lonnie settled down and could talk again, he took a slurp of coffee and said, "You're kidding, right?"

"Not hardly," Bowie answered gruffly.

"You got arrested? For what?"

"None of your damn business," Bowie growled. "Just suffice it to say that he offered me a job and I took it." He glared at Lonnie. "So you can stop cackling. You sound like you're about to lay an egg." He sat with his arms crossed waiting for Lonnie to subside. He quit laughing, at least out loud, until the look on Bowie's face, and the story itself, got to be too much, and he started to chuckle.

The more Lonnie laughed, and the more Bowie thought about the story he'd just told, the funnier it was to him, too. He started to laugh quietly in spite of himself.

The two of them were lounging back in their chairs, contentedly sipping Elvira's good coffee, when a silhouette crossed the Cafe' window. Lonnie sat bolt upright in his chair and stared out the window, trying to see through the blowing snow. "What bit you?" Bowie queried.

"I could swear that gent was riding Smith's horse!" Lonnie replied.

"What gent?"

"The one that just rode past the window."

Bowie looked at him. "Are you sure you aren't seeing things? I didn't see a rider."

"That's 'cause you were too busy watchin' Miz Patterson

pick up dishes," Lonnie told him. "I'm sure that was Smith's paint. I haven't seen too many horses around with that kind of color on 'em. But that sure wasn't Smith ridin' him." He stood up and started for the coat rack near the door. "I'm gonna go see who it was."

Now it was Bowie's turn to ask, "You're kidding, right?" His tone stopped Lonnie with his hand outstretched toward his coat and hat. "How do you know for sure it wasn't Smith? If it was ,you're dead, you know that, don't you?" He waited for Lonnie's nod then went on. "The idea was for us to see them and for them not to see you, remember?"

Lonnie's hand dropped and he went back to his chair. "Alright then, you go. Whoever it is don't know you."

"Have you seen the weather out there lately?" Bowie asked with a grimace. He got to his feet. "I know, I know, it's my job. I really hate it when work gets in the way of what's really important in life." He put on his hat and his sheepskin coat. "Keep the coffee hot," he called back over his shoulder as he went out the door.

~ 44 ~

Abel Barnes cursed and struck another match. He held the flickering flame to a small bundle of mostly dry grass and hoped for the best. He'd woke up shivering in wet blankets, and needed a fire in the worst way. At first he thought the match would be snuffed out by the flying snow, but then he saw a tiny tongue of flame creep along the grass stems. He blew gently and the flame brightened. Abel fed it some shreds of bark and the hungry flame devoured them and reached out for more. After what seemed like an eternity, the fire was crackling merrily in the gray-white morning and Abel stretched his hands to the blaze.

Abel looked around and saw Riker watching him from beneath the buffalo robe that covered the big man's bed. "We gonna go inta that town an' wait out this storm?" Abel asked. "I'm freezin'."

"No, we're not," wasn't exactly the answer he was looking for, but that was the answer he got. "So if you're that cold you'd better start buildin' some kinda shelter. You got a letter to deliver soon's you warm up," Riker told him.

"Deliver a letter? In this storm? You gotta be kiddin' me!"

"You were pretty hot to get it to Morton last night," Bronco cut in. "You know, the one that's supposed to get him away from that fightin' crew of his so we can kill him?"

"I ain't deliverin' no letter to Bob Morton!" Abel shot back. "He'll kill me if I show up on his doorstep."

"You don't hafta hand deliver it, you little weasel," Riker said disgustedly. He slid out of his bed and stamped into his boots. "You just take the letter to the stage station in that town yonder, an' I'm sure somebody in that town'll see that it gets delivered." He slung his gunbelt around his waist and picked up the axe from where it was stuck in the end of a log near the fire, then walked to a nearby thicket of lodgepole pine. It looked like he'd have to build a shelter himself. He was beginning to think that Abel Barnes had about outlived his usefulness.

Abel was grumbling to himself, which was nothing unusual for him. In fact, he'd been grumbling for the last five or ten godforsaken miles, or however far it was from the outlaw camp to town. He'd written the letter to Bob Morton, saying he was Jake Cutter's cousin and signing a fake name to it. The gist of the letter was that Jake was in trouble but he was too proud to call on his old friend, so the cousin was doing it in his stead, and could Bob come immediately. Then, just when he'd settled down by the fire in the lodgepole hut that Riker had built while Abel was writing the letter, Riker had given him a boot in the butt and told him to saddle a horse and go deliver it.

His own horse had come up lame the day before so he'd had to ride Smith's paint. The boneheaded brute had tried to kick him, then when he'd turned his back to pull up the cinch the rotten bugger had tried to take a chunk out of Abel's backside. Those huge yellow teeth had snapped closed about a half-inch from the seat of Abel's pants. And to make matters worse, when he'd gone to Riker to ask him about taking a different horse, Riker had just stared at him until Abel turned around and went back outside. So now Abel was grumbling. He was firmly convinced he was slowly freezing to death as he rode, although he had on two pairs of pants, two shirts, and a buffalo coat Smith had left behind when he went to his reward.

The paint was tired when he carried Abel down the main street of Borden City. It had been a long ten miles, and he was looking forward to a rest. Almost by instinct the horse turned toward the livery barn, only to have the man on his back yank his head around and boot him in the ribs toward the combination stage station and post office he barely made out through the blowing snow. Neither mount nor rider saw the snow-shrouded figure that followed them down the street.

Bowie watched the man on the flashy paint rein up in front of the stage station and tie his horse to the hitchrail. Both man and horse were streaked with snow and the man stamped ice from his boots on the boardwalk before pushing open the door. Through the window Bowie could see him hand something that looked like a letter to the clerk then turn back outside. Bowie ducked into a nearby alley, but not before he saw the crossdraw holster on the man's belt when his coat swung open for a moment. He'd already seen the stars on the man's boot tops that Cooner had told him about back in Sycamore Springs. This had to be the man who had shot the banker's wife. Now if he could just get all the men he had to arrest in one place, he'd be all set. He was pretty sure from what Lonnie said that Riker was going to do just that very thing for him, but he wasn't sure at the moment how he was going to take advantage of it.

Abel shut the stage station door and walked to the counter. A young fellow with a limp came from a door in the back of the room. "Ain't a fit day out for man or beast, I'd say," he told the snow-covered figure in front of him. "What can I do for ya?"

"Got a letter I need delivered ta a gent name of Don Gordon," Abel drawled. "The letter's from somewheres back east. Fella that give it to me said it was important."

"Why didn't he send it by the regular post?" the clerk asked.

"No idea," Abel replied. "All's I know is this gent give me five dollars to get it here, said it had ta be delivered as soon as possible, an' here I am." He handed the letter to the clerk, who had a puzzled look on his face.

Inwardly, Abel was cringing, waiting for the clerk to suggest that he deliver the letter himself, and as if on cue the man said, "Mister Gordon don't get to town very regular. You could take it to him. I can give you directions."

"I gotta git back yonder." Abel gestured vaguely to the south. "Otherwise I would. You'll just hafta find somebody. I gotta git." He turned toward the door, hoping the clerk would just let him go. He breathed a sigh of relief when the door closed behind him without the clerk calling him back.

Outside, the snow and wind hadn't let up a bit, and Abel wasn't exactly relishing the idea of bucking this weather back to camp; neither was the paint. Up the street he saw the welcome glow of light from the windows of the Cafe' and it drew him in. He brushed the accumulated snow from his saddle and swung up to ride the fifty yards back up the street to an alley alongside the Cafe'. He looked longingly at the hotel sign as he went by, but he knew Riker would kill him out of hand if he didn't show up back in camp when Riker thought he should. He stepped down in the alley and tied the horse at the side of the building where it was somewhat sheltered from the screaming wind. He'd have a cup of coffee and something to eat and get himself warmed up, then start back.

Bowie followed along behind the paint horse and watched as Abel unfeelingly left the horse out in the storm. It'd serve the man right if the horse died on him on the way back and he got lost in the snow and froze to death. Bowie had half a mind to arrest the man right now but it was pretty obvious that this character was the smallest fish in the pond. If Bowie wanted to catch the big fish, he'd have to let the little one go.

Bowie trotted down the alley to the back of the Cafe' and pushed open the back door. He stamped the snow from his boots and said jovially, "Dang, there's gotta be a seat in here that's warmer than that one out yonder!" He laughed and walked toward the coat rack and hung up his coat and hat, all the while watching the newcomer out of the corner of his eye. Lonnie was sitting to one side, but the man in the buffalo coat showed no sign of recognizing him. Bowie heaved an inaudible sigh of relief and strolled to Lonnie's table and sat down alongside of him, half facing the stranger.

Abel looked around when the short fat gent came through the back door. He was tense and on edge, knowing he shouldn't be here, but needing to warm up and get something to eat. It had been a long trip to town and his greatest hope now was that he could find his way back to camp.

When Bowie made his announcement to the room that the seats in the house out back were cold, Abel lost interest and turned away. He had his hands wrapped around the steaming cup of coffee Elvira had poured for him as soon as he came through the door, and he was slowly beginning to warm up. He ordered a meal and sat back to wait.

Bowie looked at Lonnie with one eyebrow raised and the young man shook his head the tiniest bit that no, this wasn't anybody he recognized. Bowie leaned over toward Lonnie and said in a low voice that didn't carry beyond the edge of their table in the noisy dining room, "The horse is mostly kind of a dark buckskin, with a white slash down his shoulder and a reddish patch on his rump." Lonnie nodded and Bowie sat back in his chair.

Abel gratefully accepted the second cup of coffee Elvira offered while he dug into his food. The plate in front of him was heaped with turkey, spuds, gravy and biscuits. A big piece of dried apple pie sat next to it on another plate. He was hungry, and it wasn't long until the pie was disappearing, too. At last he sat back with a stifled belch. He really wasn't looking forward to the trip back through the snow but he figured he'd best get at it. Now that he'd gotten warmed up, the longer he sat the sleepier he was getting. If he waited any longer he might not get moving at all.

He stood and took a dollar from his pocket, dropped it on the table, nodded to Elvira, and picked up his hat and the buffalo coat from the chair where he'd laid them. A small pool of melted snow had formed in the britches-polished seat of the chair but he ignored it and set his hat on his head, then shoved his arms into the coat. He buttoned up and headed out into the storm.

Behind Abel, Bowie and Lonnie waited until the door closed, then Lonnie asked, "I don't suppose you're gonna follow this one either, are ya?"

"What do I look like, an idiot?" Bowie shot back. "If I didn't follow Bronco Jarvis when the weather was good, why would I want to follow whoever this gent is in a blizzard?" He grinned at Lonnie. "Besides which, the poor sucker is likely as not to get lost on his way back to wherever he came from and freeze to death, which wouldn't bother me in the least. It'd give me one less outlaw to catch." He picked up his coffee, took a sip, and grimaced. "I thought I told you to keep the coffee hot."

Abel led the paint to a nearby water trough and broke enough ice for the horse to get a drink, then stepped into the saddle and booted the reluctant animal into the storm. Coming into town the snow had been blowing from his right front so he'd had to face into the stinging onslaught all the way in. Now, with his back mostly to the raging wind, he could at least breathe comfortably and the horse had a little help bucking the knee-deep snow and the even deeper drifts.

Hours later, the horse was stumbling with almost every step and Abel was walking and looking for a place to stop. The horse wasn't going to last much longer and neither was he, and with the swirling snow nothing looked familiar. He'd been too immersed in his miseries that morning to take note of his backtrail, so now he wasn't really quite sure where he was as he thrashed his way through another drift, dragging the exhausted paint by the reins behind him.

Abel stumbled and went to his knees, tumbling down a small bank. He heard a sound that wasn't part of the storm; it took him a few seconds to realize that the sound he was hearing was running water. He sat up and wiped caked snow from his face and looked around. He was sitting next to a creek and the sound he heard was water chuckling down through the rocky creek bed. The paint slid gratefully down the bank and lowered his nose to drink then jerked his head up, showering Abel with icy droplets. The horse drew in a breath and whinnied and was answered from beyond the brush on the far bank. Abel reached out a cold hand and got hold of the reins just in time to keep the paint on his side of the creek.

The half-frozen outlaw pulled himself to his feet and after two tries finally got his toe in the stirrup and managed to hoist himself into the saddle. As soon as his leg swung over the horse's back the paint stepped off into the cold water and splashed across the creek. An icy trail of horse tracks led up into the willow brush on the far side; they broke out into a small sheltered clearing where Abel's own horse greeted the paint with another whinny. Abel swung down and stood leaning against the side of the paint, glad to be out of the wind for the moment. He hoped he'd be able to feel his extremities at some time in the near future, but at the moment he wasn't holding out much hope.

"Where you been, Barnes?" The rough voice jerked Abel from his reverie. He spun and saw Riker standing behind him with a long scarf tied over his hat and under his chin to keep his hat on his head. He had a Winchester in his hands. "Unsaddle that horse and come and warm up." Abel just stared at him uncomprehendingly as if Riker had suddenly started speaking Chinese. Riker snorted in disgust. "Never mind, I'll take care of the horse. You best get inside before you're totally worthless." He pointed past the surrounding brush to a mound of snow with a blanket for a door and wisps of smoke drifting from the top.

Abel stumbled forward, pushed the blanket aside and stepped into the pine tree hut. Inside, a small fire crackled merrily. Bronco looked up at Abel from his seat across the fire, and said sarcastically, "Hurry up and get in here and shut the door. Can't you see it's blowin' a blizzard out?"

Abel let the blanket swing down behind him and practically threw himself on the fire, opening his coat and pulling off his gloves and thrusting his hands almost into the flames. "I w-w-was beginning to th-th-think I'd never git w-w-warm again," he stammered. “D-d-damn, that fire feels g-g-good.”

Riker came in and leaned his rifle against a branch near the doorway. “Your horse is unsaddled, Abel. Did ya git the letter delivered?”

“I left it with the clerk at the stage station, like you said,” Abel answered. “He’s gonna see that it gets delivered.” *I hope,* he thought to himself. *Otherwise I’d be better off to just shoot myself and save Riker the trouble.*

“Well, get yourself warmed up and fed. We can’t do anything about Morton until this storm blows itself out.” He pointed to the coffeepot and a pan full of beans that stood steaming gently at the far edge of the fire. Abel had been so engrossed in warming himself that he hadn’t even noticed them. Now that the food had been pointed out to him it wasn’t long until he was scooping beans into his mouth and washing them down with the strong black brew.

~ 45 ~

Daylight found Don Gordon and his foreman, Jeff Lane, pushing their horses through the storm to check on the cattle. Fortunately the forests surrounding the ranch gave the cow herd at least some shelter from the screaming wind, but the snow was already a couple of feet deep inside the tree line. Behind the pair, the rest of the crew had harnessed work teams to the two big sleds and headed for the stackyards to load feed for the hungry cattle.

In the main stackyard Sam Foley had unhitched his team and backed them to the derrick. The derrick served more than one purpose; in the summer it was used to stack hay, and in the winter it could be used to load the hay on the sleds, making it that much faster to get feed to the cattle. In short order the two sleds were loaded and headed for the big meadow. Sam was pretty sure that the mother cows would be kegged up on the lee side of the trees on the upwind side of the meadow, and that was where the men would spread the first of the hay.

Sure enough, when the two sleds broke out of the trees into the edge of the big meadow, the cows mobbed them. It was all the teams could do to press through the crowd until the first forkfuls of hay hit the ground. As the hay gradually strung out so did the cows, although there were always a few who followed along behind, nipping mouthfuls out from between the slats of the hayracks. Two more trips to the stack had the cows settled and happy in spite of the swirling snow. An hour later everything close to the ranch had been fed at least something, and Sam and the crew were waiting to see what the two bosses had found.

A couple of hours out from the ranch Don drew rein in the shelter of a clump of lodgepole pines. He and Jeff had seen several small bunches of cattle but all were in sheltered areas next to openings that had been kept swept clean of snow by the wind. Don brushed the snow from his coat and looked over at Jeff with a worried look on his face. Jeff spoke first. “It looks like we scattered ‘em about right this fall, boss,” the foreman told Don. “The only ones we’re gonna have to feed at the moment is that big bunch back of the house and the weaned calves, and Sam and the rest’ll have them fed before too long, if they aren’t done already. I think we’re gonna make it.”

“This time,” Don answered. “But if we have another storm like this one hay’s gonna be getting mighty short. We’ll have to move out into Bull Canyon if that happens. I wanted to save that feed as long as possible.”

“This country only gets about one big storm a year,” Jeff assured him. “Sure, it’s gonna snow some more, but we’ve been through it before and we’ll get through it this time, too.” Jeff had worked for Don for a long time and had in fact grown up in this country, so he felt like he knew what he was talking about. He had an almost infallible sense for weather and he was sure they didn’t have to worry. They might lose a few head but that always happened, whether to wolves or the weather; it was just a fact of life.

“I hope you’re right,” Don answered quietly. “What say we head back and find a hot stove to snuggle up to?” Without waiting for an answer he turned his big bay horse back toward the ranch. The snow swirled around them as they headed back down the wind toward the house.

Don and Jeff rode into the ranch yard. At the same time, there was a new arrival at the outlaw camp. “Hello, the camp!” The wind whipped Raleigh Smithers’ words away in a plume of foggy breath. He stepped down and drew breath to yell louder at the mound of snow that he was pretty sure was a lodgepole hut; his breath hissed out and he flinched when he felt cold steel pressed to the side of his head under his ear and heard the four clicks of a Colt pistol’s hammer drawing back.

“Hello yourself, bounty hunter,” a low voice said in the same ear. Raleigh forced himself to stand dead still. It had taken him two days to find what he was sure was Riker’s camp and he’d finally found it only when his horse had whinnied and been answered from deep in the willow brush along the creek. He knew that unless he played his cards right with the outlaws he was a dead man. He was sure that Riker and the others had seen him when he rabbited away from their camp when the teamster was killed, but he had an ace in the hole that he was pretty sure would keep him alive if he had a chance to play it.

Without turning his head he asked, "Is that you, Jarvis?"

"Maybe," the same low voice answered. "Are you gonna introduce yourself?"

"If you know I'm a bounty hunter, you already know who I am," Raleigh told him boldly; he was cringing inwardly at the same time, certain that his brains would be decorating the snow any minute.

"I reckon I might," Bronco told him. "And considering who you are, what's to keep me from killing you dead right here?"

Seeing as how he was still alive and Bronco was willing to talk, Raleigh figured maybe he had a chance. "Riker wouldn't like that," he said. "I know something he doesn't and it's something I think he'd pay to hear." The pistol barrel left his ear and he heard the sound of the hammer being lowered. He let out a breath he hadn't realized he was holding and turned toward Bronco. "Where's he at?"

"In yonder," Bronco pointed with the barrel of the Colt at the snow-covered hut. "Keep your hands where I can see 'em and let's go." Raleigh moved through the snow toward what looked like an entrance and pushed his way inside.

When the bounty hunter came through the blanket-covered doorway Riker rose up from where he'd been laying back on his saddle. "You!" he growled and reached for his gun. "I've been waitin' for you to show up."

Raleigh threw up his hands. "Now just a minute, Mister Riker," he said quickly. "I didn't come here to make trouble for you boys. I've got some information for you."

Riker looked him over carefully, noting the scabbed-over cuts on Raleigh's face from the fight with Bowie. "It better be good, or you're gonna be out there face up under a snow drift. So spit it out!"

Raleigh could see the cold face of Death glaring from behind Riker's eyes, so without preamble he said, "The law's waiting for you in Borden City."

Riker cursed as he got to his feet and grabbed a handful of Raleigh's coat. He pulled the bounty hunter towards him until their noses were only inches apart. "What do you mean, the law's waitin' for us? There ain't no law in Borden City, or at least there ain't no marshal's office. Bronco checked."

"There's a city marshal, but this law's from out of town," Raleigh told him through trembling lips. "This law's from Laramie."

"I told you to spit it out," Riker growled menacingly. He shook Raleigh like a terrier with a rat. "I don't wanna have to pry every word out of you. Now talk!"

The words came out in a rush. "The law's a short fat pain in my behind that Judge Martin sent out here to get you, and Bronco and Bob Morton."

Bronco interrupted. "Does this short, fat gent ride a black horse and pack a Starr revolver butt-forward?"

"Yes, he does," Raleigh answered. "Do you know him?"

"Know of him," Bronco said. "Your pain-in-the-backside deputy is Bowie Tyler." He looked at Riker. "That sucker's the one who took in Danny Galloway a year ago. Remember him?" Riker nodded. "I didn't think anybody could get Danny, but Tyler did. And if he's here, we've got problems." Bronco looked back at Raleigh. "Is he alone?"

"No, he's got some kid with him he picked up along the way. He's not a deputy or anything."

"So why are you tellin' us all this, bounty man?" Riker asked.

"Because I want to see Tyler go down, is why," Raleigh answered coolly.

Bronco chuckled. "Now I get it. He's the one who gave you those scabs on your face, ain't he?" Bronco burst out laughing when Raleigh's face began to redden. "He kicked your butt and you want to get even, but you're too yellow to do it yourself so you want us to help you. That's it, ain't it?" Raleigh didn't have to say a word, the answer was written across his face plain as day.

Riker let go of Raleigh's coat and sat back down. "Sit down, bounty man. I wanna hear more about this fat deputy that you're so scared of. What'd he do to you besides give you what looks to me like a pretty thorough whoopin'?"

Raleigh sat down and opened his coat so the heat of the fire could get inside and told Riker and the others all about the slights Bowie had dealt him, both real and imagined. He finished with, "I'll help you trap him, but I'm gonna kill him."

"From the sounds of things I don't think you can get it done, but we'll give you your chance," Riker told him. "Just make sure you don't run off an' leave us holdin' the bag like you done that fella that Bronco shot back yonder, or you won't be doin' any runnin' anymore. I'll hamstring you an' leave you for this Tyler to kill."

~ 46 ~

The storm finally blew itself out sometime in the middle of the second night. The sudden stillness woke Bowie from a sound sleep in the loft of the livery stable. He lay there for several minutes trying to figure out what had brought him out of a deep sleep and a pleasant dream, then it dawned on him that he could no longer hear the wind.

When the morning came, the sky was clear and the temperature was well below zero. The sunlight glittered on long icicles hanging from the eaves of the houses and on the crusted surface of the snow. The townsfolk were bundled up and hurried about their business, getting stoves stoked up and trying to bring some warmth into their rooms. Water buckets left near exterior walls had frozen over and sparkling hoarfrost covered many of the windows.

Bowie Tyler rolled out of his warm burrow in the hay and tugged on his boots. There were chills running through him and he shivered as he finished dressing and headed for the ladder to the ground. Bright white light from outside the barn struck into his eyes, making him squint as he made his way out into the cold.

Bowie was sitting at his usual table in the Cafe' when Lonnie came rushing in the door and slammed it behind him. "Damn, it's cold outside," the young man said as he dropped into a chair opposite Bowie.

"Ya think?" Bowie asked mildly. He pointedly ignored the glare Lonnie sent his way while he poured the boy a cup of coffee.

When Lonnie had the cup in his hands he looked through the steam at Bowie. "What are you planning on doing about Riker and them?" he asked. "Or are you still waitin' for them to ride into town and give themselves up?"

"Funny you should ask," Bowie told him. "I've been thinking that I might just ride out to Mister Gordon's ranch now that it's not snowing and see if he knows your old pal Riker."

"You're jokin', right?" Lonnie asked. "Even you ain't that crazy."

"What's crazy about it?" Bowie leaned toward Lonnie and spoke quietly. "He's never shot anybody yet that we know of, in spite of what the warrant says, and we both know that's wrong. And I think maybe paying him a visit might just stir things up a mite." He took a sip of coffee. "Elvira's cooking's good and her company's better, but I'm not getting paid to sit here on my butt, however nice that might be." He sat back with a grin. "What's the worst he can do? Throw me off the place? He does have a reputation as a solid citizen to uphold, ya know." Lonnie just looked at him over his coffee cup and shook his head.

After breakfast, Bowie went back to the livery and saddled Black. The horse wasn't especially impressed with the idea of leaving the relative warmth of the livery and humped his back when Bowie stepped aboard. He bogged his head and started to buck then gave it up as not worth the effort. He and Bowie had played that game before, and somehow, probably through some form of cheating that the horse had yet to figure out, Bowie had always come out ahead. Lonnie stood in the livery door and watched the proceedings with an expectant smile on his face. He sorely wanted to see the rotund deputy get his comeuppance from the horse but it wasn't to be. When the horse's head came back up where it belonged Bowie lifted the Greener from the scabbard under his leg, laid it over his arm, and pointed Black down the street.

Lonnie had offered to go along but Bowie had turned him down, telling him to "stay in town and keep a lookout for Riker and the rest. And stay out of sight if they do show up". The boy didn't know whether to be thankful, considering how cold it was, or indignant that Bowie didn't want him along. It wasn't that the boy wasn't good company; Bowie just kind of liked to play a lone hand. If you didn't have anybody to depend on you were less likely to look the wrong way when things went south, as they seemed to do much too often. A man who knows he's only got himself to get out of a hole with is more likely to go all out than a man who thinks he might have help.

As Bowie was passing the stage station the clerk came out with a blanket wrapped around his shoulders. "Hey mister," the man called. Bowie looked around at him and reined Black up. "You wouldn't be goin' towards Mister Gordon's place, would you?

I got a letter here for him. Fella that dropped it off said it was important." A hand clutching an envelope appeared outside of the blanket.

"As a matter of fact I am," Bowie told him. He was pretty sure this was the letter that the skinny galoot on the paint horse had brought to town during the blizzard, and he wouldn't mind getting a look at the contents. Unfortunately, he could see that it was sealed.

"Would you mind taking this to him?"

Bowie reined Black over next to the boardwalk and took the letter from the clerk. "Sure, no problem." Bowie tucked the letter into his coat pocket.

The clerk said, "Much obliged," and hurried back into the stage station and slammed the door without looking back. Bowie chuckled and pointed the black out of town.

It was definitely cold out. Bowie had a wool scarf wrapped around his face so that only his eyes showed under the pulled-down brim of his hat, and periodically he reached up a gloved hand and knocked the ice loose that had formed from his breath. His eyebrows and the horse's nostrils were rimed with frost and frost crystals hung in Black's mane. Bowie took his time, not wanting the horse to get so hot that he would be hurt by the cold when he stopped. And bucking the drifts that lay across the road to Gordon's ranch was hard on horseflesh.

By the time Bowie came in sight of the ranch yard hours later, the Greener had long since been returned to the scabbard and Black was beginning to stumble. Steam drifted from the sweaty hide in spite of Bowie's best efforts to spare the horse as much as possible. The sun was slanting down behind the ridge to the west of the ranch house and the cold, which had abated somewhat in the afternoon sunlight, had begun to return with a vengeance. Bowie's heartfelt prayer was that Gordon, or whoever the rancher turned out to be, was Samaritan enough to put him and his horse up for the night. He really didn't want to think about the possibility of having to ride that trail back in the dark on a tired horse, even if he had broken a trail through the snow on the way out.

Across the meadow, plumes of smoke lifted from several chimneys. A substantial log bunkhouse stood next to what appeared to be a smokehouse. Opposite the bunkhouse was a grainery, and a large barn with a wagon parked in a lean-to alongside it.

Two large sleds piled with hay stood side by side near the wagon shed. Corrals made up the side of a square that was bounded on the fourth side by a log house that appeared to have two stories. It wasn't often one saw a two-story log house, but there it was.

Yellow light gleamed in the windows of the bunkhouse and the main house. Bowie lifted Black into a walk across the square, figuring the bunkhouse was a good place to start, considering that the smell of cooking meat and boiling coffee was coming from that direction. He was almost to the stone stoop when someone spoke from behind his right shoulder. "That'll be far enough, mister."

Bowie lifted his hands to shoulder height and sat rigidly in his saddle without looking around. The door in front of him stayed closed. "I'm friendly," he said as calmly as he could.

"What man ain't, with a shotgun pointed at his back," the man said with a chuckle. "Who might you be, and what's yer business here?"

"Well, I might be Ulysses S. Grant, except he's taller and not so big around," Bowie said. "So I guess I ain't him." He waited for a response but the response wasn't what he wanted to hear. He cursed himself silently for being such a smart aleck when he heard the clicking sounds of shotgun hammers being drawn back. "Now let's not get hasty, friend," he said quickly. "My name's Tyler, and I've got a letter for your boss."

"It's alright, Jack," Don Gordon called from the porch of the main house. Bowie looked that way gratefully. "I don't know about the letter, but I do know his name's Tyler. I've seen him in town."

"You want I should take his guns, boss?" Jack asked as he let the hammers down on the shotgun.

"No, that's okay," Don told him. "I don't think Mister Tyler means any harm. And far be it from me to deprive a man of the means to defend himself if need be. You can go back inside. I'll be there shortly." Don looked at Bowie. "Put your horse in the barn, fork him some hay, and come to the house. There's sacking there to rub him down with while you're at it, and some corn in the bin." Gordon turned and went back inside and Bowie slumped in the saddle, letting out a deeply held breath. He heard a chuckle, again, as a tall man with what looked like a knife scar down his right cheek came around in front of Black.

"It's amazin' what a shotgun he cain't see can do for a man's posture, ain't it?" the man said to Bowie then strolled into the bunkhouse.

~ 47 ~

Bowie stepped down from his saddle and led his horse to the barn. A lantern hung just inside the door and gave enough light for him to find an empty stall and unsaddle the grateful animal. He slung his saddle over the rail at the side of the stall and led the horse to a nearby trough for a drink. The black eagerly pushed through the skim of ice to plunge his muzzle into the cold water. When the horse lifted his head, flinging water droplets across Bowie's face, the deputy led him back to the stall and rubbed him down with a piece of sacking. The manger was already full of hay. "I'd feed you some of that gent's corn but you'd probably think I was trying to poison you," Bowie told the horse affectionately. He poured a small measure into the manger anyway, and was totally ignored as the horse slicked it up then went to munching the sweet hay.

Bowie crossed the yard, stepped up on the wide log porch, and knocked on the door. "It's open," Gordon called from inside.

Bowie stepped in and closed the door behind him. Inside, the room was warm and homey, with solidly built furniture scattered across a floor dotted with rag rugs. Gordon himself sat in a hide-covered chair near the stone fireplace with his left index finger marking his place in the book on his lap. His right hand was out of sight from Bowie beyond the arm of the chair.

"Pull up a chair, Mister Tyler," Don told him. "You look a mite chilled."

"Thanks, I am," Bowie said as he sat down and opened his coat then stretched his hands toward the flames.

After a few moments Don said quietly, "I believe you said something about a letter, Mister Tyler." He was watching Bowie intently. When Bowie's hand went to his coat, Gordon tensed almost imperceptibly and his right arm moved slightly. He relaxed again when Bowie's hand came out holding just the smudged envelope. Noticing Bowie's glance at his right arm Gordon said,

"You'll have to excuse me, Mister Tyler. We've had some trouble with rustlers and we're all a little tense."

"Not at all, Mister Gordon," Bowie told him. "And please call me Bowie." He handed the envelope to Don, who laid his book down on the floor and tore open the envelope to read the message. As he read his face darkened into a frown.

"Bad news?" Bowie asked innocently.

Gordon glanced at him sharply then said, "Just another in a series of unfortunate circumstances that seem to be dogging me lately." He stared silently into the flames and seemed to forget that Bowie was there. The ringing of the cookhouse triangle calling the crew to supper startled him from his reverie. He got to his feet and said, "It's too late to start for town tonight, Bowie. You'd best spend the night here and head back in the morning. There's a spare bunk in the bunkhouse." He led the way to the door and across the yard to the cookhouse.

Inside the cookhouse the air was steamy and the smell of food made Bowie's stomach growl. Conversation ceased when Bowie and Don came through the door. "Boys, this is Bowie Tyler. He'll be spending the night with us." He sat down in the chair at the head of the table and reached for a platter of steaks. The crew made room for Bowie on one side of the long table and he set to eating with a will. It had been a long time since breakfast.

After supper Gordon went back to the house and Bowie sat with the crew and tried to learn more about their boss, but the crew wouldn't say much. It was soon obvious that the men were totally loyal to Gordon, and trying to pry too deep might just get Bowie tossed out into the snow on his butt. He really didn't want that to happen because he was pretty comfortable right where he was. All he was able to find out was that Gordon was a surveyor who went on several trips a year, and that he paid well.

It wasn't long until only Bowie and Jeff, the foreman, were still awake. The men started work early in the morning and consequently they went to bed early, too. The lamp on the table was turned low and the two sat sipping one last cup of coffee. "Have you been with him long?" Bowie asked quietly.

"Why?" came the equally quiet answer.

"Just natural born nosey, I guess," Bowie told him.

Jeff chuckled and said, "I've been working for Mister Gordon for about seven years. Been foreman for the last five or six."

"He must pay pretty good, eh?"

"Why, you lookin' for a job?"

"Not me," Bowie said quickly. "Punching cows is too much like work." He sat quietly for a minute or two then asked, seemingly as an afterthought, "Has he ever had anybody named Riker working for him?"

"Just who in hell are you, Tyler?" Jeff asked sharply. "You seem to have a point to all these questions other'n just idle curiosity."

Bowie was cussing himself mentally for pushing too hard. He already knew these men were suspicious, but Jeff had seemed to be a bit more open than the others. He held up his hands in a placating gesture. "Like I said, I'm just natural born nosey. I heard the name mentioned someplace, and the person doing the talking seemed to think there was a connection so I thought I'd ask. I didn't mean anything by it." He sat back in his chair and hoped the foreman would let it drop.

Jeff looked straight into Bowie's face. The look in Jeff's eyes was challenging; at the same time he seemed to be protecting someone or something. After several long moments of silence, he got to his feet without averting his gaze.

"Breakfast comes early around here, Tyler," he told the deputy. "You'd best be getting into your blankets. Good night." Jeff had his own room at one end of the bunkhouse and he turned toward it. At the door, he turned to look back at Bowie who sat trying to look as innocent as a newborn babe and not sure how well he was pulling it off. Then Jeff went into his room and shut the door.

"Tyler, you came close to wrecking the whole thing there," Bowie said under his breath. He went to the bunk he'd been given and crawled under the blankets but it took him a while to fall asleep.

A second door led outside from Jeff's room. When the sound of Bowie stirring around could no longer be heard from the bunkroom, Jeff slipped into his coat and went outside and up to the main house. He tapped on the door and Don called for him to come in. Jeff stepped inside and looked at Don.

"Boss, that Tyler's been askin' a lot of questions," he said.

"What kind of questions?"

"Questions like how much you pay, and what you do other

than ranch." He paused for a moment to consider what he wanted to say next then went on. "And he asked if anybody named Riker had ever worked here."

"What did you tell him?"

"I told him I was goin' to bed and left it at that, but there had to be a reason for him askin'." Jeff was the only one of the crew who knew Don Gordon was really Bob Morton. He'd known Morton's dad, and he knew Riker. It had been Jeff who had talked Bob into becoming Donald Gordon; he had also known about the ranch property, and he had helped get the ranch started. He hadn't been totally forthcoming with Bowie about how long he'd worked for Gordon. Both men were quiet, then an idea came suddenly to Jeff. "You don't suppose he's some sort of law, do you?"

"I don't know, Jeff, but I hope not," the big rancher replied, concern evident in his voice. "I hope not."

~ 48 ~

Artie Torges cracked his whip over the backs of the lead bulls in his team and shouted, "Come on, boys, look alive, it's only ten more miles." Artie had been freighting supplies into Borden City practically since the town was founded twenty years ago by Elias Borden. Artie had started with a couple of worn-out Conestogas and two teams of mules. He'd had to baby those wagons back and forth, and it had taken almost as much time at the end of each day to fix things that had come apart as it had actually moving freight. He still used the big Conestogas for most of his freighting, but the blizzard had changed his usual routine.

The big wagons were fine most of the time. Their wide wheels traversed muddy ground well, and he'd bred up a fine herd of good big mules to pull them. But deep snow made things difficult for the wide, heavy Conestogas, so he'd come up with something different for when winter came.

A couple of years before, Artie had taken some time off from freighting and traveled back to Missouri to visit his sister. While he was there, he'd had occasion to visit Springfield, where he'd seen a wagon that he was sure was just what he was looking for to use for winter freighting. The Springfield wagon, as it was called, was relatively new on the market and it was designed for rough country. The Springfields had tall wheels and a strongly built body and running gear. He'd ordered four of them on the spot.

The Springfields wouldn't haul as big a load as his Conestogas, but he'd decided that they looked like they'd get around through rough country better and should be easier to pull through deep snow. A friend back home had some oxen for sale and the big cattle were just what Artie thought he needed. He now had six of the Springfields and a herd of oxen to pull them with. Oxen were slower than mules but for "git right down and grunt" pulling he figured they couldn't be beat.

The whip cracked like a pistol shot over the heads of the

leaders again but the stolid cattle pretty much ignored the noise as they leaned into the yokes. They were used to Artie and his ways and knew their jobs as well as he did. They'd been over this route many times before.

As the echoes of the cracking whip died away Artie heard a horse whinny off in the distance, or at least he thought he did. He looked around but the snow was smooth and white as far as he could see, which wasn't very far on the north side of the road. They'd stop and water the teams at Beaver Creek, just up ahead, and he'd see if either of the drivers of the two wagons behind him had heard anything. There was always the chance that someone had been caught in the storm and would need help.

Riker heard the crack of the whip as a muffled snap through the snow that covered the outlaws' lodgepole "cabin". He reached out with his foot and nudged Abel in the ribs where he lay sleeping near the fire. Abel opened his eyes with a grunted, "What?" and glared over at Riker.

"I heard what sounded like a shot," Riker told him. "Go find out what it was."

"It was probly just a limb crackin' in the cold," Abel grumbled. "It was more than likely nothin'." He started to roll back up in his blankets.

Riker kicked him in the ribs again, harder this time. "I ain't askin' ya, you ignorant hillbilly," the big man snarled, "I'm tellin' ya. Go find out what's goin' on. Now."

Abel threw the blankets aside. "Oh, alright," he grumbled as he pulled on his boots. "But I'm tellin' you it ain't nothin'." He pulled on Smith's buffalo coat, picked up his rifle, and ducked out through the blanket-covered doorway.

He reappeared a few minutes later. "There's a bull train down yonder. It looks like they're headin' towards that town!" he exclaimed. "They're waterin' the bulls at the crick and it looks like they're buildin'a coffee fire. What're we gonna do?"

"We're gonna do nothin'," Riker told him. "They don't have the first foggiest idea we're here unless you let those bullwhackers see you. Soon's they've watered their stock and coffeed up, they'll move on." He looked suspiciously up at Abel. "You didn't let 'em see ya, did ya?"

"No, no, I stayed back in the trees," Abel said defensively.

"They couldna seen me."

"Then sit down, Abel," Bronco said. "You're gonna work yourself into a tizzy." Raleigh snickered and Abel glared at him before taking off his coat and dropping down on his blankets.

The teamsters unhitched the teams and led the oxen two at a time to water while Artie put together a small fire for coffee. When the teams had been watered and feedbags with a small ration of grain were hung on each of the animals' noses the men came to the fire and stretched their hands to the warmth. "Coffee's about ready, boys," Artie told them. "Soon's we coffee up we'll push on into town. We'll be sleepin' in real beds tonight."

The two men, brothers named Silas and Jeremiah, had been with Artie almost since the beginning. They grinned at each other. Artie always said the same thing when they stopped here.

"Either of you boys hear a horse back there a little ways?" Artie asked.

"No, but there was some gent in a buffalo coat watchin' us from back in the timber when we first started waterin' the bulls," Jeremiah said in his slow drawl. "He didn't think I seen him but he got a little too far out in the open." He paused and grinned. "First I thought maybe it was a bear, but most bears I seen don't wear a hat with a scarf tied over it."

"Why didn't you say something?" Artie demanded.

"I told Silas," came the slow answer, "but he didn't see nothin'. Then that feller went back in yonder." He pointed with his chin just in case the watcher was still there.

The three men were silent as they drank their coffee but there was always at least one of them nonchalantly facing the timber where Jeremiah had seen the man in the buffalo coat. They all kept their pistols uncovered, just in case. Theirs wouldn't be the first bull train that had been attacked and robbed, although that sort of thing was more likely to happen further south where the weather was better. Seemed like most outlaws didn't like working in the snow.

When there was no further sign of watchers the three finished their coffee, kicked snow over the fire, and hitched the teams back up. As he worked Artie worriedly kept an eye on the stand of timber to the north. A brief swirling of the breeze brought him just the faintest whiff of wood smoke, but wherever the man was camped it had to be back in the brush far enough that the smoke was invisible from where Artie was working. When the teams were hitched he climbed back up on the wagon seat and cracked his whip.

"Heeyah, you critters!" he yelled. "Let's git on up the trail!" The three wagons moved, creaking and jangling, across the creek and back onto the trail to Borden City.

~ 49 ~

The cook came into the bunkhouse with a battered old cast-iron skillet and a steel spoon in his hands and started banging on the skillet. “Roll outta them blankets you no-good sheep wranglers!” he bellowed. The voice that boomed out of the scrawny fellow in the flour sack apron was all out of proportion to his size. “Biscuits’re ready and the coffee’s boilin’ away.” He ducked back into the kitchen as a boot thudded against the wall by his head. He stuck his grizzled mug back around the corner long enough to shout, “Come and get it ‘fore I throw it to the hogs!” then he disappeared.

Bowie rolled over and sat up with a groan. Even the hay in the Borden City livery stable was easier to sleep on than the rope-sprung bunk he’d spent the night in. Somewhere along the line some of the ropes had apparently parted company with their fellows and had just been knotted together wherever they would reach. The straw tick had sagged in some rather unusual places and he’d found himself shifting position constantly just to keep from falling through the gaps.

Around the room the ranch hands were swinging their feet to the floor and reaching for their pants. Across the way Jackson, the shotgun wielding fellow from the night before, told Bowie, “You’d best get your britches and such on in a hurry, Tyler. Jonesy ain’t kiddin’ about throwin’ out the grub.” He tugged on a boot and said, “He’s mighty particular about his food getting cold.”

Never one to take the missing of a meal lying down, Bowie scrambled into his pants and boots and went into the dining area pulling his suspenders up as he went. He was greeted by the sight of a heaping platter of sliced ham sitting next to another equally large platter full of fried eggs. “Where in the world did you get cackleberries?” he asked Jonesy in astonishment.

“Outta the henhouse,” Jonesy boomed. He looked at Bowie as if the deputy was the village idiot.

"Silly me," Bowie told him sarcastically. "I didn't realize you had a henhouse, let alone hens. How do you keep them away from all the varmints?"

"There ain't many varmints left," the cook told him as the men began to meander in and sit down at the table. As Jonesy turned away and began pouring coffee Bowie hurried to a seat. He intended to get his fair share of the eggs. It had been awhile since he'd even seen one, let alone eaten any. Elvira was a good cook and all, but eggs were scarce in Borden City and she saved what she had for baking.

After breakfast was done Bowie stepped outside and headed for the barn to saddle his horse. As he entered the barn he saw that Gordon was already there, saddling a big bay horse. A gray packhorse, packs already loaded and securely lashed down, stood in the center alley of the barn waiting patiently.

"Good morning, Mister Tyler," Gordon said as he pulled the latigo up and snugged the cinch in place. "Nice day for a ride." The sun was just starting to stretch shadows across the ranch yard and the temperature was hovering near zero. Bowie grunted something unintelligible and went to where Black was stalled.

Bowie stepped up to his saddle, picked up his blankets, and swung them onto the horse's back. Black humped his back and shook the blankets off onto the floor reprovingly. "None of that this morning," Bowie told the horse as he bent to pick up the blankets, dodging a half-hearted swipe from a hind foot. "We're going back to town whether you want to or not."

"I think that horse likes it here, Tyler," Gordon told him.

"I reckon," Bowie replied. "He hasn't had corn for awhile." He swung the blankets back into place and held them with one hand while he reached for his saddle with the other. He let go of the blankets and quickly swung the saddle onto the horse's back before the black could shake them off again then reached for the cinch. "Looks like you're packed for a long trip," Bowie said nonchalantly. "Kind of a bad time to be traveling, isn't it?"

"A friend is in trouble," was all Gordon said as he led the bay out of the barn followed by the packhorse. Bowie hurried and got his saddle cinched then warmed the bit on the bridle between his hands while he led the black outside. He slipped the bit into the horse's mouth and the headstall over his ears then reached to tighten the cinch.

“Mind if I ride along with you as far as Borden City?” Bowie asked lightly. “Conversation always makes a trip seem shorter.”

“Suit yourself,” Gordon said and swung up on the bay. Bowie got into the saddle as the bay started into a ground-eating walk. Gordon lifted his hand to Jeff who had just come out of the bunkhouse with a cup of coffee in hand as the two men moved out of the ranch yard.

About the time Bowie Tyler and Don Gordon were leaving the ranch on Swale Creek Lonnie woke and lay for awhile with his hands behind his head. Last night the bull train had come in and the three teamsters had all talked about the man they’d seen watching them from the trees. From the description the man had to have been the one who had come into town during the blizzard. That could only mean that Riker and company were camped out where the teamsters had stopped for coffee. Lonnie guessed he’d better tell Bowie when the deputy got back into town. Maybe the news would light a fire under his chubby behind and he’d go take care of business. Lonnie was kind of tired of sitting in town and hiding out whenever somebody new rode in. It never occurred to him that he’d brought it on himself by tagging along with Bowie instead of riding to Laramie like Bowie had told him to do in the first place.

~ 50 ~

It was late afternoon and the sun was disappearing behind the western mountains when Bowie and Don rode into Borden City. Between the snow, and Don's pack horse slipping on the ice crossing a creek and crippling itself, the two men had been on the trail a lot longer than Bowie really cared to be. The cold had gotten deeper as the sun had moved toward the horizon, and Bowie was hunched into his fleece-lined coat so that only the end of his nose, which was red and coming close to paling into frostbite, and his eyes were visible between the collar of his coat and the pulled down brim of his hat.

Don had told him to go on, but Bowie couldn't bring himself to just ride off when the man might need some help with the packhorse. The small amount of time he'd spent with Don had brought him to a grudging respect for the man, and a feeling of kinship that Bowie couldn't seem to shake. No matter how much he tried to tell himself that the man was an outlaw and a fugitive, Don came across as a solid citizen who really wanted to make something out of this little corner of the world. When the time came, arresting him was going to take all the willpower Bowie possessed.

The two men pulled their horses up in front of the livery and stepped down to stretch the kinks out of their backs. Bowie looked at the packhorse standing with all his weight on three legs and the left hind foot barely resting on the packed snow. "I don't think that horse is going with you tomorrow, Mister Gordon," he said, stating the obvious. "He may not be going anywhere any time soon."

"I know," Don answered glumly. "I'll have to see if I can find another one. The problem is that this time of year most folks don't have anything they'll let go of. At least not anything worth buying." He led his horses into the barn and began unsaddling. Hank the hostler came out of his room in the corner of the barn.

"Dang, Mister Gordon, what happened to him?"

"Aw, this fool critter slipped crossing Camp Creek on the way into town and crippled himself. And I need him tomorrow." Don turned to Hank. "You don't know anybody who's got a good packhorse they'll part with, do you Hank?"

The grizzled fellow stood scratching his chin thoughtfully for a moment then looked up. "Why, I do believe I do," he said cheerfully. "But it'll come dear. You know Oscar Raines, out yonder past Mahogany Springs?" Don nodded. "He was in here just last week, sayin' he had a couple of horses he'd part with. But you know him, he's gonna wanna pinch you for all he can."

Don nodded. "Well, I'm kind of between a rock and a hard place here," he said. "I guess I'll just have to pay what the man wants so I can get on. Thanks." He led the horses into a stall and put up the poles behind them, then stacked his gear in a corner where it would be handy. "It's too late to ride out there tonight; I'll go in the morning." He lifted a hand to Bowie and Hank and left the barn.

"Has anybody new come into town since I've been gone, Hank?" Bowie asked casually.

"Nope, just Artie Torges and his bull whackers," Hank told him. "And they ain't exactly new, they come in purty regular, bringin' in freight an' such."

"Which way did they come in from?"

"They come in from the east," Hank told him. "That's the only way into here with a wagon."

"Did they say anything about seeing anybody camped anywhere?" Bowie asked, hoping he wasn't pushing Hank hard enough to make him wonder why Bowie was asking. But Hank was oblivious.

"Artie an' his boys said they seen a fella back in the brush out where the trail crosses Beaver Crick," Hank said. "They thought maybe they was gonna get robbed or somethin', but he just stood there an' watched 'em water the bulls and make coffee. Artie reckoned he figgered he was hid. He was wearin' a buffalo coat, and the boys thought he was a bear at first 'til they seen he was wearin' a hat." Hank chortled to himself at the image the words conjured up.

"Thanks, Hank. See you later." Bowie stepped out of the livery and turned toward the Cafe'. Down the street he could see Lonnie standing on the boardwalk out front, looking impatiently at Bowie, so naturally Bowie slowed his steps and sauntered nonchalantly down the street. "You look like a man on a mission," Bowie told him when he reached the place where the young man was standing.

"Where have you been?" Lonnie asked abruptly.

"Why I'm fine, how about yourself?" Bowie asked somewhat sarcastically.

"Very funny," Lonnie told him.

"What exactly is your problem?" Bowie asked Lonnie.

"Riker and the others are camped out on Beaver Creek," the boy said.

"I know," came the quiet answer. "Hank told me some bull whackers saw a man that sounds like the gent who was here riding Smith's horse during the blizzard."

"So when are we goin' after them?" Lonnie demanded.

"We," Bowie said emphatically, "aren't ever going after them." Lonnie started to answer and Bowie cut him off. "I'm going out there tomorrow morning, and you're staying here. This is my job and I don't need to be worrying about you while I'm doing it."

"What do you mean, worrying about me?" Lonnie snorted. "I can take care of myself just fine. And besides, I know Riker and you don't."

"All the more reason for you to stay here and stay alive," Bowie replied. "From what you've told me that's a bad man out there, and he's gonna kill you dead if he sees you anywhere in the country. And believe you me, if you go to wandering around out yonder in the snow, he'll see you. Men like that don't live long without knowing what's going on around them. So you're not going, and that's final." He turned and went into the Cafe', leaving Lonnie standing on the boardwalk with his mouth opening and closing like a trout tossed up on the bank.

~ 51 ~

"Stand still, horse, you'll wake those gents up." The quiet words drifted softly up into the loft of the livery in the pre-dawn cold. Gordon reached for his tack and slung the cold blankets onto the horse's back, followed quickly by the saddle. A stirrup thumped against one of the loft supports and Gordon swore under his breath.

Bowie rolled out of his blankets and into his coat. The white plume of his breath hung in front of his face like a misty shroud in the frosty air. Bowie slipped quietly over to the edge of the loft in his sock feet and knelt to look down. It appeared that Mister Gordon was getting an early start toward finding a packhorse to replace the lame one. As Bowie watched, the big man cinched up the saddle and with a creak of cold leather swung his leg over the stout bay's back. Without looking up he rode from the barn.

Bowie hurried back to his blankets and dove into them. As cold as it was, Riker and company probably weren't going anywhere very soon so he might as well sleep a little longer if he could. He figured on getting some breakfast and maybe a sack lunch of some sort before he headed off into the frozen wilderness east of town.

Lonnie watched from under the tarpaulin that covered his own blankets as Bowie crawled back into his bed. He was determined that Bowie wasn't leaving without him.

When Gordon rode back into town some two hours later and went to the livery to pick up his gear, he saw that the black horse was gone from his stall. He didn't realize that there was a sorrel missing as well. He loaded his new packhorse and headed east, following the tracks of the bull train. And two sets of horse tracks.

Bowie took his time riding towards Beaver Creek. The cold was hard on men and horses alike and the snow was deep; the slowly building clouds indicated that more snow was on the way. He surely didn't want to wear his horse out with a storm coming. He stayed with the wagon tracks as best he could, but where the oxen had churned up the snow it had frozen into a crusted mass pocked with the tracks of the cattle. Consequently, he spent his time picking his way from one relatively shallow spot to another between drifts.

It was well past noon when he came up to the line of trees and brush that marked the bed of Beaver Creek. He'd gotten directions from one of the teamsters, Silas Something-or-other, and he stopped Black in the dubious shelter of a clump of small lodgepole pines to consider the situation. He'd taken the wagon road that wound around the end of the ridge that sheltered Riker's camp, so he'd missed seeing where the outlaw's horses were corralled.

Up ahead, the wagon tracks curved around a knoll and started to dip toward the creek. To his left had to be the area where Artie and his bullwhackers had seen the man in the buffalo coat. Bowie looked all around, his blue eyes probing into every shadow looking for some sign of the outlaws. He was about to push Black out into the open when he heard a horse nicker. The sound was faint and had drifted to him on the breeze; it seemed to be coming from somewhere up the creekbed. Bowie stared that way until his eyes began to water, but he couldn't for the life of him see a horse anywhere. Then he smelled smoke.

Raleigh Smithers hurried up to the outlaws' lodegpole shelter and pushed aside the blanket covering the doorway. He stuck his head inside and hissed, "He's here!"

"Who's here?" Riker asked.

"That deputy! Tyler! He's just across the creek!"

Riker, Bronco, and Abel all jumped to their feet. "Whadda you mean, he's just across the crick?" Riker demanded. "I thought you were on watch."

"I was, but he must have come in on the other side of the trees. I looked across that meadow down below, and there he was sitting in the middle of that clump of little trees on the far side, just watching." Raleigh took a breath to go on but Bronco interrupted.

"Why the hell didn't you just shoot him then?" Raleigh at least had the grace to appear startled at the thought, although

Bowie wouldn't have been the first man he'd drygulched.

"It's too far over there, and all I had was a pistol," he said. "And besides, Riker said..."

"I know what I said," Riker told him as he swung his gunbelt around his waist. "So let's go take care of him." Riker picked up Smith's big Winchester and went through the blanket door and out into the frigid afternoon, followed in succession by Raleigh, Bronco, and Abel. Riker began snapping orders as he handed the rifle to Bronco.

"You go up yonder," he pointed up the creek, "And when you hear a hawk whistle, shoot his horse. Bounty man, you go down where the brush thins out and let him see you. Then when Bronco shoots his horse you'll have this deputy dead to rights. But just remember what I said about runnin' out on us."

"Where do you want me to go, Riker?" Abel asked.

"You stay with me, hillbilly, until we see how this shakes out." He looked at the other two men. "Go, dammit. We don't want that deputy ridin' right into our laps before you're ready, do we?"

Bronco took the rifle from Riker and moved off into the brush. Raleigh started forward but Riker held him back for a count of ten then gave him a shove. Raleigh slipped through the willows until he could see Bowie where he still sat Black on the far side of the meadow. Raleigh slipped off his heavy coat and flexed his gunhand, then stepped forward far enough for Bowie to see him if he was really looking. Almost immediately Bowie's head turned and he booted Black forward.

"I should've known you'd turn outlaw, Raleigh," Bowie said harshly. His voice carried easily through the calm that had settled over the meadow. "Where's the rest of them?"

"The rest of who?" Raleigh retorted as he stepped out into the open. "I don't need any help to take you." Raleigh slipped off his glove and his hand poised over the butt of his holstered pistol. Bowie kept Black moving forward, sure that the bounty hunter would turn and disappear back into the brush. A hawk whistled somewhere, and he checked his horse. It came as a shock when a rifle blasted from his left and Black went down in a welter of flailing hooves.

As Black went down and red blood sprayed across the white surface of the snow, Bowie yanked the Greener from the scabbard and flung himself clear. He was cursing himself for letting his guard down. He'd wanted Raleigh so bad he'd disregarded the other outlaws. He thumbed back the hammers of the shotgun as he scrambled for cover behind the thrashing horse. Pistol shots boomed out from where Raleigh had been standing and a bullet caromed off the horn of the saddle, throwing bits of leather and lead in Bowie's face.

Bowie blinked his eyes clear and turned the shotgun across his saddle and let go with both barrels in Raleigh's direction. The still weakly thrashing horse jarred Bowie's arm and spoiled the shot so that only the edge of the spray of buckshot hit the bounty hunter but it was enough to knock him sideways. Raleigh dropped the pistol he'd been trying to reload into the snow and lunged for the cover of the brush with his left arm hanging limp at his side.

The rifle blasted again from upstream as Bowie tried to burrow into the snow. The bullet slashed through his heavy coat and laid a hot lash across his shoulder as he tried to flatten himself behind the now unmoving carcass of the black. Bowie knew it was only a matter of time until the shooter managed to maneuver far enough around to plant a slug some place vital. As much as he hated the thought of leaving the dubious shelter of the dead horse, he was going to have to move.

Raleigh threw himself through the brush back toward the camp, thrashing his way through the willows. Sharp-pointed twigs and icy cold branches tore at his face and clothes as he went in a shambling trot through the snow. His arm where the pellets had slammed into him was throbbing and blood dripped steadily from his fingertips. To his left he could hear an occasional shot as Bronco kept the deputy pinned behind the dead horse.

Raleigh suddenly crashed to a halt against the trunk of a big pine tree. When he rebounded and looked up Riker was standing there in front of him. "Where you headed, bounty man?" the big outlaw asked, sneering. "You got a deputy to kill, remember?"

"I'm shot!" Raleigh gasped, reaching across to his bleeding arm. "And I dropped my pistol. As soon as I get to camp and get another gun..."

Riker pulled a Colt from behind his belt and extended it toward Raleigh, butt-first. "I just happen to have a spare with me," Riker told him with a grim smile. After a moment his smile faded and he said, "You still got one good arm. Now git back there and finish that lawman. You brought him out here, you take care of him."

Raleigh stared resentfully at him for a moment, then reached out to take the proffered weapon. Abel snickered from where he stood beside Riker, and Raleigh glared at him until the snicker died in his throat. Raleigh tucked his bleeding hand in the waistband of his pants to support his arm and looked once more at Riker, who stood without moving, waiting for Raleigh to go back toward the meadow. Raleigh turned resignedly and stumbled back the way he came.

~ 52 ~

Bowie reached up and untied the leather strings holding his saddlebags to his saddle and rolled them down to him. He reached in and got a cloth bag full of shotgun shells, reloaded the Greener, and stuck the rest of the shells in his coat pocket. He cautiously stuck his head up and looked around to see what might be the best way to go. Another shot blasted through the frosty air and the carcass in front of him quivered with the impact of the bullet. It looked like his best bet was to move toward the horse's tail then lunge up and head for the creekbed near where Raleigh had been standing when he first saw him. He tightened the chin strap on his hat, took a firm grip on the Greener, then rolled to his feet and ran as hard as he could through the calf-deep snow toward the cover of the willows.

A relatively quick slog was the best Bowie could manage in the snow, and as he went he felt like he had a bullseye painted on his back. The skin across his back was tight in anticipation of the impact of the next rifle bullet but he made it to the cover of the willows unscathed. He stopped in their shelter and tried to catch his breath and quiet the pounding of blood in his ears enough to maybe be able to hear someone sneaking up on him. But between the ringing in his ears from the gunshots and the beating of his pulse, he was pretty sure he'd be hard pressed to hear a brass band parading through, let alone stealthy footsteps in the frozen snow.

Ironically, it was the squeak of a footstep on frozen snow that saved Bowie's life. The sound came from behind him and he threw himself sideways to the snow. A pistol roared and the bullet cut twigs where his head had been just moments before. He rolled toward a nearby blowdown and almost made it before the second bullet tore into his calf and sent a bolt of pure agony up his leg. Involuntarily his leg jerked and he rolled on his back in time to see Raleigh standing there, swaying, with blood dripping steadily down the front of his pants from the buckshot wounds in his arm.

The wounded bounty hunter thumbed back the hammer of the pistol. "You won't be in the way anymore, Tyler!" he grated.

"The way you're shaking you'll be lucky to hit the ground," Bowie snapped. The pain in his leg had his jaw clenched and he was sweating, but he knew he had one chance. His pistol was pressed into the snow under his right hip but the Greener lay at his side and his thumb was across the hammers. If he could keep Raleigh talking for long enough, or distract him somehow, he might be able to get the shotgun into action.

"We've been in each other's way," Bowie said as best he could through the throbbing in his calf. He could feel blood running down into his boot. He looked past Raleigh and spoke as calmly as he could through gritted teeth. "You must be Riker," he said suddenly, and made his play.

Before he could stop himself, Raleigh started to glance around. The muzzle of the pistol swung just enough away from Bowie, who yanked the Greener up out of the snow with his right hand, praying that the barrels weren't plugged with snow and that the gun wasn't going to blow up and kill him if he had to shoot. His left hand streaked to the fore end and his right thumb snapped the hammers back. By the time Raleigh realized he'd been had he was staring into the twin maws of the short-barreled shotgun from a distance of roughly fifteen feet.

"Drop it, Raleigh!" Bowie snapped at the stunned bounty hunter. "You might miss but I damn well won't." The two men stared at each other, and for the briefest moment Bowie was sure that Raleigh was going to do what he'd been told. Then desperation flickered in Raleigh's eyes and his finger tightened on the trigger.

The silence around Bowie was deafening. When Bowie had disappeared into the brush, Bronco had quit trying to make mincemeat of the black horse with his rifle and stopped shooting so he could reload. The only sound was the chuckling of the creek over the rocks and the slightest of breezes whispering through the willows.

Bowie watched the knuckles of Raleigh's trigger finger whiten and said, "It doesn't have to be this way," but in the tension of the moment he felt like he could see the trigger moving.

"Ah hell," Bowie muttered to himself, and squeezed the triggers of the Greener.

Bowie's ears were ringing something fierce now, and his hand was throbbing in time with the ache in his calf as he untied the bandanna from around his neck and knotted it as tightly as he could around his leg. He didn't try to take off his boot, he just pulled the cloth deep into the split in the leather and hoped for the best.

He flexed his right hand, hoping that it wasn't broken. He'd never fired the Greener from that position before, and his hand had taken most of the recoil. He grimaced as he climbed to his feet using the shotgun as a cane. He looked at the sprawled remains of the one-time bounty hunter he'd just pulled those triggers on. "One thing about a shotgun at fifteen feet," he told what was left of Raleigh Smithers as he cracked the Greener open and reloaded, balancing on one leg, "It'll ruin a fella's day." He tried to take a step and nearly fell. He cursed again. "So does getting shot."

~ 53 ~

Lonnie booted his sorrel into a run when he heard the first shots. As his horse labored through the snow, he yanked his rifle from the scabbard and levered a round into the chamber. He'd swung wide through the timber to come in from the north, wanting to cover Bowie without Bowie knowing he was there, but he'd miscalculated how much time it would take him. "Dammit, dammit, dammit," he growled over and over under his breath. Instead of having his chance to be a hero, he'd be lucky to help pick up the pieces.

The sorrel horse burst out into the open next to Riker's lodgepole hut. It was the last thing Lonnie expected to see and he checked up the horse while he looked rapidly around the small open area for the outlaws. He was about to boot the horse back into a trot when he felt hands on his coat and found himself flying through the air. The rifle flew free to land muzzle-down in the snow at the edge of the creek. The world spun crazily around him and he crashed down on his back in front of the hut with the air slammed from his lungs. A sharp knee came down on his stomach and forced what little air remained in him out with a sharp grunt.

Lonnie was sure he was dying. He couldn't breathe and his vision was blurred as bright streaks of light flashed in his brain. He fought for breath while someone yanked the pistol from his holster and was finally rewarded by the flow of air when the owner of the knee that had come down on his belly relaxed enough for Lonnie's lungs to start working. Then he felt the muzzle of a pistol come to rest on his upper lip just under his nose.

"Boy, who are you, an' what the hell are you doin' bargin' in where you ain't wanted?" a nasal voice asked. Lonnie finally managed to focus his eyes enough to see that the man who knelt in the middle of him was the same man who had come into Borden City astride Smith's paint horse.

"His name's Lonnie, and he rode with me and Bronco and

Smith for a while," Riker said roughly as he came around the hut. "Didn't you, Lonnie?" Lonnie nodded, carefully, not wanting the pistol to go off. "Remember what I told you when you left us, boy?" Riker snapped menacingly. Lonnie nodded again and swallowed convulsively. "Well, so do I. You brought the law down on us, and now..." Riker reached behind his back and drew a skinning knife from a sheath on his belt. The late afternoon sunlight glinted along the edge of the well-honed blade.

The double-barreled bark of the Greener and the crack of Raleigh's pistol after several minutes of relative silence startled Abel. For just a fraction of time, he relaxed and looked away from Lonnie but a fraction was all the boy needed. Lonnie whipped his hand up and yanked the Colt out of Abel's hand by the barrel, nearly breaking Abel's finger. He was fortunate the pistol hadn't been cocked or he would probably have left his brains in the snow. Instead, he rolled to his hands and knees and scrambled behind the lodgepole shelter. There was a muffled thud and Riker's skinning knife stood quivering in the bark of a tree just above his head as he dove headlong into the brush and began forcing his way through the tangled undergrowth in a mad rush to get away.

Lonnie found a narrow game trail and wormed his way deeper into the willows. He stopped to listen for pursuit but all he could hear over the sound of his breath whistling in and out of his chest was Riker bellowing, "Get that sprout! I'll gut him and hand him his heart!" His breathing began to settle and he waited for the sound of breaking brush but no sound reached his ears.

Lonnie pushed his way into the middle of a hawthorn thicket, then sat down and blew the snow out of the action of the pistol he'd taken from Abel. It didn't look like the shells had gotten too wet, but he shucked them from the cylinder and reloaded the gun from his own belt, which had been under his coat when he was laying in the snow. Satisfied that he had a functional weapon, he crawled out of the thicket and began to work his way in a circle toward the source of the Greener's deep roar.

Lonnie crept along the game trail, working his way toward the creek and trying to see in all directions at once. His toe bumped something hard in the snow and he looked down to see what it was. He heard a chuckle and looked up. "Well, well, what have we here?" Bronco asked the willows around where he stood just off the trail.

Lonnie stared at him, thinking, *what else can go wrong?*

"Boy, you shouldna come back, and you damn sure shouldna brought the law with you," Bronco said, shaking his head. He held the rifle pointed in the vicinity of Lonnie's belt buckle. "And after all we done for you." Bronco laughed, but there was little humor in it, and the muzzle of the rifle never wavered. "Now what say you turn around and march on down yonder to where Riker's doing all the hollerin', and we'll see what we can do about that lawman. Then we'll settle with you." He motioned with the barrel of the gun for Lonnie to turn around.

In his misery Lonnie had momentarily forgotten about the pistol in his hand until he started to move. It hung down in his hand beside his leg, out of Bronco's line of sight. He eased the hammer back as silently as he could, covering what sound there was with what he hoped sounded like false bravado when he said, "Hey Bronco, remember what I told Smith that time you boys shot up that posse?"

"About shooting him?" Bronco asked. At Lonnie's nod, he said, "Yeah, I remember. Why?"

Lonnie whipped up the pistol and yanked the trigger. The pistol blasted and the bullet slammed into the action of the rifle, tearing metal and taking Bronco's trigger finger with it. Before the outlaw could react Lonnie had the hammer back and his second shot tore into Bronco's chest and he dropped the rifle into the snow. Bronco stared, unable to believe how quickly the worm, so to speak, had turned; a trickle of blood slowly started down his chin.

"Damn, kid, you shot me," he said. He tried to draw his pistol but his knees gave way and he slid slowly down the trunk of the tree he'd been leaning against then fell face down in the snow.

"That's why," Lonnie told him as he shucked the empties from the pistol and reloaded.

~ 54 ~

Don Gordon rode deep in thought, trying to work out some plan for the future. First he'd go and do what he could for Jake, who'd somehow gotten crossways of the law where he was living, then he'd come back and do something about Bowie. He had to find out if the man was the law, as he more than half suspected. If that turned out to be the case he'd have to figure out how to keep from being hauled in. The boom of the rifle shot that killed Bowie's horse jarred him out of his reverie as it racketed through the still air and echoed from the hills nearby.

Gordon stopped his bay horse to listen. He was about to heel the horse back into motion again when the snap of pistol shots and the coughing blasts of Bowie's Greener rolled through the timber. He recognized the sound for what it was and quickly tied the packhorse in the middle of a sheltering thicket hopefully out of harm's way. He drew his rifle from the scabbard then kicked the bay forward and went toward what was beginning to sound like a full-fledged war.

Gordon stopped the bay back in the brush at the edge of the meadow. The black horse lay sprawled in a pool of red-crusted snow at the far edge of the open expanse and at first Gordon could see no sign of Bowie. A few magpies were starting to flutter down towards the carcass already, drawn by the prospect of a feast.

Gordon took his field glasses from his saddlebag and scanned the area around the horse. He could see what looked like footprints leading toward the creek so he concentrated his efforts in that direction. Bronco had stopped shooting and the only sound was the squawk of the magpies already gathering to fight over the dead horse. Then Bowie's shotgun boomed. Gordon swung the glasses in that direction and thought he caught a glimpse of somebody or something moving but he couldn't be sure.

"I reckon you're still alive, at least for the moment, Mister Tyler," Gordon said to himself as he stowed the glasses in the saddlebag and swung down with his rifle in hand. He looked at the rifle. "I think this's gonna be more pistol work than rifle work from here on out," he said under his breath. He shoved the rifle into the scabbard, pulled the short-barreled Remington from under his arm and checked the loads. He did the same with the Colt on his hip, tied the bay to a nearby tree, and started making his way through the brush around the edge of the meadow toward the creek. He could hear shouts from beyond the creek that sounded like Riker's voice, and he smiled to himself. It was time for a reckoning.

Bowie flinched and nearly fell again when Lonnie's pistol cracked twice. He had no idea who was shooting who and it puzzled him for a moment until he decided he had more pressing things to worry about, such as finding something to use for a crutch. Short as he was, the Greener was shorter, so that wasn't going to work. And besides, he might need it to defend himself. He still had some men to arrest, if there were any left after all the miscellaneous shooting that had gone on, so he looked around for something to help him get through the snow. It never occurred to him to do anything but get on with the job.

Just ahead of him a tree a few inches thick had been broken off at just about the right length, and it even had a nice forked branch sticking out in the right place to boot. With a quick thank you to whatever Providence had left it there for him, Bowie tucked the stick under his arm and hobbled toward where he thought the outlaw camp was, based on the churned-up snow from Raleigh's travels back and forth.

Two pistol shots rang out. Riker smiled. "I reckon Bronco's done that lawdog in for us," he told Abel.

"That couldna been Bronco," Abel protested. "Them shots didn't come from nowheres near where that shotgun was."

"Well then maybe he shot that damned kid. Why don't you go make sure, Abel?" Riker suggested. "Then come back here and we'll come up with a plan." Abel hesitated. "Now!" Riker snarled. Grumping and grumbling, Abel gave Riker a black look and started up along the creek following the tracks of Lonnie's sorrel.

As soon as Abel was out of sight, Riker disappeared into the hut and came out carrying his saddle and blankets. He went to the small clearing where the horses were corralled and began saddling his own. When his horse was saddled he led it and the packhorse back to the hut and began loading supplies. He figured he had several minutes before Abel made it back, and he wanted to be long gone, preferably in the direction of Bob Morton, before the hillbilly came back to the camp. Their plan to draw Morton out obviously hadn't worked, so he'd have to take a more direct approach. If the lawdog was dead, so much the better; Bronco could catch up later. If Bronco was dead, with any luck Abel and the deputy would finish each other off. Either way Riker figured he'd come up winners.

Riker ducked into the hut and brought out the last of the supplies the outlaws had brought with them. He was just swinging the bags over the packsaddle when he heard a dragging footstep in the snow and the sound of shotgun hammers clicking back. He stiffened and started to reach for the gun on his hip and an unfamiliar voice said, "Mister Riker, I presume?"

Riker turned around slowly and his hands lifted to shoulder height. The sight that met his eyes brought a twist of humor to his lips. The short fat man who teetered in front of him, braced with a willow limb, hardly looked in any condition to arrest anyone. But the shotgun in his hands said different. The dark tunnels of the barrels didn't waver.

"Take your hands down slow and unbuckle your belt," Bowie told him through gritted teeth. The throbbing in his leg was almost enough to bring tears to his eyes. When Riker didn't move Bowie motioned with the shotgun. "I don't care whether I take you in on your saddle, or over it, Riker. Makes no difference to me." Riker just stared at him malevolently, calculating the odds. Bowie could see the planning going on behind the big man's eyes.

"Raleigh thought he could make it too, Riker," Bowie told him. "I imagine the magpies have found him by now. Now drop the belt."

"Riker, Bronco's dead!" Abel exclaimed as he came around the hut at a trot. He slammed to a halt at the sight of the tableau in front of him, taking in the saddled horses as well as the crippled deputy. Bowie inadvertently swung the shotgun toward Abel and Riker made his move.

Riker threw himself backwards, clawing his way into the brush the way Lonnie had earlier. Behind him a curse rang out and the shotgun boomed, tearing leaves and twigs from the brush around him. He felt something like a bee sting in his butt and the back of one arm, but he kept moving. He was doing some cursing of his own as he made his way deeper into the thicket.

Bowie had let fly with one barrel of the shotgun in Riker's direction, knowing as he did so that it was pointless. Now he'd have to root the man out of the brush. He swung the shotgun back toward Abel and caught him with his pistol half-drawn. Never at his best when he had to think, Abel'd been as stunned as Bowie at Riker's escape.

"Ah-ah-ah, Mister Whoever You Are, we'll have none of that," Bowie told him, wagging a finger at him. "Now what say you just slip that pistol on out the rest of the way, but this time with just two fingers, and toss it in the crick over yonder." He pointed with his chin. "Or if you feel lucky you can try pulling it the rest of the way." He stopped and watched the expressions play across Abel's face. "But I think my trigger finger's faster than yours. Especially since my gun's already pointed." He stood and waited. It was obvious that Abel wanted to finish his draw in the worst way but it was also obvious that he didn't want to die.

Abel gingerly fished his pistol out of the holster and tossed it toward the water. It splashed into the creek, and he stood with his hands at his sides. "That wasn't real brave, but it was real smart," Bowie told him. "You might get to live a while yet. Depends on the mood the judge's in when you get into court."

"What're you blatherin' about?" Abel asked. "I ain't done nothin'."

"You ain't done nothing but shoot the banker's wife back in Sycamore Springs," Bowie told him.

"That weren't me, that was Bob Morton!" Abel exclaimed, desperately trying to cover his skinny behind one more time.

"Not according to what I heard," Bowie replied. "According to the fella I talked to, you did the shooting and nearly got your head blown off by Morton for doing it."

"That's a lie!" Abel tried again. "Morton done the shootin'! I was just along for the ride!"

"Enough idle chitchat," Bowie said. "Come over here and bring me some rope. I've gotta go after Riker, and I don't want you running around loose on my back trail."

"You ain't in no shape to go after a sick chicken, let alone

Riker," Abel snorted with a sour laugh.

"Nevertheless, it's my job," Bowie told him. "Now get over here." Abel just stood and glared at him until at last Bowie said in an exasperated tone, "The way I see it you've got the same two choices Riker had before you so rudely interrupted me and let him get away: you can go out of here on your saddle, or over it. And you've got about ten seconds to make up your mind. I'm getting tired of messing with you."

The standoff between the hillbilly and the crippled deputy might have gone on indefinitely, each daring the other to move, if Lonnie hadn't appeared silently behind Abel. "The man's talking to you, mister," the boy told him as he tucked the muzzle of his pistol behind Abel's ear. "And you don't have anybody to distract this here Colt while you make a run for the brush. Now move." Lonnie stepped back and nudged Abel in the back. The outlaw raised his hands and stepped toward the saddled horses. He reached up and got the rawhide reata from Riker's saddle and held it in his hand.

Lonnie took the rope from Abel's hand and soon had him trussed up like a Christmas turkey. He kicked his feet out from under him and tied his ankles together then looked up at Bowie. "You look like hell. How you gonna go after Riker in the shape you're in?"

"I feel like hell too but I've got it to do," Bowie told him. He let the hammer down on the shotgun and opened the action to replace the empty shell. He wanted to kick Lonnie's butt for being here, but at the same time he was damn glad to see him.

"Not necessarily," another voice said.

Bowie looked toward the speaker. "Well, well, I wondered if you'd be coming along. Lonnie Grable, allow me to introduce you to Mister Donald Gordon." Gordon stepped out of the brush and came to where the three were. Lonnie hesitantly stuck out a hand toward the new arrival.

"Gordon my achin' butt," Abel squalled. "That's..." But who Abel thought the newcomer might be Lonnie never heard, as Bowie leaned heavily against his crutch and kicked Abel in the head with his uninjured foot, knocking him cold and cutting him off in mid-sentence.

"Varmints are noisy in these parts, eh Mister Gordon?" Bowie asked innocently. He settled back on his good leg with a wince. He ignored Lonnie's incredulous gaze and turned back toward Gordon. "What do you mean, I don't necessarily have to go after Riker?"

"Because I'll do it," Gordon told him matter-of-factly.

"Why would you want to do that, and why should I let you?" Bowie asked.

"Because there's been a showdown coming between me and him for a long time. I've managed to put it off for a lot of years, but this time it's going to happen. And no, I'm not planning to tell you why. Just suffice it to say that it's something that needs doing." He and Bowie exchanged knowing looks. "You and young Mister Grable here had best do something with that leg of yours before infection and gangrene set in."

Gordon turned to go around the hut and Bowie's voice stopped him. "Gordon."

"Yes, Mister Tyler?"

"Good luck."

"Thanks, but luck won't have anything to do with what happens now." Gordon moved out of sight.

Bowie moved to Riker's horse and pulled the cinch loose. He tipped the saddle off onto the ground, rolled it over with the seat up, and sat heavily down on the polished leather with his leg stretched out in front of him. "Get some coffee started, would you Lonnie?" Abel was recovering from Bowie's kick to his head; he was starting to squirm and his eyelids were fluttering. "And gag that critter before he wakes clear up. I've had about all of his voice I want to hear for one day."

~ 55 ~

Bob Morton eased his way around the hut and up to a big pine tree, where he stopped. He stood listening intently. Over the murmur of the creek and the sighing of the breeze in the pines around him, he could hear Bowie's voice and Lonnie's reply. He ignored the occasional chirps and flits of birds through the trees while he waited for Riker to stir. He knew it was just a matter of time until the man moved, because Riker had always been an impatient sort.

Several minutes went by and still Gordon waited. At last his stillness was rewarded with a stirring in the near distance and the soft snap of a twig. A moment later he heard the dragging of a stiff branch across leather. The sounds were moving away, which suited him just fine. He had things to discuss with Riker that he'd just as soon nobody else heard. With a soft sigh Gordon began trailing the sounds that would lead him to Riker.

Bob knew that trailing is more than just following tracks. A good tracker has the ability to get inside the mind of his prey. Having grown up with Riker, Bob had a pretty good idea of what the outlaw would do. He followed the big man's tracks a bit further, then left the trail and cut off toward the creek on a tangent.

Riker's brain was awhirl as he made his way through the brushy undergrowth. There'd been no room in the plans he'd made in prison for the turn of events he'd experienced in the last little while, and his first instinct was to get away to some place where he could plot his next move. He was still intent on killing Bob Morton in spite of this most recent setback.

He was sure that the deputy would be coming, and he began looking for a place for an ambush. He wanted to be where he could do the killing without risking his own hide. He could see now that he'd tried to get too fancy. He should have just ridden in and called Morton out instead of trying to bring Morton to the gun. He wouldn't make that kind of mistake again.

By this time, Riker was several hundred yards away from the camp and he started looking for somewhere to hole up. Clouds were gathering rapidly and the skies were turning gloomy; he could almost taste the snow on the wind. He crossed the creek, stopping to cup some water up in his hand and drink, then went on. He was circling the big meadow towards the trail from Borden City when he heard a horse stamp and blow.

The big outlaw froze with his hand on the butt of his pistol. He eased ahead until he found an opening through the trees. He caught a glimpse of reddish-brown hide and saddle leather, and his heart beat faster. Right in front of him was his ticket out of the fix he was in.

Riker moved slowly toward the horse, listening and looking for any sign of pursuit. He knew it was only a matter of time until that fat deputy got after him, and he wanted to be long gone before that happened. He stepped out into the open and spoke reassuringly to the big bay tethered to a willow sapling. The horse watched him suspiciously. "Ease up there, boy," Riker said softly. "I ain't gonna do you no harm." He stepped forward with a hand outstretched for the horse to sniff, then when the horse had snuffled his hand slid the hand down along the horse's neck.

Riker lifted the stirrup and checked the cinch. Whoever the horse belonged to had loosened the cinch, so Riker grabbed the end of the latigo with both hands to pull it up. When he did, the rightful owner of the horse spoke up from behind him.

"Hello, Riker, or should I say, Albert," Gordon said softly, punctuating his words with the four clicks of a Colt hammer drawing back. "Where are you planning on going with my horse?"

Riker stiffened. "Is that you, Bob?" he asked, knowing good and well who was behind him. He'd never forget that hated voice as long as he lived.

"Who else?" Bob Morton replied. "What're you doing in this part of the world? I thought you were more of a warm-weather sort."

"I came here to kill you." Riker's tone was matter of fact. Bob didn't speak. Riker held his hands rigidly at his sides. "You gonna shoot me in the back, Bob?" Riker asked. "I didn't think that was quite your style."

"Not hardly," Bob told him. "I wouldn't want to take a chance on killing a good horse just to get you. You'll have your chance at me, fair and square, even though you don't deserve it. Turn around and step away from the horse."

Riker turned to face the man he had waited long years to kill. He kept his hands in sight as he moved away from the bay. He didn't want to die, and he didn't want the horse dead either; it was his ticket to freedom once he had killed Bob. He was going to be extra careful as long as Bob had the drop. He looked Bob up and down. He hadn't seen his step brother in better than ten years, maybe longer. The years had aged him, but he looked prosperous, too. The bay horse had a high-dollar saddle on its back and Bob's clothes looked like money. "Look's like you've done good for yourself, Bob," Riker remarked. "I reckon all that work I done for your daddy that you shoulda been doin' paid off for ya."

Bob snorted. "You worked harder getting out of doing anything than you ever did on the ranch, Albert," he said, deliberately using the name he knew Riker hated. "And we both know it. Pa knew it too. Makin' up for you is what stopped his heart."

It was Riker's turn to snort. "Work ain't what stopped your daddy's heart, Bob." He grinned maliciously. "I did."

Bob's finger tightened on the trigger of the pistol and Riker thought for a moment that he'd pushed too hard. "What's that supposed to mean, Albert?" Bob demanded. "And no lies. Tell me the truth."

"Gladly." As Bob's face turned first red, then deathly pale, Riker told how he'd roped the old man off his horse and drug him through the chapparal and catclaw then jammed his foot in the stirrup and ran the horse off into a steep-sided draw. By the time Riker was through with his tale of murder Bob was trembling with fury but the pistol remained rock-steady. "That old man learned a lesson about beatin' me that day," Riker finished with a sneer, hooking his thumbs in his belt.

"You never got a beating you didn't deserve," Bob snarled through gritted teeth. He let the hammer down on the Colt and holstered it.

"Draw, you yellow cur."

Albert Riker was fast with a gun, possibly one of the fastest Bob had ever seen, and Bob Morton had seen a lot of fast guns. But he was too eager. He beat Bob to the draw, no question of that, but his first shot went into the snow between the two men. His second shot never even came that close.

Bob drew and sidestepped to his left at the same time. His first shot punched the middle button on Riker's shirt deep into his chest. Riker grunted and cocked his pistol for a second shot, working to make his arm swing to the right. Before he could bring it to bear, Bob shot him in the chest again and Riker's second bullet whistled harmlessly out across the meadow. Riker stood struggling to cock the gun again and Bob waited. He marveled that the man could still be standing with two slugs in his chest and blood cascading down the front of his shirt.

Riker coughed and blood spilled down his chin. He dropped to his knees, still trying to raise his pistol for another shot. "Give it up, Albert," Bob told him. "You're a dead man."

"Damn you, Bob," Riker snarled and his gun dropped into the snow. "I'll see you in Hell."

"Most likely, Albert," Bob replied. "Most likely." He eased the hammer down on his pistol and dropped it into the holster. "Is there anything you want me to tell your mother?"

"Ma's dead," Riker said roughly. He dropped on his face in the snow with one final gasping breath.

Bob wiped a hand across his face and walked to his horse. He untied the bay, stepped into the saddle, and reined it back toward where the packhorse was tied. He'd get the packhorse, check on that deputy, and then get back on the trail east. As far as he was concerned Riker could feed the magpies and the coyotes. He still had to go do what he could for Jake.

~ 56 ~

Lonnie went into the hut and found that the coals of the fire there still retained some heat. A small pile of pitchy slivers lay nearby and he laid one on the brightest of the coals then knelt to blow softly on the ember. A tiny flame sprang up and tasted the pitch. It burned a little brighter and Lonnie blew again. Soon a small fire was crackling and he moved the coffee pot he found there closer to the heat.

When Lonnie went back outside he found Bowie slumped over, leaning on the shotgun for support. A pool of red was growing slowly under Bowie's leg. Lonnie ran over to him and touched his shoulder and Bowie looked up at him. "We better get that leg bandaged," Lonnie told him. "Help me get you inside of that hut and we'll get that boot off."

For once Bowie didn't argue; instead he levered himself to his feet with the aid of the shotgun and Lonnie's hand. He leaned on the boy as he limped over to the blanket-covered door and pushed his way inside the hut. He shuffled through the doorway and half-fell onto a pile of grubby blankets. "You'll have to go out to my horse and get something to wrap my leg with," Bowie muttered. "He's laying out yonder in the meadow. There's a bottle of whiskey in one of the saddlebags, bring that too."

Lonnie just nodded and went back out and headed for the creek. Abel's eyes held an evil glint as they followed Lonnie over the gag tied across his mouth and between his teeth. Abel was plotting his revenge on both that wet-eared kid and that fat deputy. And when he was done with them he'd get Bob Morton too.

Lonnie came back to the hut with his hands full of bandages and whiskey. He was so intent on getting back to Bowie that he didn't pay any attention to the fact that Abel had moved from his original position and was now sitting up against Riker's saddle. It wouldn't have meant anything to him even if he had noticed. In spite of the time he'd spent with Bronco and the others he was still green enough that some things just didn't register.

When Abel had heard Lonnie coming through the snow he'd stopped what he was doing, which was exploring Riker's saddlebags as best he could with his hands bound. He was looking for anything he could find to cut his hands loose, and it wasn't long after the boy disappeared into the hut that he hit pay dirt. He had seen Riker shaving with a straight razor and he'd been pretty sure that the razor was in the saddlebag he was digging around in. When his rapidly numbing fingers had found the smooth pearl handles of the fancy razor, he slipped it out of its leather case. He began working on getting the razor opened up and held in place in order to cut the rawhide strings that bound his hands together. That damn kid had tied the strings tight but Abel had been laying in the snow long enough for the strings to start to get wet. The longer he worked, the more he could feel the strings stretching and giving him some freedom of movement. He felt the razor start to come open and grinned behind the gag.

Inside the hut, Lonnie pulled Bowie's boot off and split the leg of his pants. "Damn, kid, take it easy," Bowie grunted. "That hurts."

"You better find something to gnaw on then," Lonnie told him, "'cause I've got a feelin' it's gonna hurt a whole lot worse before I get done."

Bowie picked up the bottle of whiskey and took a long slug. He put the bottle down with a shudder. "I'm not sure what's worse, that rotgut or you banging around on my leg," he said. "Go ahead, do your worst." He brought the sleeve of his coat up and took a wad of it into his teeth and bit down.

"Roll over on your side," Lonnie told him. When Bowie had turned far enough, Lonnie picked up the bottle and poured the liquor into the oozing wound. Bowie bit back a groan when the burning pain chewed into his leg, and sweat broke out on his face. Lonnie quickly wiped what dirt he could see out of the slash in the muscle and pressed a pad of clean linen against the wound, waiting to see if the bleeding would stop. The pad turned red in spots but didn't quickly soak through so he told Bowie, "Reach down here and hold this in place so I can get it tied on."

Bowie contorted his body far enough to get a hand on the pad. Lonnie had torn some strips of linen from one of the bandages and he quickly wrapped the pad onto the wound enough that Bowie could move his hand then Lonnie tightly wrapped the rest of the strips in place knotting each one as he went. When he was done he looked up at Bowie. The deputy's eyes were closed and his face was white and he'd nearly chewed through the sleeve of his coat. "Done," he said. "You can roll back over now if you want."

The pistol shots echoed across the meadow and through the brush along the creek; Bowie jerked awake and sat up. His hand reached instinctively for his pistol. "Wha-wha..." he stammered. He'd either dozed off or passed out somewhere along the way-more than likely the latter.

"Take it easy, take it easy," Lonnie told him. "I 'magine that was Mister Gordon taking care of Riker. It's over." He rinsed a cup he found nearby with coffee from the pot near the fire, filled the cup, and handed it to Bowie. "Here, drink this. I'll go outside and wait for Gordon."

Bowie reached for the cup and took a sip. He made a face. "That's horrible coffee," he said with another grimace. "But I guess beggars can't be choosers." He took another sip. "You be careful out there. Riker could've been the winner out yonder."

Lonnie just grinned at him. "Your Mister Gordon looked to me like somebody who wouldn't have too much trouble with Riker. And I'll stay close here. If you need anything, holler." He ducked out of the hut.

When Lonnie ducked outside, his first impression was that something was missing; at first he couldn't put his finger on what that something might be. He'd been so preoccupied with getting Bowie's leg bandaged before the deputy bled to death- although as slow as the leg was bleeding, it probably would have taken quite a while for that particular happenstance to occur- that he'd clean forgot about Abel Barnes. When a wiry arm snaked around his neck and a nasal voice said softly in his ear, "You even so much as think of makin' a sound an' I'll cut your throat. You hear me?" Lonnie remembered. To emphasize the point Abel nicked him under the chin with the razor. Lonnie didn't trust his voice so he nodded slightly, slowly and very carefully.

Abel had heard the pistol shots and drawn a different conclusion than Bowie and Lonnie had. He was sure that Riker had been the winner of that particular shootout and would be headed south as fast as a horse could take him away from the snow. So Abel figured it was high time somebody paid for all the crap that had happened to him in the recent past. It didn't matter to him that these two hadn't particularly had anything to do with it; somebody was gonna pay and this wet-eared kid and his fat partner would do. He completely overlooked the fact that he'd brought a lot of it on himself; his mind simply didn't work that way.

Abel snaked his own pistol out of Lonnie's holster, jabbed the boy in the back with the muzzle, and stepped back far enough that if the kid decided to be a hero he couldn't hit the gun with an elbow or something. "Alright, kid, get in there," Abel snapped. He folded the razor and pocketed it for later. It would come in handy for what he had planned for these two.

Lonnie lifted the blanket covering the doorway and stepped stiffly into the hut. He was very careful not to make any sudden moves that would get him a bullet in the spine. Bowie was sitting up gnawing on a piece of jerky. He looked up at Lonnie. "Gordon here already?"

"No he ain't, an' he ain't comin'. Riker's done kilt him," Abel said. He sidled out from behind Lonnie and crouched in the doorway of the hut pointing the pistol at Bowie. "An' now I'm gonna kill you two."

"Did you see the body?" Bowie asked mildly. He held the jerky in his right hand and his left hand drifted casually toward his holstered pistol.

"Didn't need to see no body," Abel replied. He gestured with the muzzle of the pistol and said, "Fat man, you ain't got a chance of gettin' that shooter out 'fore I kill you, so you'd best just fork it out with two fingers and toss it over here." He cocked the pistol and pointed it at Bowie's forehead. "An' if you think I'm jokin', you just try me."

Bowie gingerly lifted the Starr from the holster and tossed it toward Abel. The hillbilly reached down without looking, picked it up and shoved it into a coat pocket. "You sit down alongside of him, boy," he told Lonnie. "I don't wanna have to worry about you doin' somethin' stupid and gettin' yourself kilt 'fore I'm ready." Lonnie moved carefully over and sat down beside Bowie.

"I guess I made a mess of things again," Lonnie started.

"Shut your yap, boy!" Abel snapped. "If I wanna hear your

voice I'll tell ya." He lowered one knee to the floor. "Now, mister high an' mighty lawman, you just put your hands on the back of your neck, and leave 'em there." Bowie's lips lifted into the faintest semblance of a smile. Abel saw it. "Somethin' funny about what I said?"

"Nah, you're just kind of humorous in general," Bowie replied.

~ 57 ~

Bowie lifted his hands to his coat collar and slid two fingers and his thumb down inside. "You know, I've been trying to figure out what you remind me of, and I finally figured it out. You're just like those coyotes that follow the wolves around the edges of a buffalo herd. You're mighty humble around the real he-dog of the pack, but as soon as the he-dog isn't looking you're snapping and snarling like you're a real wolf when all you really are is a lowdown coyote." He gave Abel a grin and the hillbilly's face paled.

Abel lifted the pistol. "I'll show you who's the coyote and who's the wolf here, fat man," he snarled.

"I don't think so," Bowie said. In a blur, his hand snapped forward and the throwing knife from under his shirt collar hummed through the air and thudded into Abel's right shoulder, going in up to the leather-wrapped handle. Abel dropped the pistol with a yowl and grabbed for his shoulder with his left hand, then he fell backward out the door of the hut.

Lonnie lunged forward and started to follow Abel out but Bowie's hand on his sleeve stopped him. "No, dammit. Help me up and hand me my shotgun." Lonnie reached down and pulled Bowie to his feet. He scooped up the shotgun and broke it open far enough to see that Bowie had reloaded it then closed it and handed it to Bowie. With his other hand he picked up Abel's pistol.

"Now what?" he asked.

"Now we finish this, one way or the other." Bowie looked around. "Where's my damn crutch?"

"You mean this?" Lonnie asked, handing Bowie the willow branch he'd used earlier.

With a nod Bowie tucked it under his arm and moved toward the door. He used the barrels of the shotgun to move the blanket aside. Although he could hear Abel howling and carrying on right outside he wanted to make sure that he led with a gun this time. He was getting damn tired of coming out on the short end of things, and he was determined that it wasn't going to happen anymore today.

Bowie ducked outside as fast as he could. Abel had quieted down some but he was still whimpering and groaning where he sat in the snow. His fingers were splayed around the knife hilt protruding from his shoulder as if he was afraid to touch it, which could very well have been the case. Blood had soaked through his coat and run down his arm and was dripping into the snow. "Usin'a knife ain't fair," he whined.

"It's as fair as you holding us at gunpoint in there," Bowie told him. "Besides which, I'd like to know who it was that told you life was fair. Whoever it was lied." That was another of Tyler's Unwritten Laws. He grinned down at Abel. "Now it's your turn to fork over the pistol. Again."

Abel looked startled for a moment. It was obvious that he'd forgotten all about Bowie's pistol in his pocket. With a look of defeat on his face he reached back with his left hand toward where the butt of the Starr stuck out of his pocket. He kept his head down so that Bowie couldn't see the gleam of cunning in his eyes. "By the way," Bowie said conversationally, although it was taking almost more than he had to give to stay on his feet, "What was in that note you left for Gordon in town that would get him to travel in this kind of weather?"

Abel's hand stopped moving toward the pistol. "Aw, we told him one of his old trail pards was in trouble back East," he said. "Riker figured it'd bring him out, then we'd bushwhack him an' kill him. But Riker wasn't reckonin' on you puttin' your two bits worth in." He reached back the rest of the way and wrestled the pistol from his pocket.

Abel looked up at Bowie. It was obvious that the deputy was about all in from the way he was weaving as he stood leaning on his makeshift crutch. The damn fool hadn't even cocked the shotgun, and that kid was standing in the wrong place, so he'd have to move around the deputy to get a shot at Abel. Abel figured he'd have one chance at the deputy. It was only right that the deputy's own pistol killed him. Then once the deputy was down the kid would be easy.

Abel slipped his thumb onto the Starr's hammer. He wasn't that good a shot with his left hand but the deputy was only about four feet away so it'd be hard to miss. The deputy closed his eyes for just a flash, the barrels of the shotgun sagged, and Abel made his move. He snapped the hammer back on the Starr and tilted the barrel up toward Bowie.

Don Gordon untied his packhorse and looped the lead rope around the horn of his saddle. He reined the bay across the meadow and toward the camp. The big horse eased into the creek at a convenient crossing point and splashed across. A few fluffy snowflakes were beginning to drift down and Don was debating whether or not to go on with his trip today or hole up in Riker's brush hut and wait out the storm. He had plenty of supplies, even with the deputy and that kid helping him eat them, and it was only a couple of days to the next town through the snow. He'd more than likely run across a deer somewhere along the way that he could kill to help stretch his food, if need be. A sudden flurry of snow made up his mind for him and he turned his horses toward where the outlaws' horses were corralled.

Don stripped the gear from both horses and tucked his saddles back in under a big fir tree with the ones belonging to the outlaws. "You boys are gonna have to do some scroungin'," he told the horses. The clearing they were in was sheltered enough and the snow was shallow, so the animals could paw down to the rich, stem-cured grass. He carried the packsacks of supplies in his left hand as he moved toward the hut. He arrived at the back of the hut in time to hear Abel tell Bowie about the fake message and breathed a silent sigh of relief.

Don came around the hut and saw the barrel of the Starr coming up toward Bowie. He could see that the hammer was back and Abel's finger was on the trigger, but the deputy didn't seem to notice. It was happening so fast that Don didn't take time to think. His hand flashed to his pistol and the Colt boomed.

Abel's head snapped back and a black-rimmed hole appeared in his forehead as he toppled over into the snow. His finger tightened reflexively on the Starr's trigger but the shot went wild. Bowie and Lonnie both tried to look every direction at once and Bowie tumbled into the snow, losing the Greener in the process. Before Lonnie could swing his pistol in Don's direction, he stepped out and held up a hand.

"Easy gents," he said hurriedly. "It's just me. Don't shoot."

Bowie sat up and reached for his crutch. "Pull me up, Lonnie," he said, and held up a hand. Lonnie holstered his pistol with a shaking hand and levered Bowie to his feet.

"Dang, losin' all that blood hasn't made you any lighter," Lonnie told him with a smirk.

"Just shut up and hand me my guns, kid," Bowie growled. He leaned on his crutch and waited for Lonnie to pick up the Starr and the Greener. "I don't need any of your lip." Lonnie bent down and picked the Starr out of Abel's lifeless fingers and handed it to Bowie butt first, then retrieved the shotgun.

"I'm assuming by your presence, Mister Gordon, that Riker is dead?" Bowie asked Don.

"As dead as I could possibly make him, Mister Tyler," Don replied in a formal tone. "And now I believe that you and I have something to settle between us, do we not?"

Bowie looked him up and down with a thoughtful look on his face. "I can't think of a thing, Mister Gordon," he said quietly. "Unless you want something to be there."

"Are you certain, Mister Tyler?"

"Positive, Mister Gordon." Bowie turned and started hobbling toward the hut. "And now I believe I'll lay down for a bit before I attempt to ride back to Borden City."

Lonnie had been watching and listening to this exchange with a puzzled expression on his face. "What the hell are you two going on about?" he finally asked.

"I'll tell you when you're older, kid," Bowie said. A gust of wind swirled snow through the little clearing and dusted Abel's upturned face. "For now, why don't you haul us in some wood, and drag that," he gestured with the shotgun toward the rapidly cooling corpse of the late Abel Barnes, "the hell out of camp. I'm going inside. Looks like there's a storm coming." Bowie ducked into the hut and for all practical purposes fell onto the blankets he'd laid on earlier. Lonnie stared after him for a few moments then stooped and grabbed Abel by the ankles and began to drag him through the snow. "And bring me back my knife when you come, would you?" Bowie called. Lonnie just shook his head and kept on going.

Don followed Bowie inside, and set the packsacks down across the fire from where Bowie was sprawled. "I think you know who I am. Are you sure about this, Mister Tyler?" he asked. "Or is it Deputy Tyler?" Don stood waiting for Bowie's answer.

Bowie reached into his coat and brought out his badge. "It's Deputy Tyler," he told Don. "And as far as I'm concerned, you're Donald Gordon, the surveyor." He tucked the badge away.

"What about the rewards?" Gordon asked.

For an answer, Bowie looked at the packsacks and asked, "Is there anything to eat in those packs, or do I need to send Lonnie out to my horse to cut us off some steaks?"

Don stared at him for a few seconds then chuckled. "I've eaten horsemeat a time or two, but you'll have to settle for spuds and bacon." He opened one of the packs and pulled out a side of bacon, a cloth sack of potatoes, and a skillet. It wasn't long before the smell of frying bacon was drifting out the door into the rapidly building snowstorm.

Lonnie came inside carrying a heaping armload of wood and dropped it near the fire. "It's blowin' up a real blizzard out there," he said. He looked at Bowie. "I brought you're saddlebags and saddle, and Riker's packsacks, up close. It looks like we're not goin' anywhere for a while." He stepped outside for a moment, and reappeared with Bowie's saddlebags in one hand and the outlaws' supplies dragging from the other. A few more trips outside and the hut was half full of the wood the outlaws had chopped and piled outside.

"He's a worker, ain't he?" Gordon commented.

"He is a persistent sort, but he doesn't always follow orders," Bowie said with a twinkle in his eye. "Kind of reminds me of me. You got a need for somebody like that?"

"I might just have a place for him," Gordon said.

Lonnie looked back and forth between the two men. "When you two get done plannin' my life for me, do you think we could eat? It's been awhile since breakfast and it's gettin' hungry out." The two older men just laughed and the three started in on the contents of the skillet, using their knives to gingerly scoop the hot food into their mouths while the wind whined and prowled around the outside of the hut.

~ 58 ~

Bowie stepped out of the Café, leaning heavily on the crutch tucked under his arm. He stood on the boardwalk picking his teeth and enjoying the sunshine. The bullet gouge in his leg was mostly healed, but it was still tender to the touch. And he didn't even want to think about putting all of his considerable weight on it yet, even though he was going to have to start thinking about getting his chubby behind back to Laramie and his job. Unless he wanted to ride one of Artie Torges' wagons somewhere then try to find his way to Laramie from wherever he ended up, he was going to have to go horseback.

He, Lonnie, and Gordon had spent three days in Riker's lodgepole hut, only venturing out when it was absolutely necessary. Lonnie's sorrel had been one of the casualties of the storm. By the time the blizzard had blown itself out, another two feet of snow had fallen and the horses had been down to gnawing the bark from the willows along the creek. The remaining horses had been so weak that it had taken two days to cover the ten miles or so miles into Borden City, and those two days were some that Bowie would just as soon not have to live through again any time soon.

When the three finally managed to leave the lodgepole hut, the snow had been so deep that the bodies of the outlaws were completely covered. Bowie was pretty sure various scavengers had had their way with the bodies anyway, and he really hadn't been in the mood to try and find them just so they could be toted into town and buried. The Good Lord knew those men had probably left a lot of folks to the coyotes and magpies in their time so it only seemed fitting, in Bowie's mind at least, to do the same for them. And after all, the critters had to eat, too.

Now Bowie was the confident sort, and he'd had a good run of bringing in outlaws up to this point. But when confidence turns to cockiness it can rear up and bite a man on the butt, and if anybody had thought to ask, Bowie would have had to admit that this time he'd gotten cocky. If it hadn't been for Donald Gordon and Lonnie Grable he'd have had more than a bullet hole in his leg; he'd've been the one laying out there under all that snow.

"Maybe, just maybe, you're getting too old for this sort of thing, Tyler," he said quietly to himself. After a moment's thought, he changed his mind. "Nah, couldn't be.".

"Talkin' to yourself?" Lonnie asked from behind him.

"Only when I'm in the mood for an intelligent conversation," Bowie told him with a grin as Lonnie stepped up beside him. Lonnie just gave him a look and held his tongue. He'd already lost more than one battle of wisecracks with Bowie, so he decided he'd better change the subject.

"So, where we headed next?"

"*We* aren't going anywhere," Bowie said seriously. "I'm going back to Laramie to file my report, and you're going to work for Gordon." Bowie had sent Judge Martin a telegram as soon as he'd gotten up and around:

Bob Morton killed in gun battle with Riker Stop Banker's wife shot by Abel Barnes Stop Barnes, Riker, Jarvis also deceased Stop Will return to Laramie soon to file report Stop Signed, B Tyler

The telegram wasn't exactly the truth, the whole truth, and nothing but the truth, but it was the embodiment of one of the most important of Tyler's Unwritten Laws: don't tell the Boss anything he doesn't absolutely *have* to know.

Bowie held up his hand to stop Lonnie's protests. "Just give it a try," he told the young man. "Gordon's a surveyor besides being a rancher. You might learn something from him." He devoutly hoped that he was right about the surveying part; he would have been surprised to find out that he was wrong. Don Gordon seemed to be a man who had a lot of cards hidden up his sleeve.

"Oh, alright," Lonnie groused. "I reckon it won't kill me." Then his face brightened, and he looked sideways at Bowie. "What're you gonna do about Miz Patterson? She kinda seems to set store by you." He gave Bowie a mischievous grin.

Bowie glared at him briefly, then sighed ruefully. "I don't rightly know," he said resignedly. When he, Gordon, and Lonnie had first gotten back to town, something suspiciously like pneumonia had set in, and between the fever and the chills Bowie had been one sick puppy. Elvira had plied him with chicken soup and other even more appetizing foods, and had spent many hours by his bedside. Doc Baines credited her with saving Bowie's life. Ever since he'd been back on his feet she'd seemed bent on keeping him fat, dumb, and happy. It was enough to make a confirmed bachelor like Bowie look to his hole card, so to speak, and keep a fast horse saddled.

"I don't rightly know," he said again. "But I guess I'd best think of something quick before I find myself swampin' out the Huckleberry Café full time and permanent-like."

The solution to Bowie's dilemma came the next morning at breakfast, or so he thought at the time. He was sitting in the Café, lingering over a last cup of coffee, when George from the telegraph office came in. "Got a wire for you, Deputy," he told Bowie as he handed over the folded sheet of paper.

"Thanks, George," Bowie said. "Care for a cup of coffee?"

"No thanks, gotta get back." Bowie tipped him a quarter and George left the Cafe'. Bowie unfolded the paper. The words were brief and to the point:

Return Laramie posthaste Stop Signed Judge Randolph Martin

Bowie felt almost guilty about the wave of relief that washed over him when he saw the words on the paper. Now he just had to break the news to Elvira and he wasn't looking forward to that prospect. He folded the paper and stuck it in his pocket.

The morning crowd had thinned and Elvira came to Bowie's table with a pot of coffee. "Bowie, we've a need for talkin'," she said as she pulled out a chair and sat down. She had, during his convalescence, gone from calling him Mister Tyler to Bowie. A twinge of dread went through him at her words; he was sure that she was going to tell him it was time to announce their betrothal or some such thing. But he hadn't reckoned on her levelheaded nature. She refilled his cup and filled one for herself.

"I've grown rather fond of you, I think you realize," Elvira began. "And I've given a lot of thought to the future." She sipped some coffee while the dread inside him grew and he tried to keep his expression neutral.

"You're quite pleasant to have around, you're generally well-kept, and you're not afraid to be helpin' out when somethin' needs doin'." She held her cup in both hands and looked at him over the rim. "But after a great deal of consideration I have come to the conclusion that it would be better for all concerned if, as soon as the weather's permittin', ye were to saddle your horse and return to Laramie."

Bowie sat back in his chair with a stunned look on his face. Here was his chance to bow out gracefully and he wouldn't even have to produce the telegram from Judge Martin! With any luck, he could get George to forget he had ever gotten it. Elvira misinterpreted his expression as shock and tried to soften the blow. Inside he was ecstatic. Or at least he told himself he was.

"I realize this is seemin' rather sudden," Elvira went on. Bowie barely heard her words. "But we are too different. I'm thinkin' we'd soon be at each other's throat. I believe it's best that we part amicably." Now it was her turn to lean back in her chair.

After taking a minute to try to think of what he should say, Bowie finally said dejectedly, "If that's how you feel, Elvira, I won't fight it. I'd rather we parted friendly myself." He let his expression brighten. "I might be back in these parts again some time, and I'm always in need of a good meal." He reached out and took her hand and brought it to his lips.

Elvira blushed and stood looking down at him. Suddenly at a loss for words, she finally said brusquely, with a catch in her voice, "The Huckleberry Cafe' is generally open seven days a week." She pulled her hand back and quickly turned toward the kitchen so Bowie wouldn't see her face. "Let me know when you're ready to go and I'll be sure you're well fed." She bustled off toward the kitchen, collecting dirty plates and cups as she went.

"Phew!" Bowie muttered quietly to himself, but there was just a hint of uncertainty in the word.

Two days later, with the first hints of pink outlining the eastern hills, Bowie reined his horse to a stop at Elvira's gate. He was riding Bronco Jarvis' horse and leading the outlaws' packhorse. He'd decided that he needed the two animals more than anybody else, seeing as how his own horse had more than likely been reduced to bones and a few scraps of hide by this time. The fact that Bronco was dead helped, and it just seemed to be a sort of poetic justice. Bowie stepped gingerly to the ground and tucked his crutch under his arm then limped up to the porch.

Elvira opened the door before he could knock. She was in her robe and slippers with her hair in a kerchief. "Come in, Bowie," she said. "Coffee's on."

Bowie pulled off his hat and held it in front of him. "Thanks, but I reckon I'd best be getting on down the trail, Elvira," he said. "I just came to say goodbye." He put his hat back on and turned to go.

"Bowie." He turned back toward Elvira. She stepped out the door and kissed him on the cheek then stepped back. "You be takin' good care of yourself, Bowie Tyler."

Bowie reached out and touched her cheek. "You too, Elvira. You too." He limped back to his horse and managed to get aboard without falling and making a total fool of himself. He stowed the crutch in the rifle scabbard under his leg and lifted the reins; the horse stepped out of its own accord. Just before he turned toward the main street of town Bowie looked back over his shoulder and waved. Elvira returned his wave, then Bowie faced forward, heeling the horse into a jog. "Come on, horse. We've got a long way to go, and a short time to get there. The boss wants us home."

THE END

About the Author

Chuck Buchanan, an associate member of Western Writers of America, lives on the family cattle ranch in eastern Oregon. He likes to hunt, shoot, load his own ammo and burn it up shooting cowboy action as a member of SASS, the Single Action Shooting Society.

Tyler's Law is his second novel in the Deputies series.

www.ingramcontent.com/pod-product-compliance
Lightning Source LLC
LaVergne TN
LVHW020541100826
845148LV00010B/1560

9780982458013